WEREBEARS OF THE EVERGLADES

A SHIFTER ROMANCE COLLECTION

MEG RIPLEY

Disclaimer

This book is intended for readers age 18 and over. It contains mature situations and language that may be objectionable to some readers.

CONTENTS

ALPHA'S SECOND CHANCE

WEREBEARS OF THE EVERGLADES

1

OWEN

I stepped out into the brisk morning air with my bare feet, stretching tall as I filled my lungs. The sun peeked over the tree tops, lighting the morning fog in oranges and pinks. From where I stood on my cabin's porch, I could just make out the glint of Shark River off in the distance. *Perfect morning for a run.*

That time of year—the wet season in Everglades National Park—the air was full of bugs in the heat of the day, but before the sun came up, the swarms were fewer and the air tasted cleaner. The temperature was just below 70, but in a matter of hours, the hot sun would raise it closer to 90. With the bugs, running would be unbearable, so I chose early mornings or late nights to tear through the forests.

I pushed down my shorts and boxers, stepping out of

them both in one swift move. My feet touched dew-ridden grass for only a moment. Seconds later, my thick, hairy paws were trampling the wet blades in their place. I shook out my black fur and stood tall, roaring louder than any natural bear would dare.

Owen! Ezra signaled to me through our shared mind link, *Up already, chief?*

Surprised to hear you rumbling around, Ezra. I didn't think you got up this early unless there was tail to chase.

There's always tail to chase, man.

I could almost hear the wink in his words. *Who else is around?*

We both paused, waiting for another voice or two to chime into our mental conversation. All was quiet in the clan.

Just you and me, Ezra said. *Though, I should clarify. I'm not up early.*

I laughed. *If you stay up all night until the sunrise, I think that crosses the line from up late to up early.*

Whatever makes me look better. Where are you at, anyway?

I crossed the edge of my property into the boundary of the park. No one was technically allowed to live on park grounds, so my hand-built cabin sat just over the line. It felt like park living, but without the legal hassle.

Touring the park before heading toward the office. You?

Umm, you think you'll need me today?

I rolled my eyes. *You are the most unreliable ranger I've ever met.*

Hey! he said back, *I didn't earn my place as your second in command by slacking off. Maybe you should ask me why I haven't slept.*

Okay. Humor me.

The cool air rustled through my fur and my nose filled with the scents of various animals. The small family of key deer who lived nearby were out foraging, it seemed. I sent a scattering of herons into the sky as I ran too close to their nesting place. Their wings stretched out far, letting the large birds glide peacefully. Smaller game bolted when they heard or smelled me, and I wished I could've assured them all, "It's okay, it's just me. I'm actually a really nice guy and I won't hurt you." Well, unless the full moon was out. Though I tried to not hunt in bear form too often, it was sometimes necessary.

Ezra took a mental breath and began his tale. *Okay. So, it started out innocently enough. I was out with some of the clan last night, Mason and Conner, and we were minding our own business, having some beers. Then this asshole croc came up to us and started some shit—*

Wait, wait, I interrupted. *Which croc?*

Dunno. I've seen him before, though. He's local. Anyway, he was all like, "Pfft. Looks like you bear boys could use some company." While he had, like, a chick on each arm. Whatever. We weren't trying to pick up any ladies. So, we were all just kind of like, "Whatever, prick," and rolled our eyes. The place was crowded, you know? And he was just calling us bears in the middle of the joint. Stupid. But then he knocked over a beer, on purpose. Of course, he was all like, "Whoops, silly me." Just being a jack ass.

Ezra, I interrupted again, when do you get to the part about why you were up all night?

Patience, oh wise, Alpha. I'm getting to it.

Is there a shorter version?

Fine. So, we ended up outside fighting the guys. Just fists, all humaned out. People were watching. Afterward, one of the chicks he was with was making eyes at Mason. I guess he impressed her with his mad fist throws. They ended up leaving together, but the croc did not like that one bit. He threatened to follow and attack them, so me and Connor beared-up and chased them home, keeping watch to make sure they were safe. The croc never showed, though.

So, you looked out for Mason while he took a booty call.

If that's what you want to call it. I just think we were being good brothers, looking out.

Get some sleep. Come in at noon.

Thanks, Boss.

Ezra?

Yeah?

Did anyone get hurt?

Not us.

Good. Now get some sleep.

He went quiet after that, and Ezra wasn't one for silence,

so I assumed he had shifted back. When I finished my run, I rinsed off in the shower and dressed for work. Being a manager of rangers at the park, I was on the first shift in the morning. It was part of my job to assign the rangers to the tasks needing to be completed, man the radios, and check in with the other departments. Then, I'd go off to do my own tasks for the day.

I parked my Jeep and entered the ranger station, heading right for my office. The office assistant, Rachel, smiled when she saw me. "Morning, Owen."

"Morning." I poured a cup of coffee and picked up the thin stack of reports that had come in overnight. They were still warm to the touch and sitting in the printer's output tray. "Looks like things were pretty quiet last night."

"Last night, they were. This morning..." She widened her eyes and blew out a breath. "You have several messages waiting for you."

"Great."

I shut the door to my office and hit the blinking red button on my phone. I was told I had five waiting messages. Rachel wasn't kidding. Usually, I had one or two at the most.

The last message had me running out the door the second I'd finished listening to it.

"Owen." It was one of the human junior rangers, Pete. He sounded out of breath and distressed. "We need your help. A kid is stuck in the grass river by the overlook. I have the small cat, but I think we're gonna need the big bear."

I tried to stay calm as I hopped into our larger utility vehicle, lovingly called the big bear. I had no idea why Pete would have only taken the smaller utility vehicle—the small cat—for something like this. And I also had no idea why he hadn't called my walkie. All the rangers carried walkie talkies so we could be reached immediately if there was an emergency, which it sounded like this was.

I drove fast over the dirt and stone paths that made up the roads and ranger trails through the park. One and a half million acres was a lot of space to cover, but luckily, Pete wasn't too far from the main ranger station. It took me only a few minutes to reach the overlook he mentioned.

When he saw me pull up, he ran over. "Thank goodness!"

"Why didn't you use the walkie?" I asked, holding it up.

"Oh, I..." He scratched his head and looked around. "Sorry, sir."

"And why in the world would you bring the small cat for a rescue mission?"

"Oh, well, it didn't seem like that big of a deal at first and I..." He turned and gestured toward the small crowd that had formed.

Two other rangers pulled on each of the kid's arms while another junior ranger watched. A crying, shrieking woman, who had to be the kid's mom, stood off to the side, loosely held back by a big man who was likely the father.

I took charge immediately. "Hello, folks. I'm Owen, the

ranger manager here. Don't you worry, we'll get him unstuck in no time."

I assessed the situation. The grass river was tricky. It looked like solid grass in many places, but water hid beneath. If you didn't know and walked too far, it was nothing but mud and muck. And this kid had walked too far.

His hiking boots were barely visible in the mud. He looked terrified and could only be about eight or so. I walked as close as I could to him without getting stuck myself.

"What's your name?" I asked.

"Robbie."

"Okay, Robbie. The first thing I want you to do is stay calm, okay? Worst case scenario, we just untie your boots and your mom and dad get mad at me for losing them in the mud."

He nodded and kept his eyes on me.

"Now. Take this rope and wrap it around your waist."

I held the end of the rope out to him and he did as he was told.

"Now, I'm going to get in my UV there and press the gas real slow, but it will give you enough of a lift that you'll start to feel yourself being pulled up and out. When you feel that, don't panic and don't fight it. Just hold on tight and let the rope do its thing, okay?"

Robbie nodded again and held the rope tightly enough to make his knuckles white. I walked back to the big bear, where the other end of the rope was attached to the back roll bar.

I watched in the rearview mirror as I slowly pressed on the gas; soon, I saw Robbie pop free and splash into the wet, swampy grass. When I got out to check, he was still mostly upright from hanging onto the rope, and he still had both shoes. I stepped into the water and scooped him up, then handed him to his grateful mother.

"Oh, thank you, thank you!"

The boy vanished from sight in a flurry of hands and arms making sure he was okay.

"Thanks," Pete said, still looking flustered.

"I want a full report by noon," I said and drove off, heading back to the station. I'd need a few more cups of coffee if the day was going to start like this.

2

ADDIE

I stretched my arm out the window, letting the wind blow over my skin and weave through my fingers. I looked at Emma behind the wheel and smiled. "This is going to be an amazing vacation!"

"Yay-ya!" Emma shouted.

Julie chimed in from the backseat. "Whooo!"

"I'm just glad to be done with finals," Emma breathed. "All those hours of studying were starting to make my brain turn to mush."

"Actually," Julie countered, "You were building stronger neuropathways that increase brain matter, not decrease it."

Emma rolled her eyes.

"Come on, now," I said. "If it weren't for the medical

geek's wisdom, you wouldn't have made it through finals in the first place."

"True." Emma looked in the rearview mirror and stuck her tongue out at Julie. "It's still annoying though."

"Say whatever you want," Julie snickered. "Just remember that when you get struck by lightning, I'll be the one fixing you up."

I laughed. "I don't think she'll have to worry much about that being a weather girl."

"Hey." Emma gave me a mock glare. "A degree in meteorology, *Adeline*, gives me a lot more opportunity than just being in front of a camera."

I was in trouble if she was using my full name. "You'd make a perfect weather girl or anything else your heart desires. I'm just looking forward to getting out in nature and using my degree to explore," I said. "And you can let us know if the weather is going to be bad."

"Maybe you'll actually figure out what you want to do this week?" Julie asked me.

I sighed. I had known my whole life that I would study animals and the environment. The only problem was, now that I had, I couldn't decide what I wanted to do with my brand-new bachelor's degree in ecology. The options seemed endless—zoologist, field biologist, ranger. They all sounded amazing, too. I hoped this vacation to Everglades National Park would help me get into nature and figure out a direction to move in.

"I can always work in a pet store," I said.

Emma dropped her head to one side. "I did not just spend the last four years studying with you and correcting your papers so you can go sell cuddly kittens to little girls all day."

"I know," I said. "I'll figure it out. We just graduated. I have time."

"Should have gone into the medical field," Julie said. "I'd give you one of my *three* job offers, but, you know, ecology doesn't really work in a hospital."

"Unless it's an animal hospital," Emma said. "Maybe you should be a vet!"

"That's an entirely different field of study from ecology," I said.

"It's still animals," Emma replied.

I laughed. "Right."

"Hey," Julie said. "We just spent four years studying and focusing on school, as Emma pointed out. Can we, like, not talk about that stuff for just this week, please? I want to enjoy this time before I have to join the real world."

"I agree," I said. I didn't need the stress of trying to figure out the rest of my life when it was only just beginning.

"Yes, yes," Emma said. "It would be a lot easier if we'd gone to the beach with the rest of our classmates. Just saying."

"Who needs all that sun?" Julie said. "The rates of skin

cancer have been increasing exponentially over the years. You do know that, right?"

"And the sand gets everywhere." I wrinkled my nose.

"Worth it," Emma said. "On both counts."

"Next time," I said. "That was the deal."

Emma sighed. "Just promise me that at least one night we'll go out and get trashed."

"Umm, yes," Julie said.

"Of course," I said.

The drive only took about an hour, but when we got closer to the Everglades, it felt like entering a different world. Miami was so built up with businesses and houses and people. The Everglades was the opposite. Few buildings and they were all part of the park. No homes or tall structures to break up the skyline. Trees and clouds and chirping birds. The air smelled cleaner and fresher. The greens were brighter, the sky bluer.

This was why I'd chosen a degree in ecology. I couldn't get enough of the outdoors. I loved to be in nature, letting my inner animal run wild, experiencing all that the natural world had to offer. It refreshed and invigorated me. I'd been in desperate need of some nature after years of college, and this was why I'd chosen the Everglades as our vacation destination. Emma and Julie had bargained for other locations when *my* vacation became *our* vacation, but I'd stuck to it. The beach was nice, but there were way too many people and not enough trees. In the end, they'd agreed, but only under the agreement that our next getaway would happen at the beach.

When Emma stopped at the check-in station, I hopped out and went inside. "Reservation under Pearson." I bounced on my toes, the excitement filling me, as the woman searched for our reservation.

The woman handed me a tag for the car. "Site 382." She pointed to a spot on a map and circled it. "Right here."

"Thank you!" I dashed out to the car with the tag and map. "Okay," I said as I buckled my seatbelt again. "Turn left up here."

I navigated to our spot. When we found site 382 and parked, I got out and stretched tall, taking in a nice long breath of Everglades air.

Julie and Emma joined me. We stood together, looking out at the trees and greenery.

"This was a good choice," Emma said.

"My hiking boots are calling my name," Julie said.

"Oh!" I ran back to the car and got the map. "There are lots of trails. Look!"

We checked over the map, noting the hiking trails and other sites to see.

"Let's try this one first," Emma said, pointing to a colored line on the map.

"We better set up the tent first," I said. I'd set up tents in the dark or near dark before and it was always so much easier with full daylight.

We pulled our bags out of the car and I heaved the tent into the middle of the site. I opened the bag and started pulling out stakes and poles and other pieces of tent, and Emma and Julie grabbed pieces and helped me. I'd set up this tent enough times to have each piece's location memorized. I directed and they followed, and within minutes, the tent was standing tall and proud in the middle of our site.

We spread out our mats and sleeping bags inside, chose a spot to set our bags, then changed into our hiking gear. I packed my small backpack full of essentials; my pocket knife, flashlight, map and compass were all tucked in their spot in my bag. I added a bottle of water and was set.

When my friends were ready, we set out toward the path. There weren't a lot of other tents set up. Being May, maybe it was still early in the season for camping. It was plenty warm and the perfect weather for camping, I thought. Later in the year, it would be unbearably hot, muggy, and buggy. July and August were difficult months for me. I wanted to be outside all the time, but I could only stand it for so long before my hair was wet with sweat and sticking to me annoyingly. Thank god my apartment complex had a pool.

"Already a half mile," Emma announced.

She was watching her fitness app and anytime we walked anywhere, she would give updates on how far we'd gone, how fast we'd walked, and how many calories we'd burned. She might claim she wasn't interested in being a TV weather woman, but she sure cared about her physical appearance as if that were her goal.

Emma was concerned about the exercise aspect and Julie was, too, of course. It wasn't that I didn't care as much about that part of it, but I got plenty of exercise. I was more interested in studying the plants and animals, seeing what sort of things lived here and what their environment was like.

I watched two squirrels tangle through tree branches, feeling complete delight at seeing them in their natural habitat. Several times, Julie or Emma called out to me to catch up. They wanted to keep a good pace so their heart rates stayed elevated, but I just wanted to appreciate everything my gaze fell across.

As we walked, our footsteps were quiet on the well-worn dirt path. We didn't make much sound, so when I heard a strange noise, I stopped immediately. It was a sort of whining chirping sound. A bird, maybe? Whatever it was, it sounded distressed.

"Guys," I whispered to my friends.

They walked a few steps back to where I'd stopped.

"Do you hear that?" I asked. "I think there's a hurt animal."

Emma took a step away. "Don't animals attack when they're hurt?"

"Only if they think you're going to harm them further," I said, trying to locate the sound.

"Here," Julie said.

I walked to where she was holding back a patch of tall grass. There, sitting hidden in the brush, was a white ibis. As it made the distressed sound again, I became more concerned; this was bizarre behavior for a bird like that.

I crouched down and got on my knees, making soft cooing sounds in attempt to let the bird know it was okay. I slowly moved closer, not wanting to scare it. Emma was right about one thing: if this bird were afraid of me, it would at least peck my hand if I tried to touch it.

I watched it for several minutes. Its wings were tucked around it as I would have expected, so perhaps it hadn't hurt its wing. Could it be sick? I moved my hand closer until I gently touched the bird's head, and to my surprise, it didn't attack me or flinch.

"Addie! What are you doing?" Emma hissed. "That thing is going to eat you."

"Shh," I said. "Ibises don't eat people. It's fine."

The bird let me run my fingers over both wings; those couldn't be the source of the problem, then. It then made a sound and fluffed its wings, and I noticed that it tried to stand, but couldn't. I carefully lifted one wing, and when I lifted the other, the bird pulled back.

Then I saw the problem: one of its legs was twisted in an unnatural way. It must've landed badly or something had hit it and broken its leg. Even if it could fly, the bird needed help. It might sit there for too long and end up starving or being attacked by something else in its vulnerable state.

I stood up and took out my phone.

"What are you going to do?" Julie asked.

"The same thing you would do if this was an injured person." I dialed the number for the ranger station located closest to our location. Good thing I'd thought to bring the map. Not only did it have trails and other places of interest marked, it had a list of numbers to call if there was a problem.

When someone answered, I explained the situation.

"I'll send someone out to you right away," the man on the other end said. "Will you stay in the area to guide our ranger to the injured animal?"

"Of course," I said. "I couldn't possibly leave this bird alone to be attacked."

I gave as much detail as I could about our location, then hung up and waited. I tried to find bugs and berries to feed the bird, but it wouldn't take anything. We heard an ATV in the distance and watched for the ranger.

When the vehicle came into view, we waved to get the ranger's attention. Two rangers rode in the ATV, wearing their khaki uniforms.

"Hi there," one of the men said. "Were you the ones who called about an injured bird?"

I opened my mouth to answer yes, but nothing came out. I stared at the other ranger, and he returned the gesture, both of us standing there in complete shock.

"Owen?" I nearly choked on his name.

"Addie."

I looked into the eyes of my high school boyfriend. It'd been four years since I'd seen him. He looked the same, but somehow, even better. He'd always been gorgeous with his black hair and blue eyes, but he'd gained some muscle over the years and the stubble across his chin was not something he'd had during our high school years. He looked much more mature. And, if I were being honest, he was downright hot.

"Good to see you," I said. What else could I say? It wasn't entirely a lie, but he'd broken my heart. If I'd had to choose any person in the world to run into, he would have made the list, but wouldn't have been high on it.

"You, too." He nodded slowly. He seemed to be thinking hard, but didn't say anything.

Finally, I broke the silence. "So, the ibis is right over here."

I pointed to where the patch of grass hid the bird, and the other ranger went to it immediately. Owen hesitated, then followed him over.

I stood back to let them do their jobs. After a few minutes, Owen picked up the bird, and I was impressed. He must be very good with animals if he'd gained that much trust in such a short time—and from an injured bird, at that. He tucked the ibis under his arm and carefully got back into the ATV.

"Thank you for calling us," the other ranger said.

"You think it'll be okay?" I asked Owen.

He nodded. "We'll have our vet take a look. I think it's just a broken leg." He stroked the bird's head. "She'll be up and flying in no time, thanks to you. If you hadn't called, she would probably have been attacked."

"That's what I was worried about."

He pressed his lips together and nodded again. "Good to see you, Addie."

"You, too."

I watched them drive off, feeling a bit saddened by the exchange. Emma and Julie turned to me with wide eyes.

"Let's hear it," Emma said.

I let out a slow sigh, then resigned myself to reliving this painful story one more time.

3

ADDIE

"From the first day we met, it was like magic," I said. We started walking again, more slowly this time so they could listen to my tale. "I was lost in my giant, new high school and dropped my books while I was trying to find my class. There were so many people that I kind of freaked out a little. I was picking up my books and he stopped to help me, and he ended up walking me to my class, even though it made him late for his."

Owen had shrugged when the bell rang. "It's the first day. They won't care."

"Thank you again." I held up my schedule. "And for pointing out my next class." I smiled and dashed into the classroom. I'd sat quickly and glanced back to the door, surprised to see him still standing there.

He smiled at me and my face grew hot. He held up a hand to wave, his smile spreading even wider, before he finally walked away. When class ended, I'd looked up and down the hall for him, but didn't see him.

I knew where to go next, thanks to him, and when I got to my next class, he slid into the seat next to me. My heart jumped.

"Glad you didn't get lost on your way here," he said. "I'd hate to think I'd miss out on one minute of being this close to you."

"He did not say that!" Julie said and they both giggled.

"We were only fourteen," I reminded them. "And his brother used to teach him to say all these cheesy lines. It didn't matter, though; I fell for all of them. And he meant them, too. Those things only come off as cheesy when the person saying them isn't sincere."

"Okay, okay," Emma said. "So, it was love at first book drop. What happened next?"

"We would talk before and after class. Usually, he would walk me to my next one. Then, one Friday, he handed me a note with his phone number and he asked me to call him over the weekend. I called that day after school, and he asked me to go to the mall with him that night."

"The mall?" Emma asked, flabbergasted.

"Yeah, the mall. Hello? Fourteen," I said.

"That's where we spent, like, all of our Friday nights, Em, and you know it," Julie said. They'd gone to a nearby high school and had been friends before college, where they met me.

"Ignore her," Julie said. "Did he hold your hand as you walked around?"

"Of course," I said. "He bought me an Orange Julius and everything."

"This story could only be cuter if you'd shared a container of fries from the food court," Julie said.

I pressed my lips together and stifled a laugh.

"You did, didn't you!" Julie said.

"I feel like I'm stuck in a teen drama," Emma said.

Julie shoved her lightly.

"We shared fries and a slice of pizza," I said. "And that was it. From that moment on, we were inseparable. We talked on the phone all night, went to the mall and roller skating and all those things we used to do when we were young teens."

"So cute," Julie said.

"Yeah, cute," Emma said. "So where did it all go wrong?"

"Well..." I blew out a hard sigh. "We dated for years. All through high school. We went to proms together, homecomings, all of that."

"Wait a minute!" Emma grabbed my arm and turned to face me. "Was he your first?"

"Yes," I admitted. "And I was his."

"This is the cutest story ever," Julie said. "I'm quite jealous."

"And then he broke my heart," I said.

"I knew it," Emma grumbled.

"No!" Julie said in a whiney tone. "He's so cute! How could he?"

"He got into a college out of state and wanted to get away from everything. So, that summer, when he told me his plans, he said he wanted to end things. He thought a long-distance relationship would be too difficult to maintain, and that it would hinder our studies."

"Boo," Julie said.

"I know," I said. "It was horrible. I cried for weeks. Then I swore off men."

"Until Sam," Emma said.

"Yeah well," I said. "I should have sworn him off, too. Jerk."

"Let's not have a Sam moment, please," Julie said. "You're done with him, and let's stay done."

"Yes, please," Emma said.

"I think part of the reason I ended up staying with him for so long was because of Owen," I said. "I just wanted to be dating, you know? After four straight years of being with the same person, it was weird to not have a boyfriend. But, I have no desire to talk about or think about Sam."

Except that now that he'd been brought up, my mind drifted toward Sam. It had been a complete disaster of a relationship. I'd expected something like what Owen and I had. A relationship that was fun and easy with someone enjoyable to be around. Owen made me laugh. Sam made me worry. He was so intense, I had never been sure where I stood with him or what was going on in his mind. The year we dated was fraught with frustration and confusion.

If being in a relationship was going to be like how things had been with Sam, I never needed to be married. I didn't want that kind of drama surrounding me all the time. In a relationship that was meant to last a lifetime, I would need someone more like Owen. Well, like Owen but with enough dedication to want to attempt something as common as a long-distance relationship.

Maybe Owen had set the bar too high. After Sam, I started to wonder which one was a more accurate representation of what marriage would be like. The best I could hope for was something in the middle.

"Maybe this will be good," Emma said. "Maybe you can remember a relationship other than Sam and can actually have someone who's good for you."

"I think the bigger problem is, I never really got over Owen."

They stopped and looked at me.

"After he broke your heart, you still have feelings for him?" Julie asked.

I shrugged. "That's the only thing he ever did to hurt me, though."

"Well, it was a pretty big thing, don't you think?" Emma said.

"It was," I admitted. "It's just hard to hate him when all my memories are good ones."

"And when he's that hot," Emma added.

"Not helping," Julie said, nudging her.

I scrunched up my face as if I were in pain. "The worst part is, he looks even better now."

Emma sucked in a breath. "Oh. Sorry."

"You should date him," I said to Emma.

"Are you crazy?" Emma said. "First of all, no. Second of all, he's your ex. Third of all, you just said you still have feelings for him! I may not be the best friend in the world, but I'm not that evil. Or stupid."

"No one's dating Owen," Julie said.

My face fell into a frown. No one was dating Owen, and none of us ever would be. He probably had a girlfriend anyhow. Maybe even a fiancé. I didn't want to be hung up on anyone, especially not my ex from high school who I hadn't seen in over four years. It was about three and a half years longer than it should have taken me to get over him. Yet, here I was, my heart still racing from our brief encounter, my mind still full of his face and voice.

I shook my head. No. "Okay, stop." I held up my hands and we all stopped walking. "I can't do this. If I'm going to get over him, I can't think about him. Or Sam. Or any other disaster in my life. I want to enjoy the fact that I just earned a degree after four years of very hard work, and so did the both of you. We made it through college, and we're ready to start our new lives. I'm not going to do that being stuck in the past. From this point forward, I am in love with no one!"

Julie pumped her fist in the air. "Down with love!"

Emma raised her eyebrow at us. "Um, how about not 'down with love' so much as, yay for strong women who don't need a relationship or a man to feel whole!"

"And that!" I said, raising my fist high to match Julie's. "Here's to focusing on our careers!"

4

OWEN

The ibis tucked under my arm nuzzled its beak into the crease of my elbow. It was warm at my side.

I should be thinking about what needed to happen for the bird now. How I should have already radioed the vet to be ready. How I would help him set the leg and hold the bird while he worked. But my mind wouldn't stay on the white-feathered creature for long; it was stuck in the place I'd found the bird.

The place where I'd seen *her*.

I don't know if I'd ever had more of a shock in my life. She had gone to college an hour away, in Miami. I didn't want to attend the same school and risk running into her or having a class with her. It couldn't be like high school. I'd never survive if there was a possibility of seeing her anytime I walked around campus.

I thought I'd chosen well with the Everglades. I could have moved to another state. Chosen another park. Joined another clan. But this had been home, and my clan was my family. I didn't want to leave the land or the shifters I'd come to rely on. Before we broke up, she'd been dreaming of mountains and snow. I expected her to go up north, fall in love with the cold, and never return.

And then, there she was.

I often thought I saw her places. I'd see a woman with the same long hair, those medium-brown locks that glinted gold in the sunlight, the way it swept over her neck. Of course, I had no idea if her hair would still be the same after so many years, but after today, I knew it was. When we first pulled up to the group of ladies, I thought it was her. But in the same way I always thought I saw her, I blew it off and refocused. Except, this time, it really was her.

When I saw her face and her shocked eyes met mine, it was as if the world had vanished. Suddenly, we were back in high school and I'd just seen the most beautiful girl in the world drop her books all over the floor. Back then, I'd been able to step in and rescue her. Saving the day made me her hero and it was easy to win her over. I wanted to save her again, but she didn't need me now.

She was her with her friends and had found an injured

bird. She was not the one in need, but I still wanted to impress her. But Addie hadn't seemed to notice.

It was all I could do to walk away from her. From the moment I saw her and got a whiff of her scent, I wanted to run to her, scoop her into my arms, and never let go again. I'd let go of her once and it had been the most difficult and stupid thing I'd ever done. If I had the chance, I'd keep hold of her so tight, there'd be no danger of us ever being apart again. My blood boiled with wanting her, with missing her, with loving her.

"Whoa, man, you look worse than me." Ezra strolled out of the ranger station as we pulled up.

"I've never seen him so quiet," Zack said. "He must be *very* worried about this bird."

Zack smirked at me and disappeared inside the station.

Ezra gave me a questioning look. "Did you see a ghost out there or what?"

"Something like that," I said, walking past him into the building.

Luckily, Zack had been in his right mind as we headed back, and he'd called the vet to meet us. I carried the bird into the exam room and held it while the vet did his thing. I sensed the animal's distress and did my best to calm it, but I was more than distracted.

Our four years together played through my mind, followed by the four years without her. Hardly a comparison. After the vet got the bird's leg fixed up, I sat in my office, trying to work, but the words on the reports didn't make any sense. I read the same page over and over, but finally stopped, setting the papers down and heading to the window, looking out over my view of the park.

Ezra came in and perched on the edge of my desk, as he often did. This was why he was my second: he knew me too well. Any time I acted out of character, he was immediately on alert.

"So, it's quiet right now," Ezra said. "I think everyone is out doing the day job thing. How about a short run?"

He knew he'd be able to read me more easily when we were in bear form. Our thoughts would be linked, but it was more than that. Just like I could sense other animals, even while in my human state, I could sense my clan even better when we were all in bear form. I wouldn't have to tell Ezra how I was feeling, he would feel it.

But I could have used a run; I thought it might help distract me. "Yeah," I said. "Get in the small cat."

I let Rachel know we were heading out on patrol, then slid into the seat beside Ezra. We drove to a spot out of the way where we could leave the UV, parked and stripped down on either side of the vehicle, roaring loudly as we changed. I stood tall on my furry legs and stretched, then bounded through the woods, the wind rustling through my coat.

I don't usually have to drag things out of you, Alpha, Ezra signaled to me. *What's going on?*

There was little point in trying to change the subject or

deny it. When my mind was so full of her, it'd slip even if I tried not to think about her. Better to just get it out.

I saw an ex-girlfriend today.

Ouch. Bummer. Did she break your heart?

I almost laughed. How I wished that were true. *'Fraid not. I broke hers.*

Oooh, even worse. She just won't stay gone, eh?

Nothing like that. I never wanted to end things with her. I was crazy about that girl.

Ezra didn't respond right away. He jumped through the trees, bouncing with too much energy. He was worse than a cub with his exuberance. But when he spoke again through our mind link, his words were full of maturity.

You're still crazy about her. What happened? Why'd you break up?

I didn't have a choice. Thinking back to that time still made me ache. I had no idea how hard it had been for Addie; I hadn't talked to her after I ended things. But I had been a wreck for weeks. So much, that my mother pleaded with my father, but he wouldn't relent. And he couldn't. I knew that, and it made everything worse.

When I came of age, my parents stepped in, I replied. *They didn't mind who I dated in high school. They always liked Addie. But she's not a shifter.*

Ohhhh. Sadness colored Ezra's thoughts. He got it.

Yeah. So, I hit eighteen and was about to graduate high school. They sat me down to have the talk. Shifter responsibilities. What we have to do for our clan, all of that. And, Addie. They told me it was better to end things. They said I could go to school further away and frame that as the reason. It was normal, they said. High school couples often broke up when they went to college. They thought that if we had no future together, there was no reason to keep dating. And they were right. I wanted to marry her. I would have. But that's not how shifter life works. At least, in our clan.

I know this too well, my friend.

You're not bound in the same way I am.

If I want to remain your second, I am.

The rule about marrying a shifter only actually applied to the Alpha of our clan. When my dad stepped down and I took over, that meant taking on everything that came with the duties of an Alpha, including the marriage rule. No one else technically had to follow this rule; marrying a non-shifter was perfectly acceptable, unless you were the Alpha. Or, in Ezra's case, a second who actually took the job seriously enough that he held himself to the same standards.

He could marry a non-shifter, but that would create a problem. In the event I could no longer lead, he'd have to become Alpha, and he couldn't if he'd married a non-shifter.

The rules made sense. An Alpha had to keep his blood pure and needed to be connected to shifters and his clan in all ways possible. A spouse outside of the clan would be a distraction to a leader. But it wasn't an easy decision. I'd almost considered giving up the Alpha position just so I could marry her. I'd almost considered leaving the clan since not all clans had rules like ours. Most didn't care if the bloodline was mixed. But some great, great, great, great grandfather of mine decided our clan would live a more pure life, so the rule had been created, and we all had to live with it.

I must've let my memories drift too far into my thoughts; Ezra heard.

This is serious, then. I can't believe you almost gave up Alpha and the clan for this girl!

She's far from a girl now. I tried not to picture her too hard. Ezra would see, and the lust flooding my veins wasn't something he needed to witness.

You need a hot piece of tail to take your mind off this human girl.

Right. Like that would happen anytime soon. Seeing her brought all these thoughts and feelings rushing back. It had taken me a long time to get to the point where I didn't ache for her constantly; I didn't want these feelings to return.

This is why you've never seriously dated? Ezra wondered. *You never got over Addie?*

That's why. I put everything into my work and my role as Alpha.

The right female will change everything. What about Hailey? I think she likes you.

She does. She'd been pretty obvious in her flirting. Hailey was beautiful and a really sweet woman. I probably should date her. At least see if anything was there. But how could I when my heart was so stuck on Addie? It wouldn't be fair to Hailey.

She's a cool chick. You should give it a shot.

Maybe someday.

Man, you've got it bad. Maybe go talk to this Addie and see how much she's changed. Maybe it'll kill your feelings for her. You've probably built her up in your memories and the real deal doesn't hold up anymore.

Yeah. Maybe.

But I didn't think that was true. Unless she'd become a totally different person in college, there wasn't a bar that could be raised high enough to match what Addie had been to me.

Well, facts are facts, man. Unless you're still thinking of giving up Alpha, nothing has changed. You can't be with her. So, let's find a way to move you on.

Thanks. I appreciated his concern, I just didn't think it would work. I'd been trying to get over Addie for four years. The guilt was still there for how I'd ended things between us. The pain of missing her was still there. It had moved to the background of my mind over the two years I spent in college. And as I threw myself into my work, I was able to go days without thinking about her too much.

It was always there, though. I'd see a happy family or couple walking through the park, and a little prick with her name on it would spike my heart. I avoided stores when

Valentine's Day was near, and every time July 20th came around, I wondered how she was spending her birthday.

If she'd found someone who would love her as much as I had.

We finished our run and headed back to the ranger station. I checked the reservations and found that Addie would be there all week. Maybe I'd take some time off so I didn't have to worry about running into her.

5

ADDIE

"How about a boat ride?" Julie asked. "We'd get to see lots of wildlife."

I nodded. "Sounds good."

"Ugh, come on, Addie. You can't just bum around over this Owen dude. He ended things. It's time to move on."

"I'm not bumming over him, Emma," I countered, getting a little defensive. It'd been a day since we'd run into Owen and I hadn't been able to stop thinking about him, but I thought I'd done a fairly decent job of hiding it.

"Then let's go on this boat ride so you can prove it," Emma replied.

"Sounds great." I tried to sound enthusiastic, but probably failed.

By the time we arrived at the dock, I was feeling hopeful.

I had my camera in tow, ready to photograph every animal and interesting plant I came across. *This is why we came here, I reminded myself. To spend time in nature and unwind after graduation. Not to spend the week being hung up on ex-boyfriends from high school.*

I'd spent enough time grieving over Owen. This time was for me.

We waited with a small group for the boat to be ready. Water lapped against the dock, and the air was cooler here. A large fan was positioned at one end of the boat, then several benches of seats. I'd never ridden an airboat before and, judging by the headphones resting on each seat, it would be loud. Perfect for drowning out my thoughts and making me focus on what was ahead, not behind.

A man walked over to the waiting group. "Hello there, folks." He waved to get everyone's attention. "I'm Aiden and I'll be your tour guide today. If you'll make your way to the boat, we can go ahead and get started on our tour."

He gestured toward the boat and the group started to trickle on. As we neared him, he smiled. "Hello, ladies."

I smiled back. "Hello."

He leaned close to me as I passed. "Be sure to grab a seat near the back. It's the best." He winked and continued greeting the other passengers.

When the three of us sat—near the back, though I honestly hadn't been trying to sit there—Emma and Julie converged on me.

"He totally flirted with you!" Emma teased, giggling.

"He's cute," Julie whispered. "Maybe he could take your mind off Owen."

I rolled my eyes and shushed them as Aiden took his place at the back of the boat, next to the large fan.

Aiden stood to address the crowd. "As we take our ride today, expect to see a nice sampling of the variety of wildlife the Everglades has to offer. We should see some gators, herons or ospreys, and maybe even a wild bull, believe it or not. Never know what's around the corner in these parts."

He smiled at me again as he took his seat. He dropped his voice to speak only to us. "If there's anything you ladies want to see, you let me know, okay?"

Emma and Julie agreed happily. I just nodded. Maybe he was sort of flirting, but it was nothing I was going to get excited over. Sure, he was cute. Lots of guys were cute. If my attraction to Owen had been purely physical, maybe that would have been enough to distract me. It was so much more than looks, though.

The large fan started up and we all placed our headphones over our ears. It was loud, but Aiden paused the boat every once in a while to explain what we were seeing or tell us something about the body of water we were riding through. He got very excited when we came across a baby alligator.

"It's very rare to see a baby out sunning like that," he said, pointing. Everyone took numerous photos and exclaimed over the sight. "I see a baby like that maybe once in a hundred rides. You folks must be very lucky." He leaned closer to us and smiled at me once more. "Or maybe I'm just the lucky one."

My face warmed and I tried to ignore it. I snapped photos and let my touristy side take over. I wasn't here to flirt or be flirted with. I was here for taking in the sights and to spend time with my friends. That was it. I turned away from the guide back toward the front of the boat.

Unfortunately, he turned out to actually be funny. Several times as he was giving commentary, I found myself chuckling at his stories. I *did* like guys who could make me laugh.

The ride ended, and as we got off the boat, he watched us file off. Emma and Julie glanced back at him.

Emma sighed. "Bummer."

"Yeah," Julie agreed.

I was confused. "What?"

"I thought maybe he'd ask you out," Emma confessed.

"Me, too," Julie added.

We walked into the building and weaved our way through the gift shop. As we made our way along the aisles of items for sale, we paused now and then to look at some trinkets and souvenirs. Emma bought three postcards and stamps.

"Here." She handed us each a postcard as we stepped out of the gift shop into the bright sun. "We'll send these to someone so we can feel like we're really on vacation."

"We *are* really on vacation," I said.

"Then why haven't I been drunk yet?" Emma asked.

I rolled my eyes. "Because enjoying nature is more interesting."

"What if you could have both?"

The three of us turned at the sound of the male voice. Just outside the gift shop, Aiden leaned against the railing. Had he been waiting for us? "There's a place out in the woods that friends of mine own. They're having a party tonight. Plenty of wild animals. Plenty of beer." He raised an eyebrow and looked at me expectantly.

I pressed my lips together. "I'm sure you'll have a good time."

"I'd have a much better time if you joined me."

My eyes widened and I felt heat rush up my neck. When Emma had said something about him asking me out, I'd been relieved that he hadn't. So much for that.

"Oh, I, umm... am on vacation," I said. "With my friends. We're doing things together this week."

"Even better. Bring them along."

I glanced over at them, which was a mistake. Both of them were pleading with me. Pleading to say yes. We hadn't been out yet. Of course, it had only been one night so far, but they were itching to let loose, and I didn't want to stop them.

"Okay," I said. "The three of us will meet you there."

"Excellent." He handed his phone to me. "Why don't you save your number in my phone and I'll text you the address."

I took the phone reluctantly. I didn't like giving out my number to someone I barely knew, but I guessed I could just block him if I had to. I saved my number and handed the phone back.

"Addie," I told him.

"So glad to be your tour guide today. I look forward to seeing you tonight, Addie." He nodded at us, smiled and turned away as he headed back into the building.

Emma and Julie squealed as we walked away.

"Thank you! Thank you!" Emma said. "Party in the woods, woot!"

"Awesome," Julie said. "And, this will be perfect. We'll get there, find your man, and conveniently disappear."

"No! You will not leave me alone with him!" I demanded.

"He asked *you* out, remember?" Emma said. "He let us come along."

"That's because I would have said no," I insisted. "I'm not going out alone here with some guy I don't even know."

"That's how you get to know people," Julie said. "How will you ever meet someone if you don't ever go on dates?"

I shrugged. "I haven't been too worried about it."

"Right," Julie said. "Owen? Still?"

"And Sam," I added, getting a little defensive. "Owen broke my heart, but Sam confused me. I have no desire to be in any sort of relationship right now."

Julie frowned. "You're going to give him a chance, aren't you?"

"He *is* cute!" Emma gushed. "And he's funny. That was a good tour."

"It was," Julie agreed.

"Just give him a chance," Emma begged. "If it doesn't go anywhere, then it doesn't. But you won't know unless you get to know him a little."

"Just talk to him," Julie added. "And drink a beer or two while you're at it."

I rolled my eyes. "We're going, aren't we? I told him we'd go, so we'll go. And I will talk to him, but I'm not going to be off alone all night. I'm going to spend time with you guys, too."

"We'll be with you all week," Emma said. "Talk to him. Maybe have a make out session." She made a kissy face.

"No," I narrowed my eyes. "Not on the agenda."

"Keep your mind open," Julie said. "No expectations. No assumptions."

Emma laughed, pulling the car door open. "You never know; he could be the one."

I shook my head as I climbed into the backseat. "I highly doubt it."

"You won't know unless you give him a chance," Julie pointed out.

"Fine. One chance," I said. "I'll talk to him. Didn't I already agree to that anyway? Give me a break, guys!"

"But we want you to take it seriously," Julie said.

"I take it very seriously. I will have a serious conversation with the cute airboat tour guide. Then I will seriously move on with my life."

"Unless you like him," Emma chirped.

"If he turns out to be the man of my dreams, you can both remind me that I was wrong every day of my happily ever after."

6

ADDIE

I hadn't packed much for going out. I thought we'd be hiking around the area and camping. Silly me; I should have known better. Emma and Julie had plenty of cute outfits with them, so they kindly helped me supplement. A top from Emma and cute, strappy sandals from Julie and we were on our way.

Aiden had texted me the address, as promised. When we looked it up, the place was about a half hour away. So much for getting away if we were just going to head halfway back to Miami. But I said nothing and rode along, knowing that if nothing else, they were happy we were going out.

We knew were getting close when the cars started to appear, parked along the side of the road. We pulled into a dirt parking lot and were lucky enough to find a spot that didn't require us to walk a quarter mile along the dark road. I felt nervous and looked around anxiously; I hoped he wouldn't show. Then I'd have had held up my end of the deal, and my friends couldn't complain that I hadn't given him a shot. I could whine all night about being stood up and make them feel bad for me.

We walked in the direction that some of the crowd meandered toward and came to something of a clearing. There was a large fire, a few kegs of beer, and someone's Bluetooth speaker playing a playlist of country rock songs. Not really my thing, but I wasn't there to complain.

"We beat him here," Julie said.

I shrugged. "Maybe he won't show."

"Not a chance," Emma quipped.

We each got a beer and then stood off to the side. It didn't take long for the guys there to notice that three single ladies had just walked in. We were like a target, much to my dismay.

Two guys walked over and started talking to us. I tried to ignore them, but Julie and Emma chatted away, laughing and smiling where appropriate until Emma went off to dance with one of them. The other walked off to get a beer and found himself caught up in a conversation.

"That didn't take long," I said, glancing at Emma and the guy she was now dancing with.

Julie nodded toward the other guy, who had now wandered off, out of sight. "He was into you."

"Nah." I sipped my beer and glanced at the small group trickling toward us through the trees.

"You really didn't notice?" Julie asked.

"I wasn't really paying much attention."

She nodded. "So that's it. It's not that no guy has shown interest. It's that you don't pick up on it."

I shrugged again. "I guess I don't really care."

She blew out a sigh, then grabbed my arm. "He's here!"

I turned and saw Aiden walking toward us. Great. I forced a smile as he approached.

"You're missing one," he said.

I pointed to Emma.

He saw and nodded. "Glad you could all make it. I'm sure you're used to fancy nightclubs and all, but this is what us locals do to unwind. You from the city?"

"I guess so? I mean, we went to school in Miami, but my family is from the outskirts. I've always considered myself more of a suburban girl than a city girl."

"Well," he said, letting his smile spread across his face, "that's just my sort of girl. Woman, actually. You're no girl."

My face warmed and I glanced down at myself subconsciously. I turned toward Julie, and that's when I noticed that she had ducked out of the conversation. I met her eyes from several feet away as she poured herself another beer and pretended to be enjoying some conversation with a few people by the kegs. She gave me an encouraging smile and turned her attention back to her new group.

I was on my own.

"So, you're...from around here?" I asked.

"You could say that. Born and raised just a few miles down the road. My family and I are pretty tight. We stay close to each other and near the area."

"That's nice."

Why was I so bad at these sorts of conversations? At dating at all? Must have been because I had no practice. Dating was much different in high school, and in college, I had already known Sam before we were alone together for any length of time. This whole concept of going out with someone I didn't know had me baffled. Relationships really started out like this?

"What made you decide to take a boat ride today?" he asked.

"My friends and I are here camping at the park, celebrating our graduation. We wanted to do something that would give us a chance to see animals that we haven't noticed around the park."

"I love the Everglades. We're so lucky to be so close to the park. I just wished I was more accepted there."

I drew my eyebrows together. "You're not accepted at the park?"

"Well, you know. Some of the rangers there don't like the local folks very much."

"Why would that be?"

"I don't know. Technically, the boating company isn't part

of the park, it's just off the property. We have permission to ride through the park, but the company is privately owned by my family. Maybe they don't like the noise; who knows."

That seemed strange to me, but what did I know of the area's politics? "Oh," was all I could say. It made sense. The rangers probably didn't like how the boats disturbed the water and animals.

"Have you met any of the rangers?"

I lifted one shoulder. "Not really. We've just hiked and kept to ourselves for the most part."

"There's this one ranger in particular." Aiden shook his head. "Owen something. He hates me."

My heart jolted. He couldn't be talking about the same Owen, could he? "Owen Bailey?"

Aiden straightened up. "I think that's his last name. Do you know him?"

"I knew him in high school, but I haven't seen him since —well, I saw him at the park, but I haven't really talked to him in years."

"I see. So, you know what I'm saying then. How much of a jerk he can be."

"Oh, I... guess so. I don't know." Could he be a jerk? I didn't know Owen now. People changed a lot in college. Maybe it was true.

"How well do you know him?"

"Not at all. We dated in high school, but like I said, that was years ago."

"Do you know about his family and friends? His brother?"

This conversation was going to a strange place, and I didn't like it. "I guess? I've met his brother."

"What about his friend, Ezra?"

"Uhh... I don't recall him having a friend with that name."

"Do you know where he lives?" he asked. "Someone said he has a cabin just off the park's land."

"When I knew him, he lived outside of the city. I really don't know."

He nodded, thinking for a moment before he kept talking. "Guys like that just get to me, you know. I get that he's a ranger. Or the main ranger or whatever his title is. I get it. I don't have a fancy degree or anything. I just know the land from growing up here. They must not like it when locals know more than they do."

I nodded absently; I really didn't know what else to say. I didn't want to be on a date, if that's what it was, talking about Owen. And not in a way that was putting Owen down. He might have been a jerk, I didn't know. But the Owen I knew wasn't, and I didn't want to think of him in that way, even if he had broken my heart.

"Have you been doing the boat thing long?" I asked. Maybe a different subject would be better.

"My family has had that business for over twenty years," he said. "No thanks to the rangers who want to shut us down.

Do you know that one time that Owen guy approached me and tried to stop me from coming onto park land?" He shook his head. "I say live and let live, you know? Why should he care if I want to make an honest living? Isn't that what we all want to do?"

"That's what I'm trying to do myself. This week, I'm hoping to figure out what I want to do with the rest of my life."

"Right. For me, it was easy. My family has this business, so if I wanted it, the job was mine. I like giving tours, meeting people, showing off the area. I grew up here, so this is all home to me. I don't think I should be chased out of it just because someone doesn't like me."

"No, I guess you shouldn't."

"So, you agree. This guy is a total jerk, and he needs to back off."

"I..." I didn't want to agree, but I also didn't want to argue with the guy. Clearly, this bothered him. "I don't know enough about the situation to make that call."

"Well, if you see this Owen again, you tell him to let me be. I never did anything to get in his way. I just want to run my tours and that's it. Meet a nice lady, which I may have already done, have a nice life with her." He smiled in a hopeful way.

"Right. That's what we all want, I guess."

"It doesn't bother you that I don't have a college degree, does it?"

"No. You have a livelihood. Seems like you enjoy it. You're good at it, so..."

"Thank you. I like to think so. What was your favorite part?"

"Umm..." I really wished Emma and Julie hadn't gone off and left me here. "I guess the baby gator. That was neat."

He nodded. "It is quite rare. That wasn't just tour talk. You're lucky; you brought me luck."

I picked at the edge of my cup. "I haven't had too much luck lately, so that's good."

"I find that hard to believe. I almost didn't work today, but something told me to just show up, that it would be good. And then you and your friends came walking along, and I knew I'd made the right call. Who needs a day off when you can spend time with a beautiful woman?"

I looked over the crowd, trying to locate Emma and Julie. I at least wanted to have an idea of where they were if I needed a quick getaway.

"Yeah, my brother and I—I have four brothers, if you can believe that—we all work on the boats. Giving tours, fixing them up, whatever needs to be done. My oldest brother even learned how to work the web site and all. We're high tech now. Did you know you could book a tour online?"

"I didn't, no."

"You can. And there's pictures, too. I took most of them. I like to think I'm somewhat of an amateur photographer. I noticed you taking a lot of photos today. That camera of yours is nice."

"Thanks. I don't really know much about it."

"I've worked with cameras for a long time. I have one like yours—the newer model, but it works pretty much the same. Great for low light. I have some of the most gorgeous sunrises and sunsets."

"I can imagine."

"I'll have to show you my collection. I have lots of photos framed and hanging in my house."

"Nice."

"I even had one printed in a local magazine," he said. "Have you ever had a photo published?"

"I have not."

"It was just a local thing, no big deal. But people around here thought it was a pretty big deal. I've sold a few copies of the print."

"That's...cool." He went on talking about himself *non-stop*. His family, the business, even his ex-girlfriend. Like I wanted to hear about her. After about twenty minutes, I was ready to get out of there and never talk to Aiden again.

What was it Emma and Julie had said about me liking him? About him maybe being 'the one?' Were they high? There was no way I even wanted to spend another half hour with this guy, let alone go on another date. I finally spotted them across a crowd.

"Well, I should get back to my friends," I said when there was a pause in conversation.

He glanced to see where I looked. "Already? I'm having such a good time talking with you. I thought we had a good thing going."

"It's just that we came together and, like I said, we're on girls' trip, so I should spend time with them."

"Well, I have your number. Maybe once your vacation is over, we can go out on a real date."

I nodded absently. "Umm... maybe."

"It's fate, don't you think?" He smiled. "I'm Aiden, you're Addie. Our names go together. Just like we should."

"Yeah... I guess they do kind of go together..."

"I think you're a really special lady." He put his hand to my cheek and stepped closer.

Shit. I didn't have time to step back. He leaned down, coming in for a kiss, and I pulled my head back suddenly before his lips could touch mine.

"I—I'm sorry, I just can't," I said, taking several steps back.

"What the hell?" his face broke into anger. "I thought we had a good time. You've been leading me on, and now you won't even kiss me?"

"I just need to get back to my friends."

I hurried away and almost ran to them.

"Here she is!" Emma held up a cup and whooped.

"Can we go? Now. Please?"

They saw my expression and exchanged a glance.

"Yeah, sure," Julie said.

"Did he hurt you?" Emma asked. "Or get rude in any way?" She put her hand on her hip and glared in his direction. "I'll kick his ass."

"Nothing like that. I'll explain. Let's just get out of here. Please."

With one of them on each side of me, we hurried back to the car, hopped in, and sped off.

7

OWEN

I shouldn't have gone. I get that now, but all I could think at the time was, not him. When Conner told me he saw Addie talking with Aiden Harvey and he asked her out, I was pissed. I hated to think of her spending time with that asshole, but it also meant I'd let her into my thoughts too much. My whole clan knew her face now, knew my feelings for her, knew everything. More than I wanted them to know. But it was too late.

Conner had been out on some kind of work errand and had been shocked to see the woman whose face had consumed my thoughts lately. Then he'd heard Aiden talking and the two of them making plans. He'd told me about it, not so much because he wanted to or thought he should, but because he'd been bothered enough by it that his thoughts reflected something. I'd had to convince him to give me details, and as the Alpha, he didn't have much room to disobey. As my friend, he wouldn't have held back information, either, if he'd thought it would help me. He hadn't been so sure it would be good for me to know this, however.

So, I'd gone to the party. I knew about these get togethers; they happened all the time. We never went, though. We liked to hang out and party in the woods, sure. Who didn't? But we didn't do it with a bunch of locals. Bear clans tended to be tight knit and kept to themselves. Crocs, on the other hand, loved to be around people, scamming them however they could, taking full advantage of the people passing through.

Even the airboat gig was somewhat of a scam. Sure, people got to tour the Everglades by water, but the Harvey family who ran it charged far too much, and most of the animals seen on the tour were staged. Either put there on purpose or faked. I'd even heard rumors that they had a baby alligator statue that they put in the water, then claimed it was a rare sight and that group was extra lucky for seeing such a "rare" occurrence. I came across baby gators all the time; you just had to know where to find them. And it certainly wasn't in an area where loud airboats passed through all day.

The rivalry between the crocodiles and bears of the Everglades was long standing, going back more years than either clan knew. Both wanted complete control over the land, though for different reasons. Each despised the other, though again, for different reasons. The bears had had their grasp on the park for decades and the crocs were all around it, just hovering outside the borders, waiting for their moment to slither in and wreak havoc. The conclave, which consisted of delegates of shifters of all types, helped keep both sides in check and stepped in if one side went too far.

There had always been issues with the crocs—usually not enough to go to the conclave over, but annoying, nonetheless. The day Addie showed up had started with Ezra telling me about their run-in with them the night before at a local bar. I was about ready to tell my guys to not even go out in public locally, but I wouldn't punish my guys for something the crocs did. I chose not to go out often because I didn't want to deal with it. And until now, my dealings with them hadn't been too personal. Of course, messing with the member of one clan is like messing with all the members, but none had ever gone after something so precious to me.

I didn't know if Aiden had any idea who Addie was to me. I didn't know how he could, but it didn't really matter why he was going for her. It only mattered that he was, and that she'd gone for it. She'd gone to the party with her friends and wandered off to spend time alone with Aiden. It even looked like he kissed her. Maybe they had a second one planned. Maybe they'd fall in love and get married, and everything I ever wanted out of life would be his instead of mine. Maybe I'd lost my chance forever.

How about getting a bite to eat? I'm starved. Mason, third in the chain of command within the clan, thought to me.

Then go eat, I responded. *I don't need a babysitter.*

When they realized what I was doing, I'd found myself surrounded by the thoughts of my clan. They wouldn't come to where I was unless I needed them to. Even my guys didn't love partying so much that they'd subject themselves to an event thrown by crocs. They were worried I'd do something stupid. And so Mason had been assigned—probably by Ezra and Conner—to keep an eye on me through the night and make sure I didn't start something they'd have to finish.

I just want to know you're okay.

I'm fine, thanks. I'm going home to sleep. I ran up to my cabin and stood out front to stretch. *Just got home, actually.*

And you're staying there?

That's the plan.

I'm heading off to bed, too. Hit me up in the morning. I'll do a perimeter run before work if you want.

That's not a bad idea. I shifted back to human form and dressed. But as I sat in my cabin, trying to concentrate on the piece of wood I was whittling, I couldn't stop my mind.

Addie didn't know Aiden. She didn't know all these croc guys were bad news. Wouldn't she want to know if she were getting herself mixed up with a bunch of assholes? The Addie I knew wouldn't have wanted to be around people like that. I thought I should just go tell her. Just as a concerned friend. To let her know what the truth was.

I got up and paced the room. Would I come off as too... controlling? I had no right to tell her what to do. If I went to talk to her and warn her of her new boyfriend, it would seem like I was just being jealous, trying to keep her from being happy. I needed a way to tell her that wouldn't make it seem like I just didn't want her to date. *Maybe I could fix her up with someone.*

As soon as I had the thought, I shook it from my mind. Okay, so I was jealous. There was no denying it. That wasn't the reason I didn't want her around Aiden, though. *Maybe admitting that to her would be enough*, I thought. *I could just say, "Yes, I know this comes off as a jealous ex-boyfriend thing, and I am jealous, but trust me, he's bad news." Maybe I could convince her.*

Without thinking too much more about it, I found myself outside, walking. If I happened to be strolling in the direction of her tent, then okay. It wasn't like it was close. If I went to her tent, there would have been many miles of ground to cover. But if I ran there...

I stepped out of the shorts I'd pulled on and shifted back into bear form. When my bones settled and muscles were ready, I leapt into the air, running fast until I was close. I slowed to a walk as I neared the camping area, though; I didn't need to take calls all day about some bear running around the woods, scaring the campers. I kept my ears open and crouched as I moved in closer.

I really hadn't thought this through. If my plan was to

talk to her, I should have come in human form. Or at least carried a sack of clothing. Maybe it was better that way.

Just don't break the ultimate command, whatever you do.

I almost rolled my eyes at Mason. *There's no chance of that.* Like I would show her my animal form and break the rule that kept all shifters from telling humans of our existence. This one secret, this one universal command, was true of all shifters. Even if sometimes the crocs danced on the line, their way of life would be severely hindered if the world knew the truth about them. It would be for all of us.

Maybe telling Addie wouldn't start some massive, riotous outbreak that would ruin all shifter life forever, but why take the chance? Even if I could tell her, I wouldn't want to; it would scare the shit out of her and she'd think I was a freak. I didn't really have a chance with her at the time, and it was my own fault, my own family and position that kept me from being with her. I still didn't want to taint my image in her eyes. It was bad enough she probably hated me for ending things how I did; I didn't want it to be any worse.

I froze when their tent unzipped and the three of them stepped out. I didn't know these friends, but I thought she'd called the blonde Emma. Conner said the other one was Julie, who began to pull a bottle of orange juice from the cooler.

"We have plenty," she said.

"Thank god," Addie breathed, setting a large bottle of vodka onto the picnic table.

Emma came over with a few red plastic cups and held them in place as Julie poured.

"To friends only," Addie said, raising her cup for a toast.

Emma sighed. "To friends, and *good* guys."

"Like I said, *friends only*," Addie countered.

Julie rolled her eyes. "It couldn't have been that bad."

"Just be glad you walked away when you did," Addie mumbled, taking a long sip of her drink. "You were spared his long tale of life as a tour guide. Even Sam wasn't as arrogant as Aiden. He talked about himself the whole time!"

"It is quite a feat to be a bigger asshole than Sam," Emma laughed.

I had no idea who this 'Sam' was. An ex of Addie's, I assumed, by what they were saying. The jealous spark flickered. *Think about what they're saying*, I reminded myself. *Calling him an asshole. Obviously, Sam is not on their good side.*

"Why is it always the cute ones?" Julie asked. "You either find a good guy or a good-looking guy, but never both."

"That's not true," Addie pointed out. She looked off into the distance and sighed.

Emma groaned. "If you say Owen one more time, I'm going to scream."

My heart jumped. What? Had they talked about me? Addie was talking about me? My ears twitched to hear more.

"Sorry," Addie muttered.

"Hey, you know what?" Julie put both hands on Addie's shoulders and looked her square in the eye. "You took a step.

You met up with a guy and you talked to him. You had a date, Addie! A date! And so it didn't go well. That happens. The point is, you did it. You're moving on. You're over Owen. You're over Sam. Now we just need to find your Mr. Right."

"I second that." Emma held up her drink and they all tapped their cups to hers.

Addie took a sip and paused. "I just wonder sometimes..."

"Don't do that," Emma said.

"But the thing is," Addie continued, "the only reason Owen ended things was to go to school. And, okay, so we were many hours apart, and that would have been hard to manage. I get it. But we're out of school now. He works here in the park and I live an hour away. That's not exactly long distance anymore—"

"To be honest, Ad," Julie interrupted, "I don't know if that was the real reason. He might have said that. He might even have thought it at the time, but guys don't want to be stuck with the same woman forever. Not right out of high school. They like to sleep around and explore, try new things—"

"And new women," Emma added.

"Exactly." Julie set down her empty cup. "He had oats to sow, and he used that as an excuse to break things off. Any guy who does that isn't worth it. It was more important to him to date other women than it was to make things work with you. And that's the truth."

I wanted to scream. My claws dug into the earth, tearing

grass and breaking twigs. I could have stood up and roared. I could have charged at them and showed my fury. But it was no use.

You okay, Boss?

Not now, Ezra.

I tried to calm down. The last thing I needed was Ezra chirping in my ear.

I knew, on some level, it wasn't Julie's fault. Or Emma's. They didn't know me, and they were going by what tabloid magazines and Hollywood told them about men. I'd even guess, based on my friends at the time, that what they said was true in many cases. It just wasn't true for me.

I'd had my eyes set on a great school, just a few minutes' drive from where Addie had been accepted. I knew I wanted to work in the park, and I had an easy in with so many of my clan working in and around the area. I was never going to leave for good. And I didn't want to. I had my family and clan, I had my career picked out and was excited about it. And most of all, I had a woman I adored, who was everything I could have imagined in a mate.

I'd also had my eyes on a shiny ring I thought she'd like.

I had a plan. We'd take a midnight stroll through the park, sneaking into the area closed at night. There was a certain spot I loved. In the middle of one of the rope bridges, if you paused, you could look both directions on either side of you and see over the water to the horizon. I'd tell her that one side was our past, full of joy and happiness, and one side was our future, stretched long ahead of us. Sometime between proposing and our wedding day, I'd sit her down and tell her the truth about me. That was the only time most of us made an exception and told a pure human—when wedding bells were ringing. Or, in the event that a child was created out of wedlock. Obviously, the mother would have to be told that her baby had a 50% chance of becoming shifter. Addie would have understood and accepted me, I just knew it.

My plan was perfect. I was so excited the day I told my parents about it over dinner, how I was going to talk to Addie's dad the next day and ask for his permission. Then, my parents dropped the news on me. I hadn't known about the marriage rules in our clan. Why would I? Other clans were allowed to marry non-shifters. Even within my own clan there were mixed marriages. But in our clan, the Alpha rule stood on some ancient desire for purity or some bullshit. My father felt strongly about it; he didn't want to upset the ancestors.

I'd been heartbroken—and angry. I tried to think of ways to get around it. I'd gone as far as packing my bags, planning to leave my family or the area, or the clan altogether, if that's what it took. But my mother must've sensed it in me and came to talk to me, sitting beside the packed duffle bag on my bed.

We talked for hours, and by the end of it, I saw my duty. I

understood my dad's reasoning, and though I didn't agree with any part of it, I felt compelled to go along with it. I wished I could tell Addie the truth, that I hadn't wanted to sow my wild oats as Julie had suggested. That I missed her every day.

That I still loved her.

As I listened, watching Addie and wanting to be close to her, she said something that made me completely unravel. I walked away, heading back to my cabin, her words still ringing in my ears.

"The truth is," she'd said to her friends, "I'm not over Owen, and I don't know if I ever will be. I want to talk to him and see if there's any chance of us trying to make this work."

I hadn't stayed after that; I didn't want to hear her friends convince her it was a bad idea. She still had feelings for me. She wanted to get *back together*. If anyone had been there, they might have expected me to be ecstatic over this.

But sadness weighed me down. It took a long time to get back home, and when I did, I crawled into bed, still naked, and wiped away a tear. It didn't matter that she still wanted me. The rules hadn't changed; there was no way I could be with her.

The day before, I would have said that was the best news I could have ever heard, but in that moment, it felt like a dagger to the heart. It was easy to want something when it seemed far out of reach. Having her there, knowing what I knew, meant that I'd have to do the hard part. If she did come to talk to me, I had to be the one to send her away. I had to reject her. Again. I had to watch her walk away, knowing we wanted each other more than anything.

I'd have to break her heart.

Again.

8

ADDIE

I woke up determined to do it. Whatever had happened last night, and whatever my friends had to say about it, I was going to talk to Owen. I couldn't live with myself if I didn't at least see. Maybe nothing had changed. Maybe they were right and his reasons hadn't been as pure as he claimed.

Whatever the case, I needed to know.

We got up late after our long, boozy night and it was already afternoon by the time we'd all showered and dressed for the day. We ate lunch around the fire, and that's when I announced what I'd decided.

"Before either of you say anything, just know that I've thought a lot about this," I started. "I'm going to talk to him and see what the deal is. Who knows, he might even be seeing someone. After I talk to him, I will move on. I will get closure, and while it certainly won't be with Aiden, I will get out and date and find someone. Or attempt to."

Emma shoved a piece of bread into her mouth and spoke with garbled words. "Go for it."

"Really?" I'd expected much lashing back and convincing against.

"You know, I agree," Julie said. "If this is what it'll take, then go for it. Talk to him. Find out what you need to find out. Then say goodbye to him forever."

"And if you need to cry, we'll be here," Emma added, hugging her arm around my shoulders.

"Just remember that he didn't come talk to you. You're going to him. Again."

"I know," I said. "And I've considered that, too. I really have thought about this for days."

"I believe it," Emma mumbled.

"I'm not making a snap decision and rushing into this."

Julie popped a chip into her mouth. "We never said you were, Addie."

I huffed. "I just thought you'd be trying to talk me out of it. I had all these arguments planned and everything."

Julie raised an eyebrow. "Do you want us to talk you out of it? Because that alone is a sign—"

"No, no," I said. "This isn't like that. I should have talked to him years ago. Seeing him again made me realize that I'm really not over him. And I need to be. You guys are right. And this will help."

Emma smiled. "Then I vote 100% yes."

"Me, too," Julie added.

I let out a long breath. "So, now I just have to go do it. What do you want to do when I get back?"

"Whatever you want to do," Emma said.

"We'll go for a hike if you need to talk. Or we can go out and get you drunk if it goes badly," Julie shrugged.

"And what if it *doesn't* go badly?" I chewed on my lip. "There's only one possible outcome, I know that. And I'm not getting my hopes up, but..."

"Then bring him back here for us to meet him," Julie chirped.

"Okay." I took several breaths, psyching myself up. "I'm going to talk to him."

They both gave me quick hugs, and I hopped in the car, headed for the ranger station nearby. It was the same one we'd called when I found the ibis, so I hoped this was the one he worked out of. The park was so huge and there were so many ranger stations, he could be anywhere.

I parked and ascended the steps, then approached a woman sitting behind a desk. Her name tag said Rachel.

"Hi, Rachel," I smiled. "I'm looking for a certain ranger, and I'm wondering if he's here."

"Sure. What is this in regards to?"

I had my excuse ready to go. "I found an injured bird a

few days back. The ranger said to call or stop by to find out how it was doing."

Part lie, part exaggeration, close enough.

Rachel nodded. "Who you looking for?"

"Owen Bailey?"

"And your name, ma'am?" she asked.

"Adeline Pearson."

She scribbled something down, then looked up at me. "I'm afraid he's not here today, Ms. Pearson."

"Oh." Disappointment washed over me. "Do you expect him in tomorrow?"

"He's off for the rest of the week. But let me make a call. I can get you an update on the bird."

"Oh, great; thanks." I forced a smile. I couldn't very well walk away and say I didn't care anymore. Even if it was an excuse, I did wonder about the bird. Wouldn't hurt to stick around to hear something about it.

Rachel disappeared into another room and came back after several minutes. "Ms. Pearson?"

"Yes." I turned from the rack of brochures and walked back over to her desk.

"I spoke with Owen briefly. He says if you'd like, you can stop by his cabin to talk about the bird, or he can have the vet give you a call if you'd prefer that."

"Oh." *His cabin? Hell yes! Yes!* I tried to act indecisive. "I'm not really sure where his cabin is."

"Well no, he wouldn't expect you to. That's why he had

me write down directions for you." She handed me a piece of paper. "It's just off the park grounds, but it can be a little tricky to find."

I took the paper and tucked it carefully into my pocket. "Thanks. We're old friends, so he probably just thought we could catch up." I tried to laugh it off.

She gave me a little smile that seemed to hint that she knew what I was up to. "If you get lost, his number is there on the bottom."

"Oh. Great, thanks."

I got back into the car and pulled out the paper. *I have his address and phone number? This information could be dangerous.* As long as I did what I planned to do and just talked to him, it'd be fine. As long as I didn't save his number to my phone and text him the next time I was drunk, or drive by his house when I was bored or suspicious, it'd be fine.

I sucked in a few breaths to steady my nerves. Once I convinced myself that I wouldn't do those sorts of things with this information, I read over the map and drove off.

I did miss one turn, but I found my way easily enough. I tended to have a good sense of direction just by taking a moment to orient myself if I became confused. When I saw the little cabin sitting there, unassuming, my heart jumped. His Jeep was there; the same red Jeep his parents had bought him for graduation. I'd ridden in it twice: once, the day he got it, and again the following day, when he took me to the park to break up with me.

Before I even got out of Emma's car, he stepped out onto the front porch. Weird that even when he was off, Rachel—whatever her position was—called him. Maybe he loved his job that much. I couldn't blame him. I would've loved to work in a national park, too.

He waved when he saw me and I raised my hand in return. Now that I was here and was about to talk to him, I wanted to leave. To turn around and keep things as they were. To not hear again that he didn't want to be with me. But it was too late. I kept walking.

ADDIE

"I heard you wanted to check up on your bird," Owen said.

Right. The ibis was why I was there. "Is she doing okay?"

I reached his porch and we stood facing each other, several feet between us.

He leaned against the railing. "She's doing great. She did have a broken leg, but the vet got her fixed up."

"Good. I was worried."

Silence fell between us for a moment. Since my big cover reason for being there had been resolved, I didn't know what to say next.

"Why are you really here, Addie?" he asked after a long while.

There seemed to be no further reason to try and hide it. "Umm, I guess just to see you again...I don't know." I sighed. I wish I could just come right out and say it. *I love you Owen. Why aren't we together?* Instead, I lifted one shoulder and gave him a tight smile. "The bird seemed like a good excuse to talk to you."

"I didn't think you'd want to talk to me. Ever again."

"Yeah. I could see that."

He laughed. "Yet, here you are."

"Here I am." I looked around, appreciating what I could see of the cabin. "Nice place you have here. Feels like it's part of the park."

"But it's not. Believe me, there was a lot of paperwork to prove it's not."

"Makes sense. I wouldn't want just anyone to be able to build on park land."

"Right. We have enough trouble trying to keep the environment in its original state in these parts."

"Yeah. Then you get idiots with loud airboats driving all through the waterways, disturbing everything." I shook my head. Whatever had happened with Aiden didn't change the fact that the airboat tours really weren't doing much to keep the natural environment as it was.

He laughed. "You've had the pleasure of meeting the Harveys."

"I wouldn't say it was much of a pleasure."

"Yeah. I heard."

I gave him a surprised look. He heard what, exactly?

"A friend of mine saw you talking to Aiden the other day."

His friends knew who I was? That seemed a little strange. 'Why' kept coming to my mind. Did he talk about me? Have photos of me somewhere? That could be a good sign.

"He invited me and my friends to a party," I said. "It wasn't really my kind of thing."

"Probably for the best. They aren't known for being the most...upstanding? They cause us some trouble. And I'll be honest, I was concerned when I heard you were dating him."

"Whoa." I held up my hands, my face growing hot. "I don't know what your friend told you, but I'm certainly not dating him. He invited us to the party and we went. I talked to him while we were there, and that's about it."

"That's all I meant," he said. "Those parties get shut down all the time. Aiden is..."

"A complete asshole?"

He laughed again. "Something like that."

"You know what's weird? Besides the fact that he tried to kiss me when I gave him no indication that I wanted him to? He asked about you."

Owen drew his eyebrows together and stood up straighter. "He asked about *me*?"

"If I knew you. He said you didn't like his family being in

the park and they weren't accepted here or something. He wanted to know about some guy named Ezra who's a friend of yours, he asked if I'd seen you and said you were a jerk."

His eyes narrowed. "What did he ask about Ezra?"

"Just if I knew him. He wanted to know where you lived. Oh, and he asked if I knew Noah, too."

"Really."

This did not seem to make him happy, and I couldn't blame him. If someone I didn't like was asking around about my family and friends, I'd be bothered, too.

"How is your brother, anyway?" I asked.

"Doing well. Just got married."

"Little Noah?" I shook my head. I sure didn't think Owen's little brother would be married before I was.

"Yup. Do you remember Tori who was in his class?"

"Mmm, maybe?"

"Really long black hair? Was a cheerleader?"

"I think so."

"Well, anyhow," he said, "she's my sister-in-law now."

"Nice. Good for them."

Awkward silence again.

"So, what's the deal with Aiden?" I asked. "Is he trying to start something with you?"

"I'm not sure, but I hope not. I would just ask—I know I don't have any right to—but please stay away from him. For your own sake. I know I might come off like a jealous ex-boyfriend or something, and I wanted a way to say something without sounding like that, but I really just want what's best for you. And I know too much about him; I don't want to see him hurt you."

"You don't have to worry about that. I want nothing to do with that guy. I already blocked his number on my phone."

"Good."

"You were going to say something about me going out with him?"

"Uh." He scratched the back of his neck. "I considered it. But I figured it wasn't my place."

"We're still friends. Aren't we?"

"Sure. I'd like to be."

"And friends look out for each other."

He nodded. "That they do."

"So, as a friend, since we're friends now, I was wondering how things are going for you. Did you find a special lady, too?"

"Nope."

"I guess you know I'm single. I dated someone for about a year in college, but that turned out to be a nightmare."

"Sorry to hear that. I hoped you would find happiness; a good man to love you like you deserve. Someone to marry and have kids with, to grow old with."

I chuckled. "I always thought that would be you. Maybe I'm just not meant to be married."

"Don't say that. Of course you are—I mean, if that's what

you want. I don't think I'll ever marry, but I want you to have everything you want."

"Is that it?" I asked. It seemed like the perfect—maybe my only—opening to finally ask. "Is that why you ended things between us? You never wanted to get married and you thought I did?"

He put his elbows on the railing and rested his chin in his hands, thinking. "No," he said after a long while. "Not entirely. I thought we'd be married once, too."

He had a far off look in his eyes and stood back up, looking past me into the woods. I waited, wanting to hear more.

"I just thought with us being at schools so far away, that it would be too difficult. I didn't want to hold you back. I thought you'd find someone in college and fall madly in love."

I swallowed hard, my throat thickening despite myself. "I did," I whispered. "I fell madly in love with you. All I wanted was for us to have a happy life together."

"How many people actually marry their high school sweethearts? I didn't want you to feel trapped like I have at times."

"You felt trapped in our relationship?"

"No, that's not what I meant. I've felt trapped, yes. Not by you. Just by...life, I guess. By my family. We all have things expected of us. Sometimes it's more than we'd like to have to bear."

"I didn't feel like I was trapped with you. I wanted to tie myself to you in every way possible. You were my first love. My first...everything. My...only love."

It took several long seconds before he would meet my eyes. When he did, his expression looked pained. A tear ran down my cheek and I swiped it away.

"I wish I could say I was over you, Owen, but I'm not. You asked earlier why I was really here. That was it. Closure, is what my friends are calling it. I just wanted to know if the distance was the real reason you ended things. The only reason. Because if that was the only reason, and if we're both still single, and now we're closer and maybe it's not a reason anymore, then..."

"Addie," he whispered.

His expression looked conflicted. I couldn't remember ever seeing him look so troubled, except for when he broke up with me. This was the exact face he'd made then, too. Right before he told me he could never see me again. I expected him to say the same now.

He took a step closer and reached out to take my hands in his.

"I'm so sorry I hurt you. Believe me when I say it was the last thing I wanted to do. I did what I had to do, but there isn't a day I don't regret it and miss you."

I fell into his arms, letting the tears flow freely down my cheeks. It was everything I ever wanted to hear him say. I looked into his eyes and made my move, leaning forward until our lips touched.

When our mouths met, it was like none of the last four years had happened. We fell immediately into the same familiar pattern of moving our lips together, his hand at the back of my neck, my hands rubbing his back.

This was how things should be. Everything felt right in the world as I kissed him. I could feel the love behind it, the delicate way his tongue slipped into my mouth, caressing me. I grew warm all over. I'd spent years wanting him and finally, there we were.

Our kissing grew more intense and I couldn't get close enough to him. I pressed my body against his, my arms squeezing tighter as he squeezed me back. I ran my fingers through the soft spikes of his hair, the texture coarse but soft, just like I remembered it. He smelled good, too. It was a different cologne than he'd worn in high school, but the smell of him made me wild. I wanted to devour him.

I felt myself getting lost in him, wanting to fully merge with him in every way. Wanting what we'd had before. It might have been young, high school sex, but we'd always enjoyed ourselves. He was a good lover, and I needed that. I needed him.

I ran my hands under his shirt and along his back. He was clammy with sweat and his skin felt as if it were almost on fire. Or was it my skin that was so hot? I couldn't tell anymore, but it was all I could do to keep from biting his neck when his fingers circled the back of mine. Chills ran through me everywhere he touched.

"Owen," I breathed in his ear, breaking our kiss for the first time. "I want you."

He made a growling sound and picked me up, wrapping my legs around his waist as he carried me inside. He lay me down on the couch and pulled off his shirt. I sucked in a breath and looked him over.

He was even more muscular than I'd thought. His biceps popped as he leaned over me, and his pecks stood out over his washboard abs. The hint of hair he'd had years ago had darkened and spread to accent his chest in all the right places. I liked the changes.

I pulled my own shirt off, letting him look all he wanted. He kissed down my neck to my chest, stopping to cup my bare breasts and take my nipples into his mouth. The feeling made me dizzy with desire, and I pressed my hips up against his.

He was hard and pushed back against me as he resumed kissing me. His hands made their way down my stomach, unzipping my jeans and sliding further down, rubbing me over my panties. I let out a low moan of pleasure; It was like torture to wait, so I reached down to unzip his jeans.

When I reached beneath his boxers to feel his warm, smooth hardness, he closed his eyes and sat up. I thought he was just moving to enjoy it more, but he stood and zipped his pants.

I was still breathing heavily, and now I was confused. I looked down at my half-naked body. Had I done something wrong?

He stood beside me and reached down to squeeze my hand. "I'm sorry. You should go."

"What?" I sat up and smoothed my hair down. "Is something wrong?"

"I can't do this, Addie. I'm sorry." He put his fist to his forehead and let out a frustrated growl. "I'm so, so sorry."

I picked up my shirt and pulled it on, stunned. I sat there on his couch, taking just a second to glance around. It was nice inside, too. Clean and orderly. But in that moment, I couldn't have cared less.

"I don't understand," I stammered, getting to my feet. I slipped back into my flip flops. "I mean. You said..." My hand extended toward the porch, indicating everything he'd told me before we started kissing.

"I know, and it's all true. But I can't be in your life. I'll complicate things. I...I just can't."

"Owen," I pleaded, "don't do this to me again. Please. I love you."

"I know," he whispered. "And you deserve better than what I can give you."

"How can you say something like that? After all this time. After the last few minutes? You said—"

"I'm sorry." He walked back out to the porch.

I sat for a moment, trying to stop my mind from spinning.

I'd gone from being nervous to overjoyed, thinking I was about to have sex, to confused. And rejected. Again. How was this possible?

I collected myself and walked out on the porch to join him. "Maybe someday, you'll tell me the truth. Why you really ended things. Why you're doing this now. Because your old reasons don't make sense. I want to be with you, Owen. I love you. I've only ever loved you, and I can't picture myself with anyone else. If you don't want me, then okay. At least I know. We had a final...whatever that was, and okay. I'll leave you alone. I'll tell myself whatever I have to in order to get over you. Somehow."

He looked down at his hands. His voice was tight. "I hope you can."

So that was it. He had feelings for me. He regretted ending things. But he still didn't think he could be with me.

"You're wrong, you know." I walked down the porch steps and looked over at him one last time. "You think I deserve better than you, that somehow you can't give me everything I want. Well, all I want is you. So, you're wrong if you think somehow that's not enough for me. There is no one better than you. All of the disasters I've been involved in since you have proven that. I attract men who...are not you. You were the best thing that ever happened to me."

He walked inside and closed the front door softly. I stood there for a moment, but when it was clear he wasn't coming back outside, I got in the car and left. I had no idea what I would tell my friends; this was the opposite of closure. Maybe they'd have some insight to share, some glaring reason I couldn't see that would explain why he wouldn't be with me. I wiped the tears falling from my eyes as I drove back to the site.

10

OWEN

I heard my phone buzz and groaned. I'd told them only to text if there was an emergency—something no one else could handle—and now my phone was going off again. I didn't even bother to look at the screen. I reached my hand out from underneath my blankets and pushed my phone off my bedside table.

All day, it'd been the same.

"Just checking in." Ezra.

"Making sure you're still alive." Mason.

"Hey, the guys said you're sick or something? Won't get out of bed? Call me." Noah.

I'd heard from every member of my clan; the ones closest to me, more than once. I got that they were worried. But they didn't get that sometimes, even the Alpha needed a few days to himself. To drink himself into a stupor. To deeply regret all the decisions he'd ever made in his life. To stay in bed sleeping all day, if that's what he wanted to do.

The light outside my window told me it was nearly evening. Again. I wasn't even sure how many days it'd been anymore. I'd taken a few days off from work to stay away from Addie. I'd done the right thing. I hadn't gone to talk to her, using the Aiden thing as an excuse. But then she'd shown up. Checking on the ibis. Yeah. Good one. Okay, so she did have a degree in ecology and a genuine interest in animals and the environment, but who would drive over here just to check on a bird with a broken leg? *Addie would*, my mind answered. And Addie did. Even if she had other reasons to talk to me, she might have called for no other reason. That's just how she was. She was perfect.

I reached my hand out again, this time to grab the bottle. It was almost empty, but I swallowed the last bit of whiskey and sat up. I rubbed my eyes and let them adjust to the room. Clothing sat in piles on the floor. Empty beer bottles littered the side table, along with wrappers and boxes from take-out food and delivery. I picked up a half-eaten burger and sniffed it, then put it back in its wrapper.

That had been the one interruption I hadn't minded as much. Ezra and Mason had stopped by, which annoyed me, but they'd brought me a huge bag of greasy food. And they just left it when it was clear I didn't want to talk or run. I couldn't shift when I was like this; it would be too easy for them to pick up on everything I was feeling. I had to get control over myself before I could let them in like that.

I trudged to the kitchen, wondering what beer I had left and what food was in the freezer. My walkie, which sat on its base near where I kept my keys and jacket, crackled.

"Earth to Owen..." Ezra said.

I snatched the walkie off its base and held down the button. "Do not use work equipment for personal communication."

"Owen! This isn't, man. We need you."

I set the walkie back down and returned to the kitchen. They didn't need me. There were plenty of well-qualified rangers employed by the park. Any of them were more than capable of handling any situation that might arise. Tonight was the last night of Addie's reservation. I'd be back at work tomorrow, after check out time. After I was sure she was gone and I'd never see her again.

"Owen!"

I heard him all the way in the kitchen.

"I know I've been bugging you when you said not to, but this is an actual emergency!"

I shook my head. Like I hadn't heard that one at least twice over the last few days. It was an emergency that no one could find Conner—until they'd realized he'd left his phone at home. It was an emergency when a fellow ranger called out sick, leaving a gap in the schedule. Until they'd called another senior ranger and got him to cover. Whatever "emergency" it was this time, they could figure it out without me.

I snapped open the top of a fresh can of beer and took a gulp. I had just enough beer and alcohol to get me through one more night before I needed to restock. If it was already getting dark outside, then I was already behind schedule. I took another long sip.

I heard the car door first. Cursing under my breath, I went to look out the window. *Ezra*. Did he never learn? Maybe it was time to get a new second. Mason could be moved up in the ranks; that might not be a bad idea.

I made him pound on my door for several minutes before I finally opened it. "If someone isn't dead or actively dying, you are turning around immediately and leaving."

Ezra hesitated. "Even if it involves Addie?"

"*Especially* if it involves her." I couldn't even say her name out loud. It'd been the only word I'd been thinking for days.

"Okay..." Ezra turned on his heel and took a few steps away.

He knew me too well. "What?"

He shrugged and didn't turn back. "I thought you might want to know about this, but you're right. I'll get someone else to handle it. Have a good night."

I narrowed my eyes and watched him get in his car. What was this game he was playing? I didn't want to give in, but if there was some kind of emergency with Addie, I did want to know, despite what I said.

"Ezra!"

He rolled the window down and stuck his head out. "Yeah?"

"What's going on with Addie?"

He gave me a smug smile before getting back out of the car. "Well, it's not directly about her, exactly."

I gave him the finger and turned away, slamming the door shut behind me.

"There's been an attack!" He shouted through the door. "I saw croc tracks. Got a turtle nest. Horrible damage. Killed a mother and destroyed her eggs."

Okay, this sort of thing happened. It angered me, sure. The crocs knew better and this was a serious crime. I'd be calling the conclave if it was found to be true that the crocs had done it. But it wasn't exactly an emergency if the turtle nest was already destroyed. If any turtles had been alive, the emergency would have been getting them to the vet, and he'd made no mention of that. So, what did it have to do with Addie?

"Not hearing any sort of emergency," I said. "And you've been demoted. Tell Mason he's my new second."

"Hey! I'm just doing my job here, man! But fine, whatever. Maybe I don't want to serve an Alpha who's such a heartless jerk."

I rolled my eyes.

"Well, anyway," he said, undeterred. "I thought you'd want to know since there was a word written in the mud near the nest. A name. After all that's happened, I wouldn't just ignore it."

"A name?"

"Addie. Whoever did it wrote 'Addie' in the mud near the nest. We don't know if they were trying to set it up to make it look like she did it. I mean, it's pretty stupid if they were because obviously, there are crocodile tracks and who would write their name where they committed a crime? Most of us think it's a threat. To you."

He waited, then continued when I didn't say anything. "We also got a call from the conclave. The crocs are complaining that bears are coming on their land. Named you, specifically."

Of course. When I'd gone to the party, I hadn't been careful. I'd gotten close and they'd picked up on my scent. But crocs went places they weren't meant to and we went places we shouldn't all the time. No one ever bothered to say anything unless something happened. Nothing happened when I went to the party except I saw Aiden and Addie together. Maybe her rejecting him pissed him off and somehow, they connected her to me. If they'd been asking her about me, then there was some connection happening.

I pulled open the door. "Show me."

Ezra nodded and pulled off his shirt. We shifted and ran through the woods. Almost the moment I changed, there was clatter in my head.

Owen! How are you? Hailey.

Glad you're back, man. Mason.

Me too, Conner chimed in. *Ezra can't run this clan. Don't ever die.*

Hey! I'm here, too! Ezra added.

I'm only here to check on the situation, I thought back to them.

Let me know if you want help. Mason again. Good guy. He made a good third.

Ezra led me to the site of the attack. Sea turtles were highly protected in the park; all animals were protected, of course, but some who were close to being on the endangered list were protected differently. In this case, no one was allowed to disturb a sea turtle in any way. All the clans in the area knew this. This was a blatant attack, and a horrible sight.

Sea turtles made what we called a nest, but was really just a hole in the muddy sand near the water. They dug the hole, the females laid their eggs, and they stayed to incubate them until the eggs hatched. Whoever made this attack killed the mother turtle, smashed and feasted on the eggs, and left the hole of the nest decimated. And, just like Ezra had claimed, near the nest in the mud was written "Addie," deliberately surrounded by crocodile tracks. It had to be shifters who did this.

I'm going to kill that asshole, I thought. *Has anyone called the conclave yet? This is a punishable crime.*

Not yet, Ezra thought to me. *We were waiting for you. We thought it'd be better if you contacted them.*

He was right. It was part of an Alpha's duty to do those sorts of things.

Maybe in this case, seeing as how it's so personal and all, I'll just handle things on my own, I said.

On your own, with me to help, Ezra corrected.

No. Stand by, but I'm going to find that jerk. He wants a piece of me? He wants to taunt me like this? Then I'm going to take care of it myself.

I took off running back to my cabin. I could feel that Ezra was following me. I could feel the questions coming from the linked minds of the clan and Ezra's gently urging of them to wait. Fine. He could take care of the clan.

And I'd take care of that asshole, Aiden, once and for all.

I dressed, put my gun in its holster at my side and slid my knife into the top of my boot. Then, I got in my car, took a moment to pound on the steering wheel to release my anger, and took off. Wearing only his shorts, Ezra stood on my porch and watched me leave. He'd probably follow me; a good second would. I wouldn't stop him, but I also wasn't going to get him involved in this fight. This was between me and Aiden, and it would be coming to an end that night.

I drove to the bar where Ezra, Mason and Conner had encountered the crocs many nights back. When I didn't see Aiden, I asked around. How convenient that no one knew where he was. I then drove over to the airboat dock and had much better luck. As I pulled up, I saw Aiden walk toward the building.

It seemed that their tours were over for the day. I guessed it was hard to convince people they were seeing a rare sight if it was too dark to actually see. Night hadn't quite fallen, but it was close.

I slammed my door shut, which made him look my way. Aiden paused with his hand on the door, watching me.

"We need to talk," I said.

He laughed. "Oh, do we?"

"Was it you?"

"You're going to have to be a little more specific if you're going to accuse me of something." He took his hand off the door and crossed his arms as he turned to face me.

"Did you come into the park and destroy a sea turtle nest?"

He put his hand to his chest and made a shocked face. "Why in the world would I do a horrible thing like that? They're protected, you know."

"To get back at me?"

"I'm sorry." He laughed. "I don't even know your name. I'm Aiden Harvey. Nice to meet you." He stuck out his hand as if I were actually going to shake it.

"Cut the shit, Harvey. You wrote Addie's name by the nest. You asked her about me. What exactly is the problem? Aside from you being a sketchy croc."

"Hey now," he said. "Let's not go calling people names.

I'm sorry your little turtles had their nest destroyed. I truly, truly am. Wish I could get a sea turtle to stay over here where my adoring customers could appreciate it for all its glory. But you know, they just won't nest here. Funny thing."

"Maybe it's because your operation is a big scam. I'm surprised you don't have a sculpture of a sea turtle to go with your 'baby gator.'" I made air quotes around the phrase.

"Well, now." He shook his head. "I didn't want to believe it when people told me you were a jerk. But coming over like this, calling me names, accusing me of things? That just won't do. I never did a thing to you. I'm sure the conclave wouldn't be happy to hear that you came over here, ready to attack me for some little grudge you're holding on to."

"I am going to say this one time, Harvey." I was close enough to poke his chest, hard. "Stay off the park land. Stay away from those turtles. And most of all, stay far, far away from Addie. Do you understand me?"

He smirked and took a step back. "Oh sure. I understand you're a sorry excuse for an Alpha. I understand that the conclave will be surprised by your actions here tonight."

"You want to call the conclave? Go right ahead. You should know, they take attacks on protected species much more seriously than anything you'll try to tell them about me."

Aiden glared. "You have yourself a good night and just remember, I didn't attack you."

"Am I supposed to be thankful for that?"

"One day, the bears will not run this park, you mark my words. The crocs will. And when that day comes, your ass is mine, Bailey. You just remember this moment as the moment you screwed over your whole clan. And Addie? She'll see the truth, and she'll come around. Then she'll be mine. All you have will be mine."

I shook my head and gave him the finger, then got back in my car and sped off.

11

OWEN

When I got back home, Ezra had left. If he'd followed me, I hadn't seen him. I slammed the door shut behind me and stripped off my clothes. I grabbed a fresh beer from the fridge and carried it into my room, drinking half of it before sliding under the covers and going back to sleep.

Apparently, sleep was not something I'd be enjoying tonight; the pounding on my door was incessant. I dug my phone out of the pile of clothing and glanced at the time. It was late, almost midnight, and I had many missed calls and unseen texts.

As I pulled myself out of bed, I heard someone come around to my bedroom side of the cabin and knock on the window.

"Owen, come out! It's Addie!" Ezra shouted with his hands cupped to his mouth.

I growled and stormed over to the window, pushing it up with a loud bang. "What the fuck are you doing?"

"Dude, this time it's serious. You've gotta get over to her tent. The crocs..." He stopped to breathe, putting his hands on his knees like he'd been running. "The crocs are up to something. I think she's in danger."

I was ready to rip him a new one until he said "Addie" and "danger" in the same sentence.

I slammed the window shut and hurried out the door. I was already undressed, so I jumped from my porch, shifting in mid-air. As soon as my paws hit the ground, I was running.

Ezra caught up quickly. *One of the crocs called Mason. Told him that something was going down. Named you and Addie.*

No one went to check on her?

I came to you first. We thought you'd want to take care of it personally.

Right. Thanks.

The distance passed quickly. I ran hard, not caring if I lost Ezra or not. I would take this guy down all alone if that's what it came to. And I wasn't worried about losing the fight. Aiden had nothing on me and my rage where Addie was concerned.

I saw her tent in the distance as we neared the camping area, and then, I smelled them. There had to be several crocs in the area. I slowed and made sure Ezra caught a whiff of them, too.

Stinks, he said.

On alert, I signaled to my clan, *we may need backup.*

I heard several confirmations in my mind as others shifted and headed our way. I wasn't worried about losing a fight between Aiden and me. But I was worried that if there were a lot of crocs, I wouldn't be able to protect Addie well enough.

They must've heard and smelled us. The crocs moved as we closed in.

From what I could see, there had to be at least ten of them surrounding Addie's tent. I didn't see her or her friends; hopefully, they were sleeping soundly and had no idea any of this was going on. I did see the car Addie had driven over to my cabin. Damn, I wished they'd chosen to stay out late that night.

I heard a rustling behind us, and when I turned my head, I smelled the crocs more sharply. They had us surrounded along with Addie and her friends.

I'm going to shift back to talk to them, I signaled to my second in command.

Ezra stayed at my side in bear form. He would need to communicate with the clan, and I needed him to be a second ahead of me if something went down. It didn't take long to shift, but it was long enough when teeth and claws were coming at you.

I shifted to human form and stood tall. "Aiden, I assume?"

I watched the crocs, waiting. I ignored the fact that I was naked and standing in the park surrounded by crocodiles. It was a bad position to be in, but I couldn't show any hint of fear or worry.

As I watched, one of the crocs whipped its tail, then shifted into human form. It was Aiden.

"We meet again," he said.

"You want to tell me what all this is about?"

"It's about time, Owen. That's what this is about."

I glared at him and balled my hands into fists at my sides. At least I knew that neither of us had traditional weapons. We were both stark naked in the moonlight.

"The crocs have lived under bear rule for long enough," Aiden said. "We're sick of it. You all think you run this whole area. You show up at our bars, you take our women, you try to control us, to keep us out. You're affecting our business. We all just want to make a decent living, and yet, you and your bears won't allow it. I don't think we're asking too much."

The crocs around him hissed in agreement. Ezra let out a low rumble of a growl.

"The only problem is," I started, "you think you own the bars that we all go to. You think you own some female that my bear hooked up with? Well, I guess she made her choice, didn't she? And she saw that bears are the better option. We're not in the way of your business, if you can call it that. I don't like people getting scammed, and that's all you do. But still, we've had a peaceful existence here, both of us living in the area. Well, that was until you killed a member of an endangered species and her nest for no reason. Until you got Addie involved in this mess. She has nothing to do with any of this."

"Oh, yes she does." His mouth stretched into a broad, toothy smile. "She's our ticket to getting you to cooperate. You should know that right now, I have my entire clan of crocs surrounding her tent. It will take only seconds for them to move in, tear it down and devour her and her friends. Unless, of course, you want to give up your territory. Give up control of the park and let us run things. Then, your precious girl will be left untouched."

"I'm not giving anything to you."

"Then we have no choice."

Aiden raised his fist in the air. He watched me, giving me every chance to change my mind. When his fingers started to open, I shouted to my clan, *Now!*

12

ADDIE

At first, there was just a rustling sound. I groaned. Had we left the trash or some food out for a raccoon to get into? I didn't worry about animal attacks, especially not from such a small animal, but I didn't want our things to be destroyed. And I'd hate to think we'd attracted bears or something big to the area where other people might be endangered.

I felt around for the flashlight. When I couldn't find it, I crept to the edge of the tent.

"What's going on?" Emma asked, half awake.

"Might be a raccoon outside. I'm going to check."

"You're crazy," she mumbled, then fell back asleep.

The rustling had become louder in the time it took me to move closer to the tent door. I thought I heard voices, too.

Maybe campers were setting up a tent nearby. Or someone out hiking had gotten lost.

I peeled down enough of the zipper to peek out, just a tiny bit since I didn't know what awaited us. If it were something big, like a bear, that would require different actions on my part versus a raccoon. And if there were people out there...

I grabbed my knife and stuck it in my sock. When I pulled down the flap, I squinted in the darkness. Then I saw eyes. Many eyes.

Everywhere I looked, I saw crocodiles. I sat back down, my mind spinning. This was not right. Crocodiles didn't group like this. They didn't move into areas and surround people.

I heard the voices again. Were people out there with all these crocs? My heart raced as I peeled the tent flap back again. There was one voice I'd know anywhere. I'd spent years listening to it and years thinking of it. Owen's voice spoke into the night.

I couldn't make out what was being said, but he didn't sound happy. Someone else was with him, someone he was arguing with.

"What are you doing?" Julie asked.

"Stay here. Something's going on."

"Don't go out there!" she insisted.

"No, it's okay. It's...Owen."

"Oh." She fell back down on her sleeping bag. "Have fun."

I'd been sleeping in sweatpants and a t-shirt. My flip flops sat right by the door and I quietly moved to slide my feet into them. Then, I unzipped the door even more, going very slowly. I didn't want to wake Emma and Julie again, and I didn't want to alert these crocs that I was here and awake.

As I stepped out of the tent, many scaly heads turned my way. I couldn't count all the crocs surrounding me. My heart raced. What was going on? What would make them act this way?

Then, two men turned to face me, Owen and Aiden. What the hell?

"Owen?"

He looked terrified. Then I noticed that he was naked. And so was Aiden.

In that second, something clicked in my mind. I drew in a slow, deep breath, letting my instincts do their thing. I'd been stupid before. I hadn't noticed. How could I not have noticed what was going on with Aiden?

Everything made sense now—well, not everything. But one thing was for certain: Owen and I were in a bad position. I didn't know if I could protect us both. I knew I could take down many of the crocs myself, but I didn't know if it would be enough.

Owen didn't make sense to me at all in this moment. Why was he naked? He couldn't be part of this. I'd offended Aiden, that was clear. Maybe he and Owen had had words after I talked with Owen and they were coming to confront me.

Aiden held out his arm to me, smiling. "Here she is."

I glared at him. I looked at Owen for some explanation of what was going on. He mouthed, "Run!"

I had a decision to make, and many things ran through my mind in that split second. Several sides to consider, several people I might anger, depending on how I chose. Several lives I might endanger.

I could do as Owen said and run. That would leave him there to fight the crocs and would leave my friends in peril. If I followed my instincts, I could protect everyone—or try— but I would risk something much bigger falling apart.

I looked at Owen's face, stretched in terror, and made my choice.

I threw myself forward, toward the ground. Before my hands landed palms down in the dirt, everything changed. My spine expanded, my limbs twisted, hair sprouted, and I stood tall, not roaring, though I wanted to. I didn't want to wake my friends or scare anyone.

And I was most definitely scary in bear form.

I leapt at Aiden. My hind feet hadn't hit the ground yet by the time he shifted. A dirty croc; I'd missed the scent. I must've attributed it to him always being on the boat and around all sorts of water animals. I was so new to this life, and much of it overwhelmed me. I thought I was better at recognizing fellow shifters, and I knew the members of my clan well, but when it came to other shifters, especially of another species, I'd missed it.

Aiden probably hadn't, though. He must've known from the start that I was a shifter. That's why he'd chosen me over my friends. He could sense the animal in me.

I spun and swatted at Aiden. No time to regret my lack of skills now; there was a fight. I didn't know what it was about, but I wasn't about to let Owen get injured by these crocs or because of me. He knew nothing of this life. I might have just endangered him by shifting in front of him. At least Aiden had, too. It wasn't only on me.

Aiden ducked my swat and his tail came flying around him, whacking me in the side with a hard thump, and I let out a whimper. Behind me, a sudden, mighty roar rent the air.

My head snapped to the bear standing behind me; the bear that had been where Owen was a moment before. For a wild instant, I thought the bear had attacked Owen. He was nowhere in sight. Then, I took a long sniff in his direction.

No. My mind seized and my body froze. Owen. Owen *was* the bear. The bear was Owen. Owen was...a shifter? Like me? We were both bears?

It took me too long to recover. In my shock, Aiden jumped on me. I felt his hard scales pressing against me, his teeth at my neck. I stood, and my height alone gave me an advantage against the smaller creature. With my claws extended, I swatted and caught his underbelly. Owen jumped at him, knocking him off me, and Aiden landed with a whine.

But he wasn't the only croc attacking. The others converged, snapping their jaws and swatting their tails. Owen moved in front of me, protecting me. I wanted to cry, but I turned my back to him, pressed against him, and faced the danger from behind. Back to back, we fought.

I swatted at a croc who advanced. I heard Owen whimper and gashed my claws across the croc's side. The croc let his jaw open and tried to bite Owen's foot instead. I reached to claw the croc again and felt teeth at my own foot.

Then I heard two screams. Emma and Julie were awake.

After the screams, I heard roars. I allowed one second's look away from the fight and saw a group of bears bounding toward us.

Owen stood tall and pounded his chest, and the bears immediately fell in line around us, forming a circle with me at the center.

I felt helpless watching them. I tried to move to the edge to help, but each time, a bear moved me back. They fought hard, and all the while, I kept my eyes on Owen. Even if they wouldn't let me fight, I wasn't going to just sit back and watch. I fought my protectors, punching through their legs and reaching past them to claw a croc.

Owen still fought Aiden. Right then, Aiden's scent was clear as day to me, and I kept my gaze on him. Owen had injured him; I saw him bleeding and he began to limp. But

Owen had been injured, too, bleeding from a wound on his back.

I didn't hear any more screaming, and I hoped that Emma and Julie were okay. I couldn't get to them, nor could I see them. Their scent lingered in the air. I didn't pick up a hint of extreme fear or sweat, like they were running or fighting, but I didn't know for certain if they were okay.

I let out a small whine and craned my head toward them, trying to see. I didn't know how to communicate with bears like this. My clan was linked through thought when we shifted. But I couldn't hear Owen or his friends.

I hoped they would understand what I wanted. When I made a move to try to break out of my circle of protection, to go to my friends, they blocked my way.

I heard Emma call my name; she sounded terrified. Owen and I both looked in her direction when she called for me, and it was just enough for Aiden to pounce and get his teeth on Owen's neck.

The rage in me lit up. Not this asshole; he wasn't going to kill the man I loved. I jumped more highly than I'd ever jumped in my life, sailing over Owen's shoulder. I knocked him down with me as I hit the ground.

The three of us landed in a heap and I brought my claws down hard. I swiped a gash in Aiden's stomach and he let go of his hold on Owen. I could have let it go at that, but I didn't. I let loose, slashing and clawing at Aiden until he stopped moving.

I put my head near his; I couldn't tell if it was just my heavy breathing or if he still lived. I wanted certainty, so I drove my claws into his chest and pulled down, tearing him open. When I moved back, my paws covered in croc blood, he was still.

The crocs around me chomped. Owen picked up Aiden's lifeless body with one paw and held it high, and the bears roared together and lunged. A split second later, the crocs took off running.

As they ran, the bears chased them, but Owen stepped in front of me to stop me from following them. I looked back and saw that we were alone.

"Addie? Where are you?" Julie sounded as scared as Emma had.

I whined again and lurched toward them. Owen stepped in front of me again, running his nose along my neck and nuzzled into me. He circled me, sniffing. Where he found blood, he licked the wound clean. Then, he started licking me all over. From head to paws, he groomed me.

I stood very still, the shock of the event washing over me as I forced my brain to catch up and realize what was going on. Owen, in bear form, was grooming me, in bear form. It was unreal.

I put my head down into my paws; I needed the forest to stop spinning around me. I stumbled over to a tree and threw up for the first time in bear form. Although it was less violent and disgusting than doing so as a human, it was still a strange sensation.

Owen put his bear arms around me and pulled me close to him, his hair enveloping me in warmth. It was even better than a human hug with sharp joints and smooth skin. This was like falling into a huge, cuddly teddy bear of warmth and happiness, and I let my eyes close and didn't move.

13

OWEN

G ot him!
Over here!
One more down.

I listened to their fight from a distance. They were doing fine; they didn't need me. More than that, they knew better. They knew I wouldn't leave Addie.

They'd all been there, linked to my mind the moment I'd seen it, and the shock crashed over me like a wave. They said plenty when it happened, but I didn't hear a word of it. My ears were ringing.

When Addie shifted into a bear, my entire world turned upside down. Nothing was what it should have been; I was suddenly in a dream. I thought they'd killed me so quickly, my brain hadn't caught up yet. I thought anything except that what I saw was real.

Ezra, thank god, had snapped me out of it. He'd said something like, "Dude, you're an idiot." The insult had made me see it. All this time, Addie had been a shifter and I hadn't known? Yeah, I was most definitely an idiot.

As the fight moved and I was left there alone with Addie, the thoughts started to sort themselves out in my mind. How in the world could I have missed this? I took a long sniff of her. Usually, I could tell in an instant when another shifter was near. No matter if it was one of my clan, another bear, or any other shifter species. There was a certain scent that came with shifters. A sort of animal smell, but different: clean and subtler than a wild animal.

Addie's scent was too familiar; that was the only thing that made sense to me. When I'd first become old enough to shift for the first time, when I'd learned about the shifter life and all that came with it, when I trained and learned what smells were what...all of that had happened when I was already with Addie. Whatever scent she had was something my nose had bypassed. Her deep spice was more like the smell of love to me. The scent of...my mate.

When we'd had sex in the past and the animal was stronger in the air from our sweat, I'd always thought it was me. God, I'd been so stupid. I was too new at it all to pick up the difference in the smell. I'd been too embarrassed, rushing to put on deodorant or take a shower, that I'd never stopped to really smell the scent and learn it and recognize it.

Even after spending so much time apart, she smelled the same to me when I saw her again. That hint of animal that I picked up on her, I'd mistaken for pure lust. Nothing more. I almost laughed at myself, thinking back on it. I thought she wanted me so badly that her lust smelled that attractive to me.

I sniffed every inch of her now, programming my mind to associate this scent I knew so well with a bear. To relearn what I knew of her body. When I put my nose to her neck and inhaled, at first, my bear brain said, "Want." My body reacted in a lustful way. It was no wonder I'd thought that was all it was. But I forced myself to look at her, to feel her hair, and to keep smelling until my brain corrected itself.

Now, I smelled her sweat. Her bear sweat on her bear skin under her bear hair. And her human was there, underneath it, taking the more subtle place while in this form. I smelled the blood and dirt and cleaned her. I sniffed until I knew every inch of her in this way.

It's over, Ezra reported. *They all took off.*

My clan returned to where we sat.

Emma and Julie are fine. I'd had Hailey watching them the whole time. *Freaked out about the bears and because they can't find Addie, but they're unharmed.*

Thank you, all, I said. *I...*

We know. Ezra sent a wave of warm thoughts to me.

They were all happy, but surprised, to say the least. Everyone was still charged from the fight, but we'd won. The crocs had taken off and none of my guys had been injured too badly; the only one dead was Aiden. The conclave would get a full report and there would be an investigation. There was much to be done, but I wasn't going to be a part of any of it.

Let me know if you need me. I'll...be a while.

One by one, they sent me their congratulations. They'd witnessed too much of my despair over the last week to not understand what this moment meant to me.

I shifted back to human form slowly. For a moment, I held Addie, still in bear form, and then she shifted back, awkwardly sitting in my lap. We were both naked.

I pulled her close and hugged her tightly, letting the tears flow down my cheeks. The complete relief of it all washed over me and I kissed her. I kissed her and didn't want to ever stop.

I was vaguely aware of the bears leaving. Not long after I shifted back, they started to drop off, returning home and back to whatever they were doing before I'd called them.

She cried, too and returned my kiss.

"Your friends are worried about you," I said after a long while.

I hadn't let her go to them before. It wasn't safe, but now, they needed to know their friend was alright. If for no other reason than if they called the ranger station, someone would come out, and things would get complicated.

"My clothes..." She'd torn everything when she shifted.

"They don't know?"

She shook her head.

"Give me a minute." I shifted back and called to Hailey in my mind, who responded quickly, so I shifted back and waited. A few minutes later, Hailey came walking out of the woods, a tote bag between her jaws. She dropped the bag and took off running back into the woods.

"It's convenient having a clan near you," Addie said, pulling the clothing over her human form.

I had so many questions. So much to say. "Addie." I reached up to take her hand. "I love you."

She smiled and got to her feet. "I'll be right back."

I sat naked in the dark for a long time, alone with my thoughts and feelings. I'd lost track of how long she was gone for, but when I heard rustling and smelled her—that scent that was more real to me now than my own—a smile took over my face and my heart flooded with joy.

14

ADDIE

Julie and Emma were in a state when I found them. They'd seen animals all around and couldn't find me. They knew I'd gone out into the night to see what was out there.

"We thought you were eaten by a bear!" Emma exclaimed.

"I'm fine. I'm sorry you were worried."

"You could have at least said you were going to find someone," Julie said.

"I thought you were still sleeping. I wasn't going to wake you up just to tell you I was going to call the ranger."

"Well, leave a note next time!" Emma snapped.

"Or at least take your phone." Julie held my cell out to me. "Why didn't you just call the ranger?"

I shrugged. "I was half asleep and saw a croc. I didn't think much about it and just ran. I guess I thought it would come at me?"

I tried to get them settled as quickly as possible. All I could think about was Owen alone in the woods, naked, waiting for me. Finally, I decided to play the one card they wouldn't argue with.

"The thing is," I said. "I wanted an excuse to find Owen. And I found him. He wants to talk."

They looked at me with surprise.

"Where is he?" Julie asked.

"Back at the station. He had to make some calls or something. But he asked me to come back to talk to him."

"You sure that's a good idea after the last talk you had?" Julie arched an eyebrow.

"I don't know," I admitted. "Maybe it was because of that that he wants to talk."

"Well, give me the full report in the morning." Emma slid down into her sleeping bag. "I'm not waiting up."

Julie slid back into her bag, too. "Take your phone this time. Please. Call if anything happens. I don't want to wake up and find you dead because you got mauled in the night by bears or crocs or any other animal out there."

"I will." I made a show of putting my phone in one pocket and my knife in another. "I'll be with a ranger. There's not much better protection than that."

A ranger who also happened to be a *bear shifter*.

As I exited the tent, I pulled my blanket out with me; better than sitting on the cold ground naked. If I had any clothes that would fit him, I'd bring them, but he was far too muscular for my shirts or close-fitting sweatpants.

I walked back to where I'd left him in the dark, spread out the blanket, then sat. He crawled onto it to join me.

"Sorry about this." He gestured to his nakedness.

"That's something you should never apologize for."

He chuckled. "It's just awkward. I feel exposed."

I picked up the end of the blanket and covered him as much as possible. He pulled me back into his lap. Now I felt a little awkward. I was dressed, though not in my clothes, and he had only the blanket.

"So, Owen," I said in a forced conversational tone. "I may not have told you, since I'm bound by secret and all—but I'm a shifter. I can turn into a bear at will or in the full moonlight. What hobbies and interests do you have?"

We both laughed and he shook his head. "How is this possible?"

"I've been asking myself that question since the first time I shifted."

"When? How? I mean...I had no idea. And that's absurd. I'm an Alpha, for god's sake. I'm such an idiot."

"Ha," I said. "You think you're an idiot? I was a shifter for twenty years and didn't even know it!"

"What do you mean?"

"My parents? They're not actually my parents."

He sucked in a breath.

"You remember how I'd always say I felt like I didn't belong in my family? There was a reason for that. I was adopted. My parents are actually distant relatives of mine. My real parents died when I was just a baby, and they were both shifters. But my second cousin, who raised me as her daughter, was not a shifter and knew nothing about it. I was obviously a late bloomer, and I was in college the first time it happened. There was a party, kind of like the one Aiden invited us to. Outside, you know? And it was the night of the full moon."

"Ohh," Owen said.

"Yeah." I laughed. "So, we were at this party and it was in the woods. It would have been fine if I'd known I was a shifter at the time since there was lots of cover, but I didn't; it was the first change since my birth shift. When I stepped into the moonlight, I felt the pull. And let me just say that from what I've heard from others, shifting for the first time under full moonlight is not the best way to go about it."

"I'd say not."

"Now, I've shifted enough that it doesn't hurt me. But you remember those first shifts?"

"I was just a kid when I began to change. It was hard the whole first year, but when I started shifting regularly, yeah, it wasn't so bad anymore. I'm surprised you didn't shift by accident while you were growing up, though. That happens fairly often during times of extreme emotional distress."

"Well, I wasn't old enough to remember losing my parents. So, that night, I obviously didn't know what was happening. I thought I was sick or had been drugged; at a party like that, it wasn't the craziest thought. Being drugged seemed much more feasible than the fact that I was turning into a freaking bear. So, I kinda flipped out. I thought I was hallucinating. I started running, and I ran far. Luckily, another bear had witnessed the whole thing go down and followed me. When he realized what was happening, he stayed with me and got me calmed enough to shift back when the morning came.

"He was an Alpha. I joined his pack and he and his wife looked out for me. They were like my shifter adopted parents, teaching me everything. It was a hard time. Luckily, the guy I was dating had broken up with me just days before that, so I used heartbreak as an excuse to be hiding out all the time. I was lonely, but my new pack helped a lot. Only problem was, they all lived about an hour and a half away, on the western side of the state."

"You don't live near your clan?"

I shook my head.

"Addie, we're not meant to be lone bears. We're meant to live with our clans. In some areas, they live together in a big compound or a shared house, if it's a smaller clan."

"I don't know of any near me. And I like my clan. They were there for me when I needed them."

"I'm glad for that," he said. "I really am, but you're making things harder on yourself than they should be."

I shrugged. "It's okay. I don't go out when it's a full moon and I don't shift often. It's better for me to just pretend like that part of me doesn't exist. With the whole secret thing, it makes it easier, too. Sometimes, like tonight, it comes in handy. It did feel good to shift. I think it's been about six months since I have."

"You haven't shifted in six months?"

"Nope."

He blinked at me in shock. "I didn't even know that was possible."

"Really?"

"The instinct is so strong."

"I guess mine isn't."

"That might explain some things. Like why I didn't pick on your shifter scent. Why you didn't pick up on mine."

I covered my face with my hand. "I thought you changed colognes."

"You have a good excuse—you're new and mostly alone. But I don't. I thought it was just lust. The best I can come up with is that we'd already been together so long when I came of age that I was too accustomed to your scent. And if you didn't know you were a shifter and had never shifted, I guess that's why my parents didn't pick up on it, either."

"We're a lot less rare than I thought," I joked.

"You're telling me." He nuzzled his nose into my neck,

taking in a long inhale. "How could I have missed it? I'm such an idiot. God! I'm such an idiot!"

"It's okay. I mean, yeah it would have been better if you'd been the one to tell me and had been there in the beginning, but it's okay. I figured it out. I'm okay now. I know how to handle it better."

"No, Addie, you don't get it." He put his fist to his forehead and growled. "I can't believe this!"

"What's wrong? It's not that big of a deal, is it? I mean, I can see you being freaked out if I were a shifter and you knew nothing of this life, but you are, too. I don't see how—"

"Adeline."

I closed my mouth and looked at him expectantly.

"Our clan believes that Alphas should only marry shifters. They want to keep the leadership pure to preserve our lineage. No second will be promoted if he's married to a non-shifter and Alphas are forced to step down if they take a non-shifter wife."

I scrunched up my face in confusion.

"Addie." He put a hand on either side of my face. "My dad was the Alpha; that means I've always been in line to be Alpha. I took over for him when I finished college, and I've always believed that I had to fulfill my duty as his son. I hated the rule. I nearly left my family and my clan because of it. Addie, the only reason I ended things with you was because you weren't a shifter, and I had to marry a shifter if I was going to fulfill my duty."

His words sunk into my mind slowly. I didn't want to get excited. I didn't want to get my hopes up. I'd just done that and it had ended terribly.

"So... you're saying..."

He let out a laugh and kissed me hard. "I'm saying, I love you. Marry me?"

"What?" I laughed, too. I clearly hadn't heard him right.

"Marry me. Please. Please marry me. Be my wife. I can't live another day without you."

I shook my head. "No, you're... this isn't right."

"What?" His face fell. "What do you mean?"

"You can't be proposing to me. You just ended things again. You just broke my heart again."

"It was only because of the shifter thing. That was it. I've wanted you so badly this whole time. I've missed you. Ask my clan how much of a wreck I was after you came by to see me and I had to send you off. I thought about leaving again. I was ready to give up everything for you."

I spoke slowly to make sure I didn't miss anything. "So, let me get this straight. You're telling me that the only reason you broke up with me in high school is because you thought I wasn't a shifter?"

"No. It's because I thought you weren't a shifter, *and* I knew I had to marry a shifter. I could have kept dating you, I guess, but I could never marry you, and I didn't want you to go through that. We talked about marriage. I even had a ring picked out. I knew how I was going to propose and everything."

"And the other day when I came to see you?"

"Same thing. There was no way I could see you and never marry you. Or be with you for any length of time and not tell you my secret. I had no choice but to send you away again."

"That's the only reason?"

"That's the only reason." He stood and I was reminded of his nakedness. "Come for a run with me."

"I don't have my sneakers or running—"

"Not as a human."

"Oh." I stood up and took off Hailey's clothes, setting them in the center of the blanket.

We both shifted and took a moment to rub against each other before taking off on the run. I followed him, partly because I had no idea where we were going, and also, because he was much faster than me. We ran until we came to a long, wooden bridge.

He shifted back and took my hand, leading me to the center of the bridge. "This isn't exactly how I pictured it. I mean, I thought we'd at least be wearing clothing. And I planned to have a ring."

He turned toward the water and stretched out his arm. "This bridge looks out over two bodies of water. If you look to one side, it's like our past, stretched out long behind us. But on the other side is our future. Wide open. Full of possibilities. Going on and on forever, into eternity."

He got down on one knee and took my hands.

"I should have said this to you long ago, Addie. I love you. I've had to live without you for too many years now, and I don't want to spend another day without you. Will you marry me? Be my mate in every way, for the rest of our lives?"

I blinked in shock, then sputtered, "Yes!"

15

ADDIE

Owen laid me down on the blanket and slid into place beside me. He'd carried me for what had to be over a mile, back to this place. He said he didn't want to waste one moment in bear form not seeing my face.

I didn't care if he was a bear or human, it just felt good to be close to him. As the hour grew later and the adrenaline faded, I felt tired. I curled into him, enjoying his warmth. Now that things had settled, another thought plagued my mind.

I hadn't let myself really think much about it, but now it's all I could think of. "What will happen to me?"

"What do you mean?" he asked.

"I killed someone. I killed Aiden. Won't I go to jail?"

"Don't worry about that." He tucked a strand of hair behind my ear and rubbed my arm.

"How can I not worry about it?"

"The rules are different for us. I don't know how it is in your clan's area, but here, animal on animal violence is a way of life. If you'd killed him as a human, you'd have to face the police. But you were in bear form. You'll talk to the conclave. They'll investigate, but with so many witnesses, not one of them would say you were in the wrong. You defended yourself. You defended a fellow bear. If we were in the same clan, it would be even more explainable. I think our history, though, will accomplish the same thing when it comes down to it."

"Accomplish what?"

"We have the conclave for a reason. It's a group of shifters who understand what it's like to be a shifter. When we're in animal form, our instincts are different. The instinct to protect and defend rises higher than when we're in human form. We're still responsible for our actions, but even if we'd all been human in that situation, you still acted in self defense. You'll be fine, I promise. And if the police come knocking, we'll bear up and never change back."

"Really?"

"Yes, but that won't happen. Besides, we have shifters on the police force and in other government agencies who make sure shifter law is carried out in questionable situations."

"We do?" I asked.

"If you lived close enough to be with your clan all the time, you'd know these things."

"I never thought it was that big of a deal."

"So, changing clans won't be difficult, Addie?"

"Changing clans?"

"When we get married, your human form will take my last name, but your bear form will take my clan."

"Oh." There was so much of this world I still didn't understand.

"Sometimes it's a very difficult transition for females. Clan loyalty is very intense, and when someone grows up in one clan, it can be very difficult to leave them."

"I'm not happy to be leaving them. They were there for me when no one else was. But I'm happy to be joining your clan, if that's how it works. They helped us. They fought with us and protected me and my friends. I don't take that lightly. And if this is part of shifter life, then my clan will understand."

"Good." He kissed my forehead. "I don't want anything else to come between us or get in our way."

"There's really only one thing standing between us now."

"What?" He pulled back, looking worried.

"This blanket."

He'd covered me up to keep me warm, but now the blanket acted as a barrier between our naked bodies. He gave me a seductive smile and slid the blanket out of the way, his hot body pressing down on mine.

"That's much better," I smiled.

"Care to pick up where we left off the other night, fiancée?"

"As long as this time doesn't end with you sending me away."

He shook his head slowly. "Never again. You are mine. My mate and true love, who is soon to be my wife. I will never let you out of my sight again."

"Unless I'm going to work or something," I laughed.

"Oh no. Not even then." He planted kisses all over my face, making me giggle. "You'll just have to get a job here in the park so I can have you by my side all day."

"Actually, I would love that."

He pulled back to look in my eyes. "Really?"

"I've been trying to figure out what I want to do with my life and my degree. You're here; I want to be with you. I want to protect the land and its animals and do the things you do. I think I want to train to be a park ranger."

He gave me a half smile. "Well, there's one way you'll be guaranteed to get that job."

"What's that?"

"Sleep with the manager."

"Hmm." My words became a moan as he kissed down my jaw to my breasts.

He moved his hand between my legs. I was wet just from kissing him and he slid his fingers around and inside me. I dragged my nails along his back, barely able to take the sensation.

"Owen," I begged. It'd been far too long since I felt him.

"Addie," he breathed in my ear.

I wrapped a leg around him, trying to pull him closer to me. His hardness pressed against me, and I rubbed up and down his shaft. Each time, at the last moment just before he slid in, he pulled away, teasing me until I could scream.

"Haven't I waited long enough?" I whispered.

"What's another few minutes?"

"You're cruel."

He chuckled, but it didn't last long. I reached down and grabbed his erection, and he moaned as I stroked him.

"I think," he breathed and closed his eyes, "I see your point."

He pushed my legs farther apart and positioned himself over me. He pressed in just the head of his dick, then sank into me.

I shuddered at the feeling of him sliding in so deep. It felt both familiar and new. We'd done this so many times, but we'd both changed over the years. As he moved in and out of me, my heart sped and the pleasure rushed over me. When I felt myself begin to shift, I sucked in a breath.

"Stop!"

"What's wrong?" he asked.

"I..." I breathed fast, trying to calm myself.

"Addie?"

"Hang on." I closed my eyes and tried not to move. The shivering sensation slowed, but it was still right there.

"Have you...had sex since you started shifting?"

I shook my head, my eyes still squeezed shut. Sam had been my last and we'd broken up just before my first shift. I hadn't thought anything of it until that moment.

"Shh," he whispered in my ear and stroked my hair. "It's okay."

When I calmed enough to keep the bear at bay, I pressed my hips up into him again. He moved more slowly, taking his time. But it didn't take long for the swell to rise again.

This time, instead of feeling my bear take over, I kept control of my body. I let the feeling of him thrusting in and out of me take over. I pushed my hips into him faster, urging him to speed up. I grabbed his ass and pulled him in deeper.

He pounded hard, but slow. I wanted him to speed up, but the slowness was sweet torture. The orgasm took its time to build, but when it flooded over me, it hit me so hard, I nearly passed out. My head spun, and I had to close my eyes and breathe slowly.

"You okay?" he asked.

"I didn't know it would be so different."

He chuckled. "Do you remember the night we went to that school play and I wanted to leave early and we ended up having sex in the back seat of my car in the parking lot?"

I thought for a moment. "I think so."

"That was my first time after. And it was so close to the full moon. I almost lost it a few times."

"That would have been...interesting."

"Right." He laughed. "I've heard stories..."

"I have a *lot* to learn about being a shifter."

"You have all the time in the world to learn it," he said. "And, you're hired."

"Whew," I said. "If we had done that for nothing..." I sat up to kiss him. "I love you. I always have."

16

OWEN

Epilogue

"Hey there, Alpha man."

I glanced over at the walkie sitting on my desk and smiled. Some people questioned our ability to work together and be married, but Addie and I loved it. Being in the park with her, running things here and in the clan with her by my side. Things couldn't be much better.

"Hello there, darling wife," I radioed back.

"If you're not too busy or anything, maybe you want to meet me in the clearing by our cabin?"

"What! Are you sure?" I jumped up and grabbed my keys,

dashing out of my office. "Gotta go!" I shouted to Rachel as I ran past her.

"Let us know!" she called after me.

"I'm already here," Addie said.

I could hear the distress in her voice. "You should have called sooner."

"Meh," she said. "These things—take time."

"Are you okay? I'm halfway there."

"Don't rush."

I laughed. "Seriously? My first cub is about to be born and you tell me not to rush?"

"It'll be—all day."

The pain in her voice made me push on the gas.

I pulled up to the cabin. Hailey's car was there, as were Noah's and several others. I'd never really been part of a clan birth, being a male and all, but they'd told me all about it.

This was how they did it, they said. The females all came together and helped the pregnant bear give birth. The father could be there, of course, but they didn't want a bunch of males strutting around, getting in the way. Fine by me to let the ladies handle it all.

I ran to the clearing. Addie was sitting up, her hands on either knee, breathing hard. Hailey was at her side, rubbing her back.

"You need to shift," Tori said.

I saw Noah then and clapped him on the back. I guessed uncles were allowed, too.

"She wants to be human," I said, moving into place beside her.

"But it's much easier as a bear," Hailey said.

We'd talked about this. Many times, Addie had insisted on giving birth in human form. Something about wanting the woman's experience. I didn't really get it, and I didn't try to. I heard what the females in my clan said, but I had to do what my wife wanted. She was the one who carried our baby, after all, and she was the one about to give birth.

"Leave her be," I said. I stroked her hair. "What do you need?"

She shook her head. Sweat stuck her hair to her neck and face. I did my best to brush it back.

"Maybe—I should," she said, wincing as another contraction hit her.

"Whatever you want to do, honey."

She nodded and tried to pull her clothes off.

"Don't worry about that." I'd gotten over the amount of torn clothing we all went through shifting, long ago. It was why I owned so many cheap t-shirts. Didn't matter when I ripped them if I didn't have time to undress before shifting.

She shifted, and, so I could speak to her, I shifted alongside her. I did have to undress, though. For all my thoughts on cheap clothing, I still wore my ranger uniform, and they were certainly not cheap. Last time I'd had to replace one, it ran me more than $80. I took off my clothes quickly, shifted, and got into position behind her.

You're doing great, I said. *I love you.*

This sucks. So bad.

I know. But it'll be over soon. I nuzzled my body against hers.

I felt her sigh. *This is better. They were right.*

We'll tell them after. Who wants a bunch of bragging bear-wives?

She started to laugh, but the next contraction stopped her. As things worsened, I felt less and less helpful. All I could do was be there. I couldn't speed it up. I couldn't take her pain. There was no way I could protect her or our baby from any part of this. I hated the feeling.

Finally, after what did turn out to be all day, she was ready to push. I pressed myself against her as she pressed against me, pushing hard. It took many minutes, and then a tiny bear cub was sitting on the ground.

She began licking it clean, and I watched in awe. When she had thoroughly groomed the baby, she looked up at me. Smiling in bear form was different than in human, but I knew her face so well, it didn't matter. She beamed, and I beamed back. I nuzzled in closer, sweeping the baby into my arms along with her.

I want to shift back now, she said.

We shifted back and I wrapped her in one of the blankets. We stayed cuddled together for a long while, the baby now suckling at her bare breast.

"Thank you, ladies," I said. "And Noah."

He looked up from where he'd been sitting against a tree, reading, and waved. They'd all stepped back to give us space. Now they stepped closer to peek in on the newest member of our clan.

"What is his name?" Tori asked.

This was my part. It was tradition to have the father announce a cub's name after his or her birth. I said proudly, "His name is James, after Addie's real father, who she never knew."

Everyone made the appropriate cooing and awwing sounds. They stayed for a little while, helping to get things cleaned up. We made our way inside the cabin and the local midwife came by to check on the baby and make sure everything was fine.

When we were alone, the three of us sat in bed, and James slept in Addie's arms. I rested my head on her shoulder to watch him sleep.

"He's so tiny," I said.

"Yeah. Didn't feel that way, though," she laughed.

"You were perfect. Thank you for bringing our baby into the world."

"Thank you for giving him a family to come into."

I kissed her head, then kissed James. With the two of them in my arms, everything was finally right at last.

THE END

FATED ATTRACTION

WEREBEARS OF THE EVERGLADES

1

BRITT

The swampland of the Everglades National Park stretched out before me as I ran, enjoying the feeling of my long leg muscles contracting and expanding with the motion. Early morning was the best time for a run. Everything still quiet and sleepy, and no one was poking around. The sun hadn't come up just yet, though I could tell it wanted to. The sky had that pinky-orange look about it just over the horizon, so I knew the sun would be peeking up before long.

I paused for a moment to listen and sniff the morning air. I licked my thick paws, tasting the ground. I could sense there was an animal nearby; I would find it and kill it. My stomach growled and I wanted to let out a mighty roar, too, but that would scare away whatever lurked nearby. I crept through a patch of brush just tall enough to hide my crouching panther form, and the dim light helped hide me. That time of year, the end of summer, the grass had dried up, making it a perfect hiding spot for my tan coat. The critter would never know a panther was sneaking up on it, and I intended to keep it that way.

A flash of movement caught my eye and I knew I had it: a deer, drinking from a stream, not paying attention to its surroundings whatsoever. *Stupid animal*, I snickered inwardly. *You're all mine.*

I moved in closer, slinking silently until I was in pouncing range. This was my favorite game. How close could I get before it smelled me, heard me, or saw me? Deer were so slow-witted, it wouldn't matter. The instant I was spotted, I'd be on it and that bastard would be mine. I licked my lips in anticipation, thinking about my breakfast.

I was close enough now. I stepped closer, almost laughing at how easy it was going to be. But a moment later, the deer jerked its head up. It didn't look my way, though; it looked in the opposite direction, toward the east.

I'd been so focused on my prey, I hadn't been on guard. *Dumb move, Britt.* Something huge came bounding along, and as I saw a flash of black before my eyes, I smelled the bear, and rage tore through my thick chest.

I leapt and the bear sailed under me, taking the deer down, sliding them both about three feet forward with the motion—just enough that I landed hard on the ground instead of on top of my target.

The bear sank his teeth into the deer's neck, and as the creature cried out, the bear sat back, pleased with itself.

But this wasn't just any bear. If it were any random black bear, I couldn't have been too upset; it was just following its instincts, after all.

Nope. This bear was a shifter, like me.

And that meant a human was behind this.

A human male.

An *asshole* human male.

I drew in a long breath of him; I wanted to remember this scent. If I ever came across this arrogant prick again, I'd get my payback. When his scent hit me, though, it sent shock-waves right to my core. The instinct stirred in me, and my hormones were screaming, "Mate! Mate!"

But with this jerk face? No way. My body would just have to chill and deal with not getting any for right now. Business was more important.

I narrowed my eyes and jumped again, this time landing on the bear. My front paws hit his chest with a hard thud and he fell back. The idiot wasn't even paying attention to what was around him, so I bit him. Not hard enough to break skin or anything. Just hard enough to let him know I was pissed he stole my kill.

He actually looked surprised by my presence. I rolled my golden eyes at him and whacked him hard with my tail.

I heard him growl as he began to shift back to his human form and sat on my haunches to watch. *Here we go...* Admittedly, he wasn't too bad to look at. Bears had their weight and height going for them, but they were usually wimps when it came down to it. Not a one of them could outrun me, but I loved to see them get cocky and try.

This one, though... The scent of him still made me tingly, but I did my damnedest to ignore the sensation as much as I could. I wasn't about to give in to him. He stole my kill, and I wouldn't stand for it.

He held up his hands, palms facing me, and made an apologetic face. "Hey, I'm so sorry. I didn't even see you. I didn't mean to. It's yours. Totally."

He backed away, and I made it a point to not break eye contact, challenging him with my stare. I hoped it would make him uncomfortable. But if he was so obviously unobservant, maybe he didn't even notice I was a female.

"Okay?" he continued. "Are we cool?" He looked at me expectantly.

If he thought I'd be shifting to talk to him, he needed to get over that idea real fast. I was hungry, and surely, there was another deer around. I just had to find it. He wasn't doing anything interesting anyway, so I ran off.

After ten minutes of hunting, I couldn't sense other deer in the immediate area, so I circled around and came back to check on my original target. Hot anger flared once more as I realized that asshole hadn't even eaten it! Instead, there was a collection of small flowers. Tiny, white elderberry flowers arranged in a way that spelled out a word.

"Sorry."

What the hell?

Well, whatever. It was there, and I sure as hell wasn't going to let it go to waste. I sank my teeth into its neck, but the taste of my loss made it bitter. I ate until my belly was full, then swiped my back paws over the flowers, scattering the bear's apology into the deer's remains. I hope he'd come back and see what I thought of his "sorry" ass.

2

EZRA

an. I yawned and it bled into my thoughts as I mentally reached out to my clan. *This is why I don't get up early. Not worth it.*

Mason picked up on my signal and shot back, *What's going on, Ez?*

Panther.

Yeah? What about it?

I was just hunting, minding my own business. I found a deer. Score, right? So, I did my thing and took it down. Only there was a panther standing there. She jumped on me, dude! Bit my neck. I guess she was there first, but I don't know. I didn't see her.

You didn't smell her, man?

Nah, I was too busy chasing after the deer. So, I shifted back to be like, hey, sorry, I didn't know. But she just sat there all prissy and watched me.

Mason laughed. *Fuck, man. So, what did you do?*

She ran off. I spelled out "sorry" in some flowers right by the carcass hoping she might see it if she came back.

Aww, aren't you sweet?

I huffed in my mind. *Well, hey. I really didn't see her. I wouldn't have done that. I'm not that much of a dick.*

Mason chuckled. *Sure, sure.*

I officially vow never to wake before noon again. Too much competition.

Ez, I was shocked to hear from you this early, to be honest. Or haven't you been to bed yet?

No, I did. Just woke up and couldn't fall back asleep. My stomach rumbled, so I got up and hunted. Next time, I'll chew on a leftover slice of pizza. What are you up to anyway? I'm still running. Guess I need to find a new kill.

Almost home. Heading to work.

Bummer. A minute or two passed, but I could sense him still there, running. *Hey Mas?*

Yeah?

You ever... get a thing for a panther?

Uh, not that I recall. Why? She hot?

She didn't shift. But man, her scent. I whistled in my head and brought the scent to my mind so he could sample the essence of it.

Maybe you should go find her.

Meh. I'm too tired right now. Think I need a nap before I do anything crazy like that.

Alright, man...well, I'm home now, so I'm gonna let you go.

Kay. Oh hey, wait. Want to meet up tonight? Owen is coming out and we can probably drag Conner along.

Sure, sounds good. See you later, Sunshine Boy.

Yeah. Catch you around.

I yawned again. Five hours of sleep was definitely not enough. Who in their right mind would get up that early to hunt? Too much competition, with shifters or otherwise. Next time, I'd wait until it was later and hotter. Most shifters didn't run then, so the kills would be all mine. Just one more advantage of my California upbringing: I didn't mind the heat one bit. The Everglades were cool and breezy compared to Death Valley.

If we'd be going out that night, I'd definitely need a few more hours to snooze. It was my day off; I'd been nuts to drag my ass out of my warm bed.

I bounded up to the forest patch outside my apartment building and shifted back as I ran. My stash of clothing was well hidden in a large tree stump hole. I pulled out shorts and a shirt and yanked them on before heading up to my apartment, where I flopped down onto my bed face first.

At any other time, I'd fall asleep instantly. My mother had always complained because I'd be sitting at dinner, and then boom! I'd be asleep in my Cheerios. I could sleep like the dead, she'd say. But in that moment, all I could smell was that panther. The scent of her massive paws lingered on my chest, so I bent my neck forward, closing my eyes as I drew in a long, deep whiff.

Man, was she intoxicating. Mason wondered if she was hot in her human form—and so did I. How could any female smell so delicious and even be average looking? I pictured a tall, curvy blonde at the beach. Hair down her back as she stood in the sun, her bronzed skin glistening as she came out of the water rocking a bright pink bikini.

I closed my eyes and grinned as I began to grow hard. It was a good image to fall asleep to, no doubt.

Maybe Mason was right: maybe I should try to find her. I couldn't stop thinking about our encounter, and I did feel bad. How many shifters didn't pick up on another shifter's scent until it was too late? Maybe I could explain that I was tired and out of my element, not paying attention. Maybe she'd forgive me and wrap her slender arms around my neck and kiss me and tell me I could take her kill anytime.

The grin spread. *Okay, dude. Get your ass to sleep or you'll be toast tonight. Stop thinking about that panther.* But the more I tried to not think about her, the more she overtook my thoughts. Frustrated, I stormed off to the bathroom and stepped into the shower. It would take a lot of cold water to get her scent and image out of my mind.

3

BRITT

I pulled on my boots and brushed the specks of dirt off my camo pants before I hopped on my motorcycle to head to the bar where I would meet Dezi and Kat. *God, this place had better not be busy*, I groaned to myself. I didn't hang with those two often, but since they were the only other panthers in the area—and Gladeswomen, like me—they were about the only people I could tolerate for any period of time.

I guess these women were technically my clan, but we didn't act like it much. Sure, if something came up or some jerk in town was giving one of us crap, we'd have each other's backs. That was a no brainer. We did have the mental link that came with being in a clan, but we didn't use it much.

There wasn't even an Alpha in our little tribe. We used to have a fourth member, but she was killed years ago. After that, we kind of distanced ourselves some; it would limit the number of people whose deaths would hurt us.

We did make life easier for each other at times, and that's what made our clan work. Dezi was a fisherwoman and often traded me fish for rabbits or whatever else I hunted up to eat that struck her fancy. Kat had the gator farm and she'd throw me one every now and then, but she was good at telling me where to find clusters of animals who came around, since she had the boat and lots of land. When a pack of something nasty was messing with her gators, she'd call on me to help hunt them all down.

Beyond that, we got together for a beer about once a month or so. Sometimes, life out there could be lonely. Mostly that was the point and main benefit of it, but every now and again, it was nice to see a friendly face, kick back and shoot the shit.

That night was Dezi's birthday, and I had a fresh osprey wrapped up for her that I'd hunted that day. She had a thing for flying creatures. Me? I'd hunt anything that moved, as long as it wouldn't bring the wardens sniffing around my place. Some things were protected, like sea turtles, and for the most part, we all kept to the restrictions. It was about preserving the land, after all, and none of us wanted to see some big shift in the wildlife because too much of whatever had been hunted out. But if something was causing trouble, protected or not, it would have to go—either by means of hunting, or a forced relocation.

I parked the bike amongst a cluster of others. *Crap. This place is damn near packed*, I thought. That joint was our best bet, though. Shady's had the only decent grub in the area, and they actually knew how to pour a beer. Every time we went to that place further in town, we got nothing but foam and hassle. But Shady's attracted the type of people we were used to and was usually good for entertainment. Someone was always pissing someone else off at Shady's, and that was part of the draw.

I walked in and spotted Kat, then Dezi at a table, and a pitcher sat between them, sweating and half empty. One unattended pint sat full and untouched. I walked over and tapped them each on the arm with my fist, then downed half of my beer in two gulps.

"Ladies," I said, taking my seat.

"About time you showed up," Dezi complained.

Kat jerked her thumb at her, "She's getting impatient in her later years."

"What are you now, forty?" I chuckled.

She smacked my arm. "Bitch, thirty is still far off from that."

"Not too far, though." I raised my glass to hers and we tapped them together.

"Watch it, there," Kat said. "I think you're pushing thirty, too, aren't you, Britt?"

"I've got six months left and I intend to enjoy them fully."

"Now that you're *thirty*," Kat said like it was a dirty word, "do you have any plans for the next decade?"

"Yup. Fish more." Dezi nodded once and poured more beer. "Maybe go north for a trip. Catch something different for a change."

"But no settling down?" Kat wondered.

"Nah."

Kat was the only one of us who bothered to marry. She had a few little cubs running around, who kept her busy when the gators didn't. Usually, her husband was the one out wrangling them when they acted up, though. She handled the business end of things when it came to selling the critters off.

We ordered some wings and they'd barely hit the table before we tore into them. With their crispy skin and hot, tangy sauce, they hit the spot just right. As I finished off the last drumette and picked the bone clean with my teeth, I sat back to give my stomach room to digest.

People had been coming and going the whole time we'd been there. I hadn't paid much attention, since that was just the nature of Shady's. People were *always* coming and going.

That's why I didn't see him. But I *smelled* him.

That fucking bear from this morning.

I was thinking about ordering another basket of wings when his scent filled my nose and distracted me. I jerked my head over and saw him and I turned back quickly, but then remembered he hadn't seen me in my human form.

I glanced over again. He didn't seem to notice me or recognize my scent. *God. How had he managed to survive so long with such pathetic basic instincts?*

"What do you guys know about the bears around these parts?" I asked.

"Bears? Black bears?" Kat asked. "They like to come and try to get at my gators from time to time."

"I mean the shifters," I clarified. "Are there many of them?"

Dezi shrugged.

"Why?" Kat asked.

I jerked my head toward the table where the bear sat with his three friends.

"I had a run-in with one this morning. Took my kill," I explained.

Dezi narrowed her eyes and turned in her seat to look. "Which one?"

"The one with the ridiculous boy-band hair." It was bad enough when women went all crazy with hair dye, but a man? He had medium-brown hair that was longer on top in jagged chunks, and the ends were tipped blonde.

Dezi turned back and raised an eyebrow at me. "And you couldn't take him?"

"I tackled him," I said. "I let him know what was up."

"What'd he do?" Kat asked.

I rolled my eyes and snorted. "I ran off and when I came back, he not only left the carcass for me like a jackass, but he wrote out 'sorry' in elderberry flowers."

They both broke into laughter. Kat almost spit out her beer.

"Go set him straight," Dezi urged.

I nodded to myself. "Yeah. I think I will."

I pushed back from my chair and walked over, making it known with my narrowed eyes that I wasn't there for a friendly chat.

He didn't see me coming—again. His side was to me, and he was in mid-conversation with the others at his table.

I shoved his shoulder. "Hey."

That got his attention. They all looked, and the one I'd shoved gaped at me with wide eyes.

"Umm..." he said.

"Pay attention when you're hunting," I said forcefully, almost shouting, and a hush fell over the crowd.

He looked to the others, then back at me.

Behind me, two men in the bar shouted, "Fight!"

I had to remember this was Shady's. Usually we were watching the fights, not participating in them. But any time someone showed a sign of aggressive behavior, the crowd liked to egg him or her on and push the fight. My demeanor and tone had been enough to alert the masses that some-thing was about to go down.

I glanced behind me and noticed my girls nodding in encouragement. Most of the people in the bar had turned their chairs to watch.

He held up his hands, "I didn't mean to do it, and I said I was sorry. I left it for you and everything. Give a guy a break, huh?"

"Give a guy a break? I don't appreciate someone creeping into my territory and going after my kills."

Behind me, a chorus of "Ooooh" went around the bar.

He got to his feet and dropped his voice. "Look, I'm not trying to start something. I'm not the fighting type. What can I do to make this better?"

"You can stay out of my way, dumbass. Pay attention to what you're doing from now on." I poked my finger into his shoulder with each word: "And stay. Out. Of. *My*. Territory!"

"Okay, okay, I will. I didn't even know it was yours; I was just out hunting."

I stood there, glaring. He wasn't even going to defend himself?

Finally, he stuck out his hand to shake mine, not to push me back. "I'm Ezra. Sorry I pissed you off, but it's nice to meet you."

I hesitated. If I shook his hand, his scent would be all over me. And right then, his scent was driving me up the wall. It was the same as before. It made me wired, like I wanted to pounce on him, but not bite him. I'd thought it was just a reaction from my animal side. It was much stronger when I was in my panther form and he was in his bear form, but even as humans, my body wanted him. Craved him.

But my mind sure as hell didn't.

I glared at his hand. "Next time, you might get yourself killed."

I turned on my heel and stormed back to my table. The crowd responded with disappointment, but I ignored them. Fuck 'em; they could get their kicks from someone else. He wasn't worth throwing fists over, and it hadn't been all that much of a deal to get bloody over. He had left it for me and apologized several times. He was an idiot but not an asshole, I decided.

I sat hard in my chair and the ladies clapped for me. They sent final glares at Ezra before turning back to me.

"Hopefully, that'll get through his thick bear skull," Kat said.

"I'll remember his scent," Dezi said in agreement. "The second he shows up somewhere he shouldn't be, I'll let him have it."

"Thanks, ladies," I nodded.

But throughout the rest of the evening, I found that my gaze was being pulled in his direction. About half the time when I looked over, he'd be looking at me already or would turn to meet my gaze and I'd have to look away fast. If only he didn't smell like that. I might have to go as far as to wear perfume to keep his stench from my nose.

"Either of you own perfume?" I asked.

They looked at me, puzzled.

"You want to get dolled up for someone?" Kat asked.

Dezi knitted her brow. "What do you want that shit for?"

"Nothing like that, guys. I want to get his scent out of my head."

Kat's mouth jerked into a smile. "Oh boy. Got it bad, huh?"

I kicked the leg of her chair. "No."

Dezi chuckled. "Defensiveness is the first sign, you know."

"I'm not interested in him or any other fool in the 'Glades. He just smells...well, I just don't want to smell him is all."

Kat held up her glass. "We've got beer. Does that count?"

Dezi snorted and I shoved her.

"You stuff it," I said. "That's not what I meant. I ain't pouring beer on myself just to chase away his scent."

"Maybe you should just embrace it," Dezi shrugged. "You haven't really dated."

"There's a reason for that," I said.

"Did he touch you at some point? Brush against you or something?" Kat wondered.

"Nah."

"Then why is his scent so strong to you?"

I shrugged. "It just permeates everything. I don't know. Maybe it's time I went on my way."

"Sit your ass down and ignore your little boyfriend over there," Dezi commanded. "We just ordered another pitcher, and you ain't getting out of drinking your share."

I blew out a breath. "Fine. But if it gets worse, I'm out."

4

EZRA

I trudged beside Owen as we walked through thick brush deep in the park. He sprayed a neon pink dot on a tree and turned to smile at me.

"Did I tell you what he did yesterday?" he asked.

I blinked at him, trying to refocus. He'd been talking so much this morning in his excitement that I'd tuned out. My mind kept wandering that day. And the night before. I tried to deny it. They were just random thoughts bouncing along my brain, that's all.

But I could not stop thinking about that woman. All morning, she'd consumed my thoughts. And now, I was about to be found out.

"Umm..." I tried to bring back some part of the conversation, but my brain blanked. "Who?"

Owen gave me an incredulous look. "James?" He said it like I was the biggest idiot in the world.

"Oh, right." Who else would he be talking about? Since his baby was born, Owen's whole world had transformed. Now it was all about how many hours the baby slept and how much he ate and how many smiles he gave. It went on and on.

"So, did I tell you?"

"I don't think so." I wanted to say yes. Anything to get him to stop going on about the baby. But if I lied, he would ask me what I thought about it or would say something that needed a response from me, and I wouldn't be able to give one. So, I had to be honest and take whatever lengthy monologue would follow.

"He rolled over for the first time!" Owen looked at me like I should be overjoyed about this.

"Oh. Is that...a big deal?" I gave an apologetic smile. I didn't know the first thing about babies.

"It's just an important milestone. It means his brain is growing and working. Before long, he'll be pushing up on all fours and starting to crawl. Gosh, then it won't be long before he's pulling himself up on things and trying to walk." He blew out a breath and ran a hand through his hair. "I have to get the baby-proofing upgraded. It's one thing when they can't move much yet. There's not much he can get into, you know? But once he's crawling, everything in the house has to be moved or covered or protected. Do we have those corner protectors?" Now he was taking out his phone. Probably to text his wife, Addie, about whatever baby-proofing crap he was talking about.

While he was distracted with corner protectors—whatever the heck those were—I looked around, trying to accomplish what we came here to do. Some trees in the area were dying and had to be removed, so we were out marking which ones would be cut down and which would be watched. The questionable ones wouldn't get the axe just yet, but if they didn't improve in the next six months or so, they'd get the chop on the next round. I spotted a tree that didn't look too promising, gave it a good sniff to confirm, and sprayed an X with the bright green spray paint in my hand. This tree was a lost cause.

When Owen put his phone away, he smiled at me. "Addie is so awesome. She already had them, of course. I should have known she would. She was planning to put them on this week, now that he's turning over. She was thinking exactly the same thing I was today!"

I nodded. "Cool, bro."

"I never knew marriage would be like this. It's just... so much better than I ever imagined, you know?"

"I don't, actually." I chuckled. I'd had girlfriends, of course. Plenty. And more short-term hookups than I could count. But none of them had ever been at the level of Addie and Owen's relationship. I doubted he ever loved anyone besides her. They'd been high school sweethearts and everything, separated for years, now together again and forever.

"When's your turn, man?"

"Funny you should ask. I was just thinking about that."

"Oh?" He sprayed another tree.

"Thirty is coming, whether I want it to or not. Maybe it's time."

"Definitely. You find the right woman, and it'll change your world." Owen beamed.

"Obviously." I rolled my eyes, but laughed.

"Sorry. I guess I do tend to talk about Addie and James a lot. They're my everything, though. I can't help it."

"Yeah... I think I know what you mean."

"Oh yeah?" He raised an eyebrow. "Does this have anything to do with the panther from last night?"

"I can't get that chick out of my head." I shook my head like I was trying to shake her out. I didn't even have to close my eyes to imagine her scent. It had taken up residence in my brain and whatever thought I had brushed against it, bringing it fresh to me. I'd never taken so many cold showers in my life.

"You gonna ask her out?"

"I don't know. I mean, yeah, I guess I want to start thinking about settling down and all that. Find my special one. I see what you have. I'm not ashamed to admit my jealousy. I just don't think the panther is the one."

"Why's that?"

"She's a panther, dude. I mean, like, I don't have an issue with that. I fully respect other species. It's not the inter-species thing that trips me up. But Panthers are hardcore; all tough and serious. And she is most definitely 110% panther." I shook my head, remembering her reaction to my acciden-tally taking her kill, then how she'd confronted me at the bar. It wasn't even that big of a deal, but she kept going on like I'd murdered her puppy or something.

"She *was* pretty intense last night, I'll give you that."

"I need someone like me, chill and carefree. Someone who won't go all ape-shit over me making a mistake. Can you imagine living with someone like her? I use my floor like a second dresser. She'd probably slit my throat for leaving my socks out if I married her."

Owen laughed. "I will say, even more laidback women don't appreciate that sort of thing. Addie has complained more than once when I left clothes on the floor of our room."

I groaned. "Somewhere in all of the Everglades, there is a messy girl who's perfect for me."

"Good luck finding her."

"If you come across her, let me know. Basically, think of the panther, then look for someone who's her total opposite."

"Got it. What about one of Addie's friends?"

I stuck my lip out in a hurt frown. "You want me to marry a non-shifter?"

"You are free to marry whoever you want."

"Not if I ever need to be the clan leader," I said. "I have responsibilities as second in command."

"Unless you're planning to kill me off so you can take over, I wouldn't worry about that. I'm not going anywhere."

"You just never know. Accidents happen. I hope I never have to take over. Honestly? It's a lot of work and responsibility. But what sort of second would I be if I wasn't ready at any moment to take the lead if I had to?"

"I'm thinking that the whole alphas-have-to-marry-a-shifter thing is unnecessary," Owen said. "Other clans don't have that rule. It almost ruined my life."

"Well, you're the one who can change that, but even still. I can't handle that panther."

"Yet, you keep bringing her up."

I paused. He had me there. Had to think fast. "I just keep running into her is all. She's, like, everywhere."

"Everywhere?"

Our walkie talkies crackled, then Pete's voice spoke to us. "Hey guys?"

"Yeah, Pete?" Owen responded.

"We got a call about a shark being possibly injured."

"We'll check it out. Send me the coordinates," Owen said.

A moment later, Owen's phone buzzed with a text of the shark's location.

"Let's head out," I said. Anything to change the subject.

We hopped into the utility vehicle and drove through the twisting back paths to get to where the shark had been last seen. When we came to water's edge, Owen shut the UV off and we hopped out.

"I just don't get why her smell affects me so much," I said.

Owen stifled a laugh.

"What?"

"And you claim I talk a lot about my wife and kid? You haven't shut up about this panther since you first encountered her."

"Well, all of our encounters have been...stressful. And painful." I rubbed my shoulder where she'd poked me repeatedly the night before. I actually had a faint bruise there this morning when I woke up.

"I wonder..." He took out his flashlight, even though it was midday, and shined it into the water so we could see below the surface better.

"What?" I asked again.

"Does it feel almost unavoidable?"

"How do you mean?" I saw a flash of movement. "There!" I pointed.

"Does it feel like she's a magnet, drawing you to her?"

"Yeah, actually. That's pretty much exactly what it's like. I don't want anything to do with her, but I can't stop thinking about her. I keep running into her, and her scent drives me freaking wild."

"Fated."

"Umm, say what now?"

"It's an old folktale, but like anything else around these

parts, most people believe it. Some people, and it happens with shifters especially, are meant to be together. For whatever reason, this is decided and then the two, when the time is right, are brought together."

"No, no, no. No way, man. Did you hear what I said? She's crazy. I can't be with someone like *her*. How could she possibly be my soulmate or whatever you want to call it?"

"Not soulmate. Fated mate."

I rolled me eyes. "If fate wants me with that panther, then fate can shove it. No way. No how." I cut the air with my hands to reinforce that there was no chance this was going down.

Owen shrugged. "Just saying. It's a thing. I see it!"

I followed his gaze and saw the shark. It was lying partially out of the water—not a good sign. We made our way over to it, keeping a distance so it didn't get scared. It was injured, with a slender gash along its body.

"Hey Pete," Owen said, getting on the walkie again. "Call the vet down here. We found it. Just has a laceration, but it'll need to be treated."

"On it, Boss," Pete answered.

There was nothing for us to do now but wait for the vet to show, then we'd get back to our tree marking.

"Who believes in this fated thing anyhow?" I asked.

"Are you *still* thinking about that panther?"

"No. I'm thinking about what you said about her."

Owen laughed and sat against a tree where he could keep an eye on the shark. "You've got it bad, man."

I leaned against the tree. "Do not."

"No point in fighting it, tough guy."

I slid down the tree's trunk to sit beside Owen. When I did, a smell hit me. A familiar smell.

"You've got to be kidding me!" I said, leaning forward on all fours, taking a harder sniff.

"What's up, man?" Owen asked.

"Her." I pointed to the patch of grass that held her scent. "She won't leave me alone!"

He made a tisk-tisk sound. "Told ya. Fated."

"Stop saying that! I'm not fated to her. I won't do it!"

"You can only resist for so long, man."

5

BRITT

I slung my shotgun over my shoulder and grabbed my pack with extra ammo, along with a bottle of water and some gator jerky. It was a work day; I'd be out for hours, until the sun got too hot for the animals and they hid, or until I killed enough critters that they had to be dragged inside and processed. I sold off the animals in a variety of ways to different folks around the 'Glades. Some wanted whole carcasses, while others were just interested in the meat or hides.

My cabin wasn't big enough to house my processing workshop, so I'd added a little building years ago to make sure I'd be able to do it all myself, right here on my land. This land had been in the family for decades, and luckily, the location of it was just right. I wasn't around in the 1940's when everything went down with landowners in the 'Glades, but boy, did people still run their mouths about it.

Especially at Shady's and other places where the locals hung out. They'd be talking about how their daddies had a hundred acres until the government came in and took it all from them. Hearing their stories, I wished I had been around back then. They made it sound so amazing; a town full of folks, all doing the same thing: living off the land, trading with each other, and most importantly, abiding by their own laws.

Shady's had a long history there. Back when the closest cops were a hundred fifty miles away, no one would show up to break up fights that got out of hand. The owner kept a shotgun or two behind the bar and, as the story went, he'd shot off more than his share of toes, trying to save his business from being torn apart by rowdy customers.

Of course, we had a decent presence of cops eventually. I didn't break the law, so they didn't bother me. And it was nice to know they were around if I had a problem. Same with the rangers. Yeah, they were going to reinforce the regulations, but they also kept us safe and protected the land.

But some shifter groups wanted to see things run differently. A group would flare up now and then, causing some kind of trouble until the proper authorities stepped in and fixed things, usually with the help of us Gladesmen and women. The one consistent headache came from those damned crocs.

The crocs caused problems for everyone who got in their way—shifters or not. They wanted full, complete reign of the 'Glades. Like a bunch of idiots who'd been dropped on their damn heads too much, they really thought they'd get things to go back to how they were back in the day. They'd run the park, kick out the police and be the authority of the land. Nothing but a bunch of dumb fucks if you ask me, and I wanted nothing to do with them.

I was just happy to be a Gladeswoman and have the skills passed down to me from my Ma and Gramma over the years. Gramma had been around back in the old days. She'd somehow—through smarts or luck—bought land that was real close to the 'Glades, but outside of park territory and wasn't subject to the government take over. If it'd been a mile or two to the east, she would have had to let it go when she passed. There'd have been no inheritance for Ma or for me. Who knows where I would have ended up if that were the case.

The men all vanished. Ma grew up with no Pa, and my Pa took off before I ever saw his face. But it was fine. We were used to it, and we didn't need no men to make things right. We were tough women, the Wilsons. Anyone who knew us would say, "Don't screw over those Wilson women, they'll hunt you down and skin you in your sleep." Gramma caused that rumor. She had plenty of stories of going after men who tried to steal from her, back before the law. I don't think I'll ever know which stories were true and which were exaggerations. No matter, though. Gramma was a master storyteller and you never cared if what she said was a total lie. It was entertaining just to hear her talk around the fire.

Gramma had taught me how to hunt, skin and process meat, while Ma made the connections that are still in effect today. Every time I sold a critter to the butcher down the way, he'd say, "Here's to your old Ma; may she be hunting in heaven." Of course, both my Gramma and Ma had been shot on these same lands, killed during a hunting accident—though with Gramma, I don't know how accidental it was. The two of them weren't panthers, either.

I guess my Pa musta been a panther and passed his shifter DNA down to me. From what I heard, if you had just one shifter parent, you had a 50/50 shot at being one. Guess I ended up on the lucky end of the inheritance.

From what my Ma and Gramma told me, I was four years old the first time I shifted, playing outside in the mud, as always. A bunny came hopping along and I went chasing after it. My little legs were too unsteady and slow to catch up, though, so I went back to playing in the mud. Well, some time later, the bunny came back, and that time, I was more determined. I ran after it, and at some point along the way, my determination went haywire. As I ran, Ma said I dropped down to all fours, screamed and then boom! I was a panther cub. That little bunny's skin still hangs over my bed today. My first kill. A proud moment.

But it was also a moment of sheer terror for Ma and

Gramma, who had no clue what was going on. Gramma was a stealthy woman, though; she poked around town and eventually discovered what was going on. She got an old panther woman—Kat's gramma, actually—to come over and talk to us, telling us what to expect. She said I might shift by accident while I was a youngin', but once I came of age, it'd be happening regularly and the full moon would force me to shift if I stepped into its light. She became like a second gramma to me, and that's how Kat and I knew each other.

Dezi had become part of our tribe not too long after. The three of us had been all we had growing up. We liked it that way; that's just how things were done in the 'Glades. You kept to yourself, you did your work, and on occasion, you'd meet up at Shady's with a friend or two for a cold one.

I kissed the barrel of my gun—Gramma's gun—and put it back over my shoulder. I always took something of Gramma's with me on a hunt for luck, like her gun or knife. I walked on through the morning light, searching for a good spot to sit up high for a while. With my panther eyes, I could see farther than most and in dimmer light. My panther genes were a real benefit to me most days. Made me a good hunter.

As I continued to make my way through the swampy forest, I caught a whiff of a scent that made me stop dead in my tracks. I took a few steps toward it to make sure and I shook my head. *Yup. That damn bear again. Ezra.* What kind of a name was that anyhow? And, more importantly, how was I going to shake that loser? If he really started to get in my way, I'd have to do something about him.

It seemed he'd just been running around and landed at my hunting spot. Fine, whatever. It was part of the park and well within his rights to do so. I'd even heard he was a ranger, so it was his job to be in the park. I just didn't personally want him so close. Had he managed to recognize my scent this time? Did he know he was close to me? Probably not. Dumbass.

I followed his scent for a short time, but it went on through the trails for a while in a direction I didn't need to be heading. As long as he wasn't lurking somewhere, waiting to jump out and mess up my kill, I wasn't worried about it. He didn't seem to have been in the area at that moment, but he was there recently. The scent was pretty fresh.

As I sniffed around, I picked up another scent. And that one disturbed me more than the bear's. I had to be sure of my suspicions, so I crept closer, sniffing all the way. I saw a paw first, then the legs, and finally, the body.

A panther lay dead, half hidden in the tall grass. Not too many panthers were left in those parts. Even if I was a shifter, I still felt a very deep connection with the creatures that were completely animal. We were the same species. That dead panther was especially disturbing, however; clearly, it had been murdered.

Across its neck were long gashes. I couldn't tell specifically what had killed it, but it must have been some kind of blade. They were clean cuts, unlike the tear of a claw. These wounds were also too intentional to be a matter of defense. The typical signs of a fight were missing; evidence of foul play, the police called it.

If two animals fought, there should have been crushed plants nearby. There would have been scrapes and wounds on the body, but they would be varied; sometimes, you didn't land a good swipe, making the gash shallow.

This crime scene was clean. It seemed like the panther had been sleeping and someone snuck up on it to slice its throat. I doubted that's how it happened, but that's what it looked like. It told me two things: one, it was not an animal attack, and two, someone was hunting panthers. No, not hunting. Hunting implied stealth and skill and purpose. I hunted for meat, for skins, for carcasses. This poor creature was left for dead. No sport involved. Pure murder of a pure panther.

Not too many things in the world upset me, but that filled me with such strong rage that I balled my fists and growled in anger, tears forming in my eyes. I would find who did this. I'd skin them alive and eat their scrawny frame while they watched. I'd pull out their fingernails one by one and watch them suffer.

I paced for a minute, trying to clear my mind. I'd be no good for anything if my head was foggy with rage, so I forced myself to calm down. I spent a bit of time sniffing all around the body; I wanted to know the scent of the killer better than my own scent.

Better than that bear's scent that kept plaguing me.

As I filled my nose with the mark of the murderer, I kept thinking of him. *Ezra.* If he really was a ranger, that would mean he knew those grounds almost as well as I did. As much as I hated to admit it, he might have been my best ally. My best chance for catching this killer and bringing him down. He'd be just as anxious as I was to get to the bottom of it. A ranger's duties are to protect and conserve, and that death broke both tenets.

But that meant finding Ezra, talking to him and working with him on some level. That meant time with him, in his presence. And that was the last thing I wanted.

Okay, Britt. Focus on what's important. Sure, Ezra is annoying and happens to be everywhere. Sure, your body reacts to his scent in ways you can't stand and can't shut off. But, admit it, he's a nice guy, even if he's an idiot and a pansy. He wouldn't hurt me, I told myself.

I sighed and went to find a place to stash my clothes and weapons nearby. I hung my things on a nearby tree's branches and shifted, then ran to the last place I'd picked up Ezra's scent and followed the trail.

6

EZRA

"I'll go ahead and file the report," Owen said once they'd left the injured shark. The vet seemed to think it would be just fine, but there was still paperwork to be done. I was happy to let him do it.

"I'll drop you at the station, then get back to the trees," I said.

Owen gave me a sideways smirk.

"What?" I demanded.

"You want to be out there where you girl's scent is? Hoping to run into her?"

"Um, no. I ran into her once and she bit me. Then I ran into her again and she poked me and yelled at me. I have no desire to run into her again. Ever."

Owen laughed. "Wait till I tell the guys about this."

"Nothing to tell, man."

We hopped into the UV and drove back toward the ranger station. My clan loved to pick on me, the kid from California who didn't grow up with a clan; pick on the one who speaks a little differently and isn't all uptight. How could they think I'd have a thing for that panther? They knew me well enough to bust on me constantly, yet they insisted I had a thing for this she-devil tormenting me.

"You know," I said, "you should know better."

He'd been looking at his phone and put it down in a hurry to keep his eyes on the path. "Sorry, you're right. Addie just sent me a picture of James. Look." He held the phone so I could see the photo of the baby on his stomach, looking at the camera.

"Cute. And no, I guess you shouldn't be on your phone while driving, but that's not what I meant."

"What then?"

"You know me. You guys all do. I've been part of this clan for like, five years now? Living and working here in the Everglades with you all."

"Yeah?"

"So, you know me," I went on. "You should know my type. And that means, you should know I'd have nothing to do with a chick like that panther."

Owen pulled over and stopped, leaning over the steering wheel, laughing so hard he held his stomach. I shoved him and he tumbled out of the UV onto the path. He lay in a ball, still laughing his ass off.

I got out and went around to his side to nudge him with my foot.

"You—" He couldn't talk, he was laughing so hard.

I stood over him, my arms crossed, glaring down at him. "Dude."

"You're friggin' obsessed!" He'd started to calm down and sat up now to wipe tears from his eyes. "This is hilarious."

"Yeah, real funny." My face felt hot with embarrassment. I never cared about their teasing; I had plenty of decent comebacks and I always got mine. But somehow, that was different. Maybe because deep down, I suspected what he said was true. Even if it was the last thing I wanted.

"Ezra, man." He got to his feet and put a hand on my shoulder. "You're my second in command. I want you to be happy. You're important to me. You're also my friend. But I have to tell you, from bear to bear, friend to friend, ranger to ranger, brother to brother—this chick is your mate, whether you want to deny it or not. Maybe just give into it and explore that. I mean, this is happening for a reason."

"What reason could there possibly be?"

"No idea. The tale goes that when the fated need each other, the universe brings them together. You don't have to believe it, but it sure seems like everything people say is true for you."

I shook my head and got back into the UV. "You're wrong. I don't need her for anything."

"Okay." He got back in and turned the ignition, then hit the gas. "I'm with you, no matter what. You want this panther? Awesome. You don't want this panther? No problem. But when you say you don't want her, then go on and on about her? You're going to get busted on, sorry." He playfully shoved my shoulder. "Nothing wrong with being a little twitterpated. Especially since you're fated mates."

"We're not fated!" I hollered.

He held up a hand in defense. "Okay. I'm sorry. I'll let it go." Then, under his breath, he added, "For now."

"Heard that."

"Figured you did."

As we neared the station, I noticed an animal running in the grass beside us, along the dirt road.

"Hey, hold up for a sec," I told Owen.

He stopped and turned to look with me, and we got out to watch the running animal. It was unusual activity for this area and time of day. And then I knew why.

"Oh fuck," I said, slapping my forehead.

Owen pressed his lips together hard, trying not to laugh.

"Just don't, man," I said. "Why the hell is she here now?"

I saw the panther's head popping over the grass as she bounded toward us and prepared for another fight. What had I done to piss her off this time? I stood with my arms crossed, wearing an unhappy scowl on my face.

She dashed out of the grass, her paws sliding in the dust as she came to a halt. The second she stopped running, she shifted into her human form, not seeming to care about the fact she was buck naked as she stood before us.

"Hey!" She came right at us.

"What'd I do now?" I asked.

"For once, this isn't about you." She gave me a nasty look and turned to Owen. "I just came across something I thought you should know about. A pure panther. Dead. Murdered."

Owen's eyes widened as mine did. "Where?"

"Follow me; I'll show you," she said.

"One sec." Owen went back to the UV to radio the station that we had a situation to check out.

While he did that, I tried to talk to her. "What can you tell us about it?"

"Wasn't an animal," she said. "The wound is too clean. I picked up the scent of the killer, though."

"Whoa, whoa." I held up both hands. "We can't assume anything like that yet."

She glared at me. "You think I can't tell the difference between an animal murdered and one killed in a fight?"

"That's not what I meant, I—"

"Why don't I murder you and see if anyone can tell I did it?"

I let out a sigh. "Nevermind. What makes you so sure it was murder?"

She spoke slowly and pointedly, like she thought I was a

complete idiot. "Did I stutter? The wounds on the animal are clean. Not from claws, but blades. The area around the panther showed no sign of a fight, and the smell is human— and male. Did you get all that or should I repeat it again for you more slowly?"

"I got it," I snapped. "You don't have to be so grumpy all the time."

"We'll see how cheerful you are when people start hunting bears."

I gave her an incredulous look. "Bears aren't protected like panthers are. We do get hunted. All the time. There's a bear hunting season; aren't you, like, a hunter or something for a living?"

She rested her hands on her hips. I'd done a good job of avoiding scanning my eyes over her gorgeous curves, but it was a lot of work to maintain my cool. I kept my gaze trained on hers and refused to look down, even as I felt my member begin to throb in anticipation.

"What the fuck is wrong with you?" she demanded.

"Aside from you showing up and hassling me over and over again?" I asked.

"Okay, whoa," Owen said, returning to us. "No time for your little fight here. And I'm sorry, Miss, what's your name?"

Owen actually stuck out his hand to shake hers and she returned the gesture.

"Britt Wilson," she replied.

"Britt," Owen continued. "Thank you for coming to tell

us. Obviously, we're highly concerned about this and we'll do everything we can to get to the bottom of this. Since we're all shifters, I'd say Ezra, let's go ahead and bear up. We'll get the clan over to sniff it out so we can all work together. My third just became a police officer, so he'll be a valuable asset."

"Good," she said. "I want this person dead. Fast."

"Shall we get a move on?" Owen asked. "The sooner we scope it out, the sooner we can find the attacker. He might still be in the area."

Britt didn't answer, but promptly shifted and waited for us. Owen and I both went to the UV and yanked off our clothes, then shifted. She took off and we followed.

You have to chill out, Owen commanded. *What the hell was all that?*

What's going on? Everything okay?

Great. Now Mason was in on this, too.

Where's Conner? Owen asked.

Here, Conner answered. *Noah and Hailey are on their way.*

Perfect. Thanks. Owen explained the situation as we ran fast to keep up with Britt. *We're following her now to the body.*

Britt, I scoffed. *What kind of a name is Britt?*

Oh right, Owen said. *I forgot to mention that the woman who found the panther is the same panther shifter that Ezra won't shut up about.*

She keeps showing up! I defended myself. *I can't escape her and every time I run into her, it's a horrible experience.*

You should hear him whining and going on. Owen did a

mental eye roll. *He's worse than a little boy pulling the hair of the girl he likes.*

I do not like her, I insisted. *I might actually loathe her.*

But her scent drives you wild, man, Mason pointed out.

It's so strong, Conner added, *that it makes me want her!* He laughed and the others joined him.

Whatever, dude, she's all yours.

I don't want to get in the middle of that, so I'll pass, but I appreciate your willingness to share, Conner amended.

It's kinda cute, really, Owen said. *I mean, when we're at your wedding, we'll think back to this moment and all have a good laugh.*

My wedding? I huffed. *You're taking things way too far. I don't appreciate it.*

Britt came to a stop and we halted behind her. Owen sent a mental map of our location and then we got to work.

We looked around, taking note of our surroundings, sharing mental images with the clan and memorizing scents. Britt was right. There was no way this was accidental or caused by an animal. I wouldn't admit it, but she was smart. She knew what to look for. She'd make a good ranger and was probably a pretty decent hunter.

I noticed these things about her, but wouldn't let the ideas become actual thoughts in my mind. If I did, the clan would pick up on them and would never leave me alone. I was grateful they were finally focused on something beside me for a change.

Owen shifted back and Britt followed shortly after. I stayed in my bear form to both connect to the clan and to avoid being naked around her again.

"Do you recognize the scent at all?" Owen asked her.

"No, but I'll be on the lookout, mark my words. I *will* find this asshole."

"There was a group years ago who thought the panthers should be taken out of the park for good; I hope they're not back. They killed a lot of panthers, and that's part of the reason you've become rare and protected."

"Yeah. My clanmate was one of them." She spit on the ground. "That's why I'm going to hunt this bastard down and make him pay."

"I'm sorry for your loss, and I understand your determination, but I have rangers on the way and the police are on their way, too. There will be a full investigation. We're all taking this very seriously. I wouldn't want you to be in danger."

"And that's why I'm going to hunt down the killer," she insisted. "If he's hunting panthers, obviously I'm in danger."

When she said it like that, the words prickled over me. I hadn't thought it through. Yeah, she was upset about finding a dead panther. But whoever did this would be hunting her, too, if he was hunting panthers. She was in danger.

Something in my heart alighted. Concern, I realized. I was worried about her. And the mention of her clanmate being killed? It saddened me. I growled at myself. Why should I be worried about her or sad for her? Of all people. Her? Well, no. I was a ranger, after all. I would be concerned about any citizen who might be in danger.

Keep telling yourself that. Mason ran up behind me and Conner was with him. Hailey and Noah were close, but still running.

Stop thought-dropping on my internal convo, I snapped.

"These are two more members of my clan," Owen explained to Britt.

She glanced over and nodded.

Whew, Mason whistled in his mind. *She is pretty hot, though.*

Umm hello? Female present, Hailey hissed.

Sorry, Mason said. *It's true, though.*

Dude, I said as a warning. *Not helping.*

What's the police's ETA? Conner asked. He was on my good side. For now.

They'll be here in a few. I'm going to shift to be ready, Mason replied, then dropped the sack he'd been carrying and shifted, dressing quickly.

It'll be alright, man. Conner nudged against me, then shifted back.

I took off into the woods. I wanted to be away from them, but I also thought I could do more trying to follow the scent than just sitting around getting ragged on.

7

BRITT

Once the rangers and police had left, I had more room to take on my own investigation. I had sniffed around the body all I could, but now that it had been removed, things had changed. Scents that had been under the body and somewhat hidden were then exposed. Of course, there were also the smells of many other people layered in there by that point, but I had stuck around just for this reason. I was careful, but I had made sure to get a whiff of each person who'd been there so I wouldn't be confused. Of course, I had no trouble recognizing out Ezra's scent. His was the strongest of them all, much to my dismay.

Once I had gone over the crime scene in full detail, I ran around my cabin to make sure the scent of the killer was nowhere near it. I wanted to identify any new odor marks and have a clear scent map of my home in my mind. If anything new came up, I needed to know; whether it was a bunny, a lizard or a person.

When that was committed to memory, I went back to the scene again, found the scent of the killer and followed it. I figured at some point, he got into a vehicle. Being human meant he couldn't get this far into the park on foot unless it'd taken him hours. And there hadn't been anyone found around the area. I still wanted to go as far as I could; I'd even sniff out the vehicle so I could recognize it.

I knew Owen didn't want me to get hurt or anything, and I'm sure they didn't want me interfering in their investigation. Hell, I sure didn't want to mess up their work, either. But I wasn't going to sit around, just waiting for this guy to show up and slash me, too. And if I could give them information that would help them nail the guy, even better.

Owen seemed like a much more reasonable bear than Ezra. It's probably why he was the Alpha, though naming Ezra as his second wouldn't have been my choice, if I were him.

Ezra. I drew in a long breath. It still didn't make sense why I reacted to his scent like I did. My body warred with my mind. My body wanted me to be closer to him, yet my mind wanted to stay far, far away.

As I followed the trail, I noted each scent I took in. Killer, Ezra, Owen, killer, Mason, Ezra, Owen, Ezra, killer, Conner, Ezra, Ezra, Ezra. I let a low growl rumble my chest. They'd apparently had the same idea and had followed the path. Well, I didn't want to be out of the loop. But as I went, it was like the scents were forcing me to think Ezra, Ezra, Ezra, over and over. Had he just run around in circles as they moved along, marking everything in his path?

Maybe I should talk to Kat's gramma, I thought. We still kept in touch, though I didn't see her much those days. Being up in age, she kept to herself even more than she used to. But I wanted to ask her what this Ezra thing was all about. Why was his scent so strong and permeable? Why did my body want him when my mind hated the idea? Unless I was turning schizophrenic, there had to be a reason for it.

I followed the trail until it came to an end on a road, as I suspected it would. I sniffed hard to pick out the correct vehicle scent, but lots of vehicles traveled this road, so I had to be careful. I noticed one that meshed the killer's scent with a vehicle's, and that had to be it. I spent time with the smell, committing it to memory, then took off to head back home.

8

EZRA

I sat in the ranger station with Owen after the panther's body had been removed. The clan had come and checked out the scene. The police talked to us and the report had been filed. Now that all of that had passed, my mind was left to wander. And, of course, it wandered to just one place.

Britt.

The hint of worry I had noticed earlier was becoming stronger. I kept seeing the dead animal and hearing and smelling Britt, and it all got tangled in my mind until *she* became the dead animal. It was too much.

Though we hadn't spent much time together, I had a decent sense of her personality. Gladesmen and women were the type of people who didn't mess around, didn't waste time, and definitely didn't sit back and wait for something to happen. If Britt thought there was someone hunting panthers—and there was a good chance there was—then she would be out in the woods trying to find him.

Most people would be smart about it. They'd leave the investigation up to the police. They'd wait to find out more before assuming this wasn't an accident or a stand-alone incident. And if they found out this was someone just going after panthers, they'd be smart about it: they'd sit at home where it was safe, not run out into the prime location for the killings. She would put her scent all over the place, giving the killer a map right to her.

From the scent, we knew the person who'd killed the panther was a pure human. And though we hadn't smelled another scent with him, that didn't mean that somehow a shifter wasn't helping him out. It wasn't like people and shifters weren't all around the park all day, every day. The Everglades National Park was a tourist attraction, after all. Whether local or distant, people came to the park to see the wildlife and experience nature.

Others were in danger, too, but my mind was on Britt and Britt alone, which was a problem for a few reasons. Obviously, I couldn't share this with my clan; they were riding my ass enough. If they heard half of what I'd been thinking all morning, they'd never let up. And without being in bear form, there wasn't much I could do anyway. What, walk around the area with a shot gun and hope the killer steps out onto the trail? I don't think so. Being a shifter, my human senses were heightened, but they were nothing compared to when I was in bear form.

The other problem was Britt herself. I was sure, without having to ask, that she did not want me around. If she knew I was trying to protect her, she'd probably attack me. She'd stop me somehow. I didn't want to be around her again, but I didn't want to be thinking about her, worrying, feeling trapped and helpless. I couldn't shift, I couldn't get my clan's help, I couldn't do anything as a human, and I couldn't find her to protect her. I was stuck.

"You okay?" Owen asked.

I guess I'd been quiet a long time. "Just thinking about everything."

He watched me for a moment. "You're worried about her."

Even in human form, I couldn't hide things from him. I shrugged.

"I know I've been getting on you, but man, if you're worried, there's nothing wrong with that. It's okay if you're attracted to her or you're into her."

"I don't think she's right for me though. Do you?"

"Can't say. Only one way to find out. If you're worried, go for a run. Sniff around and make sure she's okay."

I nodded. "Maybe I will. If she finds out and throws a fit, then I'll just say I was doing my job."

"There ya go. And it's not a lie. I do need you to help find this guy. We all need to be on the case to make sure we don't have another panther killing in the area."

"I hope it was a one-time thing," I said.

"Me, too."

I looked at the clock on the wall in his office. "I'm done for the day. Think I will go for that run."

"Let me know what you find, bud."

"No doubt, man."

I went out to my car and drove to a more secluded spot. Once there, I stripped down and hid my car key, then shifted. I stood on my hind legs and gave a good stretch, then took off running.

Without really thinking about where I was going, I ran back to the last place I'd had her scent. When I reached it and smelled it, the familiarity of it was comforting. I breathed her in, and it warmed my chest. And that made me pause. If I really didn't want to date her, or even get to know her, why did her scent affect me like this?

The whole fated thing that Owen kept bringing up seemed like a bunch of bullshit. Her pheromones made my body want her and go crazy with the wanting—that must have been it; it was purely chemical. If we ended up sleeping together ever, it would probably end this. And actually, that wasn't a bad idea. It might be the best means to the end of this obsession.

I shook the thought from my head and refocused. I didn't have time to get all riled up, and I sure as hell didn't have time to stop and take a cold shower. *A cool dip might not be bad, though*, I thought, so I dashed to the closest pond and jumped in, letting the water run through my fur and cool my body. I got out and shook off, then returned to following the scent.

As I went on, weaving through the mangroves and tall grasses, I got some insight on her hunting patterns; how she circled around nests of birds and slunk along the water's edge in places. She must have been very good at what she did.

I came to a cabin tucked deep in the woods, but off the park land, technically. It reminded me very much of Owen's cabin, but then again, there were many of those little cabins out there. They were the properties that had been outside the government takeover back when the Everglades National Park was established in the first place. I didn't know much about that time, but people still talked about how much land and property they lost. It seemed like a bunch of whining to me; the land in the area needed to be protected, after all. I'd hate to think about the ramifications all that development would have had on our natural resources if the government hadn't stepped in. But then again, I wasn't a Gladesman.

It was her property, though, and I wasn't about to trespass, so I didn't go any further. But I did pick up a very fresh trail leading away from the cabin. *She must be out hunting right now,* I thought. *I could make sure she's okay and see if she found anything.*

With that, I followed the trail and the scent grew stronger as I went.

Just then, Mason reached out. *Hey all.*

Just me here, I answered. *How goes it?*

Wish we were making more progress, but there's not much to go on.

For the panther killer?

Yeah. We haven't been able to pull evidence off the body. We've pretty much got nothing.

I'm running right now, I said. *Trying to follow a trail I picked up on to see if Britt knows something.* Right after I had the thought, I regretted it and mentally braced for the backlash.

She was helpful the other day, was all he said. *I bet she'll be a valuable resource in finding him. She has the motivation and the skills.* As it turned out, he wasn't going to rip on me after all. He must've picked up on my not-so-fully formed thoughts because he added, *She's cool, man. You could do worse.*

I'm not trying to do anything with her at all.

Okay, then. I've gotta shift and get back to work. Just wanted to check in and stretch my legs.

Catch ya later, bro.

Later.

When Mason shifted back and I was alone again, I considered what he'd said. Were they all just going to accept it going forward? Would they assume I was going to be with her and that was it? Well, that wasn't going to happen. They'd see it. I'd work with her the best I could to find the killer. Sure, we all would. But it didn't have to go any further than that.

I'd barely finished that thought when I heard a rustling and paused to listen and sniff. It was her. She had to be just over the hill from where I stood.

I didn't want to startle her, and I sure as hell didn't want to anger her. I walked slowly and loudly in her direction, and when she came into view, I saw her pounce on a raccoon, sinking her teeth in deep. She turned to look at me, holding my gaze for a long moment.

I stayed back, not wanting her to think this was going to be a of repeat of the deer incident. I wasn't interested in the raccoon, anyway. So, I sat down to watch her and waited until she was through.

She tore into the raccoon, eating a large chunk of its flesh, and I was content to watch. When she was finished, I'd shift to talk to her. But as I waited, she sat up sharply, then took off running at full speed.

9

BRITT

The timing couldn't have been worse. I'd just killed my coon and was having a nice snack, then *he* showed up. At that point, I wasn't even surprised. I'd heard him coming a long way off and then he just sat there. He was being respectful, for once. Just watching. Waiting, I guessed. Why would he have stuck around?

I had planned to talk to him; to show him the trail of the killer I'd found and see if the vehicle's scent was familiar to him at all. If it wasn't, I'd make him familiar with it. But then, I'd heard footfalls in the distance. I knew it was a human, from the sound of its steps. Most critters had distinct patterns as they moved, and it wasn't uncommon for me to recognize what something was before I even smelled it or saw it. This was no different.

I kept an ear out. If the person came closer, I'd make sure I wasn't seen. When people saw a panther, it tended to freak them out a bit, and I wasn't there to scare people. But then the wind brought me a little gift: a hint of the scent of the person—the one who'd killed the panther.

Well, nothing was going to stop me from chasing him down. Not some little raccoon snack, and not Ezra showing up. I would do whatever it took to get him. And I surely wasn't going to waste one damn second to shift back and tell that bear about my game plan.

So, I dropped the coon and took off. I was nearing the killer; nothing would stop me from tearing him to shreds. I ran hard as I could, but when I got to the place where I thought the sound had come from, he was gone.

I sniffed around and found a new trail—the vehicle—and picked up my pace. Running after a human was easy; I could outrun even the best sprinters without breaking a sweat. But a vehicle was different; much faster. And the smell was different, too; not like tracking a person or animal. Mammals had a warmer, stronger smell that my nose was built for. This task took a lot more concentration.

I was so focused, in fact, that I hadn't paid attention to Ezra. I didn't think he'd come after me—or be able to keep up, for that matter. And so, when I heard someone running just behind me, it threw me off.

The sound of paws pounding on the dirt made me whirl and pause until I realized it was him. I ran again, but now his scent overwhelmed my senses. I shook it off and picked out the vehicle scent again and ran to a crossroads.

When I got there, I found a slightly busier dirt road. This was one more heavily-traveled by visitors to the park, so there was an onslaught of odors to sort through; I couldn't tell which way the killer had gone. I sniffed and sniffed, running in circles, going down one direction, then another. *Fuck.*

I had to face the truth after several minutes of trying. I'd lost him. My gut sank and the anger ripped through my chest. It was all Ezra's fault.

I ran back a little ways until we were well out of human earshot or sight. I waited, and sure enough, moments later, he came bounding toward me. As soon as he caught up to me and stopped, I shifted back. And then I let him have it.

"Why do you always show up at the worst possible times? I had him, you asshole! Why won't you stay away from me?"

He blinked at me with his big bear eyes before he stood up and shifted back.

"How can you blame this on me?" he demanded. "I was following you to help you catch him!"

"But you didn't. You distracted me and I lost the scent."

"So, you got distracted and that's my fault?"

"If you would have stayed out of my way, I would have him right now." My rage boiled at the thought of it. "I could have put an end to all of this."

"Oh right, because you're going to chase a car now? You really think you're that fast?" he challenged.

I gritted my teeth together. "I would have followed the scent until I came to the vehicle, idiot."

"Then go ahead. I'm not stopping you."

"I can't because I lost the trail when you distracted me."

"So, you lost the trail and that's my fault, too?"

"Yes!" My hands balled into fists. "What is your problem? Why do you keep showing up and following me around?"

"I'm not. *You* keep showing up! I was out hunting and there you were, then—"

"Oh, when you took my kill? That time? When *I* was out hunting and you just showed up?"

"Then, you came into Shady's—"

"I was there first," I said.

"Whatever. But you were the one who took it on yourself to come over to me and start something. I was just sitting there minding my own business. Then you were the one who came to us when you found the dead panther, or did you forget that?"

"Hello? You're the ranger, not me. It's your job to find the killer."

"Exactly." His expression fell into cockiness, and I wanted to slap it off him. "And that's what I'm doing. So, actually, *you're* in *my* way. You got in the way of the official investigation."

"Oh, what are you going to do, arrest me? You don't have

the authority to do that."

"Of course not." He shook his head. "You're an asset to the investigation—when you're not getting in the way. I came out here to make sure you were okay and see if you found anything."

"I don't need you to check up on me. Stay away and maybe I could find something to tell you about. Or, more likely, I'll just kill him myself and not bother you all with it."

"Right, because you're better at everything? You're better than everyone? Why would rangers have any idea how to do their jobs, is that it?"

I growled low in my chest before I jumped on him, sending him crashing to the ground. I pinned him down, my hands on his shoulders.

"Who's winning now, asshole?" I spit the words at him.

"Neither of us." He held my gaze for a long moment, then did something I couldn't forgive him for. He leaned up a few inches and smashed his mouth to mine.

I pulled back and narrowed my eyes. "What the *hell* do you think you're doing?"

"Let's just get it over with. We keep running into each other. It's obvious there's some stupid attraction between us."

The fact that I was lying naked on top of him suddenly registered in my body, and warmth rushed over me. He grew hard beneath my hips and that same feeling took over. That animalistic desire.

Maybe he was right. "So, we fuck and that's it? Then we'll

be able to stay away from each other?"

"I sure hope so," he said. "Because I can't stand it anymore. Your scent drives me wild, but your attitude drives me crazy. I don't know if I should kiss you or smack you."

Just for fun, I slapped him—not too hard, but to make a point. Then, I pressed my lips against his in a hungry kiss, like I wanted to devour him. Because in that moment, I did.

He dug his fingers into my hair and pulled me closer. We kissed so hard, it hurt my mouth. My body tingled all over with wanton desire, and when I finally gave into it the feeling was so strong, it made my head spin.

He pushed up and flipped us so he was on top. His hands were on either side of my body and he lowered himself down to press against me. His skin was as hot as mine; we were fire together, stoking each other to raging. Pressing his hips into mine, his hard-on slid up and down against me; I was so wet already.

But I didn't like him being on top. I was going to show him that I was in control. I pushed up and tackled him again, reaching down to grab his cock. I had to make sure he was nice and ready, and I wanted this over fast.

He was hard as a rock, so I positioned myself over him and slid down his length, but as he entered me, the feeling overwhelmed me and shook me to the core. Before he was even fully inside me, I came with a loud moan. Any other time I had sex, it took much longer than that, and once I hit my peak, that was it. I came and moved on. Not this time.

This was just the beginning; my body was still hot and wanting him.

I sat up, pushing him fully inside me before I bounced on him, sending him deep and shallow as I rocked. I tugged on his chest hair and he growled in response, pinching my nipples so hard it should have hurt, but instead, it sent a wave of pleasure through me.

He grabbed my hips and slammed me down, thrusting harder into me than before, and his eyes stared at me intently as he pounded me faster. This was not lovemaking. Not even close. This was fucking.

"Faster!" I demanded.

He sat up and embraced me, but it was only to move me. He put himself on top of me again and slid one arm under my leg to pin it up high. From that position, he was able to go deep, but also harder. His ass muscles worked as he thrusted into me again and again. It still wasn't hard enough. Nothing could be hard enough.

"Harder!" I insisted.

He sped up, his face red with the exertion. As he pounded, I came again, feeling like a wave had rushed over me, then out of me and all over him.

He yanked back, pulling out of me so fast it took my breath before he flipped me over on my stomach. Pulling my hips up to meet his, he entered me from behind. His fist wound into my hair and he tugged as he slammed into me.

Finally, from this position, he could do it hard enough.

My ass slapped against his thighs and my wetness drenched him. That was the problem, I realized. I was actually too wet. Not enough friction.

As he sped up, putting his other hand on my shoulder to steady me as he pounded me, the friction increased a little. Before it had been just playing. Now we were getting serious.

"Fuck yes," he groaned.

I pushed back, forcing my ass into him with each thrust. His cock stroked my insides and when he cried out, I came for the third time.

"I'm coming," he announced and let go of my hair to grab my hips. He pounded me as hard as he could and cried out again. I could feel his dick throbbing inside me.

He collapsed to the forest floor, spent. I was still on all fours and dropped my forehead down to the soft ground, tingling all over. Even the soreness felt good, which seemed twisted to me, but then again, so did this whole thing. Did we really just have sex?

I faced him as he laid in the grass, breathing hard, glistening in a sheen of sweat.

"You think that did it?" I asked.

"That did something, that's for sure."

"Yeah." I got to my feet. "Now please, *please*, stay the fuck out of my way."

I shifted back to my panther and heard him calling out to me, begging me not to run off yet, but my paws sank into the soft ground as I ran.

10

EZRA

When I could finally move again, I pushed myself up. She'd ditched me, just like that? Get off, then take off? Weren't women always accusing men of doing that, calling it insensitive? She had just screwed my brains out and left.

I shook my head. How had we gone from screaming at each other to having sex? It didn't make much sense to me. But it had made perfect sense to my body. She felt so good. Even the thought made me hard again. *No*, I reminded myself. *That was it. We had sex so that we could stay away from each other.*

I shifted and took off, running back to my car and clothes. I went straight home and showered, but at least this time, I didn't have to shower in frigid water to calm my body down. I was worn out. I grabbed a beer from the fridge and fell onto the couch, but I didn't even get the can opened before I fell asleep. I knew this because when I woke in the morning, the sealed can was on the floor where I'd apparently dropped it in my sleep. At least it hadn't spilled all over the carpet.

I stretched and caught a faint whiff of her on my shirt. How that had even happened, I didn't know. I guess her scent was on me when I dressed and it had lingered. One little sniff and my cock stood at attention. *Great,* I sighed inwardly. *So much for the whole 'let's-have-sex-to-get-this-out-of-our-systems' theory.* I already craved her. I wanted more. I wanted *her.*

I doubted there was any way she'd want to see my face again. This had been a one-time thing and probably a huge mistake. My mind was already foggy with desire and want; full of nothing but her. I scrubbed my face with my hands and hopped in the shower for yet another cold shower.

When I got to work, I went straight to Owen's office, where I found him working at his computer. I sat in the chair across from him and banged my forehead onto the desk.

"Bad night?" he asked.

"Depends on how you look at it," I mumbled, my face pressed into the cool wood. "I found her."

"Yeah? Anything come up?"

I sat up to look at him. "You could say that. We... had sex."

"What!" He coughed and spit out his coffee. "How the...?"

"I found her and pissed her off like I always seem to do. She was on the trail of the killer and said I distracted her and made her lose it. So, we got into this huge screaming match and the next thing I knew, she tackled me. What was I supposed to do? She was naked on top of me. My body went crazy. So, I kissed her. Then we..."

"Of all the things I thought you might say to me this morning, this would have been last on the list, right after you telling me you were abducted by aliens last night."

"It sorta feels like that, man." I set my elbow on the desk and slumped, putting my cheek in my hands. "It's like she's taking over my whole body."

"What happens now? Are you two going to be a thing?"

"No. The whole point was to get it over with so we can be done with each other."

"She said that?" he asked.

"No, I said that and she agreed. I thought if we just had sex, the attraction would be lessened. You know how that happens sometimes? You chase someone who's hard to get and when you get them, the interest is gone."

"I guess? I've never had that."

"Well, I have," I admitted. "It sucks. More for the female, but still. The chase is over, you get what you want, then you want nothing to do with her, but now she's into you."

"Is that what happened?"

"No," I sighed. "I want her even more. And even less. I don't know what to do. This is killing me."

"You look like crap," he pointed out.

"Thanks."

"I don't know if what I'm going to say will make it better or worse."

"There is no worse."

"Okay. I'm sending you to work with Mason. I want you to join forces with the police to become part of the investigation." He looked at me, waiting for a response.

"Fine. If we find this guy, I won't have to be around her. She'll be safe, and I can move on."

"Can you?"

I stood and looked at him sadly. "Fuck, I don't know."

"Call me if you need anything."

I held up a hand to wave as I walked out.

I drove over to the police station to meet up with Mason and his team. They were expecting me, and when I got there, they welcomed me into the room where they had details of the investigation set up. We went over things, but there wasn't much new. I did tell them about Britt and I coming across the scent, then losing it, but that didn't help much. It did tell them that whoever this was, he was still in the area.

"Since you know the park best," Mason announced, "we'll team up to go on regular patrols." He flipped open a binder of photos and information. "These are our suspects. They've all been known in the community for speaking out against panthers.

Once they left the station to return to the park for their

first patrol, Mason said, "Now that the non-shifters aren't around, I can tell you the rest. We checked out each suspect already and none of them match the scent. That doesn't mean the person who killed the panther isn't working with a group, assuming this isn't just a random, one-time attack. We have to treat it like an ongoing attack and expect another incident. We're trying to find connections at this point. See if the killer knows any of our suspects. They're not truly suspects any longer to those of us in the force who are shifters, but obviously we can't just come out and tell our non-shifter colleagues that. I had no idea this would be so tricky." He shrugged. "So, any trace of the scent that we come across, we'll follow fully. We have something of a scent data-base between the shifters on the force, so I want to get a good whiff of the vehicle to share with them. That way we can see who's connected to who and try to get evidence from there."

"Great," I said. "I'll take you to the scent."

We ran to the place where Britt and I had chased after the trail; I showed him the scent and he got a good whiff.

"I don't recognize it," he admitted after we returned to our human forms. "I'll share it with the guys and see if they do. Some of the cops who've been around a while might have come across the guy before. Most criminals don't expect the police to use smell to track them down." He chuckled.

"Right," I agreed.

"You okay, man? You're awfully quiet."

"Yeah, I'm okay," I lied. My mind was tangled. Being close

to where Britt and I had been just the night before was like torture. The longing in me had grown out of control. Having sex hadn't quelled my interest; it only made it worse.

He narrowed his eyes slightly. He knew me too well, but didn't press. "We were also hoping that Britt would join us, unofficially of course, as part of the team to help patrol and search for the guy."

My eyes widened. "You want us to work together?"

"Unless that's a problem?"

I shook my head. The idea of having to be around her, to team up together to find this guy, to be out in the woods running around together, excited me; I couldn't deny it. My heart raced.

"I'll go talk to her about it. I'm sure she'd love to help. She's already on patrol, trying to find him anyway. This way, we can keep her safe."

Mason studied me again and nodded. "Exactly."

"I'll ask her and bring her back here so we can set up a plan of which directions we'll go in, how we'll report anything found, that sort of thing."

"I'll drive you over to her house," Mason offered as he grabbed his keys and headed off to his car.

I hesitated. I wanted to do this alone. As I was thinking of a way to tell Mason without alerting him to something more, an urgent voice crackled through his radio as I slid into the car.

Mason picked it up and had an intense conversation with

the person on the other end. There were a lot of codes given back and forth that I didn't understand. "Ezra! There's been another attack," he said. "Another panther has been found dead."

I didn't stop to think about it, and I didn't let him know where I was going. He'd figure it out. I threw open the passenger door and shifted, leaving my clothes in his car, and ran as fast as I could. I had to get to her.

The run didn't take me long. I came up to her cabin and didn't stop at the edge of the property, but ran straight up onto the porch and hammered on the door.

11

BRITT

Someone was pounding on my door. If it wasn't the police, it sure sounded like them. This would usually piss me off, but after everything that had went down, it worried me. I hurried to the door, but when I opened it, Ezra was there. I didn't have time to get annoyed; the look on his face was so frantic, it shot ice through me.

"What is it?" I asked.

"Another panther's been found dead."

My stomach dropped. It hadn't been just the one; this was going to keep going after all. I'd never been so regretful of being right in my life.

My shotgun wasn't far. I spun, grabbed it from the living room where it'd been resting against the wall, and came back, ready to go after the asshole.

When Ezra saw me, he looked pained.

"What are you waiting for?" I asked. "Come on."

"I know you want to get out there," he said. "But let's let the police do their job first. They're already on it."

"I'm not going to sit around and wait to be slaughtered." Was he nuts? He wanted me to just sit there?

"Please. I'll stay here with you. The second I hear something, you'll know about it. And if we can help in any way, we will."

"Get out of my way." I reached out my arm to push past him.

I hadn't paid attention to the fact that he was naked. Again. I'd seen this guy naked more than I'd seen him clothed. But after our night together, I knew what that body was capable of. When I brushed my arm against him, it was like touching fire. It made my skin tingle and my scalp prickle.

He reached out to stop me by putting a hand on my arm. He didn't grab or pull or hold me; he pleaded. "Please, Britt."

Had I ever heard him say my name before? If he had, it hadn't sounded like that.

I turned to look at him. "You don't know what you're asking."

"I do. I really do. And that's why I'm begging you. As soon as I know the park is clear, we'll go out and follow the trail."

"What good is that going to do? I have to get out there if I'm going to catch him."

"What if it's more than one?"

"It's not."

"You mean, it *wasn't*," he challenged. "What if this time, there are a few of them? What if they overtake you? Can you outrun a bullet? Can you fight off two or three men at a time?"

"Did they shoot this panther?"

"I don't know yet. But wouldn't it be good to know that before charging out there? Mason is on the scene and so are several shifters from the force. They know the scent. I even took Mason to get the vehicle's scent. I know you know these parts really well. You're a good hunter, and I know you could find him. But you're not a cop. You're trained to deal with animals, not criminals. They know more about how people like this work and think. I don't want you to get hurt. Please."

I don't know what it was, and I may never know. But something in his eyes or words softened me. And that was a rare occurrence. Being sentimental wasn't exactly in my nature. In fact, I couldn't recall being sentimental once in my whole damn life. But as I looked at him, the trouble I saw in his eyes brought me pain.

What the hell? Why should I care what he felt or thought? I'd wanted this all to go away. That was why what he'd said the night before made sense. If we just did it, just went ahead and had sex, it was supposed to end these feelings. To take this obsession from me. It hadn't worked and that pissed me off. Being so close to him naked, I could hardly stand it. And now he wanted to sit around like that and wait?

I pulled my arm away. "Do you own any clothes?" I snapped.

I turned and went inside, letting the door slam behind me. I heard it open a moment later, as I was setting my gun back down.

"Actually, I kind of ran out without thinking. I didn't bring anything. I just wanted to get here to make sure you were okay."

I gave him a slight glare, but my heart wasn't in it. I went to my bedroom and found a pair of shorts and a shirt that I thought would fit him. When I came back out, I tossed them at him.

"Thanks."

"Beer?" In the kitchen, I pulled one from the fridge. If I was just going to sit around all day, I might as well enjoy it a little.

"Sure."

I grabbed a frosty can and passed it to him. When he popped the top, it foamed all over his hand.

I laughed. "Amateur."

"Not in everything." He winked.

I rolled my eyes. "You look ridiculous." I hadn't paid much attention to what I'd grabbed, but I realized that the shorts were on the shorter side—probably why they were stuffed in the back of my drawer—and I must've grabbed the one shirt I owned that had any sort of sparkle to it: a blue tee with tiny gems on the sleeves' edges. It was subtle, but too much for me to wear—definitely too much for him to wear.

He struck a pose and made a face like he was a super-model. "It's all about being comfortable in your own skin." He chuckled and sat down on the couch, resting his feet up on the coffee table.

"Well sure, just make yourself at home." I flopped down next to him and took a long sip of my IPA.

"Nice cabin," he said.

"Thanks. It was my gramma's. My ma lived here her whole life, and so have I."

"Right. You said your mom was killed by a hunter years ago. I'm really sorry."

"Me, too." I took another sip.

This felt awkward. I didn't know him well enough to be comfortable around him, and I didn't do well with the whole getting-to-know-you thing. I didn't need to know anyone besides the people I already knew.

But desire still racked my body. A desire to know him, to be near him. It was starting to move from my bones to my emotions. And that meant it was getting dangerous. I had no reason to be with anyone; my life was just fine as it was. Alone. I'd never wanted any sort of boyfriend or partner, and I still didn't.

Except—and I couldn't bear to admit it—it felt like I was beginning to. He made me feel so...*domestic*, if that was even possible. Like I wanted to just get up and cook something for him; to take care of him. God, I was going soft and becoming a damn floozie. I had to stop this nonsense somehow.

"So, what's your story?" I asked. "Are you like, sixteen, or what?"

"Um, no. Twenty-five."

"Really?" I looked him over. "With that baby face?"

"I'm from California. It's different there."

"I'm sure. How you'd end up here, then?"

"My family moved away, but I was born here. I don't know. I got older and it was like the land itself called to me. I came out to visit family we still had in the area and I stayed. I found our original clan and they welcomed me with open arms. Everything just fit." He shrugged. "I may not be a Gladesperson like you, but it seems that I belong here somehow."

I snorted. "Is that why you highlight your hair? To remind yourself of California?"

He reached up to finger his blond tips. "I just like it."

"It makes you look ridiculous in bear form."

He grinned. "You don't like my streaks? I think they make me look distinguished."

"The first time I saw you, I thought it was dried mud. Then you shifted and I saw your hair and realized that even in bear form, you have those goofy blonde pieces."

"You should dye yours." He reached over and picked up the end of my blonde ponytail. It would look good blue or even with just a touch of red. Your hair has a hint of natural red in it."

I froze until he put my hair back down. Any touch from him seemed to make me begin to sweat. If I was going to keep a level head so we could chase this killer down when the time came, I'd have to keep my raging hormones in check. I couldn't just get turned on every time he brushed against me.

"No TV?" he asked after a minute of silence.

"Nah. What's the point?"

"Entertainment?"

"I make my own."

He crossed his arms. "Yeah? Let's see."

I raised an eyebrow. "I didn't say *I* was the entertainment. I find ways to keep entertained is all."

"Like how?"

"Going out and finding something to eat. Skinning it, selling it. Walking around or running through the park. Sometimes, I go to Shady's."

He raised his eyebrows. "That's it?"

"What else is there?"

"Fun? There is TV, but also movies, going out, dancing, hanging with friends, relaxing and maybe playing a game or two. Reading, shooting, bike rides, hikes, fishing, working out, running. Golf, bowling, painting, cooking. Then there's the local stuff like museums, zoos, arcades. The beach? I love the beach."

I blinked at him. "So, you are, like, sixteen."

"Dude! People do these things. Adult people. Adult people who want to have fun and enjoy life."

"I enjoy life."

"Do you? You seem kind of...unhappy to me."

"Based on what?" I snapped, crossing my arms.

He broke into laughter. "Well, that posture and that attitude, for starters. You're always so serious. Just have fun once in a while."

"There's no time for shenanigans. I do catch a good fight at Shady's now and then."

"So, watching two drunk idiots pummel each other is your idea of a good time?"

I lifted one shoulder. It had been. Until the night before. Now, I could think of at least one other way I wouldn't mind passing the time.

"Doesn't your clan get together and do stuff?"

"Sure," I said. "We were at Shady's the night I saw you."

"You were there with only two other ladies."

"Yeah. My clan."

"Your clan has only three people?"

"Panthers are rare, remember? We have Kat's gramma, too. But she's older and doesn't get around much anymore."

"Sound pretty lonely."

"It's not," I said, a little too defensively. I didn't need to explain myself to him. "So, what does your clan do? Sit around and play shuffleboard while drinking lemonade?"

"Shuffleboard." He tapped his lips. "That's one we haven't tried yet. Could be fun…"

"You're kidding."

"Yeah." He playfully shoved my shoulder. "Lots of times, we just build a fire on the beach and hang out, talking and telling stories. Or we go out and do things, like hang at Shady's. Usually Conner and I hit the gym together a few times a week. I go to Owen's for his wife's cooking. Though now that they have a baby, that's all he talks about. I go shooting or fishing with Mason. They're my best friends, but we have a decent sized-clan. There's eight of us. Well, I guess if you count the baby, it's nine, maybe soon to be ten. We think Noah's wife is pregnant, but no one is saying yet. Probably too soon to announce. We have clan picnics and get togethers regularly, and a lot of us work together. We're close, you know. Family."

Family. At the mention of the word, I thought of Ma and Gramma. God, did I miss their company; missed having people to just sit back with and bitch about the day to. But Ezra couldn't be that to me. We were far too different.

"Your life sounds overwhelming," I admitted.

"It's full. But it's happy. I figure it's about time I find a special lady and move onto life 2.0."

I chuckled. "Life 2.0?"

"Marriage, kids." He made a box crossing his pointer and middle fingers on both hands. "Dad life, you know."

I laughed again. "Did you just throw a gang sign at me?"

"It's a hashtag? Don't you get on Instagram?"

"What's that?"

He slapped his forehead. "You do have a smart phone, don't you?"

I pointed to the phone hanging on the wall. It was yellowed with age, its cord sagging to the ground. It was rarely used. If I wanted to talk to Dezi or Kat, I spoke through our clan's mind connection or just went to see them.

He went over to the phone and picked it up, then started laughing. "Oh my God, it has a dial tone and everything!"

He took another two beers from the fridge and tossed one to me as he sat back down. Brave little fucker, wasn't he, to just go around my place and do as he pleased.

"So, I'm guessing you have no computer?" he asked. "Wi-fi?"

"I don't even know what that is."

He whistled. "That explains a lot."

"What's that supposed to mean?"

"You're so secluded. You must really be a pain in the ass if you scared everyone away."

"Ha ha."

"Your life is really just hunting?"

"I have a garden, too. But I like to keep it simple."

"There's so much out there that you're missing, Britt. It's not even just about having fun. It's life. There's so much to experience, and you're not experiencing any of it."

"And I'm just fine with that."

"Don't you want more?" he asked. "Don't you want to see the world? Taste weird foods, see beautiful sights, meet all sorts of people and animals, do everything life has to offer you?"

"Nah."

"The Everglades is amazing. But there's a lot more to the world than just this little chunk of Florida."

"I don't think about it like that. This *is* my world. It's all I need." I paused, not sure I wanted to say it out loud. "Until..."

12

EZRA

I held my breath waiting for her to finish the sentence. Until...she gets older? Until...she wants to settle down? Until...she met me? But before she answered, my phone buzzed in my pocket.

"One sec, it's Mason calling." I tapped the screen to answer and walked out to her porch for better reception. "What'd you find?"

"The scents match, so we're looking for a serial. I was hoping you had something more."

"No. I'm with Britt at her cabin."

"Oh." Long pause. "Good. Is she up for helping?"

"Definitely." She was inside, but she could hear me talking. "We're just waiting until it's clear so we can run."

"Until it's clear? What do you mean?"

"Um..." How could I say this without Britt finding out? "When it's safe for panthers to be in the woods?"

"You're keeping her home to keep her safe."

"Of course. That's my job."

"Uh huh... Then I guess I'll let you know when we know more."

"Thanks, man. Stay safe."

He snorted a laugh. "You too, man. You, too."

I went back inside and found Britt waiting for me, looking anxious.

"Anything?" she asked.

"He just called to make sure we were both okay. They're a caring bunch, my clan." I smiled. "He'll call when they know something."

"It seems like it's taking a long time. Let's run over to where the body is at least. I want to know if it's the same guy or not. He didn't know if it was the same guy?"

"Oh..." I scratched the back of my head. Why hadn't I foreseen this? "He didn't say."

"He didn't say." She leveled her gaze at me. "He does know the scent of the first killer, right?"

"Right."

"And he's there now at the second body?"

"Uh...I think he's there. He didn't say. Maybe he's still at the station."

She narrowed her eyes at me. "Don't you think that's kind of important?"

"Well, yes, sure. But right now, they have to gather evidence. Find fingerprints, footprints, fibers, that sort of thing. DNA, you know?"

"We don't need any of that! We need to get out there." She stood and headed for her gun again.

"We have to wait. There are a lot of cops over there right now. Non-shifter cops. Mason said once they're done, the shifters will move in. It's complicated, I guess, being on the force where some are shifters and some aren't. They can't give up the secret, so they have to let them do things the human way."

"The human way is going to get more panthers killed."

"You know, maybe we should have your clan come over here and hang out. Until we know it's safe."

She huffed. "Kat has a family and a gator farm to run. Dezi is out fishing, as always."

"Do they know what's going on? Did you use that"—I pointed to the ancient phone on the wall—"to call and tell them?"

"I didn't use the phone, but they know. I gave them the scent. Can't pass a scent through the phone."

"Good point," I said. "Got a deck of cards?"

"For what?"

"To play?"

"There's a killer running around, panthers are in danger, and you want to play cards?"

"Yes." I nodded. "That's how you stay safe. He's not going

to come into your cabin and kill you. Not with all your guns and me here. Maybe we can lure him close and get him."

Her head whipped to me as if she had a sudden thought. "The second panther was a pure panther, right? Not a shifter?"

"Not a shifter."

She visibly relaxed.

"Call your friends," I suggested.

She stared off into space for a moment. "Yeah…"

She went into the kitchen and made two calls, returning much sooner than I'd thought she would. When she returned to the living room, she looked distraught. I wanted to pull her into my arms and hold her, but I wasn't sure if that would be okay. After our night together and the way it had all happened, I didn't know where we stood, if anywhere.

"You okay?" I asked.

"Sure." She dropped a pack of cards on the table.

"You updated your friends?"

"Yup."

I shuffled the cards and dealt. She sat across from me at the kitchen table, but seemed to be lost in her own world.

"So, you do care about something," I said.

"Of course, I care about something!" she snapped.

"Well, you act so tough all the time, like you don't need or want anyone, like nothing bothers you."

"I don't need anyone. What are we playing?"

"Texas Hold 'em?"

"Fine."

I dared to ask, "So, do you care about *me*?"

"I care about beating you." Her mouth quirked into a half smile.

"I'll take it."

She actually relaxed a little as we played. I don't know if it was the beers or if she was getting comfortable with me. She seemed to laugh more, and every time she did, it lit me up inside. I felt myself falling—try as I might to resist it. And I thought, just maybe, she was starting to like me, too.

I thought about kissing her. Or even starting simpler and just taking her hand. I didn't want to move too fast, but we had already slept together, so was it moving fast at all? I didn't know how to handle it, and I didn't want to mess it up.

As I was considering whether I should try to beat her or let her win the game, we heard a noise outside; a rustling of leaves and twigs. Our heads snapped to attention at the same time, then I looked at her. "Doesn't sound big."

"No, it doesn't." She narrowed her eyes.

"Probably just a coon. If you hunt them often, they'd smell it and come around. They come around here a lot, don't they?"

"No, they don't. I have several small game traps set. Something small as a coon shouldn't make it within fifty feet of this cabin."

"Guess we'd better check it out then."

We walked out onto the front porch and listened. The

rustling stopped for the moment, and I could have sworn I smelled a raccoon.

She pulled off her top and dropped it on the porch, then stepped out of her shorts. Just like that. I took off the clothes she gave me and followed. There's no way I'd let her shift and run off by herself. She roared into her panther form, and I leapt into my bear, showing off with a twist mid-air.

She glanced at me, rolled her eyes, and began to run.

13

BRITT

I took off running, looking behind me to see how close he was. *A coon. So what if there was a damn coon out there?* I laughed to myself. He'd fallen for it. I just wanted to get out and run, so I came up with the perfect excuse. They didn't bother me none; it was probably just stuck in my trap.

I wanted to mess with him, so I stopped short and ran in the opposite direction. He seemed confused, but came running after me, leaping like the goofball he was as he went. We were running parallel, and without warning, I darted to the side, crashing into him. He tackled me as payback and I let him—but only for a moment. I used my strong back legs to push him off me, then bolted again.

I almost forgot about the raccoon. It was fun, running

and playing around like that, but of course, I kept my nose on alert at all times. I didn't want to be taken off guard. But running with Ezra meant I had backup, something I didn't usually have. Not that he was the sharpest shifter around, but he was another set of paws and claws, should it come down to that. And really, he wasn't as dumb or slow as I'd thought initially. The more I got to know him, the more comfortable I became—and the more I'd respected him.

It was strange to feel this way; I'd never had this happen before. Not even with Kat and Dezi did I have the desire to just play around. It wasn't something I did as an adult, which was made even more obvious by all his damn questioning of me. Maybe he had a point. My entire life had been 100% 'Glades, all day every day. Was I missing out on the world? On relationships? I sure never thought I'd enjoy being around someone like Ezra, a goofy, blonde-streaked bear.

I fell back slightly to put him in front of me. When he was ahead, probably thinking he was beating me, I dashed forward and grabbed hold of his little nub of a tail with my teeth, causing him to whirl around in shock. I let go immediately, but it was enough to get his attention.

He jumped on me and pinned me to the ground. I started a laugh, which I'd never even attempted in panther form before, and it came out like a barking rumble. He licked up the side of my face, and I tried to move out of the path of his long tongue, but it was no use. He licked me all over, and when he was through and let me up, I rubbed my wet face against his coat.

He was much softer than I thought he'd be. He was warm and humming, making a sound similar to a cat's purr. Comforting.

He stuck his nose in the air and sniffed. *Right. The coon. We're out here to get the coon,* I reminded myself. Nothing else was around at the moment.

I dashed back toward my cabin to where the trap was, and sure enough, he was in there, struggling to get free. I sat back and gestured at the coon with my paw, letting Ezra have it, and he tore it free from the trap with his teeth. The coon was dead in a second in his strong jaw; he shook it back and forth and then set it down at my feet.

The action filled me with a sense of...I didn't know what, exactly. It felt warm, and I appreciated the kind gesture.

I put my paw on the coon and sank my teeth into its body, pulling so I could tear it in half. I gave him the bigger piece. He'd earned it. Plus, that boy needed to gain a few pounds. He worked out a few times a week? With what, jump ropes and wrist weights? I'd have to show him what a real workout was like. My body grew hot at the thought of us sweating together, and as excitement flooded through me, he looked up at me.

Damn pheromones. He must know what's on my mind. I had to keep my emotions in check unless I wanted to broadcast to the world that I wanted him.

I finished off my snack and took off running again, wanting to clear the air of my scent—and clear my head— while I was at it. I decided to do a perimeter run, circling the cabin. I did this at least once a day just to stay familiar with what was going on. If I detected any new scents, I'd investigate them so I didn't have any surprises popping up.

I ran light and easy. I even added in a little bouncy skip now and then, just to feel my paws' pads press into the earth then leave it. I realized then what that new feeling was. Happiness. I never even realized I wasn't happy before, but now that I had that warm glow about me, now that I was enjoying myself in new ways and with this bear, I liked it. It felt good and I wanted to be around him. And right then, I made my decision.

There was no reason to fight it. If I liked being with him, fine. If the sex was great, even better. If he wanted to hang out with me and enjoyed himself while doing it, then okay. I had no plans or expectations. It wasn't like I was saying I was in love or anything. In 'like,' maybe, if that was a thing. I just knew I didn't mind his company.

He stopped running and called out a little bark to get my attention. I circled back to him and he changed.

"This would be so much easier if we had a mind link like I do with my clan," he said.

I shifted back, too. "Something going on?"

"Yeah. I was just talking to Mason. He says they're going after the guy."

"The killer? They found him?"

"Kind of. They identified him. Some local guy trying to stir up trouble against the panthers, claiming all sorts of attacks and things. I guess they're going to get him now."

Something wasn't right. "So, was it the same guy or not?"

"Oh." His face fell into surprise for a moment, then he recovered. "Oh, yeah. It's the same guy."

I narrowed my eyes at him. "Did you know that already?"

His face turned red and his eyes widened. "Didn't we all assume it was?"

"Stop fucking around. Did you know for sure it was the same guy who killed both panthers or not?"

He hung his head. "I did. I just thought if I told you, you'd go out trying to find him."

"Obviously! He needed to be found. Why would you lie like that?"

He raised an eyebrow at me. "Why? You don't know why?"

"I can only imagine what sort of logic goes through your little pea brain. Why don't you spell it out for me?"

I thought hurt flickered across his face, but I wasn't sure. "I wanted to protect you. I didn't want you to be running around, trying to find the guy on your own. I thought if we went out together, that'd be okay, but then if we didn't find him, you might go when I wasn't around. I've been worried about you." He held up a hand before I could protest. "I know you can take care of yourself and you don't need me to protect you. But that doesn't mean I wouldn't worry something might happen."

I pressed my lips together. "Well, now what?"

"They know who it is. I guess someone recognized the scent. Right now, they're all going to arrest him. They had to find some kind of evidence so they could. You can't just stroll up to a human and tell him you sniffed his scent at a crime scene."

"Yeah. Sometimes, our secret's a little inconvenient. Most times not, though."

"Right. So, I guess that's it. It's over."

"Now I'm allowed to run around without you worrying about me?"

"I would never stop you. But you can't stop me from worrying, either."

I sighed. "Okay, whatever. I could use a long run. You up for it? We've been cooped up inside all day."

"All day?" He laughed. "It was a few hours."

"It seemed like all day. Come on!"

I shifted back and took off, and he was right behind me. I ran hard. This was more for exercise than anything else. I didn't know what to feel about the killer being found. It was a relief, but I was slightly disappointed I hadn't gotten to help at all. I felt responsible as a member of the same species to pay this guy back for what he'd done to my fellow panthers, shifters or not. As long as they got the guy and he paid for what he did, I couldn't be too upset. At least the park was safe again and Ezra wouldn't have to worry.

I tried not to feel smug that I'd made him worry. It was sweet. He had lied and that pissed me off; he'd better not do that shit again, but at least he had a good reason. It wasn't a lie to cover up something slimy he did; he was only trying to protect me. Couldn't be too upset about that, either. It seemed that things were kind of coming together, in a way I'd never expected. *But new doesn't have to be bad*, I reminded myself. *This is all new to me, but as long as it's enjoyable, I'll go with it.*

As I ran, a familiar scent hit me like a slap in the face. I stopped so abruptly that the ground shifted and piled under my paws. Ezra bounded past me, then halted and spun to double back. He moved his nose, sniffing the same scent.

He shifted to human. "It's fine," he explained. "This is one of the trails they followed to get the killer."

I shifted back, too, so I could talk to him. "You sure? It's pretty fresh."

He nodded. "I checked with Mason before shifting back. He says the area is clear. The killer wasn't at home, but they have information on his location."

"So, he's still at large. He could be anywhere." I looked around as if he'd come walking out of the woods behind me.

"Nah. So many people are looking for him, and there are patrols all over the park. He's human, so it's not like he could just run by someone who didn't know. Every vehicle coming or going is being checked."

I raised an eyebrow. "You know just as good as me that there are plenty of other ways into this park."

He pressed his lips together. "Maybe we should go back then. Just to be safe until they have the guy behind bars."

"It felt good to run while we could."

"Yeah," he agreed. "We'll get to run back."

"Care to race?"

He chuckled. "No. You run faster than me all the time. It's not a fair contest."

I pulled my mouth to the side. "Okay, then. Let me prove that I can have fun."

He tilted his head. "I'm listening."

I let the playfulness show in my eyes. "A game of shifter hide and seek?"

He grinned. "You're on."

"Close your eyes and count to five."

"Five? How about like ten or twenty, at least."

I put my hands on my hips. "Didn't you just say how fast I was?"

"Fast. Not silent. And I can smell, you know."

"Fine. Ten, but when it's too hard, just remember, I tried to help you out."

He laughed again. "Okay."

He shifted back and put his bear head down on the ground, then covered his eyes with his paws. The sight of a bear doing something so human made me crack up. I laughed at him for several seconds, until I realized that his little barks were numbers. He was already counting while I stood there laughing.

I shifted back and sprinted away. I had the perfect place in mind: in a little hollow near the water. The dampness would help hide my scent and I could roll in the mud or jump in the water if I needed to really make it tough for him.

I ran fast, focused on getting there before he got too close. My eyes were trained on the spot where I headed, but not on the ground in front of me, like they should have been. I ran that way when I chased prey, but any other time, I was careful to check the grounds and take care with my footing. There were hollows that could twist an ankle—human or otherwise. And there were traps. Some were my own.

I stepped into a small hollow and felt my footing go, and my heart jolted at the feeling. I yanked my leg back to avoid falling and felt the hard jaws of the metal trap close around my foot, crying out in a whimper of pain.

This was not my trap or any other I was familiar with. I couldn't even see all of it since it was down in the hole. I let out a howl, hoping Ezra was close and hadn't run off in the opposite direction. He had to have followed my scent, right? He had to be close.

I let out another howl, panting from the pain, and searched for any sign of movement that might be him.

14

EZRA

I had been running, following her scent. I didn't think she could have gotten too far ahead of me; she wasn't *that* much faster.

But then I heard her howl. And it tore through me like I'd jumped into ice water.

I ran faster. I ran so hard, I thought my heart would explode. I had to find her. I kept thinking that was it, the killer got her. We shouldn't have been out there. We should have been more careful.

My throat burned and I pushed harder. When she came into view, she was whimpering, but perked up when she saw me.

At least she hadn't been stabbed or shot, but the situation was still dire. Britt wasn't able to disengage the trap, and neither could I, not without someone else to help provide leverage. I smelled the scent of the killer and, of course, she had, too. With a look of sheer terror in her eyes, she whimpered again. I took a long sniff; the scent of the killer didn't seem too fresh. He probably wasn't nearby right at that moment.

I tuned back in to my clan. I had blocked them out because they were all going after the killer. They were talking to each other, discussing locations and details, and I hadn't needed to be a part of it. I'd been too busy goofing off with Britt, which seemed incredibly stupid in retrospect—though honestly, I didn't regret a moment of it.

You guys find him yet? I didn't think they had, but I wanted to confirm.

Britt whined.

He's not anywhere he's supposed to be, Conner replied angrily.

All of our information has been wrong or too late, Owen added.

We're not out of options yet, Mason said, *but we've been after him a long time. We're going to have to start relieving some of the guys out there so they can get some rest.*

Britt whined again, more insistent this time, and batted at me. I lifted a paw to my temple, trying to show her that I was in communication with my clan. I rubbed my nose against hers, trying to give her some comfort, then licked her face.

I have a situation here, I told them. *Britt is trapped.*

Trapped? Owen asked.

Yes, her foot is caught in some kind of trap. And the killer's scent is on it, but it's not recent. I'm not going to leave her. Have any of you guys been able to open a large jaw trap?

There was some discussion back and forth, then Conner said, *Mason and I will come and check it out. Between the three of us, we should be able to get it open.*

I sent them a mental image of our location.

Where is that? Mason asked.

I wasn't really sure. We were far from Britt's, in a remote part of the park I wasn't as familiar with. I tried to give them a better sense of where we were stuck.

We're on our way, Conner said, *Hold tight.*

I shifted back and cupped Britt's face in my hands. "I was talking to my clan. They're on their way to help us."

She nodded once, but locked her terrified eyes on mine.

"Can you shift back?"

In a moment of extreme stress like this, it would be very difficult for her to revert to her human form. If she could manage it, that would be a good sign. Staying calm was always best in these situations, and if we needed an ambulance or other help, there would almost surely be a few humans coming to our aid, too, so being a panther meant staying panther. It also meant she'd be treated by a vet instead of at a regular hospital until we could get her away from humans. It would be much better all around if she could become and stay human.

She closed her eyes and concentrated. Sweat broke out on her forehead, but eventually, slowly, her coat melted into her skin, her snout sunk back and reformed as her nose, and her ears slid down into place.

She looked up at me, tears in her eyes. "It...it hurts."

"I know, I'm so sorry this happened. Some of my clan will be here soon to help."

"Which ones?"

"Mason, who's the officer, and Conner. He's part of the search and rescue team, so this type of thing is his specialty."

She looked at me hard. "This isn't just someone stuck in a hole, I'm caught in a trap. We have to get this off. It punctured deeply, maybe even to the bone, and it smells like..." She gulped hard and closed her eyes, sending a tear down her cheek.

I leaned in closer and took a hard sniff. There was something there that didn't belong. Besides the odor of the metal and her blood, fear and sweat, along with the scent of the killer—now more vile to me than anything I'd ever smelled before—there was a musty, earthy scent that I didn't recognize.

"What is that?" I asked.

"I don't know for sure, but I've smelled it before. My gramma had some once. Some kind of poison."

"What?" I breathed.

"If it's the one I think, it's not meant to kill. Just slowly incapacitate."

I closed my eyes and swallowed hard. How was this possible? How was this happening?

I squeezed her hand hard and shifted back to check in on the guys. *Where are you guys?*

Almost at the park entrance, Mason said.

We have a problem. There's some kind of poison on the trap. Britt says she thinks she's encountered it before, though she can't recall what it is. She thinks it's only meant to sedate, but we can't be sure.

Can you at least try to get the trap off? Mason asked.

Send me an image of it if you can, Conner added.

I looked down at it, but with my clumsy bear paws, I couldn't do a thing. I sent what I could see, but it wasn't a good view since the trap was in the hole and blocked by Britt's body. *I'm going to shift back for a sec to see what I can do.*

In human form, I could get my head closer and get a better look.

"Okay," I said to Britt. "You trap all the time. You sure you can't tell me how I can get this off?"

She shook her head. "I don't use traps like these." She blinked and another tear ran down her cheek. "They're too inhumane. Too painful to the animal."

I didn't have my phone, and even if I did, I'd never get reception this far out. So trying to Google it or watch a YouTube video on how to open it was out of the question.

My heart raced so fast, it was clouding my thinking. I got my hands down in the hole with her foot, and I tried to pull open the jaws of the trap, but they didn't even budge. They were locked tight, lined with sharp teeth that sank into her skin. I rubbed my finger around the teeth and took a sniff of the poison to get a stronger scent.

"What are you doing!" she cried. "Get that off your skin!" She shook her head and muttered, "Dumbass."

At least she was still herself.

I wiped my fingers in the grass and mud. "I need to shift back to tell them." I pressed my lips to hers hard and fast, then shifted.

This is the poison, I told them, and sent the impression of the smell. It wouldn't be as strong as smelling it firsthand, but it was something. *Recognize it?*

No, they both answered.

Even the other members of my clan paid attention, and I felt them trying to place the scent.

Then I heard Hailey react. *It's hemlock,* she said sadly.

I wasn't familiar enough with it to know what it did. *What does it do?*

She could die. Hailey's words were somewhat choked. *Do you have any idea how much she was exposed to?*

It's on the trap, I said. *I don't know, but it obviously broke the skin.*

Is she having any symptoms? she asked.

I don't know what the symptoms would be.

Conner spoke up then. *Look for drowsiness and swelling,*

increased saliva, severe muscle pain. Later stages are loss of speech and consciousness before...

Before what? I asked.

You have to get her to the hospital right away, Hailey said, and I could hear the panic in her thoughts.

We're trying to find you, Conner said, frantic. *Where the hell are you guys?*

I stuck my nose in the air and sniffed and listened. There was no sign of them, so I sent the mental image again.

Not helping. I could hear the physical strain in Mason's thoughts. They were running hard to get to us. *I don't know where that is!*

I don't either, I said, and my own throat grew thick. I looked at Britt, and she had her head down, resting. Was this the drowsiness Conner had mentioned?

I shifted back and took Britt's hand. "They can't find us. Can you tell me where we are?"

She looked up at me, forlorn. "Run south and go find them."

"I am not leaving you."

"You have to. Unless you want me to die here."

I clenched my jaw and took a deep breath before I kissed her, then shifted back to bear form. I'd never shifted back and forth so much in a short time. It was making me tired, sick to my stomach, and achy. *I'm going to come find you. She told me to run south.*

15

BRITT

I closed my eyes when Ezra was out of sight. I hadn't wanted to cry in front of him, and it was bad enough he saw me shed a few tears. Now that he was gone and no one else was around yet, I let the tears flow.

The pain was intense. Not just from my foot, which had to be broken, but from whatever the poison was. I could feel it seeping into my body with each second that passed. I felt heavy all over, my muscles burning. If they didn't get there soon, I'd die. Even when they did get there, I didn't know what good it would do. I couldn't run in my condition. Even if there hadn't been poison involved, the trap had done too much physical damage. I'd say, depending on how crushed the bones were, I might even be permanently injured. I tried not to think about what that meant. If it would affect my shifting, if it would stop me from running or hunting. That wasn't the time for 'what ifs.'

I just hoped he was fast. My body was in an awkward position and I was naked. I couldn't decide if it was better to stay human or be a panther, but Ezra had said human. My mind was foggy and I couldn't think straight. I didn't like being trapped there, naked and defenseless. All it would take was one slimy man to come upon me.

I decided to change back; I needed my panther senses anyhow. I set my head down; it was becoming too heavy. It was easier to shift to panther than it'd been to shift to human. Deep inside, my core was more animalistic when under duress, so the animal side usually won.

When I shifted back, though, I realized I'd made one mistake: my human calf was thinner than my panther leg. When I'd become human, the trap had closed a tiny bit more. Shifting back, I'd forced the muscles of my leg further into the teeth of the trap. It was even tighter, sending waves of hot pain through me that were so intense, I passed out. I'd never experienced pain like that in my life. The trap was bad enough, but the poison felt as if someone had injected acid into my muscles.

I had to keep spitting, too. I was starting to think I was wrong. I couldn't recall what the plant had been that Gramma made her poisons from, but the symptoms weren't matching up. *Could I have rabies? That would mean certain death.* But no, that wasn't right. Rabies wasn't that fast-acting. I knew better, but my brain wasn't pulling its weight.

I tried to keep my attention focused on the world around me, listening and sniffing like always, on alert for any hint of a predator or, in that case, help. But the pain blocked me. My mind was sludge. I put my head down again and closed my eyes, but I didn't want to drift off. Without knowing what the poison was, that could make everything worse. But I just couldn't keep my head up or my attention focused.

I must've dozed off anyway, because I felt the sudden jolt into consciousness. A noise had woken me. I sniffed first, mostly because I didn't want to pick my head up to hear better. It wasn't Ezra or any of his clan members. My heart raced and I forced myself to pick up my head to look in the direction of the sound.

Footsteps. Two men are coming toward me.

I was so very grateful that I'd shifted back to panther and wasn't lying there naked as these men approached. Their sent was vaguely familiar. As I drew in a few long breaths, I realized that their scents were on the trap, too. It wasn't just the killer who'd set it up; those men must have been working with him.

One of them began to laugh, then they stepped into view. They looked like the local scum that ran around being assholes and starting trouble. Thick boots, dirty overalls, greasy hair, too long and scraggly, with beards that hadn't been trimmed in months.

I was in a terrible position to fight back. With one leg down the hole, I couldn't stand. I could use my front paws and maybe my one free back paw. I had my teeth, but could only use them if they got close enough.

I kept my eyes on their every move and tweaked my ear every so often in the direction Ezra had gone, listening for his return. I wanted to let out a loud howl to alert him if he was close enough to hear. I didn't think I had the strength, though. My mouth was full of saliva. I couldn't spit with my panther mouth, so the excess ran over, my drool puddling under me on the ground.

I'd seen these men before around Shady's and around town in general. Those fuckers were always up to no good. They were humans, and most likely, not the type who'd know about shifters. The only humans allowed in on our secret were mates of shifters and family members who could be trusted with our secret.

But not these two. I had to stay panther at all costs. It would be easier to stay in my condition, but I didn't like being forced into it.

"Well, looky here, Chuck. Got us a real nice panther indeed."

Chuck, I assumed, nudged his elbow into the other man. "That makes three! At this rate, we'll have the Glades pantherless by the end of the month." He then curled his lips back and muttered, "Damn vermin."

I let out a low growl. I wanted them to know I knew. I

wanted them to be afraid. I wasn't used to humans walking up to me while in my animal form and being so calm.

I searched through the fog in my mind for the bit of information that kept trying to break free, and when it did, I sucked in a breath. Now I remembered. These men had been seen with some of the croc shifters in town, so maybe they were keen on our secret after all. The crocs themselves were a sketchy bunch. Always causing trouble. Always scheming.

"Aww, nice kitty," Chuck said.

The other one came over and petted me like I was his house cat. I snarled and snipped at his hand. He pulled it back before I sank my teeth into it.

"Mean kitty," Not Chuck said.

"Well, that's alright." Chuck set his shotgun on his shoulder and aimed. "Dead kitty, soon."

I pleaded with my eyes for them not to kill me. I begged the heavens for Ezra to show up; for anything, anyone, to stop this.

Then my prayers were answered. Almost.

A third man walked up. "I told you fools to wait."

He smacked Chuck on the back of the head, and Chuck lowered the gun. "Ain't no one around, Jimmy Bob."

"How would you know? Do you even know what she is? No, you don't." He shook his head.

The new guy, Jimmy Bob, looked a lot like the others, as far as his levels of cleanliness and tidiness went. He was younger, though, with blonde hair. But something didn't make sense. When his scent reached me, the resulting growl was automatic. He was indeed the killer, but something was off. The killer hadn't been a shifter like that croc was; I knew that. Even right then, he didn't smell like a shifter.

Jimmy Bob walked over to me and crouched down, smiling right at me. He put a hand to the side of my face, then slapped me.

"No boys, this here is not just any old panther. This girl's a real, live panther shifter."

Their eyes widened. Not Chuck got a creepy grin as he continued to chew a wad of tobacco. "Huh. She a female?"

The croc nodded. Not Chuck rubbed his hands together, and my stomach turned.

When he was that close, his croc odor became an overwhelming stench. As I sorted through the details of it, I figured it out. The croc smell was there; I was also able to smell the shifter in him with no problem in that moment. But I picked up on something else that wasn't his natural scent: some kind of neutralizer or scent cover that blocked it.

It was nothing I recognized, like deer piss, but he had something on, and it had worked. It'd thrown us all off so we'd thought the killer was human. I wondered if they had been chasing after the wrong guy the whole time. Good chance of it. Well, now I'd found him—or, more accurately, he'd found me.

"I'm gonna check the area, like I told you two assholes to

do before we kill her. Can't take a chance of someone coming around, especially if she's called her clan."

With that, he stood and pulled off his shirt before dropping his pants, and Chuck twisted his face in disgust. "Aw man, ya coulda given us a little warnin'. I ain't into seein' yer naked ass." Not Chuck shook his head and raised his eyes to the canopy of the forest.

Jimmy Bob shifted to croc form and scampered off in his stupid lowdown run. Crocs looked like such idiots when they ran, like they just weren't made to move like that. No wonder they got taken down so easily on land. I could pounce on one in a heartbeat and crush the bastard good.

I still didn't see or hear Ezra. Where the hell was he? I wanted to scream and cry. The one time I'd let myself need someone, and he was letting me down.

A minute later, the croc came scurrying back, but didn't stop when he got to me. He charged toward me, and I sat up the best I could to swat at him with my sharp claws.

He had the advantage on me, obviously. Having me trapped and poisoned was the only way he could. When he swiped back, his black claws slashed my skin and I howled; there was no reason to hold back by that point, and I couldn't have controlled it if I wanted to.

I swatted and swatted, wildly waving my paw as I tried to slash him hard. I gave him a good gash across his neck. Blood poured from the fresh wound and he backed up, panting.

"Enough of that!" Chuck yelled out and picked up his gun again.

Fuck! This is it, I told myself. I couldn't stop a bullet, and I couldn't leap forward and bite him.

He pointed the end of the barrel at me and cocked the gun.

16

EZRA

We all heard it at the same time: the howl, followed by the sound of animals fighting. We didn't have to say it; we all knew what was going on. Britt must have shifted back, and if she was stuck in a trap, half drugged, she'd have no chance.

We'd been running fast, but now we sprinted, spending every last bit of energy we had to push harder and faster. I pulled ahead. It had to be the adrenaline because I'd never outrun Mason or Conner before.

I wished, for the hundredth time, that I could communicate with her mentally like I could with my clan. It was so hard being in animal form and not having the human level of communication we were used to.

More help was on its way behind us, but it would take them a while. Still, I felt some comfort in knowing that in a short time, the place would be swarming with police and rangers, all there to help Britt. But the comfort was minute compared to the extreme panic I felt. What if we were too late?

It seemed to take ages to get back to the place where I'd left her. I saw the tail of a croc first and a snarl ran up my chest. The croc turned and I pounced on him, noticing in my peripheral vision that two human men were there with him. This was an uneven fight. Two humans and one shifter against a helpless panther was too easy. But three bears on two humans and one croc? Even if they did have a gun, they'd get theirs real fast.

As my paws landed on the croc, my weight pressing him down, and I picked up on the killer's scent. *This bastard is the one,* I realized. I bit into his neck and he thrashed around, but my sheer size and weight were more than he could fight against. I punched his spine. The bony, scaled ridge of his back hurt my paw, but it was worth it when I felt his bones crack and he went still. I opened his soft throat with my claws to speed things along, and when I was sure he was dead, I turned back to the others.

The humans were pinned down, looking properly terrified—and very immobile. What the hell were we going to do with them? Well, they weren't my primary concern in that moment.

I ran to Britt. I wasn't sure what made her change back to her panther, but I guessed it had been a good thing. She was dirtier than she was when I left her, bleeding from a fresh gash across her muzzle.

I began licking her. The blood and her animal sweat all tasted alive to me, and I felt relieved. But we weren't clear yet. She was barely conscious, hardly able to move. I didn't know if it was because of the poison or the attack.

Before I shifted, I asked, *How long until someone gets here?* There was hesitation. *What?* I demanded.

There's no way a crew can get in here, Conner said. *Or maybe they can, but it would take too much time. We have to carry her out.*

How? There's still the trap.

Mason looked at the human he was holding down. He slammed his paw into him hard, knocking him out. Then he shifted and came over to the trap.

Conner shifted back and pulled off the pack he'd been carrying in bear form. He pulled out zip ties, flipped the man over, and secured his feet and hands behind his back. He put his face close to the man and growled, "I don't know why that croc decided to tell you and your buddy over there about us shifters, but you need to forget everything you've seen. If you breathe so much as a fucking word about our existence, mark my words, you *will* be destroyed. Do you understand?"

The man gulped and nodded. "I ain't seen nuthin', man."

When the guy Mason knocked out regained consciousness, Conner secured him after making a similar threat and joined us.

I'd shifted back and sat at Britt's head, cradling her and talking to her. "I know it's hard, but you have to shift back."

Her eyes closed and her head went still.

"Britt! Don't close your eyes!" After all that, I wasn't about to lose her.

Her body moved as Mason and Conner worked to get the trap free.

"There's no chain," Mason said.

"Small miracle," Conner added.

They dug at the ground, and in a few minutes, they had freed the trap from the hole.

"Britt, just stay still," Conner explained. "We're going to lift the trap out of the hole so we can get it open."

She nodded once and I watched them as they struggled to pull the heavy trap from the small hole while trying to not hurt Britt, but she twitched and winced in pain.

"Do you have other injuries?" I asked. "Something we can't see?"

She just looked up at me.

"Please shift back. I don't know what you're saying. I need to be able to talk to you." I felt the tears run down my cheeks as I pleaded with her.

She closed her eyes, and I thought she was either passing out or falling asleep, but then, I saw her tail twitch and begin to shorten. Mason and Conner worked at the trap.

Patches of her skin changed so she became splotchy with panther fur, skin and mud. Her skeleton seemed to change bone by bone, and I couldn't imagine what pain it must have been causing her. Every shifter perfected the art of changing as fast as possible; that was the only way to keep the pain at a minimum. It got so I barely noticed it anymore. But shifting slowly would hurt like someone was twisting and wrenching each limb, forcing it to break and morph forms.

"Just do it real fast and it'll be over," I said, rubbing her nose and head. I wished I could do it for her; wished I could give her my strength, my energy.

It took time, but finally, she looked up at me with her human eyes. I kissed her and stroked her golden hair while they worked.

"We need to get it flat on the ground to do it," Mason said.

Conner cursed and looked at me.

"What?" I asked.

"We have to move her so that her leg can bend. We have to be able to stand on these springs to get the trap to open," Conner explained.

They'd have to use a lot of weight to push down on the triangles, making them into flat pieces stacked on top of each other, so that the trap would release. With Britt lying down, the trap was on its side.

"Okay," I said, taking in a deep breath. I looked down at Britt. "Did you hear that? We have to turn you onto your back so your foot is flat on the ground. That's the only way they can get it off."

She closed her eyes. With their help, we turned her as gently as possible. Once she was in position, it only took a minute for them to stand on the trap and get it to release.

Her foot came free and fresh blood poured from the wound. Conner went to his pack and pulled out a roll of bandages, promptly applying pressure and wrapping the wound.

"I think our best bet is to carry her out," Conner said. "We'll have the EMTs meet us wherever they can get to."

"We're all going to walk out naked?" I asked.

They exchanged looks.

Mason said, "Actually, it might be better if we're bears. We can lay her across our backs."

"Take my pack," Conner said. "There are some clothes in there. Put whatever you can on her and you. We can get back to the car. We have more stuff there."

They shifted back as I grabbed the pack and slung it over my shoulder. In case any of us had to shift again, I'd wait to get us dressed. We couldn't afford to lose these clothes and we wouldn't have time to undress if something came at us.

Mason and Conner stood side by side, and I squatted down and slid my arms under Britt. She was sturdy and muscular, but the adrenaline still pumped through me, giving me just enough of a boost to easily lift her.

I set her carefully across their backs. "Try to hold on," I told her.

She dug her hands into their coats and they started moving, slowly at first, until they knew she wasn't going to slide off. They picked up speed and I walked fast to keep up, watching to make sure she wouldn't fall.

As bears, it would have taken only a few minutes of running, but at human speed, it was taking much, much longer.

"This is taking too long," I said. "Put her on my back."

I shifted and held the pack in my mouth while Mason and Conner helped move Britt onto my back. She wrapped her arms tight around my throat. It almost choked me, but I welcomed the pain; it made me move faster.

Once I was sure she was on securely, I took off running as fast as I could while carrying her, and Conner and Mason ran with me. It wasn't as fast as my usual bear speed of course, but I could cover more ground a lot more quickly than I could on human legs.

They're here, Conner said. He showed me where the ambulance was parked. It had come as close as it could and the EMTs were standing by, waiting.

Just before we got to them, I stopped and eased her to the ground.

See you at the hospital, I told them before shifting to my human form.

I hurried to get some clothes on us both, and once we were decent, I picked her up again and carried her out of the woods.

I'm sure Conner could have explained exactly what happened at that point, but all I remember is that once they saw us, the EMTs swarmed. They took her from me and got her on a stretcher, then loaded her into the ambulance, where they got an IV line running, gave her oxygen and began cleaning her wounds.

They asked her questions, but she couldn't answer, so I gave them all the critical information I knew. They asked her more questions, and at first, I answered for her, but then the EMT looked up at me.

"I need to assess her cognitive awareness."

"Sorry." I shut up and just sat beside her, holding her hand.

Just before they shut the ambulance doors, Conner hopped on. He got the report from one of the EMTs, then he did his own assessment and gave them more information as the ambulance took off.

They could have been speaking another language, for all I knew.

Conner told the driver, "Straight to the poison center."

I watched her carefully, hoping she'd just open her eyes and start talking to me and be fine. Conner sat beside me, still checking her vitals and doing things I didn't understand.

He put his hand on my shoulder. "You did good, man. I think you saved her life."

"You *think*?"

"She'll live. I don't know what damage has been done, but she'll live."

That was all I could ask for. I set my jaw and nodded.

17

EZRA

When we got to the hospital, I had to sit in the waiting room. I still didn't have my phone, so I couldn't call anyone. But they all knew. In ones and twos, my clan trickled in.

Mason told me, "The humans are under arrest in jail, and the body of the croc is being processed by our guys."

By "our guys" I assumed he meant shifters.

When they finally let me in to see her, I refused to leave her side. I spent the night in the ICU with her, and in the morning, the doctor said she could be moved to a normal room. Progress. They kept her one more night for observation, then I was able to drive her home.

"I don't want you arguing with me," I said as I helped her inside. "I'm staying here and taking care of you."

She hadn't been speaking much over the last few days; she'd been in and out of consciousness as they worked to get the poison out of her system. Then she'd been groggy on pain killers. She'd finally started to seem more like herself on the ride home.

"I want you to stay," she said.

I helped her to the couch and got her a glass of water so she could take her medication, then sat in a chair by her side.

"You scared me to death," I said. "Do you know that? I thought you were going to die."

"*I* thought I was going to die. When those assholes showed up...and that croc." Her jaw tightened, and I put my hand on her shoulder.

"Easy," I said. "He's dead now. You took a swipe out of him, and I finished him off. We killed him together."

She pressed her lips together. "I know. I watched you do it. I was cheering you on in my mind."

"Thanks." I chuckled.

"No." She shook her head. "I need to thank you." She looked at me with tears in her eyes. "What you did for me, saving me and protecting me the way you did...no one's ever done anything like that for me. I don't even know if anyone would."

"I'm sure your clan would."

"I don't know," she admitted. "We keep to ourselves for a reason. If they saw I couldn't get away and three guys came with guns, they might have taken off, thinking I was a lost cause."

"Well, those aren't very good friends."

"We're just not like you all. We're together for convenience. I don't doubt they'd try to help me, sure. But if it was me or them, I'd be dead right now."

"I could never treat you that way."

"I know." She gave me a thin smile. "That's what made me fall in love with you."

I sucked in a breath. "What?"

"I...I love you, Ezra."

I eyed the bottle of pain pills. "I'll believe that when you're not high."

She slapped my arm. "I knew it before the attack, you damn idiot."

I laughed. "Britt, when I thought I'd lost you, it felt like my life was over. I can't imagine my life without you. I love you, too." I kissed her and smiled widely.

"We don't need to get all sentimental about it," she said.

"Then what should we do about it?"

"There's one thing I've been thinking of a lot."

She sat up and pulled off her shirt. She wasn't wearing a bra and her bare breasts shown in the room's dim light.

I raised an eyebrow. "Yeah?"

She pulled my head to hers, forcing me into a kiss. I didn't fight back; I wanted her just as bad.

I pulled my shirt over my head and climbed carefully on

top of her. Her foot was in a huge cast, but she had it resting on the floor, out of the way.

"I don't want to hurt you," I said.

She huffed. "You really think you could?"

I raised an eyebrow. "You've been in the hospital with severe injuries and poisoning. Yes, I think you're maybe not quite 100% right now."

"Pfft." She pushed down her shorts, trying to wiggle free, but my weight stopped her.

I lifted myself and helped her get her bottoms off, pulling them awkwardly over her cast, then stepped out of my pants and resumed my position.

I was careful to hold my weight off her, though I let my hot skin touch hers all over. We'd spent so much time together being naked, but this was for a different reason. Now, I took the time to caress her breast and suck her nipple, enjoying every inch of her body.

I moved down slowly, kissing a trail to her stomach, then lower. I pushed her leg over to spread her wide, and when I slid my tongue between her folds, she let out a moan. I sucked at her clit, moving my tongue inside her, then back to her sensitive nub. She moaned and rocked her hips, then grabbed my hair and pulled my face closer. I almost couldn't breathe, but I kept at it, sucking and flicking until she cried out and her body tensed with pleasure.

I smiled up at her and she made a pleased murmur in

response. I climbed back up, laying my head on her chest and listened to her breathing.

"What the hell do you think you're doing?" she asked.

I picked up my head to look at her. "What do you mean?"

"We're not done."

"Oh." I laughed. "I didn't want to push you too hard."

She narrowed her eyes at me. "I want you inside me. Now."

My eyes widened and I couldn't help but chuckle. "Well, yes ma'am." I saluted her and started kissing her again.

It didn't take long for my cock to stiffen right up again; around her, it happened without me even trying. She had me hard all the time, my thoughts consumed with her and how to please her.

I circled my fingers around her clit, making her moan more before I slipped my finger in and out of her, spreading her wetness around.

"Come on," she said.

I raised an eyebrow. "Patience."

"I've been waiting weeks. I can't wait any longer."

"No?"

I kissed along her neck, and when she reached down to stroke my shaft, I pulled my hips back, out of her reach. I kissed down her stomach, gave her a few flicks with my tongue, then kissed my way back up.

"Ezra!"

I gave her a wicked smile. "You'll have to be nice if you want me to give you what you want."

"I don't *do* nice."

I kissed her breasts and pinched her nipples, and she tugged on my hair to bring my face back to hers. She kissed me hard, biting at my earlobe and neck, like she was going to tame me into submission with her tongue and teeth.

I was going to draw this out and tease her as long as I could. After a lot of kissing, I rubbed the tip of my cock against her clit, slipping in the wetness. She tried to buck her hips to guide me inside, but I didn't let her.

She grabbed my hair and pulled my face close to hers. She breathed, "I need to feel you inside me. Right now."

I almost obeyed her, moving the tip down to her opening. She shot her hips down, but I only allowed the head to slip in.

She cried out in frustration. "Ezra!"

This was too good to rush, though, so I pushed in slowly. Before I was fully inside her, I pulled back out. She tried to reach down to grab my ass, but the couch wasn't the place for that sort of thing. She did not have the advantage, and her cast made her even more at my mercy. That probably pissed her off the most.

If we were in her bed, she would have flipped me over, tackled me, and sat on me to get what she wanted. This might be the only time I could tease her, and I was going to make her work for it.

"What do you want, Britt?" I cooed in her ear. "It's right there." I pressed in again a little, then pulled it back out.

"Ezra," she whined. "Please."

"Oh, I like it when you beg." I smirked.

"Please," she said.

I pushed in halfway, then stopped.

"Please," she moaned, "You're killing me."

When those words left her lips, I closed my eyes and slid in all the way. I wanted to give her everything she wanted.

"Is that what you want?" I asked.

"Yes!" She managed to get one hand on my ass and gripped my cheek to pull me closer.

Her free leg wrapped around my waist and she bucked her hips as I moved slowly in and out. I still didn't want to rush things; I didn't want that lust-filled sex we'd had before.

But as I moved in and out of her, I couldn't hold back. My own hormones kicked in and my body yelled at me for being a fool. I sped up, thrusting in harder, and each time she moaned, it sent a shot of pleasure through me that made me move faster and faster.

"Yes, yes!" she shouted. "Harder!"

I pumped into her as fast as I could, my ass muscles squeezing and working. I slammed her hard, making her breasts jump and her face twist in pleasure.

"Yes!" She grabbed my ass and wrapped me tighter and snapped her hips into me as she tightened around my cock.

Her squeezing and throbbing as she came pulled the pleasure out of me, and I thrust hard a few last times as I came.

"Asshole," she muttered as we lay still.

"Oh, you love it," I said, breathing hard and enjoying the
feeling of our sweat-covered bodies sticking together.

She sighed. "Yeah, I do. But next time, don't you keep me
waiting like that. If you don't think there'll be payback, you're
dumber than I thought."

"Really?"

"Yes."

"The thing is..." I lifted my head to look in her eyes. "I
was smart enough to pick you."

She pressed her lips together. "Fine. You're smart as a
damn whip." She paused, then said, "Whip. Hmm. That
could be fun. Maybe I might just cuff you to the bed and
whip you, see how you like to be tortured."

"I might like that very much," I said.

"Yeah, yeah, Mr. I Love Life And Everything About It."

"I love everything about *you*." I kissed her. "And I will
make you love life like you never knew you could if it's the
last thing I do."

18

BRITT

One Year Later

I came up to the cabin, dragging a croc carcass behind me as I approached the door. I'd made a point of hunting more crocs since my quite unpleasant experience with the one who tried to kill me and had killed two of my kind.

Something wasn't right, though. The door was open a crack and lights were on inside. I'd left in the middle of the day, so there was no way I'd left any on. Ezra was working and wouldn't be over until much later.

My heart raced and I started my sniffing investigation. This felt too familiar. Was someone in my place? After me or panthers again?

I pulled my handgun from my side holster and pulled back the slide to load a bullet in the chamber. If someone was in there, I wasn't going to wait for them to explain.

I crept up the porch, my gun at the ready, and aimed in front of me. I kicked the door open wider as I jumped back, out of sight in case someone was right there. When I leaned my head forward slightly to see inside, I dropped my gun and rolled my eyes.

"What the hell?"

In the center of my living room sat a trap. It looked a little like the one I'd nearly lost my foot in a year before. That one, though, happened to be covered in pink fur, and rose petals were strewn around it. The trap was only plastic. A toy.

A note sat beside it that read, "You've trapped my heart."

"This is the worst damn joke I've ever seen," I called out. He was there somewhere. I walked over and shut the door, then locked it.

Candles formed a circle around the trap, flickering in the gentle breeze. The candles formed a trail that I guessed I was meant to follow, so I walked back to the bedroom.

When I pushed open the door, I laughed. The candles formed another circle. This one had Ezra in the middle, down on one knee.

I crossed my arms. "What are you doing?"

He shrugged. "I just thought the candles and rose petals would be a nice touch."

I let out a sigh. "Well, let's hear it then." But I was laughing. This was cute.

"Britt," he started, taking something from his pocket. "You've been a pain in my ass since the day I met you, when you tackled me and almost attacked me."

I shook my head, remembering our meeting, and laughing.

"Since that day, we've gotten on each other's nerves, we've driven each other crazy, we've killed together, almost died together, and made some good sweet loving. And all that was before we even really started dating. Someone—fate, maybe—brought us together to form this wacky balance of love that we have going on. But at the end of the day, there's no one I'd rather be annoyed by than you. Your insults are like the sweetest compliments."

I snorted. "Oh, Lord, this is getting thick."

He laughed, too. "You've made me see life completely differently, and I think I've done the same for you. There is no one—not even close to anyone—on this earth that I would rather annoy the piss out of for the rest of my days than you."

I put my hand to my forehead. "Is this supposed to be a proposal?"

He smiled, but turned serious. "A year ago, I almost lost you, and it felt like the world would never be right again. I don't want to go one day without your laugh or smile or quick wit. Be my hunting partner and mate forever. Britt, will you marry me?"

He held up a ring. But it didn't look like the typical diamond ring. I squinted and moved closer to look at it.

"Now, before you go having your fit, this is not a diamond. I didn't think you'd want that."

I gasped. "Is that—"

"I talked to Kat and Dezi and Kat's gramma and they assured me—"

"You didn't!"

"—that this was the only ring you'd want."

"Ezra!"

He stood and slipped it on my finger.

"Is that my gramma's jade?"

"Yep. And the band is made from your ma's necklace, melted down."

I squealed and wrapped my arms around him. I'd never been into typical jewelry, it was true. If he'd given me a gold band with a diamond, I'd wear it, but I'd try to get out of wearing it whenever I could. I just didn't like that sort of thing. But this ring? I couldn't have designed one more perfect.

"I think I'd have to say yes just because of the ring."

"Really?" He sagged with relief. "I was worried you might be pissed that I ruined two pieces of jewelry that were both super important to you."

"I can see why you'd think that. And if you'd screwed it

up, I would be. But it's perfect." I pulled back to look in his eyes. "I had no idea I could love someone like I love you. You were totally unexpected and not at all who I ever would have pictured spending my life with, if I had pictured that at all. But somehow, we're perfect together."

"We are, aren't we?"

"We are." I kissed him hard. "Now come help me skin this croc."

He laughed. "I love you."

"I love you, too." I took his hand and we blew out the candles as we went, starting out on the path to our forever.

THE END

NANNY FOR THE SOLDIER BEAR

WEREBEARS OF THE EVERGLADES

1

CONNER

From somewhere under my warm blanket, I heard my radio crackle. My ears perked and I was sitting up before the alert tones even finished.

"Search and rescue team, respond. Recovery needed."

I grabbed my walkie and pressed the button as I pulled on my pants with one hand. "Conner Griffin responding. En route."

I tossed the walkie aside so I could finish dressing, but as I pulled on my shirt, I shook my head. *No, this isn't right. I should be running.* My pants came back off, and I snatched my "go" bag from the floor by my bed, tossing my shirt and pants inside.

I was barely out the door before the familiar popping and snapping of my bones coursed through me. My skin broke out into thick, black fur, my nails extended to claws and my teeth sharpened to fangs. I roared and took off running in bear form with my pack of necessary items slung over my back. I was much faster on four feet than two.

My paws hit the forest floor, the grass still damp with dew, the morning just starting to lighten. The sun would be peeking over the horizon in the next hour or so, but for now, the hint of dawn made the world a dull orange.

At least a few members of my clan are likely up and about, I thought, bounding onward. Owen, our Alpha and head Park Ranger, would've probably known what was up if the rescue was on park grounds. That meant Ezra, who was Owen's second in both the pack and as a Ranger, might have, too— unless he was fast asleep, which was just as likely. Mason was a Ranger Officer in the area, so the situation might have involved him as well.

I tuned my thoughts into our clan's mental link. *Checking in.*

You on your way? Owen asked. *I'm on site and Mason is driving in.*

I'm running. What details do you have? I couldn't hear my walkie while running since it was in my pack, but Owen would've heard the same call go out as I had.

Looks like a body in the swamp. Suspected murder.

Murder? Mason will love that. I chuckled. He'd been in on a big case recently, but it involved animal deaths, not people.

Being new to the force, this might have been his first big shot at proving himself.

He seemed very serious.

I expected that. Mason was fun, and when we got him drunk, he was a blast. But when it came to work, he was 110% business. Important for a cop. Couldn't say I blamed him. My clan complained that I was far too serious and needed to lighten up all the time. Whatever; some things *should* be taken seriously. Life couldn't be all fun and games, no matter what Ezra said.

Exact location? I asked.

East swamp, by the northbound path. Follow my scent. Shifting back now.

Getting close. I could hear the general murmur of people moving around, talking, turning car radios on and off; life sounds.

When I got close enough to smell Owen, I stopped running and shifted back to human, then quickly dressed myself. Until I knew for sure who was around, I couldn't make myself known as a shifter. Plenty of us who worked in emergency services in Everglades National Park were shifters, and it aided us greatly, but it was a colossal secret, a great divide of us versus them. The shifters knew who was human and who wasn't, but we had to make sure the humans had no clue about our existence. It made things tricky at times, but was wholly critical for our survival. The world wasn't ready to believe that fairytales were real.

When I walked up, I saw that everyone present was a shifter; that was a bad sign. When a situation that involved shifters happened, those in charge made sure only shifters were sent to respond. Owen and one of his Rangers were there, Mason was there with his partner and two more cops, along with two other members of my team, Seth and Jamari.

I nodded to the others as I approached my team.

"Full-on murder," Seth announced.

"They suspect crocs," Jamari said.

My eyes instantly narrowed. How long were these crocs going to cause trouble? We'd been dealing with them for years by that point. They thought they were the superior shifter group. It didn't matter that the Everglades was home to bear shifters, panthers, wolves and tigers. No, only crocs should be allowed to live there, they believed. And they constantly tried to move into positions of power to take over. The rest of us all got along and worked together. That was how we'd kept them out so long, but it was getting to the point where we might have to ban the crocs from the 'Glades once and for all.

"As soon as the police are done taking photos of the scene, we're going in," Jamari added.

I stood back with them to watch. A few other rescue workers showed up, and finally, it was our time to get in the water and retrieve the bodies. It was easier in animal form, so we stripped down and shifted, then jumped in the water.

As soon as I was in the swamp, I started searching.

Being in animal form gave us many advantages, especially in the water. We could see, hear, and smell better than humans. I picked up on the scent of blood, distinct, sharp and iron-rich; few other things smelled like that. I swam in the direction and noticed a figure at the bottom of the murky water.

I made the gesture we used to let each other know we'd found something, and my teammates swam over to me. Together, we got the body free of the tangles of the grass and I grabbed hold of the shirt. *Female*, I thought.

As I swam with her toward the surface, another scent hit me; this one was much more familiar, sending a panicked jolt through me. I broke the surface of the water, then coughed and almost lost her. Adjusting my grip, I dragged her body over to the side where two members of the paramedic team were waiting.

They pulled her out as I nudged her from behind, and when they had her, I emerged from the water and shifted back immediately, sputtering and choking.

"You okay, man?" Owen asked.

I couldn't answer. I just stared at the body, inhaling her scent. Now that she was out, there was no denying it.

I had just rescued my lifeless sister-in-law.

When Owen looked at the body, he gasped and covered his mouth. Alaina and my brother hadn't been part of our clan, but they were also shifters and had come to many of our get togethers. I stood by her side, not believing the sight before me. How could this have happened? And where was my brother? Did he have any clue?

"Alaina," I whispered.

"You know her?" one of the paramedics asked.

I nodded stiffly. "My sister-in-law."

I heard a commotion behind me: Seth surfaced with another body. We had only been expecting one. My lip trembled as I saw the last thing in the world I wanted to see.

My brother, Logan, dead; his lifeless body being pulled from the swamp.

My stomach dropped and everything around me spun. I felt my knees hit the ground. Sounds turned to echoes ringing in my ears, and I turned my head and puked in disgust. My memories were fuzzy after that, but all I remember is scrambling to my feet, shifting and taking off.

"Conner, wait!" Owen called after me.

A moment later, I felt his presence as he shifted. *Oh my God, I am so sorry. I can't even... Be safe. Check in. We're here for you, brother; we're on this. We'll find the bastards who did this and fucking end them.*

Then he was gone and it was just me. Running. From something. *To* something. To what, I didn't know; I just ran.

2

JESSIE

I glanced at my phone again. Where was it saying to turn? I sighed in frustration, felt the anxiety increase in my chest, and made a turn. My phone's screen said, "Rerouting."

"Ahhh!" I growled and banged the steering wheel.

Though my sister, Nikki, assured me that Homestead was a far cry from a massive city like Miami, the area was still much bigger than our tiny little home town, which was all I knew. Of course, that was also the very reason I was moving.

Living in a town with just one elementary school and one high school, there were no nearby teaching jobs available out of college. After being turned down for the only two available job positions in the area, I ended up waiting tables at the local diner, paying huge school loans on skimpy tips. Not exactly what I had pictured for my future.

Nikki, on the other hand, had been ready to get out from the start. She went to school in Miami and moved to Homestead—right near Everglades National Park—after she'd graduated. Nikki had a stint as a waitress, too, though in a high-end restaurant that brought much higher tips. But shortly thereafter, she was able to land a position in her given industry—medical imaging—in a fancy hospital with a big fat paycheck. It had only taken her a month to find that job, and there were many hospitals and facilities within a half-hour range that she could transfer to if the first gig didn't work out.

"Jess, you have *got* to come. There are *tons* of schools out here; you'll definitely find something."

After a particularly difficult double shift, where the customers had been extra grouchy and my tips extra light, I finally decided to give it a go. What did I have to lose?

I picked up my phone again, trying to see where the little blue line was leading me. I set my phone back down and returned my gaze to the road—just in time to see a flash of black streaking in front of me. I slammed on my brakes. *A... bear? Was that a bear that just ran out in front of me?*

Once my heart stopped pounding, I drove on. I finally seemed to be getting the hang of my GPS. I'd never needed to use it before; I knew all the roads back home and ten ways to get anywhere. But driving in that neck of the woods was like being in a foreign country.

I saw flashing lights ahead and slowed. When I got to the intersection, I noticed a swarm of cop cars, an ambulance and a firetruck. Someone was directing traffic, so since I couldn't turn where I needed to, I pulled up to the officer and slid my window down.

"I need to go that way," I said, pointing left.

"Sorry, Miss. Road's closed."

Taking a deep breath, I drove straight through as directed. My GPS told me to turn around and go back the way I couldn't, and at that point, I felt like just turning around and going home. Old Miss Judy would have probably been retiring soon; I could have just gone back to the diner long enough to wait her out, or maybe sub or tutor in the meantime.

3

JESSIE

By the time I pulled into Nikki's driveway, I was completely flustered. It had taken me twice as long to get there as planned, and I'd gotten lost at least three times. Nikki came bursting out of the house before I had my seatbelt off.

"You made it!" she exclaimed as she ran to greet me.

I got out, and we wrapped each other in a tight hug.

"Let's take your stuff in."

Four trips later, several boxes and suitcases sat in her spare bedroom. I'd brought everything except furniture from my small room back home. I'd opened one suitcase and started to unpack my clothing when Nikki called to me, "Leave that! Come have tea!" I could unpack later.

We sat at a small, round table with mismatched chairs.

Her place wasn't big, but it was all hers. I was a little jealous, though the cost of her rent terrified me. "It's all relative," she'd said. "I made three times what you did waitressing alone, and my new job pays even more. You'll see."

I certainly hoped so, sipping at my tea as I tried to relax.

"I thought I'd show you around a bit tomorrow," Nikki said.

"Sure. As long as *you* drive."

She laughed. "Of course." She slid a newspaper over to me. "Most places post their listings online, but I thought you'd want to check these out, too."

I looked at the circles she'd made around several listings for teaching positions on the page of classifieds, and my hope rose a little.

"There'll be lots more online," she promised.

We chatted about Mom and Dad and life in general. She was loving her job and had made great friends over the last two years since she'd been in the area. As we were talking, her phone rang, and she glanced at the screen and smiled.

"It's Alaina. You will *love* her." She tapped the screen to answer. "Hey gorgeous!" But moments later, her face abruptly fell into confusion. "Oh, sorry," she said. Then, "What! When?" She put her hand to her mouth, nodded and listened for a long while. "W-What about Peyton?" Her voice wavered when she said, "Thanks for letting me know."

Setting the phone down, Nikki looked at me, her face pale and shocked.

"What's wrong?" I asked, my own heart racing at her expression.

"Alaina. She's...dead."

"Your friend?"

She nodded slowly. "And her husband, Logan. Both dead. Murdered."

"Murdered?" I screeched.

"They have a daughter. Peyton. She's just six."

"Oh my god! That's just awful."

She burst into tears and I did my best to comfort her, but the news was nothing short of horrific. She was mid-sob a few minutes later, and her expression suddenly changed. "Wait; you can help them." She became determined. "You have to help them, Jessie!"

"What are you talking about?"

"The person on the phone told me Peyton's staying with her uncle, but he needs a nanny. Desperately. He's a single guy and needs help; I mean, his brother just died, and he has zero experience with kids. This is the perfect job for you."

I shook my head. "I don't know, Nikki. That's not really what I'm looking for."

"Jessie! You need a job and he needs a nanny. This would be one less thing he'd have to deal with. He'll need someone good for Peyton; someone he knows and can trust."

"But I don't *know* him."

"Yeah, but you know me. That's better than hiring a stranger from a service."

I shook my head. "I have no experience as a nanny."

"But you have experience with kids. Come on, even if it's temporary; please, Jessie." Her tears spilled over and whatever shock had kept her from crying before vanished. She burst into sobs. "I can't believe this. I just saw them! I just saw them, and now..."

I got up and went to her, wrapping my arms around her and holding her close. "I know. It's horrible."

"Help them," she sputtered. "Please. Peyton is so sweet; you'll just love her. And now she—she—doesn't have parents!"

I let her sob on my shoulder for a long while, my shirt damp with her tears, her face red and splotchy. She kept saying over and over, "I just can't believe it. I can't believe they're both gone."

After mulling the thought over in my mind, I began to reconsider. *How hard could this really be, anyway? It's not like Peyton's a baby; she's six. And I do need a job...* "Okay, I'll do it, Nikki. I'll do whatever I can, even if it's just for now."

That night, I lay in bed, wondering what I had gotten myself into. It was only my first day in town; my sister's friends had been murdered, and I was going to be a nanny? Home and the diner were looking better every hour.

4

CONNER

I knew Mason was beside me. I knew Owen was there, too. I had a vague idea of where I was—in a church somewhere—and I knew the most important fact. The one undeniable, inescapable fact. I was at a funeral for my brother and sister-in-law. They were both gone. And I was about to become the guardian of their daughter.

My stomach turned and I closed my eyes to stop the room from spinning. The medication wasn't helping. The nightmares still came. The flashbacks still came. Things were getting tangled up in my mind. The years I spent on deployment in the Marines, the deaths I'd seen there, the deaths I'd seen here. Faces moved and morphed. My commanding officer was pulled from the swamp, then he became my brother, then my fellow soldier.

I woke up night after night in a sweat, reaching for someone. I hadn't been able to save Zeke when he'd been shot. I hadn't been able to save Logan and Alaina, either. I reached for them; I reached for them every damn night. And I woke up feeling inadequate with a heavy pressure on me, telling me I'd failed them all. My therapist prescribed a pill that was supposed to keep the nightmares away, another to calm my racing heart, and yet another to help quell my depression. I don't think any of them did a damn thing.

I'd been given time off from work, but the last thing I wanted to do was sit at home with my thoughts. I wanted to be out there; to be out saving people. At least let me save *someone.* Let me find some way to relieve the guilt and stress.

The service had started at some point. I hadn't noticed exactly when, but some minister began to speak. Who was that guy? Who had chosen him? He was talking about my brother. He walked over to a small CD player and pressed a button. The sound emanating from the speakers was tinny—and too quiet, yet too loud at the same time—but the melody hit me like a bullet to the chest. A sudden flash. *Logan. Me. Screaming along to this song. Goofing off. Driving too fast. Drinking too much. Dancing our asses off at his wedding.* He loved that song. And I'd never be able to listen to it again.

I stood up when the wave moved to my stomach. Hurrying out the back, I saw the bathroom sign, rushed in and heaved up the contents of my stomach. I hadn't stress puked like that in years. That was one thing my therapist had helped me with, though, the bottle of whiskey I'd guzzled down the night before probably wasn't helping, either.

Just then, I heard the lawyer's voice again. "It means that you're Peyton's legal guardian."

How was it that neither Alaina nor Logan had any other capable family members? My mother was still alive, but she was far too ill to take care of a six-year-old. She'd barely made it to the funeral, requiring the assistance of a home nurse to leave the house. "There is no one else," the lawyer said. "The will specifies you, Mr. Griffin."

If my brother's death wasn't enough to cope with, I was going to be a fucking father, too? I mean, don't get me wrong, Peyton was adorable. The times I spent with her, she always seemed to have fun, but seeing me once a week for a few hours wasn't exactly the same as living with me. What would she do at my house? I didn't have a pink room or dolls. I didn't have toys. I probably didn't have anything a child would need. And how could I? I had no idea what kind of stuff kids need to have around.

"The house is yours, too," the lawyer said. "Well, technically, it's Peyton's, but it's yours until she's eighteen. There are funds allocated for her care and education."

I figured we would stay at their house; at least she'd have everything of hers there. It would already be childproofed or whatever parents did to a house to make it safe. It would have her memories. But that meant I'd be sleeping in my brother's room. Looking at his clothes, his razor in the bathroom and his boots by the front door. For the time being, that was the plan. But I didn't know how long I would be able to take it.

Admittedly, I'd tried to get out of it. "If you don't take her, she'll go into foster care," the lawyer warned. God, I was such a selfish asshole. Peyton was part of my brother. She was the most important person on the planet to him besides his wife. How could I have abandoned her? I couldn't. And coming from shifter parents—and being a shifter herself—she couldn't be safe just anywhere; it's not like there was a shifter adoption service in the area. I didn't have a clue what I was doing, but I would have to step up and figure it out. If not for Peyton, then for my brother. That was the only thing I could still do for him at that point.

I splashed water on my face and stumbled out the door, trying to compose myself. In the lobby, a woman sat on a bench near the bathrooms. I didn't recognize her, but her curves caught my eye, making my inner bear groan. But I noticed she was on her phone, and for some irrational reason, it caused me to rage out. How dare she sit there all casual, chatting away, while my brother and his wife were lying dead in the next room?

"*Who* are you?" I barked at her.

She looked up, shocked, then glanced around. "Who, me?"

"You." I walked over to her and crossed my arms. I

wanted to yank her off the seat and throw her phone as hard as I could, watching it shatter into millions of tiny pieces.

"I... uhh..." Her face turned red and she swallowed hard. "I'm here for my sister?"

"Is that your answer, or a question?"

Her face reddened. *Good*, I thought. *She should be ashamed of herself.*

"I'm... here for my sister."

"Who's your sister?"

"Um...Nikki?" Her eyes widened slightly and she said, "Nikki. She was friends with Alaina."

"But you weren't."

"I'm new to town. I came for her, and to meet the brother of...the deceased."

"Logan," I seethed. God, she could've at least had the decency to know whose funeral she was crashing.

"Right. I'm sorry. I didn't mean to upset you, I just didn't think it would be appropriate for me to be in there since I never knew either of them. But, Logan. I understand his brother needs a nanny for their little girl, so I'm here to meet him."

"So you're a nanny?"

"No, but I have a degree in elementary education and I'm available. Nikki seemed to think that since I'm her sister and she was friends with Alaina, I'd be a good fit." She shrugged. "I need a job and he needs a nanny, so I guess it could work out."

I reassessed her from a new angle. She was dressed modestly and her mousy brown hair was pulled back. Not too much make up on. Not that any of those things meant she was capable, but it seemed like the way an elementary school teacher would be. And she was right about one thing: I needed someone immediately. I didn't know this 'Nikki,' but I knew Alaina, and if Alaina was friends with her, then Nikki must have been a stand-up person.

"384 Olive Street. Sunday at 10." I turned from her and started to walk away.

"Wait! Are you...?"

I looked back over my shoulder. "Logan's brother. Conner."

Her mouth was still hanging open as I walked back into the sanctuary.

5

JESSIE

"No, no, no," I insisted. "Nikki, he was a complete jerk! I don't even think Peyton should be subject to him; I'm certainly not going to deal with that asshole every day. Thank you for setting this up for me, but I just can't do it."

We were back home after the funeral and Nikki put her hands on my shoulders. After my encounter with Conner, I had been in shock at first, and then, was angry. Who did he think he was talking to me like that?

"Please," she begged. "I know he can be a little..."

"Of a dick?"

She winced. "I was going to say rough around the edges, but he's been through a lot."

I sighed. "I know. But I'm not ready for something so difficult. It's hard enough moving here to a new place, leaving all my friends and Biscuit and Muffin with Mom and Dad." My throat thickened when I thought about home. My parents, my cuddly cat, Biscuit, and my loyal and loving dog, Muffin, were all there waiting for me. I came to the area to be with my sister, but she was all I had there. My whole life was back home. I sat down on her couch and covered my face, sighing.

Nikki sat beside me. "Jessie, I know you're a compassionate person. I also know you're an awesome secret keeper, so I'm going to tell you something about Conner." She drew in a deep breath. "He was in the Army, and he saw some of his friends get killed. Alaina said that he has nightmares and PTSD from it and that he blames himself. He has some issues, and this is obviously making everything so much worse. That's no excuse for his behavior, but give the guy a break. He just lost his brother and sister-in-law and became a dad out of nowhere. That's going to be hard for anyone, on top of his other struggles, so you can't blame him for being in a bad mood."

My sister knew me too well. Her words tugged on my heart strings and made me feel sorry for him—and for Peyton. If he was having this trouble, the little girl would need someone to be there for her; someone who had the wherewithal to be compassionate and patient.

"Just try it for a little while," Nikki continued. "Let him get settled and get back to some kind of schedule. Let Peyton adjust as much as she can. Look, you don't have another job, anyway; any time you could devote to them would be such a help to him and Peyton—and really, to Alaina and Logan, too. They would want someone amazing to take care of their daughter, and you're just that someone."

I chewed my lower lip.

"You can always bail," she went on. "You can always find something else. But don't do either until you give it a chance. I mean, attitude aside, you've gotta admit, Conner's pretty hot." She gave me a grimacing smile.

I rolled my eyes. "Like that matters."

"He's nice to look at, is all I'm saying. I wouldn't mind having a live-in boss who looks like *that*."

"Too bad he's a complete jerk."

"Not a complete jerk. Just a...situational jerk. Once he heals a little, he'll get better. It's a lot to deal with all at once."

"Yeah." I let out a slow, long breath. "I suppose it is."

6

CONNER

"What do you want to do today, honey?"

Peyton sat on the couch and I was on the floor so that my face was close to her level. Somewhere, someone had told me you had to get down on their level so it didn't seem like you were a big giant to them. A pain struck my chest when I realized it had been Logan.

Peyton didn't respond to my question. She just looked at her hands.

"Do you want to...watch TV? Read a book? Color?"

She lifted her shoulder the tiniest bit.

"How about we take a walk?"

She shook her head slightly. I blew out a hard breath. Weren't you supposed to talk to kids and get them to do stuff? If she were old enough to be more in control of her shifting, we could go for a long run; I know it helped me deal with the pain. But she'd been spontaneously shifting as she dealt with the stress of everything. She was still in that childhood phase of being a shifter where you couldn't control it easily, and when it happened spontaneously, it was the result of an extreme situation. Like finding out your parents were dead.

"Do you have any homework?"

"We don't get homework," she mumbled.

It took me a second to work out what she'd said. "You have to get homework. All kids get homework."

"We don't."

I narrowed my eyes at her. Even in kindergarten, I was pretty sure there was homework. I'd have to...my first instinct was to talk to Logan about it. But obviously, I couldn't do that. I guess I'd have to talk to the teacher. Whatever homework she might have had would have been due days ago; before all this. How much school had she missed so far? Lord. How in the world was I going to do this?

I got up and went to the kitchen. My half-finished beer sat on the counter, slightly warm by then, and I guzzled it down; it wasn't strong enough to deal with the day I'd been having. *How much have I had to drink so far this morning?* I rubbed at my face, looking at the cans piled in the recycle bin. *When was the last time I'd emptied it? How many days' worth of drinking was that from? What day is this?*

My eyes burned and my head felt light and spun a bit, just the way I liked it to. *Has the kid eaten yet today?*

"You hungry?" I called into the living room. No answer. "Peyton. Are you hungry?" When she didn't answer again, my anger flared. *This kid had better start listening to me.* I stormed into the living room. "Hey! I asked if you were hungry, and when I ask you a question, you need to answer it, okay?"

She looked at me and her lip quivered. She shook her head.

"Fine." I stomped back into the kitchen. What was I supposed to do with a kid who didn't talk and wouldn't do anything? She was supposed to be getting into therapy; my own therapist had suggested that, but the sessions hadn't started yet. In the meantime, I was losing my mind trying to get her to do anything at all. What six-year-old didn't even want to watch TV?

A little voice in the back of my head told me, *one who just lost her parents, you asshole.*

Yeah. I wasn't cut out for this. I was failing her already and it was making us both miserable. It'd been days since the funeral—and that meant it'd been days since we were left there, alone, in her parents' house. She obviously didn't want to be there with me and, truth be told, I didn't really want to be there with her, either. I wanted my own house. My own shit. My own space that wasn't full of memories and chick decorations. *God, what a nightmare it would be to have a wife,* I thought. I couldn't take it. I'd never marry. But, I'd never planned to have kids, either, and look how that worked out.

My head swung to the side as someone knocked on the

door. People had been dropping off food and stopping by. The food wasn't bad, but I hated drop-bys. Who just showed up and didn't call first? Rude. We weren't expecting anyone, and I was tempted to ignore it. But after the knocking came again, Peyton got up and went to the door.

"I'll get it," I said. Kids weren't supposed to answer the door, were they?

I opened it to see someone vaguely familiar standing on the front steps. She must have been at the funeral or something.

"Yeah?" I said.

"Hi, um, I'm Jessie?"

I narrowed my eyes at her. "Is that a question?"

She clenched her jaw. "I'm Jessie."

"Well, what do you want? I have things to do."

"You...told me to come today..."

I tried to remember. Why in the world would I have told her to come over? I mean, she was a hot piece of ass, but... "What for?"

"I'm the nanny?"

I managed to keep myself from rolling my eyes. Why did people insist on making statements into questions?

"The nanny," I repeated. Then I recalled a moment at the funeral. Outside the bathroom. Right. "Yeah, okay. Come in then, I guess."

She walked in and looked around. I gestured toward Peyton in the living room.

"She's over there. If you can get her to talk or do anything, the job is yours." I went back to the kitchen and cracked another beer. I didn't want to make it obvious I was observing her, but I needed to know what was going on in there, so I stayed within earshot. It seemed like something a responsible parent would do. Not that I was neither responsible nor a parent.

I heard her soft voice speaking to Peyton. "Hi, I'm Jessie. I'm going to be spending some time with you, I hope. Maybe before and after school, to help out a little. Does that sound okay?"

I didn't hear Peyton respond. Of course she wouldn't. This Jessie girl had her work cut out for her.

"You're Peyton, right?"

I snorted. This girl wasn't sure of her own name or anyone else's.

"That's such a pretty name. Do you have a middle name?"

To my shock, I heard Peyton reply. "Rose. After my grandma."

"Oh, I love that name!" Jessie exclaimed. "Does that mean roses are your favorite flower?"

No response again. I smiled smugly.

"I love roses," she continued, "but do you know what I love even more? Tulips. Bright yellow and red tulips. They're so colorful and cheerful. I like to rub the soft petals between my fingers. Have you ever done that?"

Peyton either didn't answer or made a head gesture, but I

didn't know for sure. Staying in the kitchen wasn't going to work; I needed to see what was happening. I moved a few steps forward until I could peek into the living room. Jessie was kneeling down in front of Peyton, who still sat on the couch. *Yeah, I did that getting down to their level thing, too,* I thought. *Didn't help.*

Then she said, "This is a really hard time for you, isn't it?"

I almost laughed out loud. Was she serious? Of course it was!

But Peyton nodded sadly and said, "I miss Mommy and Daddy."

"I know you do, sweetheart. I'm sure Uncle Conner misses them, too. I know a lot of people loved your mom and dad, and everyone misses them."

"Did you know them?" Peyton asked.

"No, but I wish I had. My sister was friends with your mom. Her name is Nikki."

Peyton nodded. "She came over lots of times, and sometimes, she would paint my nails."

"She painted mine last night!" Jessie wiggled her pink nails at Peyton. "I'm not as good as she is, but maybe we could paint nails one day. Would you like that?"

Peyton nodded.

"What else do you like to do?"

Peyton gave a little shrug and didn't answer.

"Yeah, I get that," Jessie continued. "Nothing seems fun anymore, does it?"

Peyton shook her head and a tear ran down her cheek. Great. She had been there, what, twenty minutes? And already, she was making the kid cry. I was about to walk in there and put an end to it. But then Peyton did something. She leaned forward and nestled her head into Jessie. She started to cry and Jessie rubbed her back and spoke softly to her. I couldn't hear what she said and that aggravated me. What were you supposed to say to a crying kid?

After a few minutes, they got up. Peyton stuck her hand right in Jessie's as she slid off the couch. I thought they would come to find me, but instead, they walked down the hall and turned into Peyton's room. I inched closer to listen in.

Peyton was showing her around, telling her about her toys and stuffed animals. Actually talking. And then I heard something I couldn't even believe. Jessie must've done something with a stuffed animal; I don't know what, but it involved a goofy voice. What it did to Peyton was magic. She laughed. She actually laughed.

I shrugged and went back to the living room with my beer and sat down. In under an hour, Jessie had done what I'd tried to do for days. What a fuck up I was. I had no clue. I would've messed this kid up pretty good, though. Made sure she had all sorts of issues like me. Made sure she grew up drunk and miserable. Like me.

I sat for a while, hating myself, and both despising and loving Jessie at the same time. Either the pills or the alcohol —or the combination of both—started to kick in and my eyes drooped. I might have slept for a whole hour or two the night before. I had to take sleep when it came, and if it was coming, then I was going to get every minute I could.

I went to Peyton's door and knocked on the frame. They were engrossed in some game and both looked over at me.

"You can start now," I muttered.

In a daze, I padded off to my room, which was actually Logan and Alaina's, flopped onto the bed and passed out.

7

JESSIE

"What is this one's name?" I asked Peyton, holding up a doll with long, pink hair.

"Strawberry. Mommy named her." Her face fell and she let the doll fall to the ground. She looked at the carpet.

"Do you want to have Strawberry come and play with *this* doll?' I held up another one.

Peyton shook her head and tears ran down her cheeks.

"Hey." I was sitting on the floor and she stood in front of me. I took both her hands in mine. "You can be sad. Be mad. Be whatever you want to be. It's okay. You can cry whenever you need to."

Her little chest had started hitching. "But—Uncle Conner—doesn't like it—"

My chest squeezed, and I almost cried myself.

"Can I tell you a secret?" I whispered. I moved closer to her, and she tilted her head down to me. "I don't think Uncle Conner knows what to do when you cry. He doesn't know how to be a daddy yet, and this is hard for him, too. We have to try to remember that, even when he's being mean, okay?"

She nodded and wiped her cheeks.

"Don't ever be afraid to cry and let your emotions out," I told her. "Especially not when you're with me. Okay?"

She nodded again.

"Are you in kindergarten?"

Peyton nodded.

"Do you like your teacher?"

"She's nice."

"That's good. What's the best part of school?"

Peyton thought for a moment. "Recess."

I chuckled. "That was my favorite, too. And gym. I liked to run around."

"Me, too."

"What games do you like to play?"

"Tag. I'm good at tag."

"Oh, that sounds fun. We'll have to play sometime. Would you like that?"

She nodded.

I was relieved. In all my training to be a teacher, there had been plenty of child psychology courses and instruction on how to connect with young children. If I did end up teaching one day, at least I knew the techniques I studied worked. Peyton seemed to have no trouble talking to me. I wasn't sure, though, how much was due to my asking the right questions and how much was due to her having such a difficult uncle to live with. If I had been in her place, I might open up to the first person who didn't snap at me, too.

Hours later, Conner stumbled out of his bedroom and stood in the doorway of Peyton's room. His t-shirt was crumpled and his shorts were hanging a little too low on his hips. Even like that, with his scruffy, week-old beard and tousled hair, he still looked hot. Nikki was right about that. I didn't mind the look of him. It was everything else about him that drove me mad.

"You guys okay?" he asked.

"Yeah, we're great," I said.

Peyton looked at him, wide-eyed.

"You okay?" he asked, looking directly at her.

She nodded and inched closer to me.

"You hungry?" he asked.

Peyton nodded again. He walked away; to the kitchen, I assumed, and I stood.

"I'm going to talk to Uncle Conner for just a minute, okay? I'll be right back."

Peyton resumed our game by herself.

Enough hours had passed that I was getting hungry, too. I wasn't sure what the plan was, how long I would be there, or anything, really. I found him in the kitchen, standing in front of the open fridge with a beer in one hand and a bottle of whiskey on the table.

"So, I was just wondering...what's the plan, here?"

"Leftovers." He didn't look at me. "People keep bringing trays of food over. We have way more than we can eat."

"I mean for me. How long do you want me to stay, and when do you want me come by to stay with Peyton?"

"Oh." He closed the fridge and turned to me. "Um. She has school in the mornings. So, I guess before school and after school?"

"Do you want me to come every day or just on school days? When do you need me?"

"Whenever I work."

"And when is that?"

He pointed to a calendar hanging on the wall. Beside it, a piece of paper was taped up. I glanced at it. It listed a number of days off for bereavement, but I didn't see any sort of work schedule.

"So, you don't need me the next few weeks? You're not working, according to this."

"Just be here every day. Before school. After school. Weekends. Whatever the usual wage is, I'll add 15%."

I had no idea what the usual wage was, but I threw out a number that seemed within reason.

"Fine," he replied. "Well, are you hungry?"

"Um, sure, I could eat, if you don't mind."

He turned and took a few steps, reaching up into a

cabinet for plates. But then I saw that he was stumbling, barely walking straight or standing still.

"Are you drunk?" I accused.

He set the plates down hard. "What if I am? What are you going to do? Call the police? I know all the cops around these parts."

"No, I just...well, I'll stay then. To make sure Peyton is okay."

"Yeah." He picked up a plate and glared at me. "You do that."

Maybe I should have asked for a higher rate for dealing with his bullshit. "Look, I know you're going through a lot right now, but that doesn't give you an excuse to be so mean. People might actually like you if you were nicer." I turned and went back into Peyton's room, but when a half hour had passed and there didn't seem to be any food coming, I went back to the kitchen. I found Conner passed out at the table, hunched over his bent arms, his face smeared across the wood surface. Food sat on the counter in plastic containers, unopened.

I searched through the fridge, pulling out several other items and began to heat up some of the leftovers. He must've woken from the noise or smell because as I was setting plates on the dining room table, he sat up.

"I think you'd better eat something," I told him before going off to get Peyton and have her wash her hands.

When we returned to the dining room, his plate was

already half empty. He couldn't even have waited for us? I shook my head, but we sat with him anyway. Peyton and I ate together; she was quiet, though, and it was clear she didn't want to speak in front of her uncle.

After dinner, I rinsed the plates and loaded them into the dishwasher. Conner stretched out on the couch while I gave Peyton a bath and put on her pajamas.

"What do you and Uncle Conner usually do at bedtime?"

She shrugged and climbed into bed.

"Do you read a story or say a prayer?"

She shook her head.

"Anything like that at all?"

She shook her head again. "Do you want to read a story?"

She nodded enthusiastically. I picked out a book and sat beside her on the bed to read. By the time I was at the end, her eyes were drooping and her head drifted forward, so I laid her down and tucked her in tight.

"I'm really glad that I get to spend time with you," I whispered and kissed her on the forehead.

"Me, too," she replied, smiling and closing her eyes.

8

CONNER

I woke up somewhere in the dim hours of the morning. My heart raced, and it took a moment for me to recall where I was: in the living room in my brother's house. Not lying in a ditch in the deserts of Afghanistan. I breathed slowly, using the exercises my therapist taught me. When I had calmed my heart and anxiety, I rubbed my eyes so that I could read my watch.

4 am.

I jumped up. I'd slept enough that I was sober again, and now that I realized where I was, the night started to come back.

Where was Peyton? Where was Jessie? I glanced outside; Jessie's car was gone. I walked quietly down the hall and peeked into Peyton's room. She was in there, fast asleep. In the kitchen, the leftovers had been cleaned up, neatly put away in the refrigerator, and the dishes had been rinsed loaded into the dishwasher. The bathroom smelled faintly of Peyton's strawberry shampoo, and a damp towel hung on the back of the door. I noticed Jessie had left her jasmine hand lotion on the counter and I slowly inhaled the sweet scent. *Damn, she's beautiful.* I had to put that out of my mind, though. She worked for me, and it wasn't appropriate. But I couldn't deny that my inner bear rumbled at the thought of her lying beneath me.

I tried to shake off the thought and go back through the day, but there were a lot of holes. One thing I knew for sure is that I'd been a little harsh on Jessie, and she didn't deserve it. I'd tried to get dinner going, but when I'd passed out at the kitchen table, she had picked up the slack for me. She'd gotten Peyton cleaned up and into bed. She'd been there all day. I didn't know if she'd had any plans or other things she needed to do; frankly, I hadn't cared enough to ask. I'd been more concerned with drinking my feelings away. *What a selfish prick you've been,* I told myself.

With that realization came another, and a lump began to form in my throat. Jessie reminded me of family; of home. My mother was like her, always making sure Logan and I had food to eat—good food, too—making sure we had clean clothes and school supplies, making sure we'd actually done our homework and had managed to shower. She took care of my father, too. He worked long hours to provide for us, and she did everything she could to support that, whether it was pressing his shirts and making him coffee early in the morning before he left for the day or taking dinner to him when his hours grew long. Mom had that quiet, gentle, caring nature that I missed. And I saw it in Jessie.

My family was mostly gone by that point. My father died years earlier; heart attack, of course. He'd always worked too hard and hadn't shifted and run enough. My mother was so ill, she needed around-the-clock help, so a live-in nurse took care of her. Logan was dead. And Me? I might as well have been. I was worthless to everyone. How was it that I, the most unreliable of all the Griffin men, was the one left standing? It should have been any of them but me.

Logan, too, had the same dedication as my father, yet he'd managed to temper it a bit with some of my mother's nurturing. He was the kind of dad who woke up early on Saturday mornings after working all week and made pancakes before mowing the lawn. Or who took his daughter out for ice cream in the evening so that Alaina could have time to herself or with friends. He should have been the one to live, not me. Those croc assholes should have killed *me*.

I got up and took my meds, hoping they would lift the weight off my chest. It was so hard to breathe those days. As I set my empty glass on the kitchen counter, I looked at my printed work schedule hanging by the calendar. My boss had told me to take as much time as I needed, and at that point, I think I'd taken quite enough. I wanted to know what was going on with the investigation. I had to find a way to be active and do something about it. Sitting there all day only made things worse, and now that I had Jessie, I didn't have to.

It was well after 5. I remember telling Jessie to come before school, but I didn't think I gave her a specific time. Peyton got on the bus at 8:30, so what time would she arrive; seven, maybe? It would be at least another hour before she was there and about an hour before Peyton woke up. I changed my clothes and headed down to the basement, where Logan and Alaina had built a pretty sweet home gym. Most shifters found the need to work out hard to keep the animal instincts under control, and I was no different.

I spent an entire hour pushing my body to the limit: pushups, sit ups, pull ups, weighted squats, thrusters, bench presses; anything I could do with a barbell, I did it. I rowed and biked. I went for a three-mile run on their treadmill. After an hour, I was wet with sweat, but felt better. I had to remind myself that what my therapist said was true: exercise helped with depression and anxiety, and even kept PTSD tempered, somewhat. It was like all those emotions were somehow stored in my muscles, and when I worked out, it forced them all out of me.

I took a quick shower, brewed a fresh pot of coffee and started to make breakfast. As I was cracking eggs, there was a knock on the door. I opened it to see Jessie.

"I'll get you a key today," I said, stepping aside to let her in.

"Oh. Sure, yeah, that would be great."

"Did you eat? I'm making eggs, and there's coffee."

She gave me a surprised expression. "Coffee would be great."

I poured her a mug and set it down. "There's milk and sugar and everything." I drank mine black and took a long sip as I gestured toward the cabinet where the sugar was stored.

"I drink it black, thanks."

I raised an eyebrow at her, and she gave me the same look back.

"What?"

"You look...surprisingly well rested," she said.

"You mean sober?"

She lifted a shoulder. "You were looking at me weird, too. What was that all about?"

"I'm just surprised you drink black coffee. I figured you'd have it extra light, extra sweet, for whatever reason." I shrugged and began to whip the eggs with a fork. "I'm going to work today."

"I guess we surprised each other this morning, then. I thought I'd find you passed out on the couch and would have to poke you with a stick to get you to wake up."

I wondered if she meant it to be some kind of joke; some kind of hint that she knew about me with the whole cliché of poking a sleeping a bear. But she couldn't know. Jessie wasn't a shifter and neither was her sister. I'd given them both a good sniff to make sure. If they knew, that would mean that Alaina, or possibly Logan, would have told them. They wouldn't have dared to break the shifter code and tell someone who didn't need to know, would they?

No, that was crazy. Jessie was definitely not the type to be okay with the concept of bear shifters. If she had any idea, she'd never set foot inside that house. *Not only is she working for me, she's a full-blooded human. Just one more reason to keep her at a distance,* I thought. I knew shifters that went through the process of telling their human girlfriends or boyfriends the truth. There was a point when that would be acceptable and eventually, necessary if you were going to marry or have children with a non-shifter. But that conversation terrified me. It was the reason I'd never even considered dating a non-shifter. How would you say something like that in a way that didn't make you seem crazy or scare them out of their minds? It wasn't something I didn't have the skill to pull off.

"Peyton's bus comes at 8:30," I said. "I have to get dressed."

Jessie nodded and set down her coffee before going toward Peyton's room. I heard them talking; it was muffled but sounded friendly. Cheerful. By the time I headed back into the kitchen in my uniform, Peyton sat at the table, fully dressed, almost smiling, and Jessie was braiding her hair. The kid looked cuter than I'd seen her look since I had to start dressing her; she looked like she did when Alaina had gotten her ready for school. My heart ached, but I forced a smile.

"You look very nice today," I said.

"I like your uniform, Uncle Conner."

Jessie nodded. "Very handsome and official looking."

Was she making fun of me? I looked away from them and returned my attention to the eggs I'd been scrambling in a bowl.

"I can make those if you like," Jessie said. "I wasn't sure what you had planned there."

"I've got it." I dumped the mixture into the pan and pushed them around over slow heat until they were fluffy. I knew how to make scrambled eggs, for Pete's sake. Did she think I was a total idiot?

I scooped eggs onto three plates, and we sat at the small kitchen table to eat. That was how Logan and Alaina did it. Smaller, faster meals like breakfast and lunch were at the kitchen table, but dinner was in the dining room. Didn't matter to me, but I was trying to keep things as much the same for Peyton as they had been.

"Would you like to say a prayer?" Jessie asked Peyton.

Peyton's eyes widened. "I don't know how."

"I can say one," Jessie offered.

I bowed my head obediently. That was different. We had never really prayed. I wasn't opposed, though. We needed whatever help anyone would give, God included. After she prayed, we ate quietly at first, then Jessie started asking questions.

What would Peyton do in school today? What was her favorite subject? What was my job like? What time did I usually get home? What time did Peyton get home? What should she plan for dinner? Did anything need to be done in the house before she left or when she returned later?

I had answered the best I could, but by the time we were finished eating, I couldn't think anymore. I was used to rolling out of bed, guzzling down some coffee and waking up on my drive to work. The entire process of getting a kid up and eating breakfast together—with Jessie—would take some getting used to.

After we ate, Jessie automatically got up and cleared the table, scraping any bits of food off before rinsing the plates, then put them in the dishwasher. By the time I came back out of the bedroom with my shoes and gear, Peyton already had her backpack on, shoes tied, and was waiting at the door. I was impressed, but then I noticed Peyton begin to cry. Jessie was crouching down, talking to her.

"What's going on?" I asked.

Jessie stood and gave me a sad smile. "It's just a little hard going back, is all."

I hadn't even stopped to think about the fact that this was Peyton's first day back since everything happened. The days had been blurring together. How many had passed since Logan's death? Ten? Fifteen? It was my first day returning to work, too, but was Peyton ready to get back into the routine? *Should I be sending her to school today or not? I wondered. I can't make decisions like that. I don't know what's best for a child. I'll see what Jessie's thoughts are.*

"Do you think...?"

She put her hands on Peyton's shoulders. "We're going to be extra brave today and tell the teacher if it gets too hard, right?"

Peyton nodded and wiped away her tears, and Jessie wrapper her arms around her, giving her a squeeze.

I knelt down and gave her an awkward hug. "If you need anything, just tell Mrs. Robinson to call me on my cell, okay? Uncle Conner loves you."

She gave me a half-smile and nodded again.

We stood in the doorway until the bus turned the corner onto the road. With a final quick hug from each of us, Peyton took a deep breath and walked toward the end of the short driveway where the bus stopped.

Jessie waved enthusiastically, and I held up a hand as the bus drove off. When she turned back to us, she had tears in her eyes. "Poor little thing. This must be so hard for her. I can't imagine."

"Yeah," I muttered, running my fingers through my hair. "Guess I'm off, too."

"Do you want me to pack some of the leftovers for you to take for lunch?"

I blinked at her. In that moment, I had the thought, *I*

haven't just hired a nanny, I've hired a wife... My chest constricted and the air around me became thin as my bear threatened to make an appearance. "Oh no, thanks, I'll just get something later."

"Then, I guess I'm off until after school. Do you have a key, or...?"

"Oh yeah." I went to the junk drawer in the kitchen and pulled out the extra key, which was on a ring with a plastic Disney World keychain. They must've gotten it when they went there as a family the summer before. I swallowed hard and handed it to her. "Just use this for now until I get another made."

She tucked the key into her purse. "Hey." She smiled at me with her hand on the door. "Good luck today. I know this must be hard for you, too."

I nodded and watched her leave. I stood there for a moment, the emotions rushing over me. Tears pricked my eyes, but I refused to allow them to flow. I had work to do; whatever thoughts or feelings I had toward Jessie, I had to ignore them.

She was Peyton's nanny, and nothing more.

9

CONNER

As I drove to work, I tried to focus. I kept having flashes of that morning and the night before cycle through my head. And each time, a wave of pain and longing came.

I could not let Jessie in. I could not get close to her. When I got too close to people, they died.

That was why I kept my clan only as close as I had to, and they didn't get inside my head more than our mental clan link would allow. Even then, I'd worked hard to build my own walls. They couldn't get in. No one could.

I pulled into the station, hoping no one would make a big deal about the fact that I was back. That was precisely why I hadn't told my supervisor I was coming in that day. I took a deep breath and headed inside.

As soon as I walked in, three heads snapped in my direction. There was a chorus of "Conner!" I nodded and headed upstairs to my supervisor's office. His door was partly opened, but I knocked and waited for his response.

"Yeah?" he called.

I pushed the door open and stepped in. "Hey."

"Oh." He sat up straighter and set down his pen. "You're suited up. You working today?"

I nodded. "Any updates?"

"On?"

I had to remind myself that my brother's rescue wasn't the only mission my team had had that month. It might have been the only one that mattered to me, but my boss would've had plenty of other things going on while I was out.

"Thought maybe you'd heard from the police on my brother's case."

He nodded. "We've been working with them as much as possible, but they haven't needed us. I guess they have all the evidence there was, and now they're following up on leads. Mason would have more information; I'm sure he can give you a better update."

I nodded. I hadn't been in contact with my clan much; not that they hadn't tried to reach out, but I wasn't up for visiting or talking with anyone. I hadn't even wanted updates on the case until that day. But once I'd decided to get back to it and get something done, I wanted all the details.

"I think I'll head over to the police station," I said. "See what's going on, and if I can be of any use."

"Sure, man. Whatever you need."

My eye twitched. "What I need is to find the bastard that killed my brother and his wife, and to get back to work so that I can have some semblance of normalcy again."

"That's a good plan. You just tell me how I can help you do that."

"By not acting like I need special treatment."

He nodded and sized me up. "I get that; I do. But I also need to know that you're up for any mission I send you on. I can't have you going out there before you're ready and letting the team down."

My hands curled into fists. "I'm ready."

"Then if you don't give me a reason to question that, I'll see to it that things resume as they were before you left. Go on now and head over to the precinct. Report back with any updates."

"Thank you, sir." I turned and left, my anger slowly fading.

When I pulled up to the police station, I saw Mason's car. At first, I was relieved, but a shot of anxiety rushed through me as I parked. He might make a thing of this. I hoped he was smarter than that, but I'd been kind of MIA lately.

I nodded at the officer at reception and walked over to Mason's desk. "Hey."

He looked up, and the shock was obvious on his face.

"Conner." He set down the papers he'd been looking at and turned to me. "Back to it?"

"I'm here for an update."

"Sure thing." He pulled open a file cabinet and took out a folder. "I wish I had more to tell you. It's been infuriatingly slow going."

I sat in the chair opposite of him. "What can you tell me?"

"Besides knowing it was a croc, not much else. The swamp eliminated most of the evidence, including scent. It had been raining the night it happened, which weakened the scent around the area and washed out prints. We've been carefully questioning all those we could, but you know how it is when it's a shifter thing."

I did. Resources were limited and things had to be done more carefully. Part of the police force didn't have all the details, and they never would.

"What's being done about it?" I asked. "We had the incident with crocs killing panthers, and now this. How much further does it have to go? What do we even have a conclave for if we're never going to get them involved?"

"We are. I'm not sure exactly why Owen didn't think the panther killings were worth getting them involved over. If it were up to me, I would have, but it wasn't. I guess he thought we'd handled it."

"Or his pride got in the way," I added.

Mason shrugged. Owen was a good guy and a great

leader. I probably shouldn't have said it, but dammit, that was what the conclave was for—adjudicating shifter-on-shifter crimes—and if he thought we should handle it on our own, then I'd have to talk to him myself.

"Like I said," Mason continued. "We are going to them. We had a meeting the other night. We did text you about it."

I pressed my lips together. I'd gotten the text, then ignored it in my drunken haze.

"Well, we discussed it," Mason said, "And we are going to them to get them involved. The crocs have been running amuck and causing too much trouble."

"Good. I want them out." I punched my open palm. "*All* of them."

"It's not that simple, and you know it. We can't just demand their removal."

"I don't see how we can't. First, they attacked Owen's girl, then they went after the panther population, now they're murdering bears? Have many more innocent bystanders have to die before someone steps up and does something about these assholes? They act like they own the 'Glades, and they won't stop until they do."

"Keep your voice down," Mason whispered. "There are humans here. I hear you. I wish we could, but they have just as much right to be here as any other shifter group."

I clenched my teeth and kept my voice low but hard. "No other shifter groups are killing."

"And that's why we're going to the conclave. Talk to Owen. You should really be there when he goes."

I nodded. "Yeah. I want to make sure this is taken care of and not just sugarcoated."

Mason glared at me. "Do you honestly think Owen doesn't care about what happened? Do you think that just because Logan and Alaina weren't part of our clan, that he cares less about them? He doesn't, Conner, and you need to get past your own pain long enough to see that. He's doing everything he can. He's going out of his mind trying to solve this, and so is the rest of the clan. If you'd come around once in a while, you'd know that."

"Been a little busy."

"I know. And we're all hurting for you, but we can't help you if you shut yourself out. Talk to us. Let us know what's going on with you. Let us help you."

I slammed my palms on his desk and pushed the chair back as I stood. "I don't need your fucking help; I don't need *anyone's* help. I'll handle my shit the way I handle it. As for the investigation, let me know the second you have something. That is, if you actually decide to do your job anytime soon."

Mason's face hardened, and he set his jaw as I turned from him. I slammed the door on my way out and peeled out of the parking lot so fast, my tires spit gravel.

10

JESSIE

"So," Nikki said, curling up on the couch with a pint of ice cream, "I've noticed you haven't been complaining about Conner as much lately."

I set my purse down and sat beside her, then reached for her container of chocolate peanut butter swirl and took a generous spoonful. "I guess it's getting better. Peyton's doing well in school. I think she needed the distraction, honestly. And Conner...I don't know. I mean, he pays me well and all. But I really like Peyton. We're getting closer, and I think she feels comfortable telling me things she won't tell him. I guess that's a good thing?"

"It is." Nikki took the container back. "She needs someone to talk to. I'm sure you remind her of her mom in some ways. You're there every day, making sure she gets to school, does her homework, eats, bathes and all that. She needs that sort of caregiver, and I don't think Conner is able to be that yet. Do you?"

"I've tried to make suggestions to guide him. Like, 'Hey Conner, why don't you and Peyton go wait for the bus at the end of the driveway together?' Little ways he can spend time with her and show her he cares. But he usually just says that he wants to do things how they've always been done. I guess he's trying to keep things as consistent as possible."

Nikki sighed. "He's clueless. And it might be doing more damage. Things will never be the same for Peyton. How can he not get that?"

"I don't know. I'm trying to reach through to him. He needs time, too, and I get that. But I think we're getting somewhere. It's been, what, almost three months now, and he's finally starting to treat me like a person instead of hired help. He's been...nicer. It's been slow going, but he's just a tiny bit nicer every day." I took the ice cream container back and stuffed another spoonful in my mouth.

"Good. He's seeing someone, isn't he?"

"What?" My heart lurched, and I was surprised at my reaction. "Oh, I don't know. Is he? He hasn't brought anyone home or mentioned anyone."

Nikki raised her eyebrows and set down the container. "Whoa. Okay, what did you think I meant? Seeing someone like a girlfriend?"

My face felt hot, and I tried to play it off like nothing. "Isn't that what you meant?"

"No. I meant seeing a therapist. To deal with all this."

"Oh. He said something about that, yeah. Peyton's been going every week and they have a session coming up where he'll be going with her. I think that will be good for them both."

Nikki sat back and crossed her arms. "What I really want to talk about is the way you reacted when you thought he was dating someone."

"I was just surprised because he never said anything, and he doesn't seem...ready for that."

"You have feelings for him," she accused.

"I do not!" But even I heard the panic in my voice. "He's my *boss*, Nikki."

"Exactly. Your super-hot boss who pays you to basically be his wife."

"He does not! I'm there for Peyton, and that's it."

Nikki gave a smug smile. "Are you still applying at other places?"

"No," I admitted. "But only because it's been going really well. Like I said, the pay is good, and things are getting better, and I...I feel like they need me."

"Oh, god." She shook her head.

"What!"

"You totally want him."

"I do not." I took the ice cream and refused to give it back until I'd finished it off.

"I don't blame you. I knew him before all this happened, and he was a great guy. He'd actually be good for you."

I shook my head. "He is not my type *at all*, and again, he's my boss. I don't want to get mixed up in something like that, and I think it would confuse Peyton."

"So, you *have* thought about it."

I let my head fall back and growled in frustration. "Don't make me say it."

"Say it!" Just like she used to do when we were kids, she started tickling my ribs—which I *hated*.

"Okay! Okay!" I squealed. "I'll admit it! He's fucking hot!"

She sat back down with a satisfied smile. "I knew it."

"Doesn't change anything."

"Maybe not. But maybe it will. You never know."

"I just wish I knew how to help them both better. I'm a teacher, not a psychologist. I just feel like I could be doing more."

"I wouldn't worry about that." Nikki patted my hand. "They both have therapists for that, and it's not your job. You're there to take care of Peyton. And maybe Conner a little, too, but who's keeping track?"

I rolled my eyes. "Nannies do that. They take care of the household."

"Not as much as you do. You're like his housekeeper and

nanny in one. I mean, it's like you're his wife already, so you might as well sleep with the guy and get the full benefit."

"God, would you let it go already?" I slapped her arm.

She laughed. "Just saying."

"Well, I'm done with this conversation." I got up and threw out the ice cream container, then dropped the spoon in the sink. "I'm off to bed."

"Have sweet dreams!" she called to me. Then added, "About Conner!"

I tried to put her words out of my head as I dressed for bed, but I couldn't. Most of them were true, and that was why the whole thing bothered me so much. I *did* like him. He'd become a lot more pleasant to be around over the last few weeks, and I began to actually look forward to seeing him. I tried to talk to him and take care of him the best I could, which, yes, did involve more housework than I initially signed up for, but it was my choice. I had student loans to pay, and the extra cash he offered for doing his laundry and mopping the floor made it well worth it.

But there were days, especially when I folded his boxer briefs and tucked them away in his drawer, that things felt a little...intimate. Maybe too much so. I felt like a wife in some ways: taking care of Peyton, preparing dinner, looking out for Conner, cleaning up...but for as much as I did around the house, any emotional connection with Conner was nonexistent. He didn't talk to me like a girlfriend, or even like a close friend. More like a coworker that he spent a lot of time with and got to know by proxy.

And of course, there was zero physical interaction between us. He didn't even seem to like it if I casually touched his arm as we spoke. The first time he'd yanked his arm back from me, I'd learned to give him more personal space. I didn't know if he just didn't like being touched or it was related to his PTSD, but I wasn't about to ask.

It's just a job, I told myself as I slid into bed. *Just a job that I'm doing for the time being.* I wanted to make sure Peyton would be okay and that they were settled. Maybe one day, I'd move on and find something in the teaching field, but right then, I was happy to take care of them and feel needed.

11

CONNER

From the moment I woke up, I couldn't deny the date. As much as I tried to put it out of my head and not think about it, I couldn't. There was a notification on my phone. It was marked there on the family calendar hanging in the kitchen.

That morning, I hadn't said much at breakfast. Jessie had made pancakes, but I'd only been able to get down a bite. When she asked, I assured her they tasted fine and that my stomach was just upset. Of course, then she'd gone off to get me some antacids and a glass of water. I drank it, chewed the chalky tablets and thanked her, but I knew it wouldn't be enough to quell the wrenching ache in my gut; it was the familiar, deep down in my bones, surging through every part of me ache that nothing would fix.

Except maybe some vodka—and I made sure I had plenty around for the occasion. I'd been doing a little better, drinking less week by week. But that night? Not a fucking chance.

I checked in with Mason, as was my normal morning ritual. As usual, he answered my text with, "Nothing new. Sorry." All their leads had dried up. They were useless, as far as I was concerned.

The conclave wasn't much better. When we'd gone to talk with them, they were deeply concerned. They had representatives in the area who would be doing their own investigation, but they hadn't accomplished much, either. It seemed that everyone was content to just let it go and move on with life. Everyone except me and Peyton. We were stuck in the misery of missing two people no one seemed to give a damn about.

I made it through the day in a daze. The only mission we'd had during my shift was a simple one: rescuing a boy who got himself stuck in a tree. I watched as Jamari climbed the ladder to bring him down and made sure the EMTs were on their way to treat his wounds.

When I got home that evening, Peyton had already finished her homework and was playing a game with Jessie while dinner was in the oven. Even if I didn't think I could eat, I appreciated how good it smelled. I'd gladly pay extra if it meant she'd keep making amazing meals like she had been. They greeted me with a hello, but I walked straight to the refrigerator and pulled out a beer, gulping it down before Jessie came into the kitchen.

"I have some chicken baking," she said.

I nodded and poured myself a drink with a lot of vodka and a splash of orange juice. "I don't think I'm going to eat, but thank you."

"Oh." With concerned eyes, she watched me down a huge gulp of the drink, then top it off with more vodka. "Are you okay? You seem...out of it today."

"I'm fine."

Did she not bother to check the calendar? Did she have no idea what day it was?

"Well, I'll let you know when dinner is ready in case you change your mind."

I nodded and took my drink to the bedroom so I could be alone. I'm sure she judged me or thought I was an asshole, but I didn't care. I turned on the TV and flipped though the channels until I found something that occupied enough of my attention.

Jessie knocked on my door a little later. "Dinner is ready. Do you want to come eat?"

"Nah," I muttered.

"Do you want me to bring you a plate?"

"No, I'm good."

I heard her walk away and felt a twinge of guilt. It wasn't her fault; apparently, she didn't realize what was going on. *Whatever,* I breathed, swigging back another gulp.

I hadn't been paying much attention to the time, so I was surprised it had gotten so late when Jessie knocked again.

"Is it okay if Peyton comes in to say goodnight?" Jessie asked.

I groaned but pulled myself out of bed, stumbling to the door, and opened it. Peyton stood there, looking a little shy. I bent down to hug her and kiss the top of her head.

"Night, honey," I slurred.

She answered with a sweet little, "Night," and turned to take Jessie's hand. They walked toward Peyton's bedroom, and I closed the door.

Seeing them walk away like that gave me a sudden pang of loneliness. What the fuck was I doing? I wanted to be with them, but more than that, I wanted to be part of the relationship they were building together; not just the third-wheel drunk uncle who couldn't take care of his niece.

As wasted as I was, it hadn't dulled the pain; it flared in me hot and demanding. I heard the door to Peyton's bedroom close and the thought of Jessie leaving, of being alone in the house with Peyton sleeping, choked me. I struggled to suck in a breath and hurried to open my door.

Jessie turned to me and we looked at each other for a long moment.

"Um, did she get to bed okay?" I didn't know what else to say.

"Yeah, she's okay, I think. We talked some."

My eyebrows drew together. "Is something wrong?"

She glanced toward Peyton's door and I realized we were probably talking a little too loudly. She motioned for me to join her in the living room, and I waited for her to turn around before I moved down the hall so that she wouldn't have to see me stumble.

I sat beside her on the couch and waited for her to speak.

"Peyton was a little sad today because it's her dad's birthday. I'd seen it weeks ago on the calendar, but I thought it was better not to bring it up. I wasn't sure what it would be like for either of you, to be honest, and I didn't want to make it worse. But, this morning she told me and said she was going to draw him a picture at school."

"Did she?" I asked, my voice breaking and my throat thick. She had noticed after all; she'd known the whole time.

"She did. It was very sweet. She was..." Jessie scratched her neck and looked down.

"What?"

"She wanted to take it to his grave today. But it seemed like you needed some space, and I didn't want to bother you with it. I didn't think it was really my place to take her, either, so I said that maybe we could talk to you and see if you could go this week some time."

I put my head in my hands, but it was the wrong move. A wave of nausea rushed over me and I hurried to the kitchen; there's no way I would have made it to the bathroom. I threw up in the trash and when I lifted my head again, I found Jessie holding a glass of water out to me.

"Thanks." I took it and drank it too fast.

"Do you want me to heat up some of the chicken? It can't be good for you to have been drinking all night on an empty stomach."

I wanted to hate her for it. I wanted to scream at her to get away from me and never come back. I wanted to stop her from caring. Instead, I nodded once, numbly, and sat hard at the kitchen table to watch her pull the food out of the fridge and prepare it for me. I ate slowly, and by the time I'd finished and she took my plate, I was already feeling a little more sober.

"Thank you," I said. "It definitely helped buffer the vodka."

She chuckled. "I guess that's good. Unless you were trying to numb your pain."

"That's what I'm always trying to do."

She gave me a sad smile. "I'm sorry that there's so much of it."

"Me, too." I looked at her for a long while, then dared to ask her what I'd been longing to. "Will you...stay a little while? I...I don't want to be alone right now."

She pulled her lower lip into her mouth. "Sure, I could stay for a little longer."

"Would you like a glass of wine?" I pulled a bottle of my favorite red from the cabinet.

"Are you sure you should...?"

I paused for a moment. "Yeah, you're probably right. Iced tea?"

"Perfect."

I poured two glasses and handed her one. I tapped mine to hers and said, "To the best nanny on the planet."

She smiled shyly and looked down. "Thanks. I don't really have any experience, so it's good to know that I've been helpful."

"You have been. I don't know what I'd do without you. I think it's pretty obvious that I have no idea what I'm doing."

"Kids aren't all that hard. You just have to be in the present with them."

"And I'm not." I walked into the living room and flopped down on the couch. She followed and sat beside me.

"You've been through a lot, and having Peyton is a big adjustment in your life. I haven't known you that long, but...I'm sure with your therapist and everything, you're making progress."

I laughed. "How could you possibly know that?"

"Well, honestly, I don't." She sighed. "I just...never know *what* to say to you. I'm certainly no therapist. I was taught how to connect with kids in school. But when it comes to men, I just don't—"

"I'm sure you were able to connect with boyfriends that you've had."

"I haven't really had any."

"Oh, come on," I said. "Don't do that innocent little

schoolgirl act where you pretend to be all pure and innocent."

Her face grew redder than I'd ever seen it. I felt the embarrassment like hot fire run up my chest. God, could I say anything right to her?

"I'm sorry," I said quickly. "I didn't mean...it's just that...you're so..."

"Naive?" she offered.

"That's not what I was going to say. Beautiful. Selfless. Caring. Surely, someone in your life noticed and tried to get close to you. You must've had boys falling all over you."

"I have had dates. And I guess I could've called a boy or two from high school 'boyfriends.' But I've never been in a long-term relationship. In college, I studied hard and was the boring girl who would rather read than party. Sorry. It's lame, I know."

"I'm just surprised that no one tried to ask you out."

She shrugged. "When you stay in your dorm room and don't go anywhere except class, you don't meet people easily. I only went on a few dates. But why are we talking about this?"

"I didn't mean to bring it up. It just illustrates my point that I can't effectively connect with not only kids, but anyone. I'm always putting my foot in my mouth."

She took a sip of iced tea and gave me a sympathetic smile. "Hey, don't worry about it."

"Sorry, I shouldn't have said anything. It was stupid." But at least then I knew she was single.

"How's today been?" she asked.

"Difficult. Mostly a blur."

"Does it help? To drink it away like that?"

"For a time. But it always fades. Then the pain is usually worse."

"Why do you do it?"

I gave a half smile. "I don't know what else to do."

"Is therapy helping? I'd think talking about it would make it better."

"Why do people always think that?" I challenged. "Talking about it makes it more real, and that usually makes it more painful. After therapy, the pain is so much worse."

"But doesn't it help in the long run?"

"Doesn't seem to."

"Then why do you keep going?"

"I don't know what else to do." I set down my glass and ran my fingers through my hair. "Therapy, medication, self-medication. What else is there?"

"Having fun, spending time with friends and family, finding a purpose in life."

"Purpose." I huffed. "Who on this planet has managed to find that?"

"Lots of people."

"Have you?"

She took a moment to respond. "Partially, I think. I got

into teaching because I wanted to change lives and help kids —that's a purpose. I'm trying to do that now with Peyton."

"Maybe that's my problem. I'm not living for much."

We continued to talk, getting deeper and deeper. Deeper than I had gone with anyone in a long time, including my therapist. By the time Jessie looked at her phone, it was already 5am.

"You know, maybe you should just stay," I offered. "You're going to need to get Peyton up and ready for school soon."

She started laughing. "Look at all these texts! I didn't plan on staying so long. My sister must be freaking out wondering where I am."

"No doubt. You're gonna be grounded, for sure."

She continued to laugh and put her hand on my arm as she doubled over. "You're probably right. I'm in deep shit."

Her touch sent a flood of warmth through me, driving my inner bear wild. I wanted to pull back, but I needed to feel her close. She stood and looked in my eyes and I held her gaze for a moment. Something in what I saw there made me inch closer to her. Before I stopped to think about it, I pressed my lips to hers.

She pulled back and gasped, blinking at me. "I'm sorry, I just...wasn't expecting that."

I walked past her toward the hall. "I'll set up the bed for you. I'll sleep on the couch."

I went to the bedroom and attempted to make things look somewhat tidy, trying to not to think about the kiss. I don't know why I'd done it, and I didn't know how to interpret her reaction.

She stood in the doorway, watching me as I picked up my dirty clothes and straightened the pillows.

"Sorry," I said. "It's a mess."

"Mine is messy, too."

"I doubt that."

She leaned against the doorframe and gave me a sly smile. "You know, I'm not as sweet and innocent as you think I am."

"No?" I walked back over to her. I stood just feet from her and considered my next move. It could have gone so many ways. But I had to know.

I took her face in my hands and kissed her again, harder this time, letting my desire for her be known. That time, she let me kiss her—and she even kissed me back. But then she put her hand on my chest and broke away, looking down and resting her head on my shoulder.

"Conner," she whispered. "This...isn't a good idea. Peyton's right in the next room, and I work for you. I just think it's better if we don't do this." She met my eyes, and she looked sorry.

I was sorry, too, and took two steps back. "Well, do you have everything you need?" I asked.

She nodded and bit her lip.

I nodded and gently shut the door. In the living room, I shook the blanket from its folded square and lay down, pulling it up over me. But as soon as I reclined, the wave rushed over me, so I sat back up and put my feet on the floor.

The anxiety hit me first; then, a wave of sadness. The loneliness burned hot, right beside the rejection, making the perfectly terrible end to a perfectly terrible day. I put my head in my hands and tried to breathe.

It worked for a while. My heart slowed, my throat relaxed; I felt like I could breathe again. Then, the memory of last year on this day came to the forefront of my mind: me, Conner and Alaina, out for a night of fun. Peyton had been home with a babysitter; it might have been Nikki, in fact. Even if things hadn't gone so wrong, Jessie still might have found her way into my life.

My recollections of last year mixed with the memories of the last hour and created a perfect storm in my heart. I felt more alone than I'd ever felt in my life. I'd taken a chance with Jessie—and things had gone terribly wrong. Who knew what would happen next. Maybe she'd quit. Maybe she'd hate me. Hell, maybe she'd even fall for me. I wasn't sure which option would be worse.

I wallowed in the pain for a while, letting the thoughts and emotions take their turns wreaking havoc on my mind. When it became too much, tears filled my eyes. I let them fall, wanting to be rid of them once and for all. Weren't women always saying to just cry it out and that a good cry was all they needed? Maybe there was something to that. So, I decided to take a chance and just give in.

I found myself sobbing and then a creak of floorboards caused me to look up. Jessie stood there watching me. I quickly wiped my eyes and swallowed my tears, burying my feelings; she couldn't see me like that.

"Conner, I'm so sorry," she whispered. She made her way over and sat beside me, putting her hand on my shoulder. "Did I...make things worse?"

"I'm fine," I said. "I was just thinking."

"It's okay." She rubbed my back, and it was as if her hand radiated comfort, rubbing circles of warmth to my soul.

The tears threatened to continue, but I swallowed them down.

"You can cry," she said, leaning in and speaking into my ear.

Her closeness and warmth made it almost impossible for me to keep the tears from falling. I blinked fast and looked up, hoping they'd dry.

"Conner," she soothed, "Let it out. It's always better that way. I would never tell anyone. I would never do that to you. You're safe with me. I'm here for you."

She put her arm around me and rested her head on my shoulder. She continued to rub my back, and when I closed my eyes, I felt the comfort from not only her touch and words, but from her scent. She smelled like peace, kindness and—most importantly—hope, and I could hear the purring of my inner bear as he reveled in her essence.

I let my shoulders fall and leaned into her. I did as she

asked; I let it go. All of it. I sobbed into her and she held me, smoothed my hair and offered reassurance.

She was just *there*. I'd needed that so badly and I hadn't even known it.

I cried until I felt empty. And then, to fill myself back up, to get something that resembled peace, I looked up at her. I stared into her eyes, seeing everything I needed. I leaned forward and kissed her.

That time, she didn't pull back. She let me kiss her, and she returned the gesture just as strongly. Her fingers wound through my hair. I grew hard at her touch, and my bear begged to be closer to her, so I picked her up and carried her to my bedroom.

12

CONNER

I gently lay her down on the bed and slid into place over her. I did nothing more than kiss her for a long time, just wanting to be close to her, to share affection with someone who cared for me. I didn't need things to go further.

She rubbed my back and played with my hair. Her fingernails danced along the back of my neck and sent chills through me. *I could love her*, I thought. *I could. I could make her mine.* Why not? Didn't I deserve happiness, for once? She was there and willing and wanted to be with me. Didn't she? I knew she did. Her whole body told me so, and she certainly wasn't trying to stop me.

I kissed along her neck, inhaling her scent, moving my hand slowly under her shirt. She'd removed her bra and her breasts were firm, soft as silk. I caressed them, feeling their weight in my hands as I rubbed my thumbs over her nipples, and she let out the softest moan. That moan sent tingles through my entire body, and I felt myself stiffen. God, she was perfect. Gorgeous body with curves in all the right places. I let my hands explore under her shirt a little more and she responded to my touch, nibbling on my ear and running her hands along my spine.

Her hips lifted to press into my erection and my head swam with the feeling. She wanted me. It was clear. I didn't know how far she wanted to go, and I wouldn't push her. If she didn't make it clear that she wanted more, I wouldn't try it.

Her hands found their way under my shirt, and she pulled it up and over my head. She pinched my nipples gently and played with my chest hair. Her hands felt so good; it didn't matter where she touched me or how. Her presence alone was so enjoyable, I wanted that moment to last forever.

Pulling the hem of her shirt up and off her body, I planted a trail of kisses down her neck to her breasts. I took her stiff peaks into my mouth, one by one, and she let out a soft "oh," moving her hips in response.

She wiggled her hands under my shorts and squeezed my ass, and in return, I slid my fingers over the front of her pants, gently rubbing slow circles against her, and she moaned again, pressing into my hand. I slid her pants down and let them fall to the floor. Feeling the dampness of her panties, I slipped a finger underneath and explored her wetness.

She was soaking with desire, so I slipped a finger gently inside her. She let out a loader moan—still quiet, but more insistent—and moved against me as I slid my finger in and out of her entrance.

"Yes," she whispered.

I hooked my fingers in the lace waistband of her panties and guided them over her hips, letting them pool at her ankles, and got on my knees to work her with my mouth. I kissed along her thigh, then let my tongue flick over her sensitive nub and between her folds. I reinserted my finger and moved it in and out as I sucked her into my mouth. She swiveled her hips, moaning with the pleasure of the feeling.

Letting out a more fervent cry, louder than any of the others, I felt her tighten around my finger and she came, her juices flowing over my hand as she dug her fingers into my hair. Her body shuddered as the rush of her orgasm pulsated through her, then she went still.

She breathed more slowly, recovering. I came back to her, kissed her again, and lie beside her. She flung her leg over me and pressed herself against me, sliding her hand under my shorts and pushed them down, along with my boxers. I helped her get them off as she took my stiff cock into her hands and stroked me. I was hard as a rock and every movement of her hand sent waves of pleasure through me.

I wanted her so badly; to just lay her down and thrust

inside her, but I held back. I didn't want to pressure her into anything she wasn't ready for.

I was close to the edge when she suddenly stopped.

"Conner," she whispered. "I want you."

"Are you sure?"

"Yes. Please. Make love to me."

I closed my eyes and swallowed. There was no way I could say no to that. I moved back into place on top of her and pushed her legs apart, rubbing her slickness onto my throbbing member. I pressed my head at her opening and moved inside her gently.

Pushing back against me, she gasped as I filled her to the hilt. "Oh god, Conner."

I plunged into her slowly at first, but as I sped up, she bit her lip. She let out a moan and I found a rhythm that seemed to feel good to her. Lifting her hips, she pushed me in further; harder. She slammed into me, and as I picked up my tempo, she moaned and gripped my ass, pulling me into her even deeper.

I responded with harder thrusts and faster movements. If she could handle it, I could give it. When she started to moan, I went as hard and fast as I dared. She cried out and pulled me in, contracting around me, and I came, slamming into her hard with each thrust. She tugged my hair hard and cried out, more loudly than she had before.

She shuddered again and breathed heavily into my ear.

When I had emptied myself into her, I panted and set my forehead on her shoulder.

"My god," she said. "Wow."

I laughed once. "Good." I slowly pulled back to slip out of her, then lay beside her.

"That was amazing."

I kissed along her neck and jaw, nuzzling my head into her. Her warmth soothed me and I fell asleep almost instantly.

13

JESSIE

I woke happy and warm in Conner's arms. I lay still for a long moment, just soaking in his closeness. It felt good to have him around me, and what we'd done the night before had felt incredible. I stifled a laugh and bit my lip. My sister was going to flip when she found out that I'd just had sex with Conner. I could hardly believe it myself. But it had been everything I'd wanted it to be; maybe, even better.

I checked the time and felt a rush of panic at the thought of Peyton finding me in there, naked, with her uncle, so I slid carefully out of bed and got dressed. She would probably notice that I was wearing the same shirt, though. I glanced in the closet and saw Alaina's clothing hanging there. *Not happening.* But then I spotted a few items I'd seen Conner wearing; the messy shirts on hangers at the end of the closet had to be his, too, so I chose a button down and hoped Peyton wouldn't recognize it.

I tied the shirt in a knot at the side to make it fit better and padded off to the kitchen to start the coffee and make breakfast. Peyton would just think I'd gotten there at my usual time and would have no reason to believe otherwise.

I woke her, and as I helped her into the outfit we'd picked out together the night before, I heard Conner head into and shower. A few minutes later, we met in the kitchen and ate together, as usual.

I had to hold back my grin; I didn't want Peyton wondering why I was on cloud nine, and it didn't seem right, given the difficulty of the day before.

I couldn't read Conner. He was usually quiet in the morning and often appeared grumpy. That morning, he was much the same as always, although to be honest, I'd hoped he would have been a little happier. He looked well-rested, but his mouth didn't twitch when I snuck him a smile behind Peyton's back. He looked away when my eyes met his.

Once we'd gotten Peyton on the bus, we came back inside. I went to him to wrap my arms around him, but he stepped back, shaking his head.

"You have to go," he said.

I winced in confusion. "What? What are you—"

"You can't be Peyton's nanny. I have to find someone else."

My heart skipped. Did he want something more, then? To start a relationship? Perhaps, like I had, he thought it wasn't appropriate for us to be sleeping together while I worked for him.

My mouth fell into a smile and I opened my mouth to say something, but he cut me off.

"I can't be with someone like you." His words were cold and hard.

My heart sped even faster and tightened. "What do you mean?"

"I have too much baggage and—"

"We all have issues, but after last night, I thought that—"

"Don't ever mention last night to me again." He glared at me and set his jaw.

I took a step back, shocked at his sudden harshness. "I told you I would never tell anyone, and I meant it. What happened between us—all of it—was special, and I—"

He started to laugh. "Special? You think that was special? You let me sleep with you after I made a fool out of myself and made you feel sorry for me."

"That's not what happened." My face grew hot and my jaw ached from clenching it so tightly. "You needed someone to be there for you, and I was." My words came out choked as the tears filled my eyes.

He rubbed his face with his hands. "Look, I wasn't even

trying to manipulate you, but I did. I'm a fucking asshole—and a mess. And that's why you have to leave. Now. And don't come back."

I gasped. He couldn't mean that. "But Conner..." My arm trailed helplessly through the air. "I can't just leave; I can't do that to Peyton. At least let me talk to her after school so I can explain what's going on."

"Give me your key."

I blinked at him for a moment, then went to find my purse and fished out the Disney keychain. I handed it to him and he snatched it from me.

"And take my brother's shirt off. What right do you think you have to wear that?"

I glanced down at it, mortified. "I thought it was yours. I'm sorry. I didn't want Peyton to—"

"Take it off!"

His booming voice made me jump. I unbuttoned it as I hurried to the bedroom, pulled it off and hung it back where I'd found it before yanking my own shirt over my head. I did a quick sweep, making sure I had everything of mine. My head spun; I couldn't believe what was happening.

"Conner, please, can we talk about this? I'm sorry if I did something to upset you. I never wanted to hurt you." Tears ran down my face.

"Just go." He closed his eyes and pointed to the door.

"Conner..."

"Go."

I didn't know what else to do, so I did as he asked. Picking up my purse, I closed the door behind me. I got into my car and drove halfway down the street before the tears became too much.

I fumbled for my phone, trying to call Nikki, but after almost crashing into a curb, I decided to wait. I drove home as quickly as I could, and when I got there, I ran inside and called out for her. She popped her head out from the bedroom; when she saw the anguish on my face, she rushed over to me.

"What happened? Are you okay?" She looked me over and wrapped me in a hug.

I could barely speak, but somehow, I managed to tell her most of what happened: that we'd had what I thought was a long, amazing talk, we'd slept together, and then that morning, he kicked me out and fired me.

"He did *what*?!" The rage was obvious in her eyes.

"I just don't understand," I stammered, the tears still flowing. "What did I do wrong?"

"Nothing at all." She paced the room in tight circles. "That asshole. I'll kill him. I'm going over there right now, and I'm going to fucking kill him."

She stood, and I grabbed her arm. "No. That would only make it worse."

"He can't treat you like this!"

"I know he has issues; we both know that. Something must've just...set him off. I don't know. Maybe he's embarrassed. He did say never to mention last night to him. He really opened up to me, and maybe he regrets that."

"Well, fine. He can regret that, but he doesn't get to sleep with you, then treat you like this. It's such complete bullshit!"

Her words made my tears flow harder. "I know. And Peyton. What's she going to think? I hope he doesn't tell her that I ran out or quit suddenly or something like that. I don't want her to think I abandoned her. It kills me to leave her like this. I didn't even get to say goodbye! She'll come home and I'll just be gone. Just like her parents. Doesn't he see what that will do to her?"

"He shouldn't have her. I think we should call Child Protective Services."

"No!" I swatted her arm. "Are you crazy? And have Peyton get stuck in the foster care system for the rest of her life? Conner's far from perfect, but he's her blood relative. He wants to take care of her. He loves her; he just has a lot to learn. Being taken from him would be so much worse. And removed from her own house like that? No, no."

Nikki sighed and sat back down, hard. "You're right; that would be terrible. But he can't do this! It's not right."

"It's not," I agreed. "But there's nothing we can do."

She huffed and crossed her arms. "Well, there is one thing that might make this whole situation a tiny bit better."

"What's that?"

"Yesterday, while you were at work, someone called. They want to interview you for one of the positions you applied for."

A tiny shred of hope wiggled its way into my chest and I sighed. "Well, that's good timing."

14

CONNER

I watched until she pulled out of the driveway, then drew the curtain shut. Pure anger ripped through me, and I balled my fists and screamed. I wanted to punch something. I *had to* punch something. Luckily, I had a scrap of sense left and dashed down to the basement. I stood in front of the punching bag and let loose, throwing fist after fist into it until I'd worked up a sweat and the knuckles of both my hands were covered in blood.

But it wasn't enough. I tore off my clothes, barreled up the stairs and shifted as I made my way past the back yard. *Let the neighbors see. I don't give a flying fuck.* I ran hard, sprinting for as long as I could. I refused to think about anything except pounding the ground with my heavy paws, faster and faster.

I'd gone miles; so far, that I was getting into territory I didn't know well. I slowed to a more leisurely pace and let my mind release from its tight place of rage. And then, I realized I wasn't alone in my head.

Is there something I can do for you? Owen asked.

Leave me alone.

We're worried.

You should be.

I felt him leave the mind link. Good. He was listening and giving me space. I sat down and let myself really think about what the hell was going on.

I was freaking out. I could feel myself losing it; feel that reality was slipping away.

Feel myself going batshit crazy.

I'd let Jessie not only see me cry, but I'd sobbed in front of her like a baby. I'd told her far too much about me, but still not the worst parts. She'd been so perfect. Just thinking about it made my eyes sting. She'd been everything I wanted, everything I could have dreamed. She'd shown me more care and love in those hours than anyone had in a long time— more than I'd *let* anyone in a long time.

And that was the problem. Not only had I given her all I could in that moment, she'd taken all of me. Willingly. After all I poured out to her about my nightmares, my guilt, the horrible things I'd seen at war and on my job. The way I had to save people or I felt like I couldn't breathe. She knew more about me than my therapist or my own mother. All parts of me were opened to her.

But she still didn't know my biggest secret.

I looked down at my bear paws, hating them for the first time. Jessie could accept me as broken. She already had. But she wouldn't be able to accept my bear. If I tried to tell her, she'd be scared. She'd look at me like I was a freak. A monster. And I couldn't stand the thought of it. Just picturing how she might look at me, the raw rejection she might give me in that moment, made me want to tear my fur out and pull out my claws. Made me want to never shift again.

I'd fallen for her. Like an idiot, I'd let myself love her. A *human*. So then, I had to make sure I never saw her again. I wasn't boyfriend or husband material. I wasn't father material, either. *Peyton. God, what am I going to tell her?* I had to find someone else to care for her. I would hire the best person I could, and I'd leave. Or maybe I could send her to one of those fancy schools where the kids all stay there. I'd tell her it was like Hogwarts, but without the magic. She could make friends; be away from all the things that reminded her of her parents. Being in that house had to be making it worse, right?

Jessie had left. Just like that, she walked out. Of course, I'd yelled at her first; I'd had to. It was the only way to make her leave. I'd wanted her to go. But I'd wanted her to refuse. Some desperate, twisted part of me wanted her to fall at my feet and beg me to let her love me. To let her stay. I wanted to hear her say she would refuse to leave because she refused to give up on me.

But she'd left. After just a few harsh words, she'd left, taking every remaining piece of my heart with her.

The pain was so sharp, it made my head spin. I threw up. I was shaking and collapsed on the ground, my face much too close to the vile things that had just poured out of me. I deserved it. I deserved to drown in my own disgust and take myself away from the world so I couldn't hurt anyone else. Surely, I'd hurt Jessie; probably badly. What would that do to a woman? Giving herself away like she'd given herself to me, then to be turned away like that?

Did she feel used? Manipulated? Did she feel like I'd violated some part of her heart? She must have hated me; she should've. *I* hated me. I hated Logan and Alaina for dying. I hated the world for letting it be them. Most of all, I hated the croc who was responsible for their deaths. When I found out who it was, I would shred his skin and make him suffer. *Maybe I'll just start killing all the crocs*, I thought. Eventually, I'd kill the guilty one. And in the meantime, we'd be rid of our croc problem forever. Yes. That was the plan. What had Jessie said? Purpose.

I'd finally found my purpose: I would rid the Everglades, then the world, of every last crocodile shifter I could find. With my newfound sense of determination, I rose to my paws and started running back. I'd stay in the park for as long as I could and pick them off, one by one. I had tons of energy that day, more than I'd had in a long time. I could've gone all day.

But as I ran, it hit me: I hadn't had a nightmare the night before. *No, that couldn't be right,* I thought as I mentally flipped through the ones that often recurred. None of them had played in my mind; I had slept all night without a single nightmare. That might have been the first time it'd happened since I'd been in Afghanistan. Then, I thought of Jessie's soft body curled up against mine as we slept. *Pfft. Must have been a coincidence,* I told myself. *She couldn't fix me. No one could.* I stood tall on my hind legs, roared, and beat my chest.

We're here. It was Owen. And then suddenly, damn near all my clan was there.

Where are you? Mason.

We want to help you. Ezra.

We'll come to wherever you are. Noah.

Please, Conner. Don't do it like this. Hailey.

I'll head over to your place and be there when Peyton gets home. Addie. *Take your time and deal with whatever is going on. Please. For your sake, for Peyton's sake. For the clan's sake. We can't watch you do this anymore.*

Is this a fucking intervention? I demanded.

If that's what you want to call it, fine, Owen answered. *But we're not going to let you suffer. You have to talk to us.*

I talked to someone. And it was the worst thing I could have done.

What happened? Ezra asked. *Was it something with Jessie or Peyton?*

Where are you? Mason demanded. *Don't make me get the force and your own team on the case to search your ass out.*

Why didn't you show up for work? Ezra asked.

In a brief flash, I received a mental image of Owen and Addie at my house. Their little boy, James, was with them.

I growled. *Great. Now I can't even go home.*

Yes, you can, Owen said. *Please, man. What's going on with you? Do you want me to call your therapist?*

Do you need something more? Mason offered. *An inpatient stay somewhere? This is worse than it's ever been.*

I stopped running. There was only one way to escape of all the chatter: I shifted back.

I walked through the woods, naked. It took a long time to get home on human feet; long past the time Peyton would have been off the bus. I hoped Addie and Owen had stayed to bring her inside; I'm sure they had. I'm sure, too, that people were looking for me. I'd be harder to find in my human form, but not impossible. It was a huge park. One and a half million acres would take them a long time to cover.

I walked in the direction of home. My mind settled some during the hours I walked, and by the time I saw my back-yard—Logan's backyard—I was ready to face whatever or whoever was waiting for me.

A tan panther leapt up and I groaned internally. *Britt.* That meant Ezra was somewhere nearby. Then, I heard his footfalls and he ran at me in bear form, but quickly shifted back to human and threw his arms around me.

"Two men hugging naked outside is not the best way to keep our secret from the world," I said flatly. I pushed him off of me. "Nor is it at all comfortable."

He wiped tears from his eyes. "We've been so worried about you, man. We thought you..." He shook his head.

"You thought I what?"

"We thought you might have done something very stupid. Peyton is at Owen's. She's fine. She's spending the night there."

A spare key was hidden in the backyard under a piece of the wooden border around the garden.

"Dammit," Britt said. "I smelled nickel and thought it was the nails. Nice spot."

I glanced at her, then unlocked the door. I wanted to slam it in their faces, but they anticipated this and moved ahead anyhow.

I flopped down naked on the couch and they joined me. Britt smirked and went outside, and when she returned, she was wearing clothes and tossed some to Ezra. Then, she tossed me a small pouch.

"Herbs," she explained. "My gramma came up with this blend and it works really well. You can even put it in your beer."

"What does this blend do?" I sniffed in the bag, and my nose picked up on a mixture of things.

"It'll calm you down and help you sleep."

"Take some now," Ezra said.

I set the pouch down. "That's alright."

"Dude," Ezra insisted. "It wasn't a question or an option. Take some now."

I glared at him, but pinched a good bit between my fingers, then dropped it into my mouth and swallowed. It tasted like lavender and rosemary...and cedar sawdust.

I winced. "Nasty shit." I picked up a half empty beer bottle and washed it down.

"Said it worked, not that it tastes good," Britt admitted.

Ezra watched me, waiting.

"If this does something crazy to me, I will come after you," I threatened.

"That's fine," he said.

Britt got up and took a bag into the kitchen. I heard the microwave start. My stomach lurched, but the burning numb sensation from the herbs helped to keep the contents of my gut in place.

"You can start talking anytime you want," Ezra said.

"Nothing to talk about."

He sat back and crossed his arms. Maybe it was in my head, but I felt my heart slow. The anxiety faded and the heaviness in my chest lifted some. I blinked back tears. When Britt set a plate of fried chicken and mashed potatoes in front of me, I ate like I hadn't eaten in years.

I set the empty plate down and looked at them.

Ezra said, "Now. What's going on?"

I told them as much as I could without getting emotional. Britt was more like one of the guys than Ezra's mate, so that helped me feel comfortable saying what I had to without feeling like I was offending someone. She'd just come out and tell me if I did something stupid. They listened and nodded and didn't interrupt.

When I was done, Ezra raised his eyebrows. "Is that all of it? That's what has had you so messed up all day?"

"Isn't that enough?" I demanded.

"It's a lot," Britt agreed.

"Conner." Ezra leaned forward in his chair. "Dude. There's no reason to put yourself through this. You fell for her. It happens. It's not a bad thing. Go after her, apologize, tell her you freaked out, and get her back."

I shook my head. "It'll never work between us."

Britt laughed. "I thought that once, too. Turns out this idiot is my perfect match." She shoved Ezra and he rolled his eyes.

"You're both shifters."

"But we're different species and we couldn't be more different in every way," Ezra explained.

I waved my hand. "She couldn't handle the shifter thing."

"Oh, I thought you said you didn't tell her," Britt said.

"I didn't."

"Then you have no idea how she'd respond, do you?" she challenged.

"She's a human, 100%. I know I seem like a total idiot, but I'm actually not."

"Don't get worked up," Ezra said. "No one's calling you an idiot. If she has feelings for you, you could be surprised at what she might accept."

I shook my head slowly. "I can't take the chance. It would ruin me."

"But the thing is," Ezra continued, "you already have. You took the chance and let her in. You let yourself fall for her. That's huge. You opened up to her on an emotional level; you already did the hardest part. Talk to her and find out what she feels for you. I guess if she hates you, don't tell her, but I'll bet she doesn't, man. I'll bet she's just as crazy for you as you are for her. You won't know until you make the move and try. That's what I did. You remember how I was."

I rolled my eyes. "Good god, you were obnoxious. It was so obvious to us that you had it bad, but you wouldn't see it."

Ezra raised his hands. "Hello? Listen to what I'm saying. It's obvious now that *you* have it bad. That's why you're freaking out. Just like it was clear to you that I had to talk to Britt and get over myself, it's your turn."

"This is totally different."

"Yup," Ezra said. "Except it's not."

I narrowed my eyes at him.

"Dude! You're already miserable! You're already hurting, in pain and feeling rejected; it can't get any worse. Not really. But if you don't talk to her and find out, you'll never know.

And then you'll have to live with that forever. Every time you feel lonely, every time you have a nightmare, every time you want someone to talk to or to be there, you'll wonder if it could have worked out."

I pictured it. He was right. It *would* kill me. And it was already terrible. I already felt like my insides were on fire, roasting me from the inside out. How much worse could it be?

"Fine," I said.

"Fine...as in, you'll talk to her?" he asked.

"I'll talk to her. I'll at least apologize and feel her out. Then, I'll decide from there."

"Perfect. My job here is done," Ezra said. "Now go get some sleep, man."

15

JESSIE

I hopped into my car after the interview and picked up my phone to send a text to Nikki.

It went great!

She'd been anxious to hear about it, so I wasn't surprised when she responded right away.

Awesome, I knew it would! You'll have to tell me all about it when you get home. I'll have a tub of chocolate peanut butter swirl ready for ya! xoxo

As soon as I arrived, I dropped my purse by the door and Nikki shoved a spoon into my hand. "So, what did he say?" she asked.

"He was so impressed by my education," I answered, sliding the spoon through the crisp, cool ribbon of peanut butter. "And even by my experience as a nanny! He said it would really help."

Nikki hugged me tightly. "See, I knew you could do it!"

"Thanks for helping me." I smiled as I took a mouthful and exhaled through my nose, allowing the sweet and salty flavors to melt on my tongue. I'd almost packed up and gone back home after the whole Conner thing happened, but Nikki had convinced me to at least go on that one interview. I had nothing to lose and only a crappy job back home to gain. My pitiful paycheck from the diner looked pretty sad compared to what I'd been making as a nanny. Heck, I'd thought about possibly looking for another nannying job if the teaching position didn't come through. As rough as it had been, I'd loved being there. I still missed Peyton and hoped that the transition hadn't been too hard on her.

The next day, I received a call telling me that I'd been awarded the job and Nikki took me out for dinner to celebrate. After our Mexican meal, I was stuffed, so I decided to end the night on our couch watching a cheesy romantic comedy. While I was excited to have a new job, I couldn't deny that I still felt upset about Conner and Peyton. I missed them badly. It had already been over a week since I'd left, and I didn't think I'd be seeing them anytime soon. Maybe not ever.

I had almost two weeks to kill before my job would be starting. It was like torture to have that much idle time. Curiosity got the best of me one day, and I found myself driving past Conner's house, just to see if I could catch a glimpse of them, but I saw no one. I wished I would run into them somewhere, but Conner didn't go anywhere—except for work, anyway.

I busied myself by reading and cleaning everything there was to clean. I even thought about picking up a small job in the meantime, but what could I do for less than two weeks? I found myself taking long walks, but my mind would always drift to memories of Conner. Our night together. Where I went wrong. What I could have done to make it better. I still didn't have any answers.

By the time the day finally came for me to start, I was ecstatic. Smoothing the skirt of my new outfit, I spun for Nikki. "Good?"

"Perfect teacher attire."

"I can't believe I'm actually a teacher!" I squealed. All those long years of college had finally paid off.

I got in my car and tried to stay calm as I drove to the school. Luckily, I'd been given a tour after my interview, so I knew exactly where to go. I checked in with my supervisor, then headed to my classroom. The other teacher I'd be working with was there already, and she looked up at me with a tired smile.

"Hi there," I said cheerfully, sticking out my hand. "I'm Jessie Miller, the new teacher."

"Yes, I know," she replied. "I hope you can keep that attitude past the first hour."

My smile faltered and I dropped my hand. "Well...I hope so, too. I've wanted to be an elementary school teacher for most of my life."

"Well," she sighed, "it's much less teaching than what they probably told you. Half the reason they can't keep anyone in this position is because they have a nasty habit of painting it differently from what it's really like."

I swallowed hard. "What do you mean? And I'm sorry, I didn't get your name."

"The kids call me Miss Marcy."

"Nice to meet you, Marcy."

"*Miss* Marcy," she corrected.

I flushed. "My apologies, Miss Marcy. How is it different?"

"Oh, you'll see. Just be prepared to yell a lot."

I furrowed my brow, but I didn't have time to ask her more questions. A boy rushed into the room and threw his backpack down on the floor so hard, it made me jump.

"Who are you?" he accused, pointing at me with an angry look on his face.

I took a deep breath. *Here we go.* "I'm Miss Jessie." I held out my hand to him. Instead of shaking it, he slapped it hard and ran around the room in laps.

"Aiden! Sit! Now!" Miss Marcy hollered at him, but he didn't stop. "You're losing your recess time right now."

"Ahhh!" He covered his ears with his hands and kept running.

I watched in horror. The man who interviewed me, my

new supervisor, had said that I would be working with a
small group of students who couldn't be in the mainstream
classrooms for various reasons. "Most of them," he'd
explained, "need a little extra help." He'd made it seem like
they possibly had learning disabilities or special needs; I'd
been prepared for that. But I had not been prepared for kids
removed from class for behavioral issues.

I looked at the clock. The rest of the class would be
arriving any minute. *Maybe it's just Aiden who's like that,* I
hoped. *Maybe the rest of the class will be more like what I was
expecting.*

But by the time mid-morning rolled around, I knew I'd
been wrong. Every single one of my students was a handful
—and using the term "handful" was being polite. Unfortunately, Miss Marcy had been right. I yelled more than I ever
expected to yell. I'd pleaded with one girl to stop pulling out
her hair. I had to restrain a boy from kicking another student
and was told that sending him to the principal wouldn't do
much, so not to bother. I'd tried to teach them something.
Anything. But as soon as I got one settled, another would
act up.

At the end of the day, I sat in my car, fully exhausted, and
cried. That wasn't what I'd gone to school for, and it certainly
wasn't how I wanted to be spending my days. I wasn't a
teacher to those kids; I was little more than a prison warden,
trying to keep them from rioting or killing each other.

My mind drifted to Peyton and Conner. My heart ached

for them. Peyton, my quiet, sweet little girl. Even with her, it had taken time to get her to trust me; maybe that's all it would take with those kids. If I tried to connect with them differently, maybe I could get through. I thought of that movie where the teacher just had to find a way to get them interested in learning before she got through to them. Maybe I could, too. Maybe I could turn things around and help those kids after all.

I had planned to make dinner that night. Nikki was working a late shift and wasn't going to be home to eat with me, and after a day like that, I was tired and needed a little pick me up. Instead of cooking, I decided to treat myself to a frozen pizza instead—and maybe some ice cream. That would make the night better.

I drove to the local market and pushed my cart around slowly, the frustration of the day settling deep in my bones. I didn't want to go back, despite whatever hopes I had earlier. Even if I could eventually get them to learn something, it would take time and a lot of hard work, and I didn't know if I had the stamina or the ability to make it happen.

I ended up buying a pepperoni pizza, a tub of chocolate chip ice cream, a package of soft chocolate chip cookies—in case I decided to make an ice cream sandwich—and a bag of salt and cracked pepper potato chips. At least I could eat my way to happiness for the time being, right? But as I was heading to the checkout line, I caught a glimpse of someone from behind.

No.

My blood ran cold. The man turned to the side, showing me his profile, and I almost fainted. I held my breath and then turned sharply, careening down another aisle to avoid having him see me. Of all the times I'd hoped to run into Conner somewhere, I didn't want it to be then. All the things I thought I would say left my mind. I couldn't handle it that night.

I searched around, paranoid, as I slowly made my way to the checkout. I kept looking over my shoulder, making sure he wasn't coming. What would I say if I saw him?

To my relief, the checkout girl was quick and I hurried out to my car with a bag in each hand. I tossed the bags in my backseat and looked around one last time. I'd done it. I'd avoided him.

I jammed my key in the ignition and noticed a text from Nikki.

How was it? she asked.

I have a frozen pizza and junk food for dinner. Will tell you all about it later.

Yikes! Sounds like a rough day :(

I set my phone down and shrieked when someone knocked on my window.

Conner.

I put my hand to my chest and tried to calm down before lowering the window.

"Sorry, I didn't mean to scare you," he said.

"It's fine." *Of all the ways I'd pictured this moment going down...*I thought.

I saw you shopping and I...well...I'm sorry." He rubbed his face. "God, Jessie, I am so, so sorry for what I did, for how I treated you; all of it."

I didn't know what to say. In all my picturing of that moment, I never expected an apology, either. I imagined telling him off, screaming at him for hurting me, pleading with him to get better help...

"I don't even know what to say. I have no excuse for what I did," he continued. "I panicked. And I handled it so wrong. I miss you. Peyton misses you, too."

My throat burned and the tears didn't take long to reach my eyes. I closed them and breathed slowly. *This has to be a dream*, I told myself. *After such a nightmare of a day, I must be hallucinating.*

"Jessie?"

His voice was so raw and pained, so I decided to open my eyes. He looked close to tears himself.

"I miss you both, too," I replied. "But it was horrible to have to leave like that."

"I know. I'm the worst. Can I...Will you...go out with me? Like, on a date? We've never done that, and I'd like to talk to you. To see you again. If you'll have me, that is. If you can ever forgive me."

I opened my car door and got out, then put my arms

around him in a tight hug. He squeezed me back so hard, it hurt a little.

"Okay," I said. "I'd like to talk to you. And see how you're both doing."

He sagged with relief. "Thank you for giving me a chance. I'll text you. How's Friday?"

I thought of my day and how drained I was after working. "How about Saturday?"

"Perfect."

I gave him a sad smile. "Tell Peyton 'hi' for me, okay?"

He nodded and waved as I got back in my car and drove off. When I got home, I texted Nikki.

WTF. You are not going to believe what just happened when I was leaving the market...

16

CONNER

I sat across from Jessie at the restaurant table. Somehow, everything I'd wanted to say to her had left my mind. I stared at my hands, trying to think back to what Ezra and I had talked about. I never thought I would have found myself getting romantic advice from him, but he'd actually been a big help when it came to preparing myself for that night.

"How have you been?" she asked after a long silence.

"Okay, I guess." I had to be honest; I knew that much. I wanted to keep the same level of openness I'd given her that night. "Since I last saw you, I've been tearing myself apart over how I reacted. My clan's been worried about how I've been acting in general, and they're trying to help."

"Your what? *Clan*?"

Shit, I wasn't ready to go there. I would, when the time was right, but I couldn't start with, 'Oh yeah, I forgot to mention that I can turn into a bear.'

"My group of close friends. I call them my clan."

She nodded. "That's a...weird term. But it's good that you have them to lean on, regardless. I didn't realize you did."

"Yeah, they've saved my ass more than a few times..." I trailed off, trying to think of the right words to say next. "Look Jessie, I was a complete asshole to you, and I just want you to know how awful I feel about what happened. And after we...I didn't want you to think I was just using you or that my reaction had anything to do with us sleeping together."

The waitress showed up at the worst time possible. We ordered, and when she left, I returned my gaze to Jessie.

"Did you think it was because of that?" I asked.

"I honestly didn't know *what* to think. I knew that was a possibility; it happens in movies and books all the time. Sleep with a guy and he vanishes. Of course, I didn't think it would happen to me, but I guess no one ever does."

"Well, it wasn't because of that. You know that things haven't been good for me for a long time; I've been dealing with a lot of shit coming at me from all angles."

"I know. I wish there was a way for you to find peace in the midst of all this. I tried to help you; I really did."

"That's the thing. You *did* help me. That's why I freaked out. I never let anyone get that close. Jessie, I told you things that my therapist and even my own mother don't know."

She raised her eyebrows. "Wow, I'm...honored, I guess. Surprised, I mean, I don't know what I did to earn that from you, but I'm glad I did and that I was there. I hoped it helped."

"It did. I told you about my horrible nightmares."

She nodded.

"But that night we spent together? It was the first time in years that I didn't have a single one."

"That's great. How has it been since?"

I shrugged. "They came right back. But it was nice to have one night without them. At least I know it's possible. And now I realize it's *you* who made it possible."

"I don't think I really did anything. Maybe it was finally talking so much about your experience and all you've been through that helped."

I shook my head. "It's you. I feel safe with you. Comfortable. Like I could tell you any secret in the world and it would be okay."

Well, almost any secret.

"You can. Whatever happened between us, and whatever we end up being, you can call me. I'll listen whenever you want to talk."

She reached across the table and put her hand over mine. My inner bear surged and I wanted to jump across the table and kiss her right then.

"I really want you to come back. I've been relying on a nanny service and my friends to help take care of Peyton, but we both miss you so much. Please come back."

"I have another job," she said apologetically.

My heart sank. Things weren't going along with my master plan. I wanted her to come running back to me, but I had to remind myself it was my fault. *I* sent *her* away. And it'd been weeks earlier. I couldn't have expected her to sit around and wait for me to wise up.

I let out a breath. "Well, I'm glad you were able to find something. If anything ever changes..."

She smiled. "You'll be my first call."

The food arrived, and for a while, we didn't talk much. But I still had one thing left to do. I had to make my feelings clear. But how? I couldn't just blurt them out. I played around with different ways to tell her in my mind.

"You okay?" Jessie asked as the waitress brought the check. "You got so quiet."

"I'm sorry, I'm not good at this. Maybe we can go somewhere more private to talk?" I'd been feeling exposed the whole time we were there, wondering if anyone had been overhearing me.

"Sure."

I paid the bill and we walked out to our cars. "Peyton is at my friend Owen's for the night. Would you like to come back to the house? Just to talk."

She chuckled. "I guess I could do that." She flashed me a smile and followed me back to the house.

When we arrived, I got us each a glass of water and sat her down on the couch. "So, is the new job going well?"

"It's okay; I'm still getting used to it." She looked down at her glass, tracing the edge with her finger. "You know, I have to admit, not being able to say goodbye to Peyton made me feel terrible. I worried it would be like losing someone else close to her."

I swallowed hard and recalled that day. "You're right. It was the worst thing I could have done. She cried. She even yelled at me. Luckily, I have some really great friends that have been helping, but...things haven't been good. She doesn't like her new nannies."

Jessie's eyes filled with tears. "She's been through so much already..."

I reached out and wiped a tear away, then let my hand linger on her cheek. "It my fault. I'm so sorry; I ended up hurting you both so much."

I dropped my head in my shame, but when I looked back up, her eyes were full of compassion. I couldn't resist kissing her. It was short and sweet, but I had to let her know somehow that I loved her. I didn't think I could say it out loud, but I wanted her to feel it all the same.

"I do miss you," she said. "My job isn't exactly what I thought it would be. It's very hard. So hard, I actually kind of hate it." She laughed. "But I've only been there a short time. I don't think I could just quit on them. The kids I'm supposed to be teaching are very troubled. They can't keep anyone in that position very long, and I don't want to abandon them, either. But I'd love to spend time with Peyton. Anytime I'm not working, I can come."

I nodded. "I understand. I really messed this whole thing up for all of us."

She put her hand to my cheek as I'd done to her moments ago. "You're human, Conner. You make mistakes like we all do."

My bear bellowed at her touch, and the ringing in my ears served as a reminder of why things could never work between us. How the hell could I possibly explain who I really was—or more accurately, *what* I really was—to her?

"*This* is a mistake." I took her hand and pulled it from my face, holding it in my lap. "I'm fucked up—in so many ways you will never understand."

She shook her head. "What? Conner, stop. I know you have issues. But so do I. Everyone does! I'm afraid of every-thing. I didn't even want to leave my tiny home town because it's all I knew. I've been sheltered and allowed myself to be caged in. I can't be strong and brave like you are every day. I have my own issues. Believe me."

"You don't get it. I have secrets that would terrify you."

She raised an eyebrow. "I doubt it. I know you were deployed. I assume you've killed or at least shot people. I know awful things happen over there."

"It's not just that."

"Then what is it?"

"If I told you, I'd never see you again."

"It can't possibly be that bad. Did you kill someone outside of the military?"

I considered the question. As a clan, we had to take down animals from time to time. Some were shifters. Technically, that was killing people, wasn't it?

"Sort of," I admitted.

She breathed out hard. "Have you beaten someone badly?"

I pressed my lips together. "Yes. And of all of this is part of the bigger secret."

She narrowed her eyes. "Are you some kind of spy or government agent? CIA or FBI? Something like that?"

"No. There is an organization I'm part of, but it's not government-related."

Her eyes went wide. "The mob?" she whispered. "Are you in the mob or one of those biker gangs?"

"No. Not quite that...criminal. What we do is more just, I guess. More like when members of the military or law enforcement have to take a life in the line of duty."

"Well, that's about the worst I can think of. Unless you're going to tell me you sell babies on the black market."

"No." I gave her an incredulous look. "Nothing evil. I swear. Nothing even criminal, really."

"This is sounding like the CIA all over again." She blew

out another breath in frustration. "Just tell me. I can't take this guessing. I'm sure it's not half as bad as you think it is."

"Or it's worse."

"But I know you. And after our time together, I feel like I know more of you. I can't see you being bad. Not like that. Not evil. You'd never hurt anyone on purpose, I don't think. Except for maybe whoever killed you brother, but I think most people would feel that way."

I pulled my mouth to the side. "I've never had to tell anyone this before. I'm afraid it'll come out sounding insane."

"Just say it and then explain if you have to."

"You have to promise that no matter what, you will keep this an absolute secret. Understand that if the public knows about this, it will put a lot of innocent people in danger. Thousands and thousands of lives are at stake. No matter how afraid you are, you have to promise to never tell anyone. Ever."

"It's nothing evil, you swear? Because if you're some kind of serial murderer, you can't expect me not to tell."

"I swear it's nothing like that."

"I promise. Now what is it?"

I squeezed my eyes shut. I remembered what Ezra had said. It sounded stupid now, but I had nothing else to go on and my mind was spinning. I took her hands in mine and squeezed them.

"Just know that I don't want to hurt you. I don't want to

lose you. I know this will be hard to hear and if you need time, I get it. It's okay. You can freak out if you have to, but just promise me that at some point, you will talk to me again. Please."

"I promise." She already looked terrified.

"God, this is going to sound fucking crazy." I took a sip of water and looked deep into her eyes. "You've seen movies or read books that have...werewolves in them, right?"

She nodded her head slowly.

"Well, they're not completely fiction. Creatures like that exist. It's not exactly like most movies and books describe, but the basics are there. I'm sort of like that."

She closed her eyes. "Just don't tell me you're some kind of sparkly vampire."

"To my knowledge, vampires don't exist. But shapeshifters do. People who can become animals and then change back to their human forms. I'm a shifter. I can become...I can become a bear; a huge, furry black bear. I can control it completely, unless I step out into the light of a full moon. Then I have to shift, but other than that, it's under my control."

She pulled her hands back. I watched her face to see if she was freaking out.

"You can become a bear. And this isn't a joke."

"I would never joke at a time like this. In fact, when have you ever known me to joke at all?"

"Never, actually; but if this is true, *how*? How do you change into a bear?"

I shrugged. "If you're asking what made us like this, I don't know. Some flaw in nature? Some genetic mutation? I don't know, and I don't know anyone else who does. We just have to deal with it."

She stared at the wall for a long moment. Okay, she didn't seem to be freaking out too badly. Maybe it would be okay after all. I felt the hope flicker but stamped it out quickly; it was far too soon for that.

"What other questions do you have?"

"Are you yourself when you change or do you just go crazy and eat people? Is that why you said you killed people?"

I shook my head. "I'm me all the time. It's completely under my control."

"Except during the full moon."

"In the light of the full moon, I have to shift, but I'm still me. It's slightly different. More intense, but it's still me. All the time. I don't attack people. The people I've killed...well, as you can imagine, there are plenty of politics in the shifter world just like the human world. There are different types of shifters, and when someone gets out of line, we can't just throw them in jail in the same way. We have to keep this an absolute secret. So, sometimes, we have to take the law into our own hands. Judge, jury, and execution."

She closed her eyes. "I need to see."

"No way."

"Conner, you just told me you're a creature from fairy-tales. If I'm going to believe it, I have to see it."

"It'll freak you out too much."

"I'm pretty freaked out already, so just do it."

I sucked in a breath. She was either holding it in or was in shock. Crap. And I thought it had been going well.

"I don't want you to be freaked out."

She gave me a surprised expression. "Did you honestly think I wouldn't be?"

"Of course I thought you would. I didn't think it would go this well, actually. What are you thinking right now?"

"Just that...I don't know what to think. But I have to see it. It won't seem real until I do."

"Jessie, please, don't make me do this."

"Conner. Do you want me to believe you? Do you want me to be okay with this or not?"

"Yes. More than anything."

"Then show me."

"Okay." With that, I stood and pulled off my shirt. "Um, shifting rips clothing so we usually strip naked first."

"Okay. I've seen you naked before, so it's fine."

"Right." I pressed my lips together and pushed my shorts and boxers down. I stood in front of her, naked, more vulner-able than I've ever been in my life. "Just know this is incred-ibly difficult for me."

"To shift is difficult?"

"To shift in front of you, knowing what it might do to you."

She only stared back, waiting.

"Just remember, I promise I won't hurt you." I closed my eyes, leaned forward to drop on all fours, and, as slowly as I could, shifted into my bear form. I kept my distance from her, not wanting to make it worse in any way. She breathed heavily, her chest rising and falling fast, and her hands went to her mouth. Tears streamed down her face and she covered her eyes.

I shifted back. "Jessie?"

She shook her head and kept shaking it. "No, no, no, no... this...can't be...real..."

"Talk to me. Please."

She kept shaking her head and slowly stood up. "I won't tell anyone. I promised that. I promised I would talk to you again." She closed her eyes and tears ran down her face. When she spoke again, her voice wavered and she broke into sobs by the end. "But I have to go now."

She snatched her purse and ran out my front door. She got into her car and backed up so fast, she almost hit a car driving down the road. As she turned and sped off, her tires squealed, leaving black marks in the road.

I stood there for a long while, staring at the marks left behind. I had expected this. *Exactly* this. Everything Ezra said was bullshit. They'd been wrong. They'd all been so wrong.

My phone buzzed. In my desperation to talk to her and know everything was okay, I leapt across the couch to grab it from the coffee table. It was Mason.

I threw my phone down, but he kept calling. On the fourth call, I finally answered.

"For fuck's sake, what?!"

"We got him. The bastard that killed Logan and Alaina. He's in custody right now."

I heard his words. They bounced around my mind, but I couldn't process them. "Thanks for letting me know." I heard him shout my name as I tapped to end the call. I let the phone fall to the floor and the world spun in streaks around me.

17

JESSIE

I couldn't talk to anyone about what I saw. I kept telling myself that. Not my sister. Not my parents. Except maybe Conner, if I could've worked up the nerve to. The worst part was, I'd had my own secret to tell him; something I'd wanted to say so badly. But the way he was going on about it, I had to know his first.

When I got home, I tried to sleep. I thought after a good night's rest, everything might seem different. That was often the case. But as soon as I lay down, the image of him came back: a big black bear standing in front of me. How could it be? How in the world did a human become a bear? It didn't make sense. It wasn't possible.

Maybe it was some sort of an epic gag? No, Conner didn't joke. He wasn't the trickster type. So that meant it was real.

Conner could become a bear at will. And apparently, so could thousands of others. But why? What was their purpose on this earth? Why would such creatures exist? I got up and went to my computer; I had to see what was out there.

I started searching. Shifters, werewolves, were...*bears*? Anything that made sense and might have given me answers. Surely, shifters themselves were online, too. They must've had a forum where they could've chatted with each other, right? Or a shifter version of Facebook? I chuckled at the thought.

I was so engrossed in my search that I hadn't heard Nikki come home. She opened my door and asked, "You're still up?"

I shrieked and almost fell off my chair.

"Sorry," she said. "You okay?"

I rushed to shut my laptop so she wouldn't see what I was looking at.

"Um, do you suddenly have a werewolf fetish?"

She'd seen. Shit! I'd only known for a few hours, and already I'd screwed up. I gaped at her with wild eyes.

"Oh," she said. "Oh, okay. Did Conner...?"

"Did Conner what?" I snapped back.

"Tell you something tonight?"

"What do you mean?" I was aware that I was talking too fast and being sketchy. I didn't know what to do. I was panicking.

"Something about himself. A secret that you have

to keep?"

I studied her. What was she saying? Did she know?

"Jessie, you look out of your mind. Did you see Conner tonight?"

I nodded.

"Did he tell you a secret?"

I nodded again.

"Did that secret have something to do with what you were looking up online?"

I nodded a third time.

She sighed. "So, he told you he's a shifter."

"What?!" I screeched. "You know? I thought it was this big secret!"

"It is. It definitely is. Logan and Alaina told me. I was so close to them, they thought I should know."

"They thought you should know that Conner is a shifter?"

She sat on the edge of my bed. "I guess he didn't tell you everything. No, they thought I should know that *they* were shifters."

"Wait, Logan and Alaina were, too?"

She nodded. "Which means Peyton is, too."

"No!" I gasped. "She's not anything like that! She can't be!"

"Shifter parents have shifter babies."

"No!" I covered my face with my hands in horror. "Don't say that! It can't be true!"

"It's not that big of a deal. Kids don't really shift much. But if you were her nanny, you should have known. I think it can happen by accident sometimes, but I'm not really sure. Conner would have to explain it."

I slowly shook my head back and forth. "No... freaking...way..."

"Jessie, relax. It's not that big of a deal."

"It *is* a big deal, Nikki!" I grasped her forearms, gripping her for support. "You don't understand. I...I..."

"Calm down. God, you're sweating and all worked up. It's okay. I'll make you a drink." She got up.

"No!"

"Okay. Sheesh." She sat back down.

"Do you remember that I slept with Conner?"

"Um, of course. So?" she replied. "Sleeping with a shifter doesn't make you one. You're not going to become a bear, if that's what you're worried about. It's not like those movies where you can be bit. There's no way to become a shifter except to be born as one."

"Exactly. Shifter parents have shifter babies?" My words were failing me. They came out like a squeak.

"Yeah..."

"Well, I'm pregnant. And now I'm going to give birth to a cub instead of a baby."

"Holy crap." She blinked at me. "Wait, are you sure? How late are you? How could you not have said anything sooner? Did you take a test? Did you see a doctor?"

I answered her slowly, hoping that the world would stop spinning around me. "I took a test just the other day. I had this date with Conner, and I thought I should tell him first. I was going to tell him tonight. I have a doctor's appointment for next week, but I can't keep it now. They'll probably do an ultrasound; what if they look and I have a tiny freaking bear inside me!"

I crumbled to the floor and broke into sobs, rocking back and forth, holding my hands over my ears like I did when I was little and didn't want to hear what was being said.

Nikki hugged me for a long time and tried to soothe me. Finally, she resulted to yanking my hands away from my ears.

"First, you have to tell him. Talk to him. I doubt you have a bear in there; I don't think it works that way. But he'll know the details. And he needs to know, anyway."

"I can't. I can't be with him. I can't have this baby. What am I going to do? I can't even give it away! I couldn't give someone a baby that might become a bear at any time! Oh, my god, I have to get an abortion, don't I? But Nikki, I can't do that! I can't kill my baby! But I can't have a bear, either! What the fuck am I supposed to do?"

I kept rocking and sobbing.

"Jessie...I don't know what to say. You have to talk to

Conner. I'll support you in whatever decision you make, but I can only help you so much; I hardly know anything about shifters. I'm sorry you're going through this. I can imagine why you're freaked out; I would be, too. But Conner is the best person to help you right now."

18

CONNER

"This is all your fault!" I screamed at Ezra through my phone. "I never should have told her! I shouldn't have said anything! Now, everything's fucked up."

"Okay, man, calm down. You said you were going to talk to her again. Give her time to let this sink in. It's a lot to hear."

"You asshole! I never should have listened to you!" I stormed back and forth in my living room, still fuming from my encounter with Jessie. Once I'd snapped out of my daze, the rage had taken over. And I had just one place to unleash it. "Don't ever talk to me again."

I hung up on him. He called back immediately, and I ignored the call. He left a voicemail and I refused to listen. I wouldn't give him the satisfaction.

I did have one solution, though. There was something more productive that I could've been doing with all that fury. I stripped down and went out back, then shifted before I took off running in the direction of the jail.

Conner!

Fuck off, Ezra.

Dude, come on. Just see what happens. You don't even know how it'll turn out!

I refused to answer him.

Hey man, let's talk about this, Owen said. *I can't have you guys fighting.*

I ignored them both.

Where are you going? Owen asked.

I felt him listening to my thoughts. It was a sort of an intrusive feeling, like someone prying at your scalp.

Get out! I screamed back.

Do not go over there, Owen warned. *Conner! This is not how we do things.*

This is how I do things.

Absolutely not. I forbid it.

As the Alpha, he had that power over me. Usually. But not that day. It didn't matter what the consequences would have been. He could've kicked me out of the clan. He could've had me killed. I would've welcomed that, even. It didn't matter. I was going to tear that croc to shreds.

The conclave is meeting tomorrow, Owen said. *You'll have your chance then. There will be justice for this.*

Yup. About two seconds after I get my hands in that cell.

I wasn't that far away. I was closing in on the jail and I could almost taste the crocs's blood.

But then I smelled Owen.

He ran into me, crashing hard and interrupting my stride. I fought back for a moment, trying to get away from him. We wrestled, but in the end, I let him pin me. I gave up.

I don't want to see you get killed or be in trouble for this. Let the conclave do their job.

Like they've done so far? I barked. *Why didn't they step in sooner? Why didn't they do anything after your mate was attacked or after the panthers were killed? You thought we could handle it, that's why. And now we're handling it.* **I'm** *handling it.*

You're not. I can't let you do that. I know this is the worst time of your life. And it seems like it keeps getting worse. I get it and it sucks, but it will get better. It has to.

I tried to push him off me. *I don't need your patronizing words right now.*

That's not what this is, he promised. *I just want to help you. We all do. Look, why don't I have Addie talk to Jessie? Woman to woman. I think she can get through to her.*

It doesn't matter. I'm done with her. I'm letting her go. I can't take the pain anymore. I almost choked on the words. He backed off a bit, and I could breathe better.

Don't give up yet. You love this woman. Give her a chance to get used to our world. *Bring her to meet the clan. Let her see that we're all just human on some level. We're not monsters.*

I lay back down and stopped struggling. *I'm hiring a permanent nanny. I'll figure out how to be a single dad, and I'll move on. I don't need her. I need to see this croc die, though. That's all I need. I don't need anyone else.*

He will face justice. I swear on my life.

If the conclave doesn't take him out, I swear on what little life I have left that I will.

If the conclave fails us like that, which they won't, I'll help you.

Fine then, I snapped.

I'm letting you up now. Don't make me regret it.

Just to prove I was the stronger bear and had let him pin me down, I kicked up with my back legs and sent him flying.

Point made, he said. *Why don't you come just hang out for a while? You and Peyton. She's having a blast with James.*

I want to be alone for a while. Can you keep her tonight?

Sure, man. But she needs you. This is a hard time for her, and you're the only family she has left.

I know.

I ran home more slowly than I had when I'd left. When I felt Ezra shift in, I admitted, *I'm sorry, man.*

It's okay, he said. *I'll pay you back next time I see you. Heard from her?*

No. And I don't expect to.

Then maybe you should hurry home.

Um, why?

Just hurry. But maybe shift before you get there.

I picked up my pace. *Could she be there? Is there any chance?* It was so late. I could see the hint of dawn breaking; she had to be sleeping. But when I got closer, I spotted her car. I shifted back and went to the shed to get an extra set of clothes I had there, got dressed and walked around to the front to meet her.

Her eyes were red and swollen. She looked distraught and as out of her mind as I felt.

"Come inside." I unlocked the door and let her in.

She sat on the couch, stiffly. Her hands were on her knees, her back straight. She looked straight ahead.

I stood in front of her, moving my weight from foot to foot. I was so nervous, I felt ready to explode. She certainly didn't seem happy.

"So...?" I dared after a long silence.

She didn't look at me. "There is something I need to tell you."

"Okay." I blew out a breath. "Go ahead."

"I'm pregnant. In light of recent developments, I've decided not to have the baby because I don't think I can handle having a bear cub, but I thought you should know."

I didn't think I was still capable of being shocked. I thought that because so much shit had happened, nothing would have phased me any longer. But that? The news rocked my world so hard, I actually stumbled. I made it to the couch and dropped down, taking a moment to replay her words in my mind.

"You're pregnant?"

"I believe so, yes. I took a test and it was positive, but I haven't been to see a doctor yet, so I suppose there's a chance the test is wrong."

"Does that happen often?"

"Not that I know of."

"Okay. Well. I mean, obviously it's mine, there's no question there, right?"

"Of course."

"Right," I said. "I know that. I wasn't questioning it. I'm sorry, I was just...I'm just trying to get my head around this."

"I would guess that this isn't quite as big of a shock as finding out that the father of your unborn child turns into a bear at will."

"I guess not. I wouldn't know; I was raised in this world. And I made a point of not letting people in who weren't shifters know so that I never had to have that conversation."

"Then that's just one more thing you've messed up, isn't it?"

Her words cut me. She never spoke like that to me. Never. Her judgment of me, of my failure, made it seem final and irrevocable. Not just a mistake, but a grave error that would scar me for life.

"I'm sorry, Jessie. I didn't plan this. I didn't plan to have my brother and his wife die. I didn't plan to become a single father. You came to me, remember? You said you'd be Peyton's nanny. I needed someone and your sister was friends with Alaina, so it made sense. But I didn't think..."

"You didn't think *what*?" She finally looked at me and began to sob.

"Just don't do this, please. Let's at least talk about this and think things through before you make a decision. I mean, that's my baby, too. That's my son or daughter growing inside you."

As I said it, the words sunk in. *My child. I had a child.* Tiny, growing, inside the woman I loved but couldn't tell.

Her body shook violently as she continued to cry. "But I'm—I'm so scared, Conner. How am I going to do this?"

My throat thickened. I needed to find the words to get through to her. "Jessie." I slid down in front of her and took her hands in mine. I pressed her hand to my cheek and let the tears flow. "I love you. I know I'm not perfect; I'm not even close. But you make me better. You make me want to be better. This baby—" I dared to put my hand on her stomach and was relieved she didn't push it away— "This baby is here now. It's part of you and me. That means something. It's a new life. In the middle of all this death, there's something new. I've never done this before. I've never been in love, and I don't know how to do it. I don't know how to be a father. I'm failing Peyton every day. You know that better than anyone. But I want to be better. You can help me do that; you already have. I can be myself with you. I can let go and be free. I feel safe with you, and I haven't felt that since I was a kid. And now... You said we all need to have a purpose. I haven't had one. But I do now. This baby, our child, us..." I looked up at her, blinking through my tears to see her face. "You're my purpose. Our family—you, me, Peyton, and this new little baby—you're my purpose."

She blinked back at me. I wanted her to say something. Anything. I pleaded with my eyes, but she just stared. And then, I had another thought: I would have to prove it to her.

"Jessie Miller. I need you more than I've ever needed anyone in my life. I love you. I want to be with you forever, and I want us to share a family and a life together. I want to raise this baby with you and be the man I know I should be; the man I can be with you by my side. I promise I will love you and sacrifice everything for our family. I will do whatever it takes. I'll clean up and get more help. I'll learn how to be a father. I'll do better. I'll *be* better. I'll be whatever you need. Please. Stay with me. Love me. Marry me. Be mine forever."

Her mouth popped open. "What?"

"Marry me. Please."

She swallowed and licked her lips, then, very slowly and softly, responded. "I will."

19
JESSIE

He bowed at my feet and cried.

My *fiancé*.

I couldn't make the word sound right. Had I just gotten engaged? Had he just proposed? I put my hand on his head. His crying became wracking sobs that shook his shoulders. I knew he needed this; he needed to let out so much pain he'd kept buried inside for so long.

I wondered if he could really do all he promised. Could he really stop drinking? Could he really learn become a good father? He seemed genuine, but I was still in shock from everything so much, that I didn't know what to think.

He looked up at me, his eyes as red as mine had been earlier. "I'm sorry I don't have a ring. I didn't realize I'd be proposing today."

"Yeah, it's kind of been a crazy day."

"To say the least. I have something else to tell you, too."

I braced myself, not sure if I could handle much else. "Is everything okay?"

"More than okay. They found the bastard who killed Logan and Alaina."

"Are you serious? That's incredible!"

"It was a shifter who did it. A crocodile. We've been—"

"Crocodile? There are crocodile shifters?"

"In the Everglades, we have crocodiles, panthers, wolves, and of course, bears."

Okay then. At some point, I'd stop being shocked by this. Just not yet. "Wow."

"Yeah." He pulled his mouth into a half smile. "Usually, we all get along. But the crocs don't want other shifters in the area, so they've been causing problems. My clan leader, Owen, had to save his now-wife from being attacked by one. We just dealt with a huge panther attack, and now this. We have a conclave—a group of representatives from all different types of shifters—that's like our judicial system. They're going to come and decide what to do with him. He'll likely be killed."

"Ah. That shifter justice system you mentioned before."

"Right."

"Wait, so is Peyton in danger? Are you? Am I?" My hand went to my stomach instinctively. I still worried about giving birth to a bear, but knowing Conner's commitment of being with me through it all made it easier to handle.

"Not that I know of specifically. The crocs are somewhat of a threat to shifters in general, but that's what we're fighting to stop. And so far, it's been just them. And once we find out why, we can end it. A lot of us want to ban the crocs from the 'Glades altogether."

I nodded. "I think I like that plan."

He flashed me a grin. "Are you okay with all this?" he asked. "You must be tired, if nothing else. It's nearly morning, and it's been a long night."

"I'm exhausted."

"Can we just go to sleep and talk more in the morning?"

"Where's Peyton?"

"At Owen and Addie's." He stood and held out his hand. I put mine in his and let him help me up, then lead me to the bedroom. "I can't wait to introduce you to my clan. You'll love Addie and Hailey. Ezra's girl, Britt, is a panther, so she's not part of our clan in the same way, but she's still considered a member and is always around. She's cool. We're all like family."

"They're all shifters?"

"In our clan, yes." He gave me an apologetic smile. "Does that make it weird?"

"What's weird about hanging out with a bunch of people who turn into animals?" I laughed.

"Right. Well, they're all very welcoming." Once we

reached the bedroom, he pulled his shirt off. "Do you want something to sleep in?"

I shook my head as I unhooked my bra and slid it out from under my shirt, then stepped out of my pants. He kicked off his shorts and slid into bed in his boxers. Seeing him again—all of him—gave me that same thrill I'd felt before. His hard, muscular body, adorned with tattoos, all there for me to see. And I was going to have *that* by my side forever? I couldn't believe it.

"I hope our child looks like you." I slid in under the covers and snuggled close to him.

"Are you kidding me? I hope he or she is even half as gorgeous as you are."

He pulled me close and I melted a little. I'd wanted this so badly. As freaked out as I'd been, as angry and confused and distraught I'd been all night, what I really wanted was to be able to be close to him again. I hadn't thought it would have happened. And there I was. Not only with him, but soon to be his wife.

"Are we really engaged?" I asked. "Are you really going to marry me?"

"Are you already having doubts?"

"Yes."

I felt him stiffen.

"I can't believe this is happening," I continued. "I'm doubting all sorts of reality today."

"So, does that mean you don't know if you want to be my wife?"

"I do. More than anything. I love you, Conner. I've loved you for a while now."

"You have?" His voice wavered.

"I should have told you sooner."

"You should have. You know, no one has ever said that to me before."

"I'm sure your parents did," I corrected.

"You know what I mean. Not in the romantic sense."

"Not to me, either."

"First loves never die, isn't that what they say?"

"Who's this *they*?" I asked. "*They* also say there's no such thing as werewolves and vampires. I don't trust *they* one bit." I laughed. "Conner?"

"Yes, love?"

The pet name washed over me like a warm shower. I smiled. "Is it true that there's no way to become a shifter? Like by being bitten or something?"

"It's true. You're either born a shifter or you're not."

"Am I going to give birth to a cub?"

He sucked in a breath. "Well, there's no chance at all that the baby will born in bear form. But there's a 50/50 chance that he or she will be a shifter."

"Huh?"

"When shifter women give birth, if they're in their animal form, the baby is born in animal form. If they're in their human form, the baby is born in human form. If both parents are shifters, like in Peyton's case, it's a 100% chance that the baby will be a shifter."

"Yeah, Nikki told me about Peyton. I still can't believe that tiny little thing is capable of morphing into a bear."

"Huh. She knows?"

"She said Alaina told her."

"I wonder why. Did she tell you about us outright?"

"No, she happened to come up behind me when I was researching shifters on my laptop, and she asked me a lot of questions until I admitted that you'd told me a secret related to my search, and then she put two and two together..."

"Okay. She knows it's an important secret, though, right?"

"Definitely."

"Okay, then. Let's sleep now."

"Conner?"

He let out a sigh. "Yes, honey?"

"Will you make love to me first?"

He chuckled. "Are you kidding?" He nuzzled his nose into my neck and started to kiss me. "Tonight, tomorrow, and every night for the rest of our lives."

"Mmm," I moaned as he sent chills over my skin. "I like that arrangement."

He kissed down to my nipples and sucked on one and I reveled in the sensation. They were even more sensitive those days; I wondered if anything else would feel different because of the pregnancy.

"How do you like *this* arrangement?" he asked, yanking my panties off and making his way down to the apex of my thighs with his mouth.

"Oh god," I moaned as he teased my sensitive bundle of nerves with the tip of his tongue. "I love when you do that."

"How about this?" He slid a finger inside me. A wave of pleasure ran over me as he moved it in and out and continued to flick me with his tongue.

I answered him with a moan. I could feel my wetness as he moved his finger around, plunging it in deeper. But his finger wasn't enough. I wanted more of him.

He kept working me until I couldn't take it anymore. I didn't want to come just yet, I wanted to draw it out; to wait until I couldn't hold back any longer.

When I got too close, I gently tugged on his hair and he crawled up my body, kissing me along my neck to my jaw. He pulled my lip into his mouth and sucked gently.

"My turn," I said.

He raised an eyebrow. "Okay..."

"Lie down."

He obeyed. His cock stood at full-mast, thick, rock-hard and begging for attention. I took it in my hand, feeling its smoothness as I stroked it. I watched his face; I liked the way he closed his eyes and clenched his jaw at the pleasure of my touch.

I leaned forward and slid my lips over his member, stroking its base while I sucked him, moving my mouth up and down along with my hand. I took him as deep as I could, opening the back of my throat a bit to accommodate his length.

"Oh god," he moaned. "Yes."

He put his hand on my head, running his fingers through my hair. "Damn," he pulled back suddenly and gave a half chuckle. "You're a little too good at that. I don't want to come just yet. Why don't you come over here?"

I gave him a satisfied smile and climbed on top of him, my breasts pressed flat against his chest. I rubbed against him, letting his shaft get wet between my aching folds, driving myself mad in the process. He reached down and positioned himself at my opening and I sat up slightly, letting him slip inside me before I began to grind against his cock.

Grabbing my hips, he pulled me down harder, driving himself even deeper. I liked being on top; it gave me more control. As I rode him, every time our eyes met, his stare thrilled me.

He pulled me down close to him and grabbed my behind. "I love this ass."

I answered with a moan.

"I want to see you touch yourself," he said.

"Yeah?" I kissed him and began to buck my hips against him even faster.

I stuck my fingers in my mouth, then dragged them down my torso, reaching for my pleasure pearl. He gave a wicked smile as I started to rub myself in circles—slowly, at first, but then picking up speed to match the rhythm of his thrusts. Feeling tiny jolts of electricity beginning to tingle in my extremities, I added another finger and worked myself even harder, knowing my climax was just moments away. As I moaned out, constricting more and more tightly around his shaft, he pounded into me even faster. The sensation rushed through me so hard, it sent me over the edge, crying out loudly as he grabbed my hips, thrusting into me with full force. Seconds later, I felt his dick throbbing with his heartbeat as he reached his peak, filling me with his essence.

I lay flat on his chest, breathing fast.

"Did you like that?"

"Are you kidding?" I breathed.

He chuckled. "Good. I just want to make you feel good. Forever."

"I want to let you."

I didn't remember falling asleep, but when I felt him slip out of me, it seemed like hours had passed and the day had grown light. I nuzzled into him and drifted back to sleep.

20

JESSIE

"You have nothing at all to worry about," Conner said for the tenth time.

"But there's just so many of them," I said.

Peyton bounced in the backseat. "Clan time, clan time," she sang.

"See? Even Peyton loves them."

I glanced back at her, her pigtails bouncing as she moved from side to side.

"Yeah, but I think she's actually just on a sugar high."

In the months since I moved in with Conner and Peyton and had left my awful job, Peyton seemed to have become a different person. She was thrilled to see me again, just as much as I was to see her. We'd had a tearful reunion, followed by a long talk where Conner apologized and shared his feelings with her more than he ever had. He asked her if she wanted me to come back as her nanny. She gave him an emphatic yes and jumped into my arms.

When he asked her what she thought of me moving in, she squealed with joy. And then, when she found out we were going to have a baby and get married, she ran around the room in circles, cheering.

Conner had looked at me with wide eyes. "I haven't seen her like this in months."

We still had plenty of sad moments, and Logan and Alaina would always be sorely missed. We talked about them as much as we could. By then, I felt like I knew them in a way, from everything Conner and Peyton had told me about them and all the photos and videos I had seen. It seemed to help Peyton to sit with Conner and me and reminisce about their family trips and times together. She would always cry at some point and we would hug her; often, we cried along with her. Conner, especially, had gotten much better about letting his grief out and allowing Peyton to see him cry. The first time it happened, Peyton had looked at him and gave him such a sweet hug, it brought tears to my eyes—not that it took much those days, with all the extra hormones circulating around my body.

We were on our way over to Owen and Addie's house. I'd met them briefly a few times, but that day, I'd be meeting the entire clan, spending time getting to know them. It was both an engagement party and pregnancy celebration, they said.

Addie had promised that we'd also have a baby shower when the time grew closer, where we could kick the men outside and oooh and ahh at the tiny baby clothes to our hearts' content.

Addie had emphatically told me I was not allowed to bring anything—so, I'd baked cupcakes. Once they found out that the color of the filling inside would reveal the baby's gender, I figured she couldn't complain too much.

When we pulled in, the sight of the decorations and lights and so many people made me feel even more overwhelmed.

Conner squeezed my hand. "These people are my very best friends and they'll become yours, too."

"Right. Unless they hate me."

"Not a chance."

Peyton had thrown off her seatbelt and was running toward James and Addie. We walked over and Addie came to greet us.

"Hey! What is this?" she asked, taking the white bakery box from me.

"Cupcakes. But not just any cupcakes! Gender reveal cupcakes."

Her face broke into a beaming grin. "Oh my god, how awesome! I can't wait to find out!"

She set the cupcakes down and came back to escort me around. Her own belly was quite round; she was due in just a few weeks and had already invited me to be there. It was apparently a shifter thing to have people around when you gave birth, like women used to do to help each other back in the day, but she'd assured me that no one would be offended if I decided to not do that. Most of them preferred giving birth in animal form because it was easier, so that limited the choice of venue a bit. Addie pointed to a grassy section and a tree at the edge of the yard and said that James had been born right there.

It seemed very bizarre to me. I couldn't imagine it, but I would get to see a birth before I had to decide. And Conner had told me many times that we could go to a hospital or do whatever I wanted to do.

I was introduced to all the ladies of the clan, and even though I was a little overwhelmed, I tried my best to remember all their names: Britt, Hailey and Tori. Then Conner had me meet the men, Noah, Ezra and Owen. Mason was apparently missing. They were all really great, actually. They asked questions, told me stories, and I felt like I was already accepted as part of their group. The ladies talked about married life as shifters, how difficult it was to keep clothes stashed all over the place and to find deals because things got ruined so often.

When I asked if Britt and Ezra had any kids, Britt coyly replied, "Not yet. But maybe we'll think about having a little bundle of fur soon." She'd glanced over at Ezra and made a roar face at him. He responded with a wink.

"But, you're a panther and he's a bear, right?" I asked.

"I know. Crazy, right? But we make it work somehow."

"So, would your baby be...?"

"Definitely a shifter. Interspecies couples don't happen all that often, but from what we can gather, it's about a 50/50 shot: 50% it'll be a Florida panther like me and 50% it'll be bumbling bear like Ezra."

I nodded. Such a strange world. I didn't know how I'd managed to accept it. It had taken me some time, but I finally had. Only recently had I stopped freaking out when Conner shifted in front of me. Once, Peyton had done it, sort of by accident, but she'd had a really bad day and then Conner had been a little short with her. When he'd first quit drinking, there had been a rough period when he'd been more than a little grumpy. Peyton had been upset and then she'd dropped a mug that her mother had given her, which shattered and cut her foot in the process. She'd howled in pain and misery and started to shake.

I'd screamed for Conner. I thought she was having a seizure, but he knew what was going on. He'd talked her through it as she shifted, and then shifted back a few minutes later. I wasn't sure which of us was in the worst shape that night. Conner had assured me it was rare for kids to shift until they hit puberty. He'd said it would be very unlikely that, if our baby were to be a shifter, he or she would spontaneously shift for at least the first few years of his or her life.

"I was wondering one thing," I asked them as we

continued to discuss shifter life. "For us, if it's only a 50/50 chance, will we just have to wait until it happens accidentally one day or until the child is closer to puberty to know?"

They exchanged glances, seeming to decide on the answer. "It depends," Hailey finally said.

"Sorry, that's a terrible answer," Addie added.

"With my brother," Hailey continued, "his wife is human, and it wasn't long after their baby was born that he could smell she was a shifter."

"You can smell it?"

Addie nodded. "But with kids, it can be tricky. Not all of them give off the scent early. And it can be faint. Honestly, if I didn't know for sure James was, I would guess he wasn't."

"He hardly has the scent at all," Britt agreed.

"I know. Weird, right?" Addie said. "So, it might be years."

"Or you might know right away," Tori offered. "When my cousin had her baby, we all knew as soon as the baby was making his way out of her." She laughed. "Of course, that boy is a handful and a half. And he shifts a lot."

I nodded, my worry increasing with each story.

"It probably won't be years and years," Hailey said. "My friend said all four of her kids shifted when they were two, the first time they had a tantrum."

"I know someone who's baby shifted when she was just a day old," Tori added. "The poor thing had some kind of heart condition. I guess it was so much that the little thing just couldn't hold it back. Turned out to be a good thing, though.

It straightened something up in her little body and she was fine after that."

"A day old?" I repeated. Conner had assured me that wasn't possible.

"That's very unusual," Addie said, putting her hand on my shoulder. "Peyton has the scent, and since she's Conner's brother's child, maybe your baby will, too."

"Mason!" Someone shouted and I turned with the group to see a man approaching. He held up a hand to us and hurried over to Conner.

They had an intense conversation, then Conner made his way over to us. "I found out where Mason's been. Turns out that the croc who killed Logan and Alaina is dead. The shifter in the cell next to him didn't like him much, either and clawed him to death. A wolf."

I searched his face to see how he was taking it. Justice had been served, but he hadn't had a part in it.

I turned him to me and hugged him. I whispered, "You okay with this?"

"Yeah," he said in my ear. "At least I don't have to worry about him again."

By the time we left that night, our spirits were high. Peyton fell asleep in the car on the way home, having played so hard. I felt wholly accepted and thrilled to be joining the clan, and Conner had found some peace, knowing his brother and sister-in-law's killer was finally dead. The question of why it was Logan and Alaina had been answered weeks ago, when the conclave interrogated the croc. The two of them had witnessed a crime: the croc had a truckload of poison and was about to contaminate the clan's water supply. They'd been spotted, and later that day, turned up dead, conveniently before they could identify the croc who'd tried to wipe out the entire clan. Knowing that, and now having the killer gone for good, seemed to bring some sense of healing.

As we lay in bed that night, Conner tracing circles over my little baby bump, I said, "I have a confession."

"Oh yeah?"

"I'm a little jealous that I'm not a shifter. I think, if it were an option, I'd want to become one. To be more like you."

He kissed me. "You are like me. More so than some of my clan."

"You know what I mean. Especially with that mind link. Could be handy."

"It can also be a pain."

"Even still. I hope the baby is a shifter."

He pulled back to look at me. "You do?"

"I do. After meeting your clan, I know that it would be a good thing." I saw something by his ear and turned his head. I broke into laughter.

"What?"

"When they smashed that cupcake in your face, they did a good job." I swiped my finger just inside his ear and showed him the light blue frosting.

He licked it off my finger. "Still yummy."

"I can think of better places to put that finger."

"Oh, can you now?" He wiggled his brow and tickled me.

"Stop! Stop!" I laughed and tried to get away from him. "Wait! I have a name idea!"

"What?"

I pulled my lip into my mouth. "You can say no, and it's totally fine. But I thought it would be a nice tribute to name him Logan."

Tears rose in his eyes, and he kissed my stomach. "I can't think of anything more perfect."

21

JESSIE

EPILOGUE: TWO YEARS LATER

"Logan William Griffin!" I shouted. "Put that down right now!"

My toddler held a metal fork just a little too close to the electrical outlet. He was going to shove it in; I could see it in his eyes.

He stared at me, and as I moved closer, he defiantly jammed the fork into the socket and I screamed. "Don't!"

Sparks flew and he shrieked. I heard Conner's footsteps running closer and Peyton called from somewhere in the house. The lights didn't flicker, so that must have been a good sign.

"Logan!" I screeched. "Are you okay?" I turned him over, frantically scanning his body for burns. He cried loudly, and when I took the fork from his hand, he threw himself down on the ground and pounded his fists on the floor.

Conner reached us and bent over him with his stern daddy face on. "Logan, stop this right now."

"Fork! Fork!" he yelled.

As he twitched and cried, I saw his tiny body start to shake. It reminded me of when Peyton had spontaneously shifted.

"Conner..." I said. "Is he...?"

"I think so. Just give him room."

With a hideous shriek, black fur emerged from Logan's delicate skin. His mouth stretched wide and his teeth grew into fangs. His little hands, still sticky with jelly from breakfast, lengthened and sprouted claws.

He stood there, a tiny bear cub, looking shocked and scared. Conner pulled off his clothes and shifted, then he grabbed him in a hug and held him as I watched in awe.

My son was a shifter. We hadn't been sure. For all the talk of the scent, there hadn't been much of anything either way. Some of the clan said he definitely was, some said there was no way. There'd been a pool going since he was born two years earlier, and in that moment, I laughed to myself, wondering who had won.

Peyton came to see what was going on and sat with me, petting Logan and nuzzling into Conner. After some time, Logan shifted back and fell asleep and I took him from Conner, who shifted back himself.

"Well, now we know," Conner said. "Logan takes after his namesake in more than just looks."

I smiled at my husband. "I wonder what this one will turn out to be."

Conner put a hand to my swollen belly. "I guess we'll know soon...or at least in a few years."

"I'm glad it's a girl this time," Peyton said. "Since I already have a brother."

I patted my belly, and the baby moved. "She's glad, too."

"Can we name her Alaina?" Peyton asked.

I met Conner's eyes and we smiled at each other. We'd had this conversation already and thought it would be a fine choice for a name. We'd use my mom's, Michelle, for a middle name since we'd used Conner's dad's, William, for Logan's middle name.

"I think that's a great idea," I said, pulling Peyton in close to join our hug.

With a loving, devoted husband, two amazing kids and another on the way, my family was complete. My heart swelled at the thought; I could ask for nothing more.

THE END

RELENTLESS MATES

WEREBEARS OF THE EVERGLADES

1

GRACE

I walked into my family's dining room and plopped down in my seat at the table. "I'm starving!"

My dad and brother, Tyler, were already sitting there, waiting.

"Got some good steaks tonight." Dad rubbed his hands together.

A few minutes later, my mom placed our meal on the table. For the first few minutes of dinner, we ate so hungrily that we didn't talk. But, as we slowed down, conversation crept in.

"I think I found a law school," I said after my brother mentioned that he'd applied at Miami University.

I'd been looking at schools for a little while, deciding where would be the best place to take my degree in biology to the next level to become an environmental lawyer. Living in the Everglades, I saw a lot of conservation efforts going on at all times. Not all were successful, though, and I wanted a hand in helping to make sure the 'Glades were preserved.

I thought they would be happy that I'd decided; my mom especially had been asking me about it. But I noticed my parents exchange a look.

My dad set down his fork. "Grace, we've been talking."

Something in his tone made me nervous. "Okay…"

"What if you went over to the park and became a ranger?"

"Well, that's not exactly what I want to do. Being a lawyer is much different."

"But isn't it kind of the same thing?" my brother asked.

I gave him an incredulous look. "No. A ranger does the conserving and runs the park, taking care of issues that happen only there. I would be a lawyer, going to court to help clients with issues dealing with conservation. Like how the local paper plant keeps polluting the water. They just pay the fine and go on polluting. I would represent the state or the county or whoever wanted to stop them and help them to win so that the water stops being polluted."

Tyler rolled his eyes. "I know *that*. I'm not an idiot."

Before I could respond, my mom jumped in. "I think he just meant that both positions are focused on preserving the environment."

With a full mouth, Tyler said, "Yeah, that."

"I guess they are similar, but they're two very different jobs," I insisted.

"Here's the thing, Grace." My dad sat forward with his serious face on. "I'll just get right to it. We need you. The clan needs you. You're the only one of us crocs who's qualified to work in the park as a ranger. We need a presence in that park if we're going to survive."

I blew out a hard breath. So it was more than just simple conversation, then. It was planned, and they were trying to coerce me. "Dad, I know that's important, but I can do a lot of good for our clan and all shifters by being a lawyer."

"I don't doubt it," he said. "You'll be good at whatever you do. But this can't wait. Tyler is just starting school this year. It'll be at least four years until he graduates, maybe longer."

"Hey!" Tyler protested.

My dad raised an eyebrow at him. "What year were you supposed to finish high school?"

"I only flunked one year, and I've changed since then!"

My mother held up her hands. "Okay. This isn't about that right now. The point is, Grace, you're the only who can get in there now or anytime in the near future. And we need information on things that are happening."

"Things?" I asked. "What things?"

"There've been some rumors," my dad continued.

My mom got up and started clearing the table. I collected plates and took a stack over to the sink to help, and Dad followed, carrying an empty platter.

"The clan is saying they've heard of a bear attack coming. Against us crocs."

"Why would they do that?" I asked him. Sure, bears and crocs hadn't gotten along over the years, especially in the Everglades. That didn't mean they would just attack us unprovoked.

"That's what we need to find out. If we had someone in there who might easily overhear conversations, who might pick up on who is where at what times, who is friendly with whom, that sort of thing..."

"So, you want me to work in the park to spy on the bears." I gave him a flat look.

"You can think of it like that, or you can see it as a way to fulfill your desire for preservation in a more...*direct* way, while also helping to preserve your clan and very species. The more we know, the better we can protect ourselves."

"You can always go to law school later," my mother added. "Once we get this thing with the bears settled once and for all."

"And what does that even look like?" I asked. "Is it possible to settle anything with them if they're always so against us?"

"That's exactly what you'd be helping to do," my dad said. "You would get to know them and then use your future lawyer knowledge to help us all come to an agreement. Your award-winning debate skills would come in mighty handy in that case."

I rolled my eyes. "Laying it on a bit thick."

"But he has a point," my mom added. "You want to be a lawyer for a reason, and doing so well on the debate team in high school and college proves that you're good at winning debates and talking to people. You're perfect for this task, and what more important case would you have to win than one that will keep your people alive and bring the clans and the entire Everglades peace?"

"Yeah, no pressure, though," I snickered.

Could I do that? Could I really give up my dream of becoming a lawyer—or least postpone it for a few years—to become a park ranger?

"I'll have to think about this."

A few minutes later, while I was helping my mom with the dishes, there was a knock on the door. My dad got up from the living room to answer it.

From the kitchen I heard him exclaim, "Well, look who it is!"

Two sets of footsteps made their way toward us.

"Adam's stopped by to see us," my dad announced.

"Hello," my mom said and wiped her hands on her apron.

I nodded at Adam and kept at my task of scrubbing the pan.

"We were just talking about the rumor of the bear attack," my dad said. "Grace here is thinking about becoming a park ranger so that we can get some inside information and stop the attack before it happens."

Adam's eyes grew wide. "Wow, Grace. I can't tell you how much that means to the clan and to me, personally. I mean, it would give us so much information and really help us get to the bottom of this situation once and for all. You might be saving many lives doing this. I always knew you'd end up doing something grand and selfless. That's just the kind of croc you are."

I set down the pot and turned to him. "Thanks. But even if I do this, there's no guarantee they'll hire me."

He beamed at me as if I were his favorite person on Earth. "With your degree and credentials? There's no way they wouldn't."

I didn't smile back. "We'll see."

"You know, Grace, I've been watching you for a while."

He stepped closer to me and looked down at his feet. I think he was trying to look vulnerable. Humble, maybe? But it came off as somewhat creepy. Then I noticed my parents had snuck out of the room, leaving us alone in the kitchen. *Real subtle, guys.*

"Yeah?" I asked. "Why would you do that?"

"Besides the fact that you're stunning?" He met my eyes and gave me an intense stare. "Even back when we were in school together, I saw how special you were."

"We weren't even in the same grade."

"Upperclassmen know things about lowerclassmen.

People talked about you. How amazing you were, and I have to agree. You do something like this for the clan, and they'll all adore you even more than they already do. I'd even say you would make a fabulous co-Alpha."

"I appreciate that, Adam. But I wouldn't want to steal your glory. You earned your role, and you do it well. You deserve to be Alpha alone."

"Well, if you were by my side as not just co-Alpha, but a partner, we would be a team—and I think we'd make a great one, you and me. We could be one of those power couples, you know?"

I had to remind myself that he was the Alpha of our clan. I couldn't say what I really wanted to because of his position. If I were just outright rude, it wouldn't have been appropriate.

"The only problem with that," I pointed out, "is that we're not a couple."

"That can be easily fixed."

He stepped closer, and I worried he might do something very stupid, like try to kiss me. He wasn't a bad looking guy, but I knew him too well and had known him far too long to have any sort of feelings or interest in him whatsoever.

I held up my hand. "Adam, I'm focusing on my career right now. This isn't the time for me to be in any sort of relationship."

"I can be patient."

"Really, I appreciate your kind words and all, and I'll go

ahead and try to work at the park to help the clan. I know we can work together for the greater good of our people, but I'm just not interested in a relationship like that."

He gave me a sideways smile. "I don't mind a challenge. You let me know when you hear from that park. I'll make sure we throw you a nice party for doing something so big for us."

"Thanks." I turned back to my dishes and let out a sigh of relief when he went off to find my dad.

I could help my clan, I'd decided. Who was I to put myself over helping the entire population of croc shifters in the 'Glades? There was too much danger for me to just ignore it and go on with my plans. Maybe I'd get back to law school one day. Or maybe I'd find enough satisfaction in winning the fight, like my dad had said. I was willing to at least give it a try. School would always be there, but if someone didn't step in and put and end to these clan wars, we might not be.

2

MASON

I drove to the Ranger Station, as I often did in the late morning. The Everglades general Park Rangers and Law Enforcement Rangers were closely tied and often worked together. Since the 'Glades took up such a massive amount of land—1.5 million acres—we always were each other's eyes and ears for whatever was going on in the park. It also happened that two of my best friends and clan mates worked as Rangers there. Owen, our clan's Alpha, was also the supervisor of all the Rangers. His second in command, Ezra, also worked as a Park Ranger. I loved being able to do my job serving and protecting while also hanging out with my friends. A real win-win.

I strolled into the Ranger Station and waved to Rachel, the office assistant. "Anyone in?" I asked.

She smiled at me and nodded. "Owen's in his office. Not sure where Ezra is."

That was typical. Ezra tended to be late or off doing who knew what. I knocked on Owen's door with our special knock.

"Hey, Mason."

I walked in and sat down across from him. "What's the word?"

He scrunched his face and tapped his fingers on the desk as he glared at his computer screen.

"Something wrong?" I asked.

"I don't know yet, man."

"Care to elaborate?"

"We hired a new ranger."

"And...?" I pulled my eyebrows together, and he kept squinting at his computer screen. "That doesn't sound like a problem unless there's an issue with the new hire himself."

"*Her*self," he corrected me. "And I don't know if there's an issue or not." He turned from his screen. "She's a croc."

I sucked in a breath. "Okay, well, you must've hired her for a reason."

"I didn't hire her, my boss did. She has impressive credentials—assuming they're all real."

"Are you questioning that?"

"I'm questioning everything at this point until I know for sure if she's a threat or a phony or just plain stupid."

"What do you have there?" I gestured to his computer, where he kept refocusing his attention.

"Searching her name and her school to make sure she is who she says she is."

I nodded slowly. "Everything checking out?"

"So far." He sounded disappointed that he didn't have a reason to turn her away.

"Maybe it won't be a bad thing. We've been trying to settle our differences with the crocs for years. Maybe she can be a bridge."

"Or a spy," he said.

I shrugged. "Or a spy. I guess we'll have to be careful until we know for sure."

"I've never dealt with a situation like this. I'm not sure how to proceed."

"Owen, you're the sharpest man I know. You'll figure it out. I'm sure you'll just keep an eye on her and an ear open. There's nothing else to do, really."

"So far, she's done nothing wrong. At all. I can't even write her up for being late. It's like she's..."

I raised an eyebrow at him.

He continued. "Trying too hard. I hate to make assumptions, but it's like she's up to something. Like she's here for a reason."

"Yeah, I get it. The crocs have not exactly been willing to intermingle on friendly terms."

"She's just so *nice*." He made a disgusted face. "I wish she wasn't so pleasant. It's hard to hate her."

I laughed. "She's a croc. That limits her likability automatically."

His radio crackled and he pressed the button on its side. "Go ahead."

"I checked out the swarm and everything looks good." It was a female's voice on the other end.

"That's her," he said to me. Then, into the radio, "Go on and head back in then."

"Have you heard anything from the conclave lately?" I wondered.

They'd supposedly been aware of and trying to figure out our problem with the clans fighting for a while now. But they never seemed to do much to help us.

"Same as always. I report to them, they listen and take notes and file them, and that's it. Sometimes they make 'helpful' suggestions." He rolled his eyes, then looked up. "Oh hey, Grace."

I turned toward the door to see the new hire. I could smell the croc in her before I even turned. But when my eyes rested on her face, my heart jumped. She might have been a croc, but she was drop dead gorgeous. Like, model gorgeous. I swallowed hard. How could Owen work alongside someone like her? Oh, right, he had his own beautiful wife, Addie. Well, I didn't. I was single, and I'd take my time looking, thank you very much.

I nodded at her. "Welcome to the team."

"Thanks." She smiled and the sight lit up my heart.

"This is Mason." Owen gestured toward me. "He's one of the Law Enforcement Rangers here at the park. If anything questionable goes down here, he'll be on his way."

She met my eyes and her smile grew. "Nice to know we're protected."

"Indeed." I tipped my head at her.

Owen was all business. "Why don't you go on and check on the new calls that came in today. See if there are any you can handle on your own."

"Sure thing, Boss." She smiled at me again, then spun on her heel and left to chat with Rachel.

I gave Owen a wide-eyed look and mouthed, "Holy shit!"

He closed his eyes and slowly shook his head.

The moment she left the station, I was on my feet, leaning on his desk. "I'll keep an eye on her, look her up. Whatever you need."

He smirked back. "You do that, Mason. You do that."

"I will." I tapped my finger on his desk, then hurried off.

I wanted to know all there was to know about that woman.

3

MASON

O wen had called me first and gave me a heads up.
I was grateful because I'd planned to go out on
patrol. When he said Grace was coming in for
her fingerprints and background check, I parked my butt
right behind the front desk, under the guise of doing
research.

And, technically, I *was* doing research. I was looking up
everything I could on Grace. No criminal record or history of
arrests. Nice. Meant she was probably a good little croc.
There wasn't even a mention of her having called the police
to report anything. That could've meant two things: either
she'd never been involved in anything that required a call, or
she had, but hadn't reported whatever crime was going
down. For the time being, I'd give her the benefit of the

doubt. Her DMV record didn't have as much as a speeding ticket.

When the door opened and it was her, I tried to play it cool. "Hi there. What can I do for you?" Then I feigned a moment of recognition. "Oh, it's Grace, right? Owen said you'd be stopping by."

"Hello." She stuck out her hand and I shook it. "Grace Osborn."

"Mason Rowe."

"Nice to meet you."

I pulled my mouth into a half smile. "You, too. Ready to get started?"

"Yup."

I gestured to the seat at the desk. "The background check for new employment asks a lot of questions. Just answer the best you can."

I planned to print a copy of her information for my own purposes later, but for now, I took note of particularly interesting pieces of information. Like her birthday and the fact that she was 26, which was conveniently only a few years younger than me. She'd lived in the 'Glades her whole life, even at the same address. Her family had been in the area for a long time; old crocs. I didn't really have a concept of if the problems we'd been having were more with the newer clans or older, but it seemed like good information to tuck away.

Once that was done, I retrieved the fingerprint kit, set it up and walked around to her side of the desk. I stood close to her and took her hand to roll her finger in the ink, then pressed it down on the page. She was so close, I couldn't help but take in deep breaths of her scent. I thought the croc in her might bother me, but her scent drove my bear wild. It made my heart race; made beads of sweat begin to gather at my temples. I moved slowly, trying to make it seem methodical and careful, but really, I just wanted an excuse to linger near her longer.

When we were through, I handed her a wipe for her fingers. I perched at the edge of the desk, closer than I was when I'd been behind it.

"So, how are you liking the new job?"

"Pretty great so far. Everyone is really nice."

"Owen and Ezra are two of my best friends. They're good guys. Owen's been at this a long time. How about you? Did you dream of being a park ranger when you were a girl?"

She laughed, and the sound was like ecstasy to my soul. "Not exactly. I've actually always wanted to be a lawyer."

I let my shock show. "Then how in the world did you end up working in the park?"

"Well, I wanted to go into environmental law, so it's not too far from my original dream. I guess you could say it was family duty."

"Your clan made you?"

She glanced around, then let out a nervous laugh. "I wasn't sure if it was safe to talk."

"There are a few non-shifters on the force, but none of them are here right now."

"Oh. Well, they didn't make me, but it just seemed that staying local would be better," she explained.

"We all make sacrifices for our clans, I guess."

"Did you? Or did you always want to be a cop?" She leaned against the desk, just feet from me.

"I had no idea what I wanted to do. I spent a lot of time just running and being with my clan. I guess I did sort of the same thing you did in the end. I thought it would help keep all shifters safe, and I wanted to keep the park safe for everyone."

Our conversation came easily; naturally. I could have sat there talking to her all day. We had several things in common, I was pleased to find. Besides being shifters both working to better the park and protect and serve people, we both liked the same kind of movies and music. We even had the same favorite beer—one brewed locally by 'Gladesmen called Beast. I'd never seen nor heard of a woman liking Beast. She just laughed it off and said it was what her dad and uncles all drank, so it was the first thing she tasted when she was a kid sneaking sips just to see what all the fuss was about. I shared my story of doing the very same thing.

It seemed like every sentence of our conversation brought up something else we had in common, until the phone rang, interrupting us. I let it ring a minute, but when no one answered it, I reached back and picked it up.

"Hey," Owen said.

"Oh, hey man. Got something?"

"Was wondering if *you* had something, actually. Grace? Is she still there?"

I glanced at her. "Yeah, she's here."

"Is there a problem?"

"No, why?"

"She's been gone for almost two hours."

I checked my watch. We'd been talking for a long time. "Ah, yeah, I guess it is getting late."

He sighed. "Just send her back, please. I have things to go over with her before I can leave for the night."

"Sure thing."

I replaced the phone on its receiver and pressed my lips together. "That was Dad calling. He says you're out past curfew."

When she made a confused face, I explained.

"Owen. Wondering what's taking so long."

She looked at her phone and gasped. "Oh, my goodness." Her face turned red. "I've been gone a long time. I'm sorry, I'd better get going." She grabbed her purse from the desk and slung it over her shoulder. "I guess it's too late to try to come up with an excuse?"

"Probably."

She pressed her lips together.

"It's my fault," I confessed. "I shouldn't have kept you talking so long."

"I loved talking with you."

"Then maybe we can finish our conversation over dinner?"

"I would love to. You have my number in all that information somewhere?"

"I do." I patted her file sitting on the desk.

"Then I'll be expecting your call." She walked to the door and paused to look back at me before pushing her way through and walking away.

I sat down with a hard sigh. It felt like little hearts were floating around me, and I grinned. A date with Grace. I wondered if it was it too soon to call her right then.

4

GRACE

I nearly danced out to my car as I left the police station. Mason was so adorable and funny, and we had so much in common.

My buzz was killed slightly when I got back to work, though. I felt bad about being gone so long and hoped it wouldn't be a mark against me. My cheeks must have been red as I walked into the station because they felt like they were on fire. I went right to Owen's office and knocked.

"I'm so sorry," I blurted out the moment I entered the office.

He waved me off. "Mason can be a chatter. I need you to do the afternoon drive through and make sure all is right."

"Sure thing." I turned to leave but thought better of it and turned back around. "I really am sorry. I won't let it happen again."

He nodded and returned to his computer screen.

I hopped in the utility vehicle, grateful to be out of the station. He hadn't seemed too upset, though, so my worry faded and my buzz from earlier returned as I cruised through the park, taking in the sights of all the trees and wildlife, all the scents around me.

That night at home, the questions seemed endless.

My dad raised a thick eyebrow. "Well, aren't you in a good mood."

"Isn't that allowed?" I asked.

"Just wondering why is all," he said.

But my mom was there, and she looked at me more carefully. "Wait a minute." Her mouth spread slowly into a grin. "Did you meet someone?"

Damn that mother's intuition. There was no way I could tell them I had set up a date with a bear shifter. They'd probably disown me. They certainly wouldn't be happy, and I didn't want anything to dampen my excitement.

I quickly dropped my smile. "Meet someone? At work?" I huffed. "It was just a good day is all. I like my new job."

"What have you found out so far?" Dad asked.

"Nothing really. The bears all seem pretty nice, actually." I almost mentioned how I'd taken too long at the station and Owen didn't seem mad, but then they'd wonder what took so long, and I didn't want to have to keep lying. "My boss especially really just wants to make the park safe and enjoyable for all who visit and for the animals who live there."

My dad narrowed his eyes. "Well, you just keep your ears out."

"Of course, Dad."

That night, I was in my room going over the Ranger handbook when my phone buzzed.

Mason. I sighed and grinned.

Hey there. I know there's some man code about waiting so many days before asking a lady out, but I couldn't do it.

If you wouldn't have told me, I never would have known, I replied. *See, some secrets are better kept.*

I almost giggled as I held my phone, watching the little dots showing that he was typing.

LOL. So, when can I see you? Tomorrow?

I'd love to. Where? When?

There was a bit of a pause. *Hadn't gotten that far yet. I'll send you details tomorrow.*

He sent a smiley face and I sent one back, and I fell asleep thinking of him with a grin on my face.

The next day, work seemed to go on forever. When it was finally over, I headed home, trying not to seem too obvious about my excitement. I told my family I was going out with some friends, hoping to meet some guys. Luckily, they didn't question it much since they were twenty minutes deep into some documentary on hunting.

As soon as I got to the restaurant, I saw him. I thought

he'd looked hot in his uniform, but he looked even cuter in his polo shirt and dark blue jeans. He probably looked good no matter what he wore. Then, my mind started to wonder what he'd look like if he wore nothing at all, and I had to snap back to the moment. *Easy, girl; not time to go there—yet.*

He gave me a warm hug and took my hand as we went inside and were seated. From the moment we sat down, he charmed me and had me laughing; god, he was just all-around amazing. I had felt like that once before, with my longtime high school boyfriend, but that had taken weeks. I was already feeling myself go crazy for Mason.

Halfway through our date, though, the cloud I'd been dancing on burst. Adam appeared across the restaurant and walked over to our table, and as he neared, I felt my smile fade. *Shit.* There was no way he wouldn't know that Mason was a bear; his scent was too strong. I swallowed hard and looked at Mason fearfully. He sent back a confused expression and it only intensified when Adam paused at our table, putting his hands down and bending over toward us.

"Well, hello there," Adam said.

"Hi, Adam." I tried to keep my cool. I wasn't doing anything wrong; we were just two people having a meal. I gestured to him. "This is Adam, my clan's Alpha."

Adam nodded, smiled at Mason, and they both looked at me expectantly.

Mason spoke up for himself. "Mason Rowe." He stuck his hand out to Adam, who shook it hard. "Nice to meet you."

"You, too," Adam replied, giving a phony smile. "I had no idea my Grace here needed entertaining tonight. Why didn't you call me if you wanted to go out, honey?"

I had to be extremely careful. I didn't want to upset either of them. "Uh...sorry?"

"I know you said you needed some time before we could really start dating," Adam continued, "and it looks to me like that time has come. Good to know. We can pick up right where we left off."

Adam looked over at Mason and smirked, then spoke to me again. "I know you must feel like you owe this jerk something, but you don't, honey. If he gives you any trouble, just let me know and I'll take care of it." He leaned closer to Mason. "But I'm not expecting any trouble from no bear. And I expect all of your kind will keep your distance from mine."

Mason narrowed his eyes, but said nothing.

"Mason is a police officer," I pointed out. "I don't think I'm in danger."

"Is that so?" Adam stood up and ran his tongue over his teeth. "Well, Grace, my darling, you just keep your head up and don't do anything wrong, and if he tries to accuse you of something, we'll stand by you. Don't worry about a thing."

"Thanks, Adam. I'm not worried."

I gave him a thin smile, and he leaned down to hug me before walking off.

I stared at Mason in shock and horror for a long moment. We'd finished our meal and had been just sitting, chatting.

"Can we go?" I whispered.

He nodded and slid out of the booth. Neither of us said a word as we walked outside and toward my car. When we stopped in front of it, I turned to him.

"I am so, so sorry about that. Adam...he's the clan leader, like I said, but he also has a thing for me. I've never been interested in him, and he doesn't like to take no for an answer."

Mason visibly relaxed. "That's what all that was? Jealousy?"

"Yes." I covered my face with my hands and tried not to cry from sheer embarrassment.

"Hey, it's okay."

He put his arm around me and the tension melted. I leaned into him and inhaled his wild scent.

"I'm so mortified that he would act that way. My parents would be thrilled if I ended up with him, I'm sure," I sulked.

"I have to say, this worries me a little."

I stood up and looked at Mason. "Oh, I don't think he'd come after you or anything like—"

"No, no." He chuckled. "I'm worried about *you*, silly. I'm rather well-trained to fight and shoot, and the fact that you told him I'm an officer would mean higher charges if he came after me." He put his hand to my cheek. "I just don't want him coming after you and trying to pull something. Do you have a gun? Some way to protect yourself?"

"No, it's okay. I don't need anything like that."

"Hang on." He dashed over to his car and returned a moment later. "At least keep this with you. You know how to use it?"

I looked at the small black canister and saw its little red trigger. I'd never used pepper spray before, but it didn't seem complicated. I saw where the lock was, which would prevent it from accidentally going off.

"Yes. Thank you." I tucked the spray into my purse.

"The only thing I'm sorry about is that he interrupted our night," Mason said.

"Then I guess I'll have to make it up to you next time." I gave him a coy smile and he pulled me in close.

He pressed his lips to mine. They were soft and warm, and kissing him was the best thing I'd experienced in years, it seemed. I didn't want to stop. But I was vaguely aware that we were in a parking lot and that Adam wasn't far. Finally —*regrettably*—I had to step back and break the kiss.

"Thank you so much for a wonderful night," I said.

"Thank you for tonight. And for all the nights to come." He winked and opened my car door for me, and as I drove home, I replayed his kiss over and over in my mind.

5

MASON

I woke up early the next morning for a clan run. It wasn't something we'd always done, but over the years, it seemed more and more necessary as the clan grew and our responsibilities increased. It had become like a weekly meeting, but rather than sit around in some room, we got out and stretched our legs, tearing through the park like the pack of bears we were.

Here! I announced with my mind when I'd shifted in.

I was greeted back as everyone else checked in and we all ran to our meeting point. Once everyone was there, Owen began.

Hey all. Thanks for coming. On the agenda for today is the clan picnic. We all ready?

No one objected, so he turned and took off running, with Ezra directly behind him, then me.

I think we're settled on the date, Owen continued, *but what do we want for entertainment, food, all that?*

Beer, Ezra said.

Duh, Hailey added.

I'm good with those things, but I'd also like to add a guest, I mentioned.

Who? Conner demanded.

I know who, Ezra said in a singsong sort of voice.

Wait a minute! Hailey sounded offended. *Are you seeing someone? And I didn't know about it?*

We've only been out once, but I think this could be it. As I thought of her, my chest warmed and I sighed in delight.

Oh, wow, Conner said. *Gettin' serious, bud.*

They could all sense my feelings as I thought about her.

Tell us everything! Hailey was paying close attention to every thought and feeling that came from me.

I sighed once again. *She's perfect. We have so much in common. She even works with Owen and Ezra at the park. She's funny and amazing. And stunning.*

That's so great, Hailey said. *I hope she stays awesome. You've been out with some...interesting women.*

I laughed. *That's a nice way of putting it.* I'd been in some bad relationships over the last few years. They either went crazy on me or cheated on me; I certainly hadn't been the luckiest in finding love thus far. But that was about to change.

Tell them the rest, Owen added.

She likes me back? I offered. I didn't know what he meant.

And... Owen said.

Uh? She's a great kisser, but I didn't think you'd want to know that.

Owen sighed. *Dude, she's also a croc.*

I felt silence and shock emanating from each member. Well, except Ezra, who already knew that detail about Grace.

I tried to play it off like it wasn't a big deal. *Yeah, she is, and she's dedicated to making the park great for **all** animals, just like we are.*

Wait, why is there a croc working in the park in the first place? Conner asked.

I felt my defenses rise. *Wow, prejudiced much? Are we not allowing other species to have jobs now?*

Okay, okay, Owen interrupted. *Let's not get into a thing about it. I just thought everyone should know ahead of time so they won't be surprised when you show up with a croc at the next event.*

I'm not showing up with a croc, I said, my mental voice getting snippy. *I'm showing up with my...girlfriend? Whatever she is, I'm showing up with a date. A **person** who I'm very much into. That should be all that matters.*

You're right, man, Ezra said. *Most of us haven't even met her, but I can say that so far, Grace has been great to work with. She's really nice.*

That's her name? Grace? Hailey asked.

It felt like she was looking for something to say; something that didn't come off as prejudiced or judgmental, but she was having a hard time with it.

That's her name. Grace Osborn.

There was a long silence.

Then Hailey added, *I can't wait to meet her.* But the excitement she'd had about a minute before was lost and her words sounded forced.

I just don't get it, Conner said. *With all the issues we've had with the crocs, how could you do this?*

I tried to remember that Conner had even more of a jaded position against the crocs than any of us. His brother and sister-in-law had been murdered by crocs and he'd been part of the search and rescue team that had pulled their bodies from the water.

She didn't have any part in what happened to your family, I reminded him.

Conner, we'll discuss this at a more appropriate time, Owen said. *For now, we're not going to hold anything against her that she hasn't done.*

I just don't see how this will work out, Conner said.

And I don't see why it matters one bit, I snapped. *She hasn't done anything wrong. She hasn't done a thing to you.*

Noah spoke up then. He'd been quietly listening this whole time. *You've only been out with her once?*

So far.

Okay. Then you're not too attached.

What does that mean? I asked.

If there's an issue, it shouldn't be a big deal for you to move on, he explained.

There already is an issue, Conner added.

Well, thank you all for being so supportive and understanding, I snapped.

This is why I just said we're not doing this, Owen demanded. *If there's a problem, we'll figure out how to handle it as a clan.*

I wasn't ready to let things go so soon. *You guys go ahead and judge all you want. If you want me to leave the clan over this, then that's what I'll do.*

I ran the opposite direction, away from all of them for a few feet, then shifted back. I was far from home, but I didn't care. I wasn't going to listen to their bullshit anymore. I didn't want to think badly of Grace, and I didn't want anyone else to, either. Especially since she'd been nothing but a complete sweetheart. I would hate for her family to judge me simply for being a bear.

As I walked back, being careful to stay in the shadows since I was naked, I considered that there was a good chance her family might have a problem with me. Maybe we'd have to run away somewhere to have peace if we wanted to be together.

It was a long walk back, and by the time I got home, I had texts waiting for me.

Owen: *Hey man, sorry. I'll talk to Conner. He still holds a lot of resentment toward the crocs.*

Duh. Obviously, he wouldn't get over someone killing his brother and sister-in-law, but that didn't mean Grace was somehow responsible just because she happened to be the same species as their murderer.

And Conner had sent a text, too: *This is already causing problems in the clan. You're better off just ending things now before you do something really stupid, like fall for her.*

I decided to ignore them both and talk to the one person I actually wanted to hear from.

Hey there, beautiful. How's your morning going?

It didn't take long to get a response from Grace that made me smile.

Better now, she responded, along with a smiley face.

I sat on my couch with my phone in my hand and a smile on my face, and let my clan and their drama fall away.

6

GRACE

I set down my phone after finishing my chat with Mason. My heart was beating out of my chest; we had another date for that night and I could hardly wait.

I hopped downstairs to get something to eat and my mom was there in the kitchen, cooking eggs.

"That smells amazing!" I gushed.

She turned to look at me suspiciously. "You're in an awfully good mood this morning."

I shrugged. "Just happy, I guess."

She narrowed her eyes at me. "Any reason in particular?"

"I'm not allowed to just be happy? Thanks, Mom."

"Of course you're allowed, I just don't see why you are all of a sudden."

"Life is going well. I have a great job doing something

good for the clan. What is there not to be happy about?"

"*I* know why you're so happy."

My heart jumped and I spun at the sound of Adam's voice as he stepped into the kitchen. Was he going to say something? I glared at him.

"Why is that?" I demanded.

"Because you're working hard for your clan, to get to know the bears and see what they're up to. It's a big sacrifice. And I see you taking your task very seriously." He raised his eyebrow slightly in a challenge.

"Right," I said. "I was just telling my mom that I was enjoying my job and knowing I was helping the clan."

"And I know you'll be a big asset." He smiled at me widely, and I noticed a hint of warning in it.

"I sure hope so." I gave him a flat smile and turned back to my mom to serve myself some eggs.

He didn't say anything about me being out with a bear, but the whole encounter had me shaken up so much that by the time he left, I went back to my room to text Mason.

"Hey, so, given what happened the other night with Adam showing up, could we go somewhere tonight that's maybe less public or a little out of the area?"

I hated to have to even ask him, but I didn't want to be paranoid the whole time, either. I wanted to fully enjoy every second I spent with him.

"I have the perfect place in mind," he responded.

I sighed in relief. I didn't want him to think I was

somehow ashamed to be seen with him; it had nothing to do with that. I'd love to tell the world about him, but the bear and croc rivalry worried me.

Later that evening, after I met Mason and we got into his car, he drove for a long time before pulling into a park.

"I thought maybe a quiet picnic in a distant park would be best," he said as he lifted a basket from his trunk.

"This is perfect. Thank you for understanding." I wrapped him in a tight hug and kissed him.

We set up the picnic together, spreading out blankets and pulling food items out of the basket. He'd brought buttery rolls, chicken salad with fresh herbs and a bottle of Merlot. He poured the wine into a pair of plastic glasses and handed one to me, then held his up to toast.

"To us," he said.

I tapped my cup to his. "To us."

"I had an idea," he said as we started to eat. "There was that incident with your clan leader. My clan isn't too thrilled about things, either, and I was thinking that maybe there's a way we can kind of smooth things over with both your clan and mine."

"How?" He hadn't told me before that his clan was unhappy about us, too. It tightened my stomach.

"We're having a clan picnic, which we often do. I was hoping to bring you along so everyone can meet you. Then they'll understand why I can't keep away from you."

He twisted his fingers through mine, and I thrilled at his

closeness, but his suggestion made me nervous.

"And maybe you can take me to meet your family and clan, too," he continued. "That way, we can be sure no one will have a problem with us being together; they can just let us be happy."

I pulled my hand free from his. "I don't think that would work. I mean, my clan definitely won't be okay with it. My leader already isn't. He made it clear today that he expects me to use you to get information about the upcoming attack, and if your clan already has a problem, too, then I think...I don't know. I don't know what to do."

"Wait a minute. He wants you to use me to get information on *what* attack?"

"There's a rumor going around. It's part of the reason I got this job at the park: to get information and make sure everything was good between the clans."

"What is this rumor, exactly?" His voice started to take on a hard edge, and I could feel myself getting upset.

"That the bears are planning a big attack on the crocs."

"And you believe this rumor?"

"No, not necessarily. I mean, I guess I didn't know before. But that was before I met you and Owen and Ezra."

"You really think we would attack your whole clan?" He looked hurt.

I felt myself grow near tears. "I don't think that now. I've told them there's nothing like that going on and that all the bears want is to keep the park safe."

He shook his head and let out a long sigh. "It's working already."

"What is?"

"They're already coming between us, turning us against each other."

"I'm not against you! Are you against me? What did your clan say? You never told me anything about that."

"I was too mad to talk about it, and I wanted to talk to you in person. They're just not happy that I'm dating a croc."

"And?"

"And, that was basically it. They think that with all that's happened over the years from the crocs that it might cause problems to have you and be so close. I guess they think you'll do exactly what your clan wants you to do: use me to somehow get information that will hurt us in the end."

I blinked and a tear fell down my cheek. "I never said I was doing that or that I wanted to. I told them I was going to work in the park to get information, but I hoped that I could get to know some bears and make things better between the clans. That I could become a mediator of some sort. I want there to be peace, Mason. So that we don't have to hide out and anger our families to be together."

"That's what I want, too. I swear, we would never plan any sort of attack. We'd defend ourselves if something came at us, of course. You can't fault us for that. And we do want to stay safe, given the fact that there have been croc attacks against us in the past, but we're not—nor have we ever—planned to attack anyone."

"I didn't believe you were." I wiped a tear and he leaned in close to kiss me.

"I don't want to upset you. Maybe it would be best if we met everyone and came out in the open. Stop hiding. Tell everyone that there is no attack and bring peace once and for all."

"I don't know. It might just start a big fight and give us more trouble."

"Maybe." He moved closer and put a hand to my cheek, then kissed me. "Maybe we can accomplish what Romeo and Juliet never could."

He kept kissing me and drew me into his lap. His body pressed against mine, warm and strong. It felt so good to be close to him. In that moment, I'd do anything to be with him freely; to not have to hide or worry about my family being angry. I just wanted to be with him and have everything be copacetic.

"I'll think about it. Maybe there's a way I can ease my family into the idea so they'll accept it."

"Good," he breathed into my ear and kissed along my jaw.

I closed my eyes and let him kiss down the column of my neck and back up to my lips. I ran my fingers in his hair, pulling him close and taking in long inhales of his scent.

"You smell so good," I murmured. My heart raced as he

ran his hands along my back.

"So do you."

We kissed for several minutes, getting more and more tangled in each other. Then my phone started buzzing. I ignored it at first, but after a while, it became annoying.

"You'd better check that," he said, brushing his lips over my ears.

I sighed and turned to look at my phone's screen.

Are you with that bear right now? It was Adam. He'd sent several texts in a row. *People saw you, so don't try to hide it.*

When I didn't answer he continued, *So much for trying to get information on the bears. You're changing sides now? Do I have to worry about you?*

And finally, the last one said, *I thought I could trust you, Grace. I thought you were going to be a leader in this clan. But you're nothing more than a bear lover. Does your family have any idea where you are right now, traitor?*

By the time I had read them all, I was shaking with fear and anger. Tears sprang to my eyes. "I'd better go."

"Everything okay?" He started packing up the picnic, but I couldn't move.

"No," I said softly. "Adam is giving me crap. Somehow, he knows I'm with you. He called me a traitor."

Mason set down the basket and came to take me in his arms. "We'll figure this out somehow. I promise."

I wanted to believe him, but the pit in my stomach kept growing.

7

GRACE

I didn't know how to respond to Adam, so his text went unanswered. I said goodbye to Mason with a growing feeling of dread, and by the time I reached home, that dread had increased exponentially, then exploded when I pulled into the driveway. Adam's car was there.

I wanted to turn back and take off; to never come home again. We could've gone somewhere, Mason and I. Somewhere that didn't have clan issues like the ones we were facing. I swallowed hard and got out of my car.

My father met me at the door as I walked in. "Come on into the living room, Grace. We need to talk."

He looked pissed, to say the least. I followed him into the living room and found my mother and brother sitting on the couch, and Adam on the chair. My mother's eyes looked red from crying. Tyler glared at me. My dad gestured to the love seat and I sat obediently. My dad stood in the middle of the room, his arms crossed, facing me. The room was tense with silence. Then it felt like all the anger exploded at once.

"Adam has told us some very disturbing information," my father said.

"Please say it's not true," my mother added, her voice wavering. "You're not really dating a bear, are you?"

"Can't believe my sister is a freaking traitor," Tyler said.

Adam just laced his fingers and gave me a smug look. They all stared at me.

"The bears aren't what we thought," I explained.

"So, it's true?" my mother said, sounding pained.

"I'm seeing someone, yes. And he happens to be a bear, but—"

"Ohhh," my mother wailed and put her face in her hands. "Why, why, why?"

My father clenched his jaw. "Grace, this is *not* acceptable."

"How can you even stand the smell?" Tyler asked.

I thought of Mason's scent and how it drove me wild; how he kissed me, touched me. Suddenly, it all seemed so far away.

"How did this even happen?" my father asked. "You were there to work and get information, not hook up with one of them."

"I *did* get information. There is no attack planned," I said.

My father turned to Adam, who spoke up then. "We've got some information of our own."

"Looks to me like you've been helping them rather than us," my father accused.

"I haven't helped them!"

Adam stood and pulled a map from his pocket. He spread it out on the living room table. The map was of the park and had several places circled in red.

"Right here." Adam pointed to one of the circles where the word 'attack' was written beside it. "Is this not your boyfriend's handwriting?"

I looked at the letters closely. I had only seen Mason's handwriting a few times; not enough to recognize it. "I don't think so."

There were several other places on the map that also said 'attack' beside a circle.

Adam took another paper from his pocket: a traffic violation ticket. He pointed to several lines of writing. "This ticket was given and signed by your boyfriend. Notice how the As and Cs look exactly the same."

I looked at where Mason had written 'traffic violation' and compared the letters, and admittedly, they did look close. And there was no denying that Mason had written the ticket. His name was printed and signed at the bottom of it.

"What do you make of this?" Adam demanded.

"I...I don't know, but I'm sure there's some explanation," I said. "They wouldn't do this."

"So, even when you see proof of a pending attack, you're going to take their side?" my father fumed, his hand forming a fist.

"I'm not taking their side, I'm just—"

"How can you do this to your family?" my mother cried. "Is dating this guy worth getting people killed over?"

"No. That's not going to happen," I insisted. "Mason is not like that!"

"Yet, we have his handwriting here." Adam pointed again to the map. "You agree that it's his handwriting, yes?"

"I don't know. It looks like it, but I don't know that—"

"So, you agree that your boyfriend wrote the words 'attack' on this map near several circles?"

My mouth hung open.

"Well do you agree that's his handwriting or not?" my father barked.

I jumped in surprise. "Well, it looks like his handwriting," I admitted. "But that doesn't mean—"

"Then you have to see how highly suspicious it looks," Adam said. "He writes 'attack' on a map that has several locations circled? Do you still not believe anything's going on?"

My mind was spinning in a thousand directions, my heart racing. I was near tears but couldn't let them see me cry, especially Adam. When I looked at what he had, it did seem like proof. How could I deny that? But it didn't match with what I knew of Mason. He wouldn't do that. He wouldn't lie about it, either. Would he?

"How well do you even know this bear?" my mother asked. "How long has this been going on?"

"I've only been out with him a few times." I thought that was going to be good news, but she turned it on me.

"So, you don't know him at all! He might have you completely fooled, making you think he has feelings for you."

"He charmed you, said all the right things, and you fell for it," Dad added. "We don't blame you for that. These bears, they're masters at that. But you need to make this right. You need to end things with him immediately and never see him again."

"Well, of course she's not going to see him again," my mother said, indignant. She looked at me for confirmation. "You wouldn't dare see him again after all this proof, would you?"

"I..."

"Grace, I don't think I have to tell you how disappointed the whole clan is," Adam said. "Our leadership had very high hopes for you and your mission. We had faith in you, trusted you to do right by us. Now that you've turned and proven to be a traitor—or at least have been taken by these bears if they've managed to manipulate you—we have to think differently about you. About your whole family."

"My family?" I whimpered. "But they didn't have anything to do with it. It was just me—"

"Don't you see how this affects us all?" my father

demanded. "Your actions reflect on us as a whole. On this family, on this clan, on all crocs everywhere."

"It's not like that! I swear, it's not like that." The tears broke free; there was no stopping any of it now. I tried to keep my chest from hitching as I cried and breathed through it.

"Adam needs to hear that you're not going to see this bear again," Mom insisted.

What could I say to that? How could I possibly still be thinking that dating Mason would ever work? If everyone was up in arms about it and they were coming against my family because of me, because of what I'd done, how could I put my wants ahead of what was best for so many people?

"I won't see him again," I said softly.

"Of course you won't," my father said. "Because if you do, you'll be out on the street so fast, your head will spin."

I swallowed hard and the tears kept coming.

"We're putting you on probation," Adam said. "It's not a mark against you—yet. We're just going to watch your actions for a while and make sure there's nothing question-able happening. If we do find something, some kind of proof that you've been giving the bears information, then there will be a more formal investigation that could lead to your removal from the clan. Do you understand?"

I nodded, but didn't look up. I couldn't believe what was happening. How could something that seemed so perfect and necessary just hours before suddenly seem like the most terrible thing I'd ever done in my life?

"I'll keep an eye on her," my brother said.

I sent him a glowering look.

Adam nodded. "I expect all of you to report regularly with anything you see that might be suspicious. The more we know we can trust the Osborns, the faster your names will be cleared."

"Why couldn't you just find a nice croc boy to date?" my mother hissed.

"It's not for lack of interest, I'll tell you that much," Adam said. "I've been trying to get Grace to like me for as long as I can remember, and then I see her running off with this bear. I'm starting to question my own abilities."

"Oh no," my mother said. "You are a fine-looking man and a good leader. Don't you go doubting yourself just because of Grace's poor choices."

"And I'm sure Grace will be making better choices in the future, won't she?" My father looked at me expectantly.

"Yes," I whispered. "I never meant to hurt anyone or make anyone look bad. I didn't tell him anything that would hurt anyone or give anything away."

"We know that you're the victim here," Adam said. "That Mason and these bears are the real ones to blame for taking advantage of you. But you do understand that we have to take precautions and make sure his hold on you is broken for good."

I nodded.

"Good." Adam stood and shook my father's hand. "I think my work here is done for the night."

My mother stood to hug him and whispered something to him that I couldn't hear.

"Grace, if I might have a private word?" Adam said as he walked toward the door.

I followed him out and he stopped on the front porch, waiting until I closed the door behind me. I didn't meet his eyes. He leaned in close, so that his arm was touching mine.

"Grace," he said softly, "I know this is a lot to take, and I don't want you or your family to be negatively impacted by this. Just keep your head straight, and soon enough, it'll all blow over."

"Thanks," I muttered. "I never meant to cause anyone any trouble."

"I know." He put his hand on my shoulder. "I know you've needed time, but I want you to know that if you're looking for someone who won't manipulate you, someone your family will be thrilled to have you be with, I think you know that I'm here. I want you to be mine, Grace. I think we could do great things together."

"I know."

"Okay, well, I just didn't want to leave any doubt. Think about what would make your family happy. You can fix all of this very easily, you know."

"I know."

"Grace…"

I finally looked up at him. His gaze was intense and he leaned down toward me. I turned my head from him.

"It's been a really awful night," I said. "I need to get some sleep."

"Right. You do that and call me in the morning, okay?"

"Sure."

I turned from him and ran up to my room before anyone else could say anything to me. I picked up my phone and sent the most awful text I'd ever had to send.

I'm so sorry, Mason, but I can't see you anymore. Adam told my family and the whole clan about us. My dad will kick me out of the house if I see you again, and my family might even get kicked out of the clan because of this. It's a huge mess and I can't keep bringing them harm just to satisfy my own wants. I'm so sorry. I know you'll understand why it has to be this way.

I powered down my phone and pressed my face into my pillow to sob. It was bad enough that they all knew, that I was causing all this trouble for everyone, and that the bears might actually be planning an attack. But at that moment, all I wanted was for Mason to hold me and tell me it would be okay somehow. For us to figure this all out together. But instead, I'd just promised my clan and family that I'd never see him again. The day couldn't have been any worse, and I just needed it to end.

8

MASON

I read Grace's last message again, for the hundredth time. And then the long stream of texts I'd responded with that had gone unanswered.

My first reply was, *What? What is going on? Can you call me?*

When she didn't call—and avoided my voicemails—I'd followed up with, *Grace, please talk to me. Tell me what's going on. It can't just end like this. We're adults. They can't keep us apart unless we let them.*

Later that night, I'd written, *Please. I'm going out of my mind here.*

I hoped that in the morning, somehow, things would have been better. But she still hadn't responded. Throughout the day, I'd sent many more texts, called many times, but still to no avail.

I didn't know what to do or what to think. And my clan sure wasn't being helpful. They'd all just seemed relieved that it was over.

But I couldn't let it be over.

Grace had taken two days off work and it seemed like she'd quit, disappearing from my life completely and instantly. But on the third day that she was supposed to be at work, the fifth day since I'd talked to her, she showed up.

I got a text from Owen. *She's here, but don't do anything. Just keep your distance.*

At least it was *something*. Someone I knew would have contact with her. I knew where she was, and I could figure out a way to see her and talk to her.

How does she look? I asked.

Awful. She came to talk to me to make sure I knew what was going on. She was concerned for her job and asked if I could make sure she doesn't run into you, that it would be too hard.

She did? What did you say?

Of course I agreed, he said. *What else can I do? She's still an employee of the park, under my direct supervision. I could be fired if I somehow let you see her against her wishes.*

I don't want you to get in any trouble, I replied. *I would never ask you to do that. I guess I just hoped you would defend me a little? Or find out what happened?*

It's not my place to get into personal matters.

Right. I know that, I admitted.

Maybe just give her some time. Obviously, it was a shitstorm when everyone found out. Let it blow over and maybe she'll talk to you again so you can get some closure.

Closure. That's what they all thought I needed. Well, I wasn't about to let things go and just forget her. I couldn't.

I did wait a little while. For days, I didn't text or call her. I showed up at the clan picnic and felt even more alone knowing I had wanted to bring Grace. I sat off to the side, not talking or mingling much, just sipping on a beer and wallowing in my misery.

At one point, as the day stretched into evening, Ezra and Owen came to talk to me.

"She looked better today," Ezra said. "I think she's moving on. It's best if you can do the same, man. I know it's hard, but you've gotta let her go."

"I don't think I can." I picked at the label on my beer bottle, trying not to think about the fact that Beast Brew was something Grace loved, too. "I've never felt like this about anyone before. I can't sleep; I can't stop thinking about her, and my bear is driving me up the friggin' wall. I just have to find a way to talk to her. To see her. I...I love her."

Owen put a hand on my shoulder. "I know this is difficult, but the thing is, you have to remember that she ended it. She won't text you or call you. She's asked to not have to work with you at the park. It's clear she doesn't want to see you."

"It's not a matter of you trying harder, buddy," Ezra added. "It's over. You don't have a choice but to move on."

I left the picnic early and felt even worse than I had before I'd gone. Everyone had the same sort of things to say, that it was better to just forget about her find someone else. But I couldn't, and the longer it went on, the more out of my mind I felt.

When it had been a week since I'd heard from her, I decided to do something. I couldn't just show up at her house. I knew that. I couldn't just show up at her work, either. But there was one thing I could do.

I headed to the Ranger Station, as I always did, and made it seem like I was just going about my usual business. While I was there, I checked the territories for the day. Owen broke up the park into sections, and if anything happened in a certain area, the Ranger assigned to that section would be sent to check it out.

I saw where Grace would be stationed for the day and found the best spot in that area—secluded, but with easily identifiable landmarks. I set up my tent there, where no camping or tents were allowed, then I dialed the number for the main office and used a fake voice to place the call, which I knew would be answered by Rachel, the office assistant. She knew my voice, but not well enough to notice I was disguising it. She also wouldn't be suspicious of a call like that, where Owen might be.

"I'll send someone to check on it," Rachel said.

I'd given her a description of where my tent was and called in to complain that someone had set up a tent in an unauthorized area. Then I waited. I worried she wouldn't come, or that if she did, she'd pick up my scent and take off.

I had a view of the road and watched from the tent. When she pulled up in the utility vehicle, my heart skipped. My stomach twisted into knots as I saw her get out and make her way toward the tent.

"Hello there," she called out from several feet away.

I unzipped the tent's door and looked at her, and when she saw me, she froze. I gestured for her to come closer, to step inside. She swallowed hard, took a minute to look around, then ducked down to enter the tent.

I wanted to scoop her into my arms right then and kiss her madly. But she had ended things, and I didn't know where I stood.

"I'm sorry," I said. "I was going out of my mind and I hadn't heard from you. I just couldn't take it anymore."

She sat down across from me, leaving a few feet between us. "I couldn't. It would have been far too difficult to talk to you."

She looked down and wouldn't meet my eyes again.

"Tell me what we can do. How can we make this better? There's got to be something we can do."

"There isn't. I'm sorry, I shouldn't even be here." A tear fell from her eye and she stood.

"Please don't go. Please, Grace. I love you. I want to be

with you, and I'll do whatever it takes to make that happen. I don't want our clans to come between us. We can leave; go where no one cares about who we are. I just want to be with you. More than anything in the world, I want you."

Grace stopped and pulled her lower lip into her mouth. I stood and braved putting my hand on her arm, and she didn't pull back or flinch from my touch.

"You...really love me?" she stammered.

"I do. So much. This has been the hardest week of my life."

She turned to me and had tears in her eyes. "Mine, too."

I was flooded with relief by hearing those words. Tears burned in my own eyes. "Please tell me we can find a way to make this work. I can't live without you."

She fell on my shoulder, crying. I pulled her close, soaking in the sweet feel of her body pressed against mine. I didn't know if I'd ever get to feel her again, and I enjoyed every moment. I drew her scent deeply into my lungs, filling my mind with it in case it would soon be gone again.

"I don't see how we can make this work," she admitted. "Can we really just leave everything behind? Our whole lives?"

"I don't know, but if we have to, if that's what it takes, then I will. I'll give up everything for you."

9

MASON

Grace looked up at me, her expression hopeful. "Really? You'd really do that for me?"

"Of course. I love you, Grace. I'm crazy about you."

"I love you, too," she whispered. "I have to ask you something, though."

"Anything."

"All I need is for you to tell me the absolute truth."

"Okay..."

"Adam had a map." She sucked in a slow, shaky breath. "It looked like your handwriting. There were several places circled on it and by each one it said 'attack.' Do you know anything about it?"

That question explained a lot. I pulled out my phone, my

emotions whirling in turmoil. Was that what they'd used to turn her against me? I scrolled until I found what I needed and showed her the image on my phone. "This map?"

Her eyes widened. "Yes."

"I can only imagine what they tried to tell you this was. I wondered where it had gotten to, but now I know it was stolen from the Ranger Station, not lost. Must've been after Owen and I marked it together. It's a map of all the places there have been croc attacks in the last few years. All the places that *crocs* have done the attacking on either other animals or other shifters."

I pointed to the different places on the map. "This is where a dead panther was found. This is where Owen's wife Addie was almost killed and our clan fought back. This is where Conner's brother and sister-in-law's bodies were found. This is where Britt was trapped and almost killed. This is where a nest of sea turtles was desecrated, killing all the turtles, including their eggs, and Addie's name was written in the mud as a warning after Owen started digging around to investigate some crocs in the area. Did you know Aiden Harvey?"

She blinked at me and looked back to the map several times. "So, this isn't a map of where the *bears* were planning to attack? This isn't your plan to retaliate?"

"Do you know anything about the situations I mentioned? Each one was dealt with at the time. Aiden, who killed the sea turtles and attacked Addie, was killed when his troop attacked and we fought back. The croc who went after Britt and the panthers was killed in the process of him trying to kill us, and the croc who killed Conner's brother and sister-in-law went to jail, but was then killed by an inmate because he pissed off the wrong person. These are only the major attacks that affected my clan directly. There have been hundreds of reports of smaller incidents over the years. If we were going to retaliate, we would have done it long ago, but we've been busy trying to make things work, trying to keep the peace all this time."

She put her face in her hands and started sobbing again. I wrapped her tight in a hug and let her cry against my chest.

"I'm sorry," she mumbled. "I'm so sorry. They said— they told us—"

"Look, both our clans are trying to convince us of the reasons we shouldn't be together. But they're wrong."

"How can we do this?" She looked up at me with wet eyes and cheeks.

I wiped away her tears. "I'm not sure, but I want to try. We have to try. I won't just give up and let them keep us apart. Especially not because of a bunch of lies."

"I'm sorry I ever questioned you. I should have known." She shook her head.

I put my hand to her cheek and kissed her. Feeling her lips against mine again was pure heaven; I couldn't stop and neither could she.

Having been apart for days and being forced into something neither of us wanted drove us to cling onto each other desperately, and we kissed hungrily.

"I never want to be away from you again," I whispered in her ear.

"I don't either. We have to find a way."

"We will." I kissed along her neck and back to her mouth.

I sat and tugged her hand to join me on the floor of the tent. When she did, she sat in my lap, facing me, with her legs wrapped around me.

I dug my fingers into her hair, pulling her closer. She ran her hands along my back, in my hair, sending chills through my body. God, I needed her; I just had to have her.

I laid her down on her back and moved into position over her, kissing her until she pulled my shirt over my head, forcing me to let my lips leave hers for a moment.

Her nails trailed along my skin. I slid my hands under her shirt, feeling the firmness of her full breasts, and she moaned against my mouth. When I pinched her nipples gently, she reached down and tugged at my jeans. I helped her unbutton and unzip them before she pushed them down. She wiggled out of her Ranger uniform and, for a moment, I remembered that she was on the clock. Someone might have come looking for her.

"Wait, Grace, should we...?"

She pulled herself up to meet my mouth and crushed her lips against mine as she took my stiff cock in her hands and stroked me. That seemed to be the only answer I was going to get.

I moved my hand down between her legs and she opened herself to me. I slid a finger inside her, feeling her wetness.

She moaned and bit gently on my earlobe. "Please, Mason. Don't make me wait any longer."

I slid my finger out and moved my member into position, then slipped slowly inside her.

She gasped and dug her nails into my back. "Oh, god," she breathed in my ear.

I thrusted in and out of her, every second sending a wave of pleasure through me. She rocked her hips up and around to bring me in deeper.

"Faster," she demanded.

I sped up and felt myself get so close, I had to ease back for a moment. I wanted to make sure I gave her the most pleasure possible and didn't want to let things end too quickly.

"Don't slow down!"

I half chuckled into her ear. "I have to for a sec."

She reached back to grab my ass and forced me into her. Slamming into her hard several times, I came just as she cried out and shuddered beneath me. She gasped as I felt her contracting around my throbbing length.

Letting out a shaking breath, I lowered myself to my elbows. She'd felt so good, I didn't want the moment to end.

But I was also faintly aware that a call had come across on her walkie. She had to get back to work.

I moved back, slipping out of her slowly, and she sighed and closed her eyes. Collapsing beside her, I was no longer able to hold myself up. I panted and she turned to lay on my chest.

"We'll have to be extra careful not to be seen or found out," she whispered.

"You sure you want to do this?"

"I love you, Mason, and if you love me, too, and want to make this work, then we have to try."

I kissed the top of her head. "I want that more than anything. I want *you* more than anything."

"Me, too. And after *that*, I have to be able to see you again."

I chuckled. "You'll get no argument from me there; that was amazing. You'd better get back to work, though. I don't want to get you in trouble or raise suspicions."

"Right." She sat up and gave me a sad smile. "When will I be able to see you again?"

"Whenever you want; tonight, even. Why don't you save my number under a different name in case anyone sees your phone, then call me and I'll come get you."

She pressed her lips into a smile. "Okay."

"We'll figure this out." I tucked a strand of hair behind her ear. "We have to end this feud between the clans once and for all. We're the ones who can, I just know it."

She nodded and pulled on her shirt. "I do have to make you aware, sir, that there is no tent camping allowed in this part of the park."

"My apologies, ma'am. I'll be sure to take it down right away."

I stood and pulled on my pants as she finished dressing. She smoothed her hair down. "Do I look obvious?"

"You look obviously gorgeous." I kissed her and she sighed as she pulled away.

"Tonight."

"I'll be counting the hours."

10

MASON

I worked that afternoon and evening, but they were the hardest hours I'd ever put in. With all the turmoil of the past week on top of what had happened earlier that day, my brain was scrambled. I almost couldn't believe it had happened. Had I really seen Grace, really told her I loved her and she'd said it in return? Had I actually made love to her right there in a tent in the middle of the park? It was like a dream. And, thankfully, it would be just a matter of hours until I'd see her again.

I didn't know what the future would hold for us. How we'd keep things a secret and for how long. I didn't know how we'd end the battle between our clans. But I knew that as long as we had time together, we'd be fine. We'd figure out a way because nothing could stop our love. They'd tried and almost succeeded, but I hadn't let them and neither had Grace. We wouldn't let them do it again.

I drove around my usual patrol, watching the scenes of the evening. Every time I sat somewhere that I could see people, I watched the couples, happy and in love. I thought about Grace and I grinned.

A call came in over my radio. I picked up the receiver and held in the button to respond. "Officer Rowe here. Go ahead."

Dispatch answered with, "We just got a call. Looks a possible assault in the park."

"On it."

I started my car and headed down, following the map to the exact location as it came across my monitor. When I arrived, I saw a Ranger's vehicle there with Owen and Ezra, as expected. An ambulance pulled in right behind me, lights and sirens going strong. But then I saw Conner's crew pull up in the first responder truck. This wasn't just a simple assault, then.

I called in that I had arrived and sent for backup, then went right to Owen.

"What's the word?" I asked.

"Got a call about someone found in the woods. Possible assault. Still waiting for all the details."

"Why's the search and rescue team here?"

"Wasn't sure what we'd find."

I nodded and headed over to Conner. "Are you guys ready? Let's head in."

As soon as my backup arrived a minute later, we armed up and made our way toward the location of where the victim was to be found, with search and rescue right behind us. As we got deeper into the mangrove, we heard someone moving not too far from us.

"There!" One of the officers called out and we moved toward the sound. "I see someone. Ma'am? Can you hear me?"

The group closed in around the victim. I didn't have a clear view of her, but I listened intently for my cues.

"Let's get her out of there."

"On the stretcher," Conner said. His team moved in and loaded up the woman. "Cut the gag."

Gag? I moved to get a clear view and saw that the woman on the stretcher had her hands bound behind her back. Her back was to me. Her clothing was torn and muddy, her hair mixed with twigs and leaves. *Probably a sexual assault*, I assumed and my heart dropped. Those were the worst kind of calls. And in the park? I hated to think something like that could happen there.

"Can you tell me your name?" One of Conner's team members shined a light at her, checking her pupils. "Ma'am? Can you tell me your name?" he repeated.

She let out a sob. "I...don't know."

When the words hit my ears, ice shot through me. *No. No fucking way.*

I rushed over to the front of the stretcher, and that's when my worst fear was confirmed. I would recognize her voice anywhere. But the last place I wanted to hear it was right then.

"Grace!" I shouted and pushed through the crew working on her to be by her side.

I looked her up and down, checking for any signs of injury, already knowing I would tear anyone who hurt her to shreds.

"Are you okay? Are you hurt? What happened?" I asked, taking her hand.

Though her clothing was torn and dirty, it was still in place. The closer I looked, I thought my initial assessment of sexual assault was likely false; she didn't have any signs. *Thank god.*

She looked up at me, horrified.

"Grace? Are you okay? Talk to me." What had happened to her? Why was she looking at me like that?

I put my hand to her cheek and she flinched, so I placed it down at my side, not wanting to upset her.

The team moved through the woods to get her onto the ambulance. I jumped in behind them and tried to talk to her more while they worked on her.

"Vitals are good," I heard Conner say.

"You're going to be okay," I told her. "What happened?"

She shook her head slightly and tears formed in her eyes. "Do I know you?"

"You're probably in shock. It's okay. It's me, Grace. It's Mason." I kissed her hand and set it back down. "I'm here. I love you."

"I...I can't remember anything."

I looked to Conner, not sure what to expect. He was all business, though. Of course he would be. He wasn't going to hold anything against her in that moment, when he was there to do his job and save her life.

Conner moved into place beside her. "I'm going to ask you a series of questions that will help us determine your injuries, okay? Just answer the best you can, and if you don't know, just say, 'I don't know.'"

He shined a light in her eyes, watching how her pupils dilated. "Can you tell me any part of your name?"

She shook her head.

"Do you know what year it is?"

She thought for a moment, then admitted, "I don't know."

"Do you know where you are right now?"

"In a..." She gestured around the ambulance, but didn't seem to know the word.

"Do you know where this vehicle is located? The town, state, or country?"

She took a long time to answer, then finally said, "America?" She looked over at me, still terrified.

"Do you know the names of any family members or people we should notify?"

She shook her head again.

"I do," I offered.

Conner nodded to me and motioned for me to step off the ambulance with him.

"She's suffering from some sort of amnesia. It happens sometimes with head injuries. I'm hoping it'll probably clear up in the next few hours. If you could notify her family, that would be great."

"I..." I sucked in a breath and swallowed hard. "I can't. They hate me and they'll be pissed if they know I'm here. I'm sure Owen has contact information for her on file."

Conner nodded and walked over to Owen.

And that's when it really hit me. I couldn't ride in the ambulance with her. If her family found out, they'd be furious. She'd said her dad threatened to kick her out of the house, and her clan had said they'd kick her family out if she was found talking to me. I couldn't take the chance of making things hard for her, not when this was all so new.

Owen made the calls and I stood there, watching the ambulance pull away with a knot in my stomach. What if this was somehow related to what we'd done earlier in the day? What if someone had found out we were together? I couldn't go to the hospital to make sure she was okay. I couldn't call to check on her. I was helpless.

I turned to Owen and pleaded, "Go to the hospital and

make sure she's okay, please. You know I can't go. It's killing me. I—I—" I started to breathe heavy and got dizzy. Black spots dotted before my eyes.

I sat quickly and Owen knelt beside me. "Put your head between your knees, man."

I did and it helped some, but I still felt like I could throw up at any second.

"I'll go," he assured me. "I'll make sure she's okay and tell you everything I can."

"I love her," I whispered.

"I know." He patted my shoulder. "I'm sure she'll be okay. Hang in there, bud."

11

GRACE

I woke with a splitting headache like none I'd ever experienced before. Looking around, I had no idea where I was. I thought I knew what sort of place I was in, but the word wouldn't come; it was whatever you'd call a place people went to when they're sick.

A nurse came in the room and did something to my arm. "Is your name Grace?" she asked.

"I don't know," I admitted. How strange to not know your own name.

Three people rushed into the room.

"Here she is!" the woman said. "Grace, honey, we're here."

She held my hand and the man looked worried, too.

"We got here as fast as we could," he said. "What happened?"

I pulled my hand from the woman. I had no idea who these people were. The nurse pulled them aside to talk to them, and the woman gasped and held a hand to her mouth. The young boy with them looked at me, then looked away.

When the nurse left, they sat in a circle around me, asking questions and discussing things I knew nothing about. They said something about us all being croc shifters, which meant that apparently, we could turn into crocodiles. That's when I couldn't take it anymore. It hurt my head and after a while, I had to do something.

"I need to sleep," I said. "This is too much." They had to be crazy, these people. No one could turn into an animal. It had to be some kind of joke, and I certainly wasn't in the mood.

They all fussed when I asked them to leave, but they left me, eventually. I felt more at peace alone. What did that mean? How could I not remember my parents, if that's really who these people had been? How could I forget my brother? But I had no recollection of them at all.

I drifted in and out of sleep on the medications they kept giving me. The doctors said I'd been attacked and lost my memory. They didn't know when it would come back, if ever.

Sometime in the night, when the windows in the room were showing only blackness, a man came into my room. I recognized him, though I didn't know him. He was the one who had been there in the woods. He'd held my hand and said he loved me.

"Hey," he whispered and slid into the seat beside my bed. "How are you feeling?"

"Scared and confused."

He nodded. "I don't blame you. Me, too."

I drew my eyebrows together. "Why?"

"Do you know who I am?"

"You were there. In the woods."

"Is that all you know?" he asked.

I nodded. "That's why I'm scared and confused. You don't know me, and I don't know what it means, who could have done this to you. I'm worried that it's my fault."

"You think you did this to me?"

He shook his head. "Of course not. Grace, I love you more than anything, and I will protect you with my life. But things haven't been easy for us. Our clans, our families, don't want us together. We're in a sort of secret relationship. I'm worried that someone found something out and did this to you as a result."

"Why would my family not want me to be with you? Are you bad? What do you mean by clan?"

He picked up my hand and I let him hold it. Even though I didn't know him, I felt better when he was around. Not like when my supposed family was there; they'd made me feel crazy and even more afraid. But that guy...I wished I could've remembered his name. He made me feel comforted somehow. I wanted to believe him.

"I don't want to put too much on you," he said. "Do you remember any of your family or clan?"

"I don't know what you mean by clan. Am I in a cult?"

He shook his head. "We're all shifters. Your family, me, you. I'm a bear shifter, you're a croc, and that's the problem."

Tears returned to my eyes. Now he was saying this, too? This animal thing? "Yeah, I guess it is a problem that people keep telling me I can turn into a crocodile."

He put his hand to his face. "I can't even imagine what it's like to not remember you're a shifter. God, Grace, this is just terrible." He looked at me with tears in his eyes. "I'm so, so sorry this is happening to you. I wish I could stop it or fix it somehow. I swear that I will end whoever did this to you."

"Can you show me?"

"Show you?"

"That you can turn into a bear?"

His eyes widened. "I've...never shifted in front of you before. I don't know if this is the best place or time, with so many humans buzzing around."

"Please. I feel like I'm going crazy, and I don't know who to believe or what to think. If you don't want to do it, I'll change. How do I become a crocodile?"

"No, don't do that. When you get out of here, we'll work on that, but not now, not here. If you really want me to, I will."

"Please."

He got up and locked the door, then proceeded to take his clothes off.

I gasped. "What the hell are you doing?"

"Oh, sorry. I can see why that would be disturbing. When we change, our clothes don't, and since our animal bodies are bigger, it rips our clothing. If I'm going to walk back out of here and not draw attention for walking through a hospital naked, I need to take my clothes off so they don't get ruined."

"Oh." That did kind of make sense. And I didn't mind the look of him without a shirt, either.

"I'm going to change, then change right back. This is really risky to do it here like this."

I watched as he pushed down his pants then got on all fours. It happened very quickly. He was a man one moment, then sprouted fur and his body expanded into the form of a bear. In another minute, he was back to human, dressing quickly and unlocking the door.

"Are you okay?" he asked, panting.

"Why is it risky?"

"The world doesn't know about us. There are a lot of shifters, but we keep it a secret."

"So many secrets."

"It's not a secret that I love you." He sat back down and picked up my hand again. "Are you okay? I never thought I'd shift in front of you for the first time like that. I can't believe you're not freaked out."

"I am. Sort of. Like, my head is freaked out? But in my

body, it's like I know that it's right, if that makes any sense. Nothing really makes sense right now, so I don't know."

"Can I show you something?"

I nodded.

He took out his phone. "Where's your phone?"

I pointed to the device on the table and he picked it up and turned it so I could see the screen. He went to the text messages on both phones and I saw that they matched. It was a conversation between the two of us.

"We use code names. Your clan, being crocs, doesn't want you to be with a bear. That's the problem. But here you can see what you've said to me and what I've said to you."

He handed me the phone and I looked over the messages, reading how I'd said I loved him and apparently had had sex with him recently and enjoyed it. That made my cheeks hot, but if I was doing that with him, and it seemed like the proof was there, then I could believe him. I kept reading back through and saw a message that bothered me.

"I broke up with you?" I asked.

"Your clan made you. Look at what it says. Your family said they'd kick you out of your house, and your clan threatened to disown your family."

"Just because I'm with you?"

"There's been a feud between the bears and crocs for a long time in this area."

"Is that why we used the code names Roman and Julie? It's like we're Romeo and Juliet?"

He chuckled. "Basically. You thought it was cute when you came up with it."

"Oh. That was my idea?"

He nodded. "Can I do one thing?"

"What?"

"Can I kiss you? If you don't feel comfortable with it, that's okay. I understand. I just want to feel you. I don't know what's going to happen with all this. It might be my last chance."

I nodded and closed my eyes. I didn't remember anything, but he knew it all and now he was going through it alone, like I was. Yet, he was there, helping me, so I wanted to do whatever I could to help him, too.

His lips touched mine and he kissed me sweetly. My heart raced and when he pulled back, it was too soon. I didn't want him to stop; it felt right, even though I couldn't remember ever kissing him before.

"Did that happen to trigger any memories?" he asked. "I've been reading all I could, and I came across something that said memories can be uncovered by certain things."

He looked so hopeful, I wanted to lie to him. "I'm sorry, no. But I liked it. A lot." I gave him a half smile. "I can see why I love you."

His smile grew and he kissed me on the forehead. "I will find a way to make this better. I promise."

"I believe you."

12

MASON

I hadn't slept well and I woke feeling groggy. In my temporary state of confusion, I wondered if that was what Grace felt like all the time. The investigation hadn't given me much information yet, and I was frustrated with the lack of evidence. What we really needed was for Grace to remember something that would help us find out what happened and who did this to her.

I went to work and spent hours reviewing evidence, trying to see things from a new angle. By lunch, I was out of ideas and out of coffee, so I made a fresh pot and sat down to get back to work. I checked my phone, which I hadn't done in almost an hour, and noticed a text from Ezra:

Call me right away.

I rolled my eyes. Who knew what it would be about.

Probably something I had no time for. But, I wanted to get up and stretch my legs, so I called him from outside the station with plans to make the call short so I could get back to deciding who to interview next. The crocs had to have something to do with what happened.

"Got your text, Ez."

"Yeah, good. I'm glad you called back. So, I noticed a certain smell when Owen and I were out searching around the spot where Grace was found. I had Britt come and check it out because I thought she would know what it was. She's really good with herbs and all that, you know?"

"Yeah." I rubbed at my face, hoping he would get to the point.

"So, she came and sniffed around and sure enough, she knew exactly what the smell was."

"Okay..."

"It's some kind of herb that can be used to cause confusion and memory issues."

"What herb?" Finally, something that could help.

"Uh, I forget what it's called."

"Is that supposed to be a joke?" I gritted my teeth.

He laughed. "No, but that would have been a good one. It doesn't matter, man; Britt has an antidote for it, and it's almost ready. She had to distill it, or something. I don't know; that's her thing. But I thought you'd want to know."

"Yeah, of course. Can I come see Britt and talk to her about it?"

"Yeah, man, sure thing. Hey, Britt!"

I held the phone away from my ear as he shouted into it. Sometimes, I didn't know how Ezra managed to become an adult. He always came off as scatter-brained surfer, but then, when you needed him, he was there. He might have frustrated me at times, but there was a reason Owen had made him his second.

"She said it'll be ready in like fifteen."

"Perfect. I'll see you in twenty."

In just forty-five minutes from the time of my call, I had completed my interview with Britt, getting all the details she had to give, and I had a vial of the antidote. Britt claimed it would return Grace's memory quickly, but that she'd, "likely puke up her guts," as well. I was prepared for both. But now I had to wait.

I'd had people checking on her during the day—Owen and Ezra mostly, since they worked with her and had a viable excuse to be there. They'd said all sorts of crocs were in and out of her room all day long. I worried that they would overwhelm her, but there wasn't anything I could do about it.

Just when the afternoon was feeling like it would go on forever, I got a text. The name on my phone said 'Julie' and my heart skipped a beat.

Are you coming back? she'd asked.

Did that mean she wanted to see me? Or was it somehow a trap? Had they figured it out? My paranoia was on overdrive with all that had happened. I didn't want to leave her hanging, though.

I sighed and began to tap the screen with my thick fingers. *Yes, I'll stop by later.*

Thank you, she sent back.

I was happy to get the text from her, whatever it meant, but it made the hours pass even more slowly. I finished my shift with no progress on her case. On my way home, I stopped by the restaurant where we'd had our first date and picked up a slice of the peanut butter pie we'd shared that night. It would serve several purposes: one, it would be a nice treat for her since she'd loved it; two, I hoped it would bring some memories back; and three, if the antidote made her nauseous, she might want something to put back in her stomach. I also grabbed a box of crackers in case the pie made her stomach more upset, being so sweet.

When the hour finally grew late enough and visiting hours had long since ended, I went to the hospital. I showed my badge as I had before and walked right past security, then the nurses' station, to her room.

Grace was sleeping when I'd arrived; she had her phone gripped tightly in her hand. I carefully slid it from her grip and looked at the screen. She'd been reading our texts. It filled my heart with warmth, and I sat to watch her for several minutes. She looked so beautiful; so perfect and innocent lying there asleep. I hated to wake her, but I had to see if the antidote would work.

I rested my hand on her arm and whispered her name. She stirred and her eyes flickered open, and when she saw me, she broke into a smile.

"Roman," she said.

"Julie," I said back with a wink. But then I wondered, *Does she even know my name?*

"I'm glad you're here."

"Me, too." I gave her a quick kiss on her forehead. "I brought some things for you."

Her face fell. "It won't help me remember. People have been showing me things all day."

"I'm sorry. It has to be frustrating not to remember. This is different though, I hope." I took the vial out of the container I'd brought it in. "You work with a guy named Ezra. He's been here to see you a few times with Owen." I didn't pause to see if she remembered. I figured it was less stressful for her if I assumed she didn't until she told me otherwise. "Ezra's wife is a master at herbs and things like that. She recognized a smell at the spot where you were found and thinks she knows what was used to make you confused like this."

Grace's eyes widened and she sat up. "She does?"

I held up the vial. "This is an antidote. If Britt is right, it should bring back your memory quickly."

She reached for the vial, but I pulled it back.

"I should warn you, though. She also said it would probably make you sick to your stomach. We should get a trash can or something for you to throw up in."

Grace pointed to a can a few feet away. "I don't care. If it works, I'll throw up all night."

I unscrewed the top and handed it to her. "Drink it slowly."

She didn't listen, pouring the vial down her throat and swallowing the contents in one gulp. She sat there staring at me and we both seemed to be holding our breath. Moments later, her eyes went wide and she covered her mouth with her hand. I shoved the trash can right under her chin just in time.

I did my best to help hold her hair back and soothe her. When she seemed to be finished, I got her a glass of water and sat as she drank it, then wanted more.

I didn't want to keep asking if she remembered anything, but it was like torture to wait. After a few minutes of us staring at each other, I showed her the other things I'd brought her. She ate some of the crackers gratefully and said it helped her stomach feel better. A little while later, she took a bite of the peanut butter pie.

"This is *so* good," she mumbled with a full mouth. "You have to have some."

"Oh no, it's all for you."

"Wait a minute." She pointed the fork at me and narrowed her eyes. "We've had this before."

I tried not to get too excited, but my heart jumped.

"At Mason's," she continued. "We've had this before!"

I grinned and tried to contain myself. I wanted to jump for joy, though.

"Is that right?" she asked.

"Almost. Close enough, though."

"No, no. Tell me what it was, so I know. I don't want to remember things wrong."

"Well, we did have this before, on our first date. But you were *with* Mason. The place was called Antonio's."

Her face reddened. "You're Mason."

I nodded.

She slapped her hand over her face. "I'm sorry. I should know that. I knew something wasn't right about Roman, but I couldn't remember what."

"Those are codes names."

"That I came up with because we're like Romeo and Juliet and our families don't want us together." She gasped. "But we're going to be anyway, and we're going to end the feud."

I didn't say anything. It was better to sit back and watch her come to life, come back to me, and just let it happen. I watched her excitement as she recalled things and blurted them out.

"Oh, that jerk, Adam. Do you know he came here and tried to tell me that he and I were dating? I'm so glad you came that first night, because that's how I knew he was lying. I knew not to trust him, even if he is my clan's leader. I think the title of Alpha goes to his head." She narrowed her eyes. "He did this."

"What?" My hands balled into fists. "Adam did this to you?"

"Not directly; I knew them, though. It was three crocs who attacked me. They made me drink something, then they started talking to me. Saying horrible things about you. They tried to brainwash me, and they tried to make me forget you."

"Tell me everything you can think of."

"You're a Law Enforcement Ranger." It wasn't a question; she knew it was true now. "Can you take this as an official statement so I can press charges?"

"Yes." I took out a notepad that I had put in the bag of things I brought. "Write down what happened in as much detail as possible."

13

MASON

I rushed to the station with Grace's statement clutched tightly in my hand. Finally, we had something concrete to go on. I had to show it to my chief to get a warrant for the arrest of these assholes. I went into his office and told him what had happened.

As he read over the statement, he sighed. "This is great, but it's not enough."

"What do you mean? Since when is the victim's statement not enough?"

"When the victim has amnesia and is highly susceptible to suggestion. You did this without any witnesses; it'll never hold up in court. I can't rightly issue a warrant. And I don't think you'd want to take the chance of them getting off on a technicality and losing the case forever."

No, I certainly didn't want that; I wanted them to pay. But I couldn't hide my anger. I pounded my fist on his desk.

"I know," he said. "It sucks. But we have to do this right if we're going to nail them. Find more evidence."

I snatched up the statement and went to my desk. I sat there for an hour, drumming my fingers on my chair, trying to think of ways to get something—anything—that would help. Could I try to track the herb somehow? Get a secret confession through Grace? I had to get some sleep, so I made myself go home and took some medicine to knock myself out. When I woke, I had a new idea.

Owen had talked to the conclave a dozen times. Each time a new incident came up with the crocs, we went to them. They were supposed to be a group of representatives from all clans of all species who would oversee and make rulings on shifter crimes and help keep the peace. They hadn't been too much help to us, at least from what Owen said.

I trusted Owen. He was our Alpha and had always been a fabulous leader. But he wasn't a cop. If the conclave was some sort of law-keeping organization, then maybe I could do more than he could. Maybe he somehow didn't get across just how bad things had been with the crocs.

I hated to do it, but I had no choice. If I was going to talk to them, I had to do it behind Owen's back. As his third in command, it wasn't my right place to make that call. But I didn't think I had much of a choice. He felt there was enough peace. Each incident had been dealt with at the time, and the latest one with Grace would be dealt with, too. But as a whole, it was all too much to not do something more.

I made the call and finally got the right person on the line. After I took the time to explain the full situation—all that had happened over the years—I told him that we wanted to find a way to have peace between the clans once and for all.

He thought for a moment, then responded. "Most of the time, when there is an ongoing feud, it has to do with lack of representation. You said there are no crocs working at the park except for this new Ranger, Grace, correct?"

"Yes."

"And how about your local conclave chapter?"

Our what? "We don't have one. I didn't know we could do that."

"It's not a common thing to have. Most times, clans get along, but if this has been going on for all these years and you truly want to stop it, perhaps you should assemble one, giving the crocs equal representation. If the territory is causing so much of the issue, give the crocs a reservation, a part of the land that is only theirs, that no other shifters can enter without their permission and that no other shifters have a say over. Put the crocs in shared leadership with the bears and panthers and whatever other species you have down there in the Everglades. Have regular meetings and votes on what happens in the area."

"So, you're saying democracy is the way to answer all these croc attacks."

"That or war. Which, by the way, we would not condone or support in any way. The conclave does not believe—"

"Yeah, yeah, I know. No shifter on shifter killings."

"Peace is always better in the end. Look at the humans and their wars. They haven't achieved much, have they?"

"No, but the humans in this country also don't stand by and let violence go on unpunished. Don't you believe in justice?"

"Sure. But our definitions of justice are likely very different."

I knew I wasn't going to get anywhere with that guy, so I decided to wrap up the call. "Well, thank you for your input. I appreciate your suggestion." I wondered if he could even pick up on my sarcasm.

I hung up more pissed off than I'd been before. Give them a section of the park? So, they'd gone around attacked different species, and we were going to answer that by giving them a gift? And then by letting them make decisions and have a say over what happens in the 'Glades? When they couldn't manage to uphold the rules we already had in place? The rules we've had for decades?

What an idiot. No wonder Owen didn't see a reason to run to the conclave. They were useless, as far as I was concerned. As the day went on, though, I started to think differently about his suggestions. Maybe I was just angry over the thing with Grace and that was affecting my feelings about it all. I texted Owen and Ezra and asked for a meet up, just the three of us.

After work, we went to the small playground near Owen's house. His kids ran around, playing on the slide and swings with Conner's niece.

I told them what I had done. I expected Owen—and maybe Ezra—to be mad about my going over their heads and talking to the conclave myself.

Instead Owen said, "Well, now you see what I've been dealing with."

I explained what they'd said and Ezra had a similar response to mine.

"Reward them for their crime sprees? Yeah, okay, great plan, dude." He shook his head.

"That's what I thought," I agreed, "but I didn't know if it was just my anger getting in the way."

Owen was quiet for a moment, looking off into the distance toward where the kids were. "Well..."

We both turned to him.

"I obviously don't want to just give them part of the park and a bunch of control when they haven't handled their current business well at all." He scratched his chin for a moment. "But there is one thing that makes some sense. The rules we have now? The crocs weren't here when all that was decided; they don't have a say in what happens in the 'Glades. We've been all thinking they shouldn't because of what they've done, but maybe they've done all this *because* they don't have a say. Maybe we could have some sort of meeting with the clans and try to come to a resolution. Some kind of treaty?"

"You think that would work?" I asked.

"I don't know, but if finding peace is our goal, I don't know where else to start. With you and Grace together, maybe you'd be the perfect ones to find a compromise for both sides."

"Or it'll break you up and carry the battle on," Ezra added.

"I don't think that would happen. She's not happy with her own clan right now, anyhow."

"Then maybe it could work," Owen said. "I'd be willing to try."

Grace was released from the hospital once her memory had 'miraculously' returned. I'd put in an order to have a full legal workup done to trace any amount of the herb that might still be in her blood. I had given her one of my guns to make sure she was protected. The pepper spray I'd given her before hadn't even been on her at the time of the attack, but from that point on, I made sure she carried it everywhere she went. She also wrote herself a letter in case something like that happened again.

She was as pissed as I'd been with the legal system and decided to hire a lawyer and find a doctor to clear her and confirm that her memory was perfectly intact. She was thrilled about a possible meeting between the clans, but dreaded the thought of returning home. I suggested staying at my place, of course, but she declined. She did, however, take me up on my offer to pay for a hotel. She wasn't ready to be at home.

Now, we just had to move forward with our plan.

14

GRACE

"Grace, I wish you would just come home and stop this nonsense," my mother spat in her voicemail message.

They hadn't liked it when I said I was going to stay at a hotel for a while, but I couldn't trust them. The way the attack happened, that the crocs who did it seemed to know exactly where I was and that I was alone all seemed too obvious. I hated to think it, but they might have been in on it themselves. Even if they weren't, I couldn't have been at home; it was just too stressful. Aside from that, I wanted the freedom to be with Mason.

I responded to her voicemail with a text. *Make sure you and Dad are at the meeting tonight. A lot will be explained there.*

We'll see you there, she responded.

Perfect. Even if they hadn't had any part in my attack, they needed to hear the truth. They needed to know whose side they were taking.

When the time for the monthly clan meeting came, I drove over there feeling nervous, but determined. I had several things to cover and hadn't talked to Adam beforehand to make sure I could have time at the meeting. I would have to rush in and just take over.

I got there as people were still arriving. I took a seat and made it seem like I was just there for the meeting like everyone else, and when the time came to start, Adam walked to the microphone at the front of the room.

He said his usual greeting. "Hello, my fellow crocs. Welcome and thank you for coming."

I jumped up from my seat near the front. He gave me a confused look as I walked up to him.

I said quietly to him, "I have a few words to say, if that's okay?"

He smiled and nodded, then took a step back. Idiot probably thought I was going to thank him or some crap.

"As you all probably have heard by now, I was recently attacked and my memory was temporarily lost. I've now made a full recovery, and as it turns out, I know exactly who attacked me." I pointed to the three crocs in the crowd and called them out. "These three men followed me home, jumped me as I got out of my car, and dragged me into the woods. They bound and gagged me, and then forced me to drink the liquid that erased my memory. They tried to confuse me and turn me against the bears. They tried to keep me quiet when I found out the truth. Luckily, my boyfriend knows someone who was able to make me an antidote to restore my memory."

I let that sink in for a moment. There was a lot of murmuring and when I saw my parents, they looked confused and angry.

Adam stepped up and covered the mic with his hand. "What do you think you're doing?"

"Adam doesn't *want* you all to know about things like this," I shouted to the crowd. "Right now, he's trying to stop me from telling you the truth. I'm in love with a bear shifter and ever since Adam found out, he's been trying to break us up. He told my family, who threatened to kick me out of the house. He said my entire family was being watched and he put me on probation with the understanding that I could be removed from the clan and so could my family. Does this break that probation?"

I gave Adam a challenging look. He took his hand off the mic. "Grace has been under a lot of stress lately. We all need to understand what she's been through and how difficult it must be for her. I know that you're still having some confusion, so maybe things aren't as you think they are."

"Oh no," I said. "I have zero confusion. The problem all these years hasn't been the bears, like we've been told. We've been lied to and led astray, made to think it's their fault and that they're evil. But that's not the case at all."

I took the map from my pocket; the one that Mason and I had made that was a duplicate of the one Adam had stolen. "Adam showed me this map and tried to say it was evidence of the bears' planned attack on us. It looks like that, doesn't it?"

People in the crowd agreed and seemed to grow more concerned and agitated.

I continued, "But the truth is, these areas marked are attacks that have already happened. Attacks that crocs made on different species. Panthers, bears, even sea turtles, who aren't even shifters! These facts have been covered up and the truth has been altered."

"These are all lies," Adam said, trying to take the map from me. "I know for a fact that the bears are planning an attack."

"What proof do you have? I know the bears. Not only do I work with two of them, I'm in love with one of them. They are the kindest people I've ever met. Unlike a few members of my own clan, who attacked me and tried to brain wash me."

"I think you've been brain washed by *them*," Adam seethed. "We've seen what the bears are capable of. How many of these incidents involved the bears killing a croc? Somehow, no other species has killed crocs like they have."

"Right, so that's why I was attacked to make me keep quiet? Because the *bears* are so innocent?"

"I don't know, Grace. I don't see an arrest being made. If you're so sure you know who it was, why are they sitting here and not behind bars?"

"We're working on it," I pointed out. I should have known Adam was going to try to defend himself and make the bears the looks bad, but I didn't have a good answer for that question. It was frustrating that they hadn't been arrested.

The crowd started to turn on me. Questions were being shouted at the two of us from both sides.

"Why are crocs doing so many of these attacks?" someone asked.

"Where are the maps of all the other species' attacks? I know those happen, too!"

"How do we know Grace isn't the one lying? She's the one that's a traitor!"

I stepped back up to the mic and yelled to be heard over the chaos. "I know you have questions, and that's understandable. But the bears want peace. They want the attacks to stop. There will be a meeting between the bears and any crocs that want to come."

I turned to Adam and spoke so only he could hear. "Owen, the bears' leader, wants you to come to the meeting to talk. He wants peace and he hopes an agreement can be made to achieve that peace. I'll make sure everyone knows if you're not there, if you don't attempt to make peace with the bears once and for all."

"I should have kicked you out already," he snapped back. "But I guess that wouldn't matter to you. You'd just run off with your bears."

"I want now what I've always wanted. Peace for every clan in the area."

15

MASON

We headed to the room we'd booked to meet in. Since Owen was the head Ranger, it was easy for us to get a room at the park in one of the event pavilions. No one usually used them at night, anyhow.

Grace and I arrived first with Owen and Ezra, but it wasn't long before bears and crocs alike started to trickle in. When the time came for the meeting to start, we waited another few minutes to make sure everyone who confirmed they'd be coming was there. But really, Owen and Adam were there, and they were the most important members in attendance.

I looked over at Grace and squeezed her hand. "Ready to do this?"

"So ready."

We stood and I called out to get everyone's attention. "We're going to get started with the meeting now, if everyone would quiet down please."

Grace said, "Thank you all for coming. I think we all know that this feud has been going on too long. We all want the fighting to come to an end."

I nodded and added, "This is the first of what we hope will be a long understanding between the clans. We're hoping for a way we can all work together to make the Everglades National Park the best it can be for everyone who wants to come and enjoy it."

"Without having to worry about attacks or prejudice or anything else," Grace added.

"Is this just about your relationship?" someone in the crowd shouted.

"It is," Grace admitted, "but only a small part of it. We don't think anyone should be threatened just because they want to date someone of another species. But it's much more than that. Our clans haven't been at peace for many years. It's time the attacks and the killings and yes, the prejudices, come to an end."

"We want to make sure both sides are heard, and that both sides have equal representation," I said. "That's why we're all here together. To find an agreement between us that works for everyone."

"Are you giving us the park, then?" a croc shouted.

Grace jumped in. "That wouldn't be what's best for

everyone. The park is a huge area and it can't belong to just one clan or another. That's why I work there now. To help balance things out."

"But you're a traitor," another croc said. "You'll just do what's best for the bears."

Grace shook her head. "When Adam came to me, with my family, and asked me to give up my dream of becoming an environmental lawyer to go work in the park, I did it. Adam was actually using me to spy on the bears, but there was nothing to find out. But when my own clan attacked me and attempted to brain wash me and keep me quiet about the truth, I knew I had to do something. I am loyal to my kind. But we need leaders who won't lie to us, and we need to know the truth on all sides."

"We have a few ideas to make things in the 'Glades more equal," I said. "It's been suggested that the crocs have a sort of reservation in the park, a sanctuary area just for them."

"So, let's give them what they've attacked us to take?" Noah shouted. "How is that what's best for everyone?"

"The crocs weren't here many years ago when the initial shifter rules were put into place," I explained. "They didn't have proper representation like the other clans did."

"That didn't help the panthers," Conner said, looking over at Britt.

"There's no denying that there have been major issues," Grace said. "The crocs have not gone about things the best way. That's why we want—"

"Why are the crocs always the ones to blame?" Adam got to his feet and marched toward us. "I've been sitting here, listening to you two go on and on about how terrible the crocs are. It's bullshit. It's nothing but lies. We've been pushed aside, pushed out, given nothing but rules and no say."

"That's exactly what we're talking about," I said. "We're trying to find a place of more equal representation."

"No, you're trying to control the crocs even more," Adam said. "You want us to feel like we have more power, when we won't. I know how the bears do it. The same way they've taken over the entire Everglades and have put themselves into all the ruling positions over the other clans. Why would they suddenly play fair?"

"We've always played fair," Owen said, joining us at the front of the room. "We've made rules that protect everyone. We've kept the park safe for all. We were one of the first species on this land and had to set things in place the best we saw fit all those hundreds of years ago. This is what our ancestors planned. And now things have changed and we recognize that."

"Bullshit." Adam stepped up into Owen's face. "This is just a trick. This whole meeting is probably one big ambush. You want us dead, and now you've planned this meeting to get us all together so you can kill us all at once."

Owen tried to respond, but it was too late. When Adam spoke those words, the crocs reacted. They were on their feet, shouting and pushing each other. The room exploded in chaos.

I waved my hands to try to get everyone's attention, but it was impossible.

Then I heard someone shout, "He has a gun!"

I couldn't tell who had said it or who supposedly had a gun. All I knew is that the next time I looked out into the crowd, I saw many guns and knives being pulled. I saw fists flying and more pushing and slapping.

I looked at Owen, who had his defensive face on, and we moved forward as the crocs came toward us. I wouldn't have thought a scene like that was possible; not amongst civilized people. But it was a war.

I hadn't heard gun shots, but as I dodged a punch, I heard someone smash a chair into a wall. There was so much shouting, I couldn't even hear myself think. We had to defend ourselves. And we had to do it in a way that didn't end up with a bunch of shifters dead.

I grabbed a man's hand and twisted his knife away from him, kicking him in the knee to drop him to the ground. He lie there, cursing me and holding his knee, but he was down and out of the fight for the moment.

My gun was on me, but I kept it holstered. It would be too easy for me to start taking crocs out, and I didn't want to resort to that; not unless we absolutely had to. I still had a responsibility to uphold the law.

A croc came charging at me and I used his momentum to

send him flying into a mass of chairs. I turned to make sure Grace was still by my side, but I didn't see her. She had been right there a moment ago. Panic flooded over me, and I searched the room for her.

I stood on a chair and finally saw that she'd been pulled across the room. It looked like Adam was holding her. I pushed my way through the fray to her.

Adam pointed a gun at me. "She stays with her kind."

I weighed my options for a moment. In the end, I knew my years of training as an officer had to outrank whatever training he might possibly have, so I lunged forward, ducking, wrapping my arms around Grace's waist. When I had my arms around her, I spun, throwing my elbow into Adam's side as I freed her from his grip.

I let her go for a moment, then threw an uppercut into Adam's stomach. He bent forward just enough that I was able to twist the gun from his hand.

As Adam tried to claw me to get his gun back, someone grabbed it from my hand. I looked over and saw Grace holding the gun. She pointed it straight in the air and fired several times.

16

GRACE

The loud shots rang off the walls, creating an almost deafening wave of sound. The room went quiet and my ears rang; I'd never shot a gun before, and it was much louder than I'd expected. I shouldn't have fired it so close to Mason, but he seemed fine. I assumed he was probably used to that sort of thing as a cop.

I waited a few seconds for everyone to look in my direction, and as I opened my mouth to speak, tears came to my eyes. I swallowed to blink them back, but they still made my voice waiver.

"This has to stop," I said. "This fighting gets us nowhere except hurt or killed. Even now, as we all come together to find peace, the crocs have acted first. Don't you see this? Adam convinced you all that the bears were lying, that they did this as some sort of ambush, when there was no proof of that at all. Where is this ambush? Where is their big attack? I see bears taking weapons from crocs and not using them. In fact, look around. Who has the weapons? Who is using them? Who is really doing the fighting and attacking here?"

There was murmuring as they looked around. They had to be seeing what I saw, that it was the crocs, once again. We'd been at fault so many times over the years. I had to find a way to get them to see it; to see that we should be grateful for any olive branch of peace from the bears.

"In the midst of all this, it was a croc, my own leader, who held a gun to my head, then pointed it at Mason to keep us apart. I don't blame Adam. I've looked into the history of our clan and I know that there's a long line of lies before him. He's been lied to by those above him, and he's believed those lies and is now passing them on to us. But know this. They *are* lies. You can choose to believe whatever you want, but look at the proof. In the last few years, there have been more than ten attacks committed by crocs in the 'Glades. Do you know how many attacks the bears have committed? Or the panthers? Or any other species in the park? If you add up all the attacks committed by non-croc shifters in the last six years, you get a big, fat zero on the other side of our more than ten. You tell me what the truth is. We've been brought here to find peace; we don't deserve that. We haven't been a beneficial part of the 'Glades; we've been a blight. Yet, the bears are still willing to go out of their way to make it better for us. Which side do you really want to be on?"

I lowered the gun and tucked it in my waistband. "Take a moment and really think for yourselves for once. Do you want the fighting to stop? Do you want things to be fair? Or do you want to keep attacking and being responsible for the killings in our homeland? Do you want to be on the side of peace or war?"

Mason pulled me in for a quick hug. "Is anyone seriously injured?" he asked the crowd. "We do have people here who can give first aid."

Noah came to the front with a cut over his eye. Then a few crocs made their way forward, too, with similar injuries. By the time we'd sorted it all out, there didn't seem to be much more than a few bruises and cuts. No one stabbed or shot. No one killed. That alone was a miracle.

"This gives me hope," Mason said loudly to the crowd. "In a room of so many people, with so many weapons, no one was killed or seriously injured. That shows me that we all want peace. We don't actually want to hurt each other, and I'm grateful for that."

Once everyone had been cared for by those shifters who worked in the medical field, Mason stood to address the crowd again. "I know it's getting late and that we've been here for many hours. But I'd like to see our leaders sit down and talk. Anyone who would like to stay is welcome, and anyone who needs or wants to go is also welcome. There may be a vote at some point."

I was at his side and couldn't stifle a yawn. We had been there a long time, and we'd likely be there much longer. "I saw my parents once after the fight. They were fine. Have you seen them again?"

He shook his head and looked out over the crowd. "Maybe they decided to go. Is Tyler home?"

I nodded. "I'll text them to make sure they're okay." I sent a quick text to my mom, and when I didn't get an immediate response, put my phone back in my pocket. They'd been fine after the fight, so there was no reason to think anything was wrong. They were probably just driving.

Mason gripped my hand and squeezed it tightly. "I thought I was going to have to call for back up for a minute there and pull the cop card."

"It was bad," I agreed. "But, like you said, no one got seriously hurt. Even if Adam did point a gun at us both."

He put his hand on my cheek. "I want to make sure nothing like that ever happens again. I'm glad my training allowed me to act quickly and not have to shoot him."

"Me, too. That might have escalated the whole situation."

He nodded. "Let's see if we can get this settled."

He pulled me back toward the front of the room. "Owen. Adam." He gestured for them to come forward. Owen came first, then as Adam realized that the crowd was watching him, waiting for him to make a move, he came to the front, too.

"Let's sit here right now," Mason said. "And hear both side's terms. What will it take for there to be peace? What are your demands to make some kind of treaty that will end the fighting?"

We pulled up several chairs and all sat in a circle. The crowd was still loud and moving around, but had settled considerably during the time that the injuries were being assessed and taken care of.

Once we all sat, they thankfully quieted even more. My throat was already aching from having to shout so much, I wouldn't want us all to have to keep straining our voices to be heard.

Mason looked at our clan leaders, taking the natural position of mediator. I loved seeing him in a place of leadership; he really excelled in the role. I wondered briefly how he'd come to be third in command behind Owen and Ezra and thought I'd have to ask him the story sometime. It would be interesting to see how the bears decided their hierarchy and compare it to our system. Our leaders were decided mostly by force under the guise of a vote. Whoever fought the hardest for it, got the votes. The candidates would usually coerce and manipulate to get votes, sometimes even threaten. Adam had been in power for two years now and had eight years left in his term, unless something changed. There had to be a better way.

Mason asked Adam and Owen, "Who wants to speak first?"

Adam didn't hesitate. "If the bears had the park for so long, we should have it now," he said.

"I'm sure we can work out some equal agreement, but we're not going to just hand over complete control of the entire Everglades to you," Owen countered. "You haven't proven you can handle it."

"You haven't given us the chance! We've always been repressed. We had no choice but to fight back."

"I'm sure it seemed that way," Owen said. "But you always have a choice. Will you agree to stop attacking? To stop coming against us in every way?"

"That depends. What will you give us to do it?"

I heard the crowd start to speak up again, but they couldn't be allowed to get involved now. It would only derail things and interrupt progress.

"Please," I said loudly. "If everyone can sit down. I'm sure there will be time for a vote, but for now, let's allow our leaders talk this through. That's why we've chosen them to lead us, after all."

Adam gave me a look. I wasn't sure what it was, exactly. Appreciation maybe that I still considered him my leader and that I was letting him take charge? I didn't care as long as they could figure it out.

"What do you think about having some kind of sanctuary for just the crocs?" Owen asked. "A part of the park that could be all your own."

"We want half." Adam crossed his arms.

"There are a lot of species who live in the 'Glades," Owen countered. "We can't just let you have half of it. I'm talking about a section where no other shifter is allowed to go. If you want a bigger role in the leadership of the park as a whole, we can work that out, but if you're going to be unreasonable, we're never going to get anywhere."

"So, you're still trying to control things," Adam snapped.

Owen put his face to his hands. "The bears are in the position of authority, currently. It is actually well within our rights to not only remove all crocs from the 'Glades, but also, given the number of attacks, to ban the crocs forever, and according to the old laws, hold the croc leadership accountable for those past attacks with their lives."

Adam ground his teeth and raised a fist like he was going to punch Owen.

"But," Owen said, holding up his palm. "We haven't done any of those things, have we? We've never done one thing that's been unfair to the crocs. We've tried to have peace, and we've defended ourselves and others when necessary. We've only killed when an attacker couldn't be brought down and out of self-defense."

Adam crossed his arms. "How much of an area are you thinking?"

"I don't know for sure," Owen said. "We'd have to find the best place for it. Somewhere with plenty of saltwater or brackish water, of course."

"And you're saying this would be our land where no shifter could come and no one could have a say over it?"

"You'd still have to obey the general laws of the land, of course, but it would be croc territory. And might I point out," Owen said to the crowd, "that no other clan or species has a sanctuary of land like that. Yours would be the first."

That seemed to finally resonate with Adam. "Okay. We'll agree to that as long as we get a nice chunk of quality land. At least a few hundred acres."

"I'm sure a few hundred acres would be just fine," Owen said. "But I want a guarantee of peace. And the understanding that any attack by the crocs will end whatever treaty we hold, including your sanctuary."

"We can't hold all crocs accountable for one croc's actions," Adam demanded.

"Then it'll be your job as leader to carefully select who gets to stay on that land; to make sure everyone knows the rules and follows them. If you can prove that you're taking action against any rumor of attack and that you're willing to reprimand your own if something happens, then maybe we can work in some conditions that would allow the uninvolved crocs to remain if there were a situation like that."

"We'll be policing our own lands for sure. I don't want anyone coming onto our territory who shouldn't be there. And I don't want anyone messing it up for everyone else." Adam glared into the crowd, daring anyone to act out.

17

GRACE

"Okay then." Owen let out a long breath. "We have Grace on the Ranger team. In that position, she speaks for the crocs in whatever decisions need to be made in the park. I would welcome any other croc who wanted to be a Ranger."

"Or to join the law enforcement branch," Mason added. "We don't have any crocs, and I suspect they didn't think they'd get hired or that we would treat them well. I think we need some crocs on the force."

"I think it'd be best," Owen continued, "if we did make a local chapter of the conclave. A group where all species can be represented equally and the decisions can be made together for the good of all. We could hold monthly meetings to discuss and decide issues."

"And the crocs would have equal say?" Adam asked.

"I think the fairest way to do it is to mirror how other branches do it, by having one representative from each species in the area. That way, each clan gets a vote." Owen looked to Adam for a response.

Adam nodded. "That would make things better. As long as it's equal."

"It will be. A true democracy," Owen said. "You decide who represents the crocs. We can set up some kind of process of voting for the candidates and let the people decide who should represent them."

Adam narrowed his eyes slightly. "You'd take the chance they might not vote for you?"

"Of course. I'm the Alpha, but in the bear clans, that's more of a born position than chosen. I think it'd be better to have someone else represent the bears in a local conclave, actually. I can't be the only one making all the calls. In fact, I might require my clan to choose someone else. Any of my clan would be a find choice to represent us all."

Adam nodded slowly. "I'll have to think about that process some. We'd get to decide how to pick ours?"

"I can't see any other way, as long as you make it fair for all crocs. If there's a dictatorship in choosing representation, I don't know if things will really improve."

"Then maybe we best set something in place for that. To decide how we'll decide," Adam said. "So that in the future, we don't end with a bad leader in place."

Owen nodded. "I could agree to that."

I wondered if Adam was thinking of his own election and all the hassle he'd gone through to win. Or maybe he was hoping to change things before the next one so that he could stay in the leader position longer. Owen had said the bears were born into it. I wasn't sure how long Owen had been Alpha, but it had been many years, and I guessed it would be for life. I didn't know if that was the best way to go, either. If you had a good leader, like Owen, it was great. But what if you had a leader like Adam, who wouldn't think twice of using his own people to suit his own purposes?

Either way, I was glad to hear that they would decide on a way to choose the clan representatives. We didn't need another pushy croc trying to gain power. I thought, depending on how it happened, if I were able, I'd likely run for the position. As one of the two driving the peace treaty from the start, who better to see it through to the next stages?

"And we can agree to peace," Adam said. "I'll make sure my people know that these are new times, and new times call for new actions. I will get to the truth of what happened in the past. I want to know what lies I've been told, too. I do take these accusations very seriously." He shot a look at me. "And I want to clear things up once and for all."

"Let's start writing all this down," I said. "Get it on paper now so we can walk out of here with a set plan."

I had a notebook with me and took on the role of secretary. Mason went over the points we'd decided on so far. That there would be a local conclave chapter and that each clan would have a single representative to speak for the species as a whole. We would decide on a process to choose that individual, by some kind of vote. The crocs would get a chunk of the park as a sanctuary, with the understanding that any attacks would end the treaty and they'd be removed from their sanctuary and possibly the park as a whole, depending on what the crime was.

I wrote all that down as Adam and Owen agreed that that was what had been decided. I wondered what Adam would do to police the new lands. I couldn't be watching it if I were doing my ranger duties for work. Sure, I'd check on it, but someone should be there at all times to watch things. I made that suggestion and Adam nodded.

"What we need are croc cops," Adam said. "But we don't have anyone who can join the force. We haven't had any crocs interested in law enforcement in a long time."

"It would be the best way to keep things equal in all areas," Mason said. "Maybe talk to some of your young men and women, some who are just going into college or just getting out, to see if anyone has any interest."

"I would like to make a suggestion as well," Owen said. "I've never turned down a croc application in the park for a Ranger. Do you have anyone who is interested in becoming one?"

Adam gestured to me. "Looking at her. And we had to convince her to do it."

"That's what I thought," Owen continued. "In that case, here's my suggestion. Since there is no other croc on staff and no one interested in taking that position, I will promote Grace to be my co-head Ranger."

I blinked at him. He wanted to promote me? To give me more leadership and power?

"Wow," I said. "I would be honored to take that position. Don't you have bosses to talk to first?"

"Not as head Ranger." He winked at me.

Mason squeezed my shoulder and smiled. I wasn't sure how that had just happened, but I'd just gotten a huge promotion. I was too shocked to even be excited about it.

"I will be sure to speak up for the crocs," I said. It was great working with Owen and it'd be great to work even more closely with him. I knew I could learn a lot from him. He had many years of experience and seemed connected with the park as if it were part of him.

They did decide easily that when it came to choosing a representative for the conclave, the simplest thing would be to have anyone interested in the position add their name to a list, then have a simple vote. When I explained a little of how the other croc elections had gone, there were additional parameters set that guaranteed no campaigning beyond a one-time, debate-style discussion between all candidates. If anyone was found to be forcing or bribing people to vote a certain way, that person would be removed from the list and could never be a candidate again. If someone outside the candidates was forcing votes, that person would be arrested and face charges. They weren't taking any chances that a bad leader would get such an important role.

Toward the end, when it seemed that things were winding down, someone brought out a map and Owen and Adam marked the spot that would be the croc sanctuary. When everyone was satisfied, they drew the area out in thick black marker. Several people took a photo of the map on their phones.

A date was set for the vote to choose conclave reps, as well as for the first official meeting. The meeting would be a time for grievances to come out and for decisions to be made about them. It was stipulated also that law enforcement would be called in the event of an attack or criminal issue, even if the matter was taken to the conclave first.

The whole thing had come together much more easily than I thought it would have. But, it seemed that once Adam understood not only that we didn't deserve what they were giving us, but that we were getting a lot—most importantly equal say and power—he finally saw the benefit in getting along.

When everything had been written out, we turned back to the crowd for the first time in hours.

"Let's vote," Mason said. "I think we can make this simple with a show of hands."

He glanced at Owen and Adam and they both nodded.

"Anyone opposed to any part of the treaty, raise your hand now."

We all watched. Just one person raised his hand.

"Anyone in favor of all parts of the treat, raise your hand now."

Hands went up all over the room. I suspected that a few people didn't vote, and that was their choice, but the overwhelming majority was for the treaty. I did wonder who the croc was who had been against the treaty and which part he had issue with or if the whole thing was an issue. It wasn't the time to find out something like that, and it didn't matter why in the end. We had an agreement and the people had voted.

I watched with tears in my eyes as Mason handed the pen to Owen, who signed the bottom of the paper. Then Adam took it and signed as well. It was done. I would have the whole thing typed up more officially and copies given to all so that everyone was clear on the points. Someone had said we should frame the original handwritten notebook paper as a piece of history. I thought it sounded like a fine idea. I was glad to be part of making history. Glad that I had been there to not only witness it, but to participate in it and to be one of the ones who helped make it possible in the first place.

What would have happened if I hadn't agreed to work in the park? Would I have met Mason? Would any of those decisions have been made that night? Our love was strong and we needed each other. But it seemed that our clans needed us to be together, too. So much depended on us coming together. What if Mason had let me go when I'd tried to end things? The thought turned my stomach. What if I hadn't gotten my memory back?

I shook the negative thoughts from my mind. It had all happened and now there we were. There would be peace between the clans. Finally.

18

GRACE

As the meeting was coming to its end, Mason stood up suddenly. "I have one more idea." He turned to face the crowd, then turned back to me. "One more way that we can bring our clans together."

"But the treaty is already done," I said.

He gave me a wide smile and stood in front of me, taking both my hands in his. Then, he knelt down in front of me.

"Grace, from the moment I met you, I have been taken by you. Everything about you drives me wild. I know it's been hard for us to even be together, but I want to make sure that nothing ever separates us. I want us to be united forever, not only through love, but through marriage."

He reached into his pocket and took out a ring, turning

the silver band in his fingers so that the diamond caught the light and sparkled.

"Grace Osborn, will you marry me?"

"Oh my god, yes!" I pulled him into a hug and kissed him.

He slipped the ring over my finger and we heard cheers from the crowd. My mother and father rushed toward us. I hadn't heard back from them after I texted them, but they must've stuck around. I was glad they had been there to see it all.

They joined us at the front of the room and I gave them a wary look. I didn't know how it was going to go down. They'd never been a fan of Mason or us being together.

I watched, as if in slow motion, as my father stuck out his hand to shake Mason's. Then my mother hugged him.

They came to hug me next and my mother said, "As long as you're happy, we're happy."

"If the clan doesn't have an issue with it, then I don't, either," my dad added.

I'd take it. They weren't trying to talk me out of it. They weren't acting unhappy. I was sure that deep down, they were a little disappointed, but they didn't show it.

Owen and Ezra congratulated us and the rest of the bears followed. A few crocs came to add their congratulations as well. Then Adam was there. He walked over and begrudgingly shook Mason's hand.

The clan was watching and he knew it. He gave me a forced smile. "I hoped we would end up together one day, but

I see that you love him, and he's willing to fight for you. As long as he doesn't ever hurt you, then I wish you both happiness."

"Thanks, Adam. I appreciate it." It felt like with those words, I had my clan's permission. Whatever threats had been spoken before were long gone.

As the crowd dispersed and went on their way, I hugged Mason close. "How long have you been planning that?"

He pressed his lips together. "I got the ring right after your memory came back and I knew I never wanted to lose you again. But I hadn't decided how to actually propose until about two seconds before I did."

I laughed. "Well, it was a fine move. And it saves us the trouble of having to tell everyone. They were all there!" Though I did have a few friends out of the area and my best friend, Sophie, was still off at grad school. But that was way at the back of my mind in that moment.

I inspected the ring, watching the light shine through the round stone. "It's beautiful."

"Not as beautiful as you."

He put his hand to my cheek and kissed me, and the joy and relief of the day rushed through me. As he kissed me, I grew warm all over.

"I think we should get out of here," I said.

"Why?" He looked around, concerned.

"Because I want to celebrate and we can't do that with clothes on." I pressed my body to his and kissed him again.

"Oh." He chuckled in my ear. "In that case, why aren't we already in my truck?"

He took my hand and we said quick final goodbyes as we got into his truck. To celebrate, when we got to his house, he poured us some wine.

"To us and being one forever," he said.

"One forever," I repeated and clinked my glass against his.

I had only drank a few sips when he started to run his hands all over me. We were in his living room and I set my glass beside me on the end table so I could turn to fully face him.

"I'm thinking," he said, running his hands under my shirt and along my back. "That we both have far too many clothes on."

"Hmm. That is a problem."

He pulled my shirt over my head, and I did the same with his. He reached back to unhook my bra and then cupped my breasts in his hands.

"You are so goddamn sexy," he said. "Just perfect."

He leaned down to kiss along my chest and teased my nipples, sending tingles through me.

"We still have a problem," I whispered.

He looked up at me questioningly.

"Pants," I explained.

He unbuttoned my jeans and pulled the zipper down before pushing them to the floor. I reached for his and when we were both completely naked, he lay me back on the sofa.

"Mind if I finish my wine?" he asked.

I chuckled, but said, "Sure," thinking he was just going to gulp it down.

Instead, he picked up the glass and tilted it until the cool liquid formed a pool around my belly button, then teased me as he lapped up the wine with his tongue.

He placed the glass on the table and moved his mouth downward to kiss my thighs. I let my legs fall open, desperate for his touch. He read my mind and began to flick between my folds, and the exquisite feeling made my toes curl in pleasure.

He pressed his tongue more firmly against me as he ran his hands along my legs, and the ecstasy building from deep within my core was warming me from head to toe. Gripping the sofa cushion, I tilted my hips to position myself even closer to his mouth, and I moaned as I felt myself growing close.

I was so worked up, all it took was him slipping a thick finger inside me to push me over the edge and I came, shuddering in utter bliss, and he continued his ministrations as I rode out the ebbing waves of my orgasm.

Mason returned to meet my gaze, then planted a trail of kisses along my collarbone. "That was just the preview."

"I can't *wait* for the main attraction."

He kissed me passionately for a few minutes, but I started

to grow impatient. I bit his earlobe gently. "Just how many previews are there?"

"I thought maybe you needed a minute."

"It's been more than a minute."

He reached his hand between my legs and began to rub my clit in torturously slow circles. I moaned and pushed my hips up into him.

I felt his hardness at my entrance and he penetrated me with his entire length in one quick movement, and I let out another moan as he filled me and pounded into me again and again. He felt absolutely amazing.

"This has got to be a five-star performance," I breathed into his ear.

His lips crashed over mine as he sped up his thrusts, and when I grew close to my peak again, I told him, "Harder."

He slammed into me faster, harder, until I dug my nails into his back and reached down to grab his ass, pulling him into me as I came yet again. With a few hard thrusts, he let out a moan as he reached his own climax.

He dotted my face with kisses, making me giggle from the ticklish feeling.

"I can't believe I really get to make love to you forever," he said.

"You," I touched the tip of his nose and smiled, "are a dream come true."

He continued to lie on top of me; there wasn't room on the couch to lie side by side. "Do you ever wish I was a croc?"

"Definitely not."

"Why?"

"Do you wish I was a bear?"

"No," he admitted, "but it would make things easier for us if we were the same species."

"That's no fun. If we were, maybe things would have been different. I love you just how you are, fuzzy bear fur and all."

He ran a fingertip over my hard nipple. "One of these days, you'll have to actually shift in front of me so I can appreciate that scaly skin of yours."

I slid out from under him and got down on the floor on my hands and knees. I was already undressed, so I figured, why the hell not? I felt the familiar cracking of my bones as my limbs shortened and my skin hardened.

I looked at him with my reptilian eyes and playfully snapped my jaw. He ran his hand over the ridges of my spine, then along my underbelly, feeling the smooth scales of my skin. "You're magnificent, even as a crocodile."

I waved my tail and shifted back, then sat on his lap, facing him. "We really are two vicious beasts."

"Indeed. Two, about to become one."

"Forever."

19

GRACE

I walked down the aisle slowly, my long, white lace train trailing behind me. Mason met my eyes. He beamed and my smile grew wider.

Everything had turned out perfect. The flowers were beautiful in their purples and blues. The aisle had been scattered with purple petals just moments ago by Owen's boys and Conner's niece, son, and daughter. There were quite a few kids on the bear side of things, and I hoped we'd be adding to them soon. We'd just found out on the night of our bachelor and bachelorette parties that Ezra and Britt would be welcoming a little cub—or panther—of their own in a few months.

That day felt like the moment that everything was finally coming together. My side of the church was filled with crocs.

My family was there, my mom teary eyed, of course, holding onto my father. Bears took up most of the seating on Mason's side, and I knew of at least one panther or two as well. There were a few humans scattered here and there, too; all close enough to our clans to be trusted to know the truth.

The first meeting of the Everglades Chapter of the Conclave had met, with the representative elections having been held just weeks before. With Mason as the rep for the bears, me as the rep for the crocs, Britt for the panthers, and a man named John for the wolves, I was confident we'd all be able to keep the peace. We were family on more than one level, and as long as we kept each other in the front of our minds, we couldn't go wrong.

Even our wedding party was a fine mix of species. My maid of honor was Sophie, who'd been my best friend in the clan since we were croc kids trampling through the swamps together. She was finally back from grad school after being gone for ages. Behind her stood Addie, a bear; then Britt, a panther; Tori, a bear; and finally Jessie, a human. With Mason was Owen as his best man, then Ezra, Conner and Noah, and finally, my brother Tyler.

I felt proud of our mix. We had four species in strong representation and had even invited John and his wife as a good faith measure, which sprinkled in just enough wolf to bring the count to five species. They were all sitting together, smiling, happy for a croc and bear to be getting married. The happy part was a feat in itself, but after the meeting and our very public engagement, interspecies relations in the area had slowly been getting better.

When I reached Mason, I handed my nosegay of lavender roses and blue delphinium to Sophie and the ceremony began. Toward the end, after we'd said our vows and exchanged rings, we had another special part planned.

We brought a small table to the center of the aisle, in the middle of everyone there, where a clear glass bowl had been placed, filled with stones that we'd collected from the park. Mason lightly cut my palm and I returned the gesture, then we dripped our blood over the stones, symbolizing the coming together of the crocs and bears forever.

We had our first married kiss and bounced down the aisle hand in hand, alight with joy, and next, it was time to party. At the start of the reception, after we'd had our first dance, we'd asked Owen and Adam to give a toast.

Owen went first. "I know it hasn't been an easy path for you two, but you worked together to overcome everything against you and found a way to be with each other. You refused to give up and even managed to end a feud between two species in order to make this day possible." He paused to look around for effect. "Nothing you'll come across in married life will be as difficult as that, so I think you're pretty much set." The guests laughed. "I wish you both all the happiness in the world and I look forward to many long years of peace with the two of you representing our clans."

Owen handed the mic to Adam and they shook hands as

they did. "Well." Adam sighed. "He pretty much took my speech, so I'm not sure what to say now..." Everyone laughed again. "I'll just say that any couple who can triumph over what Mason and Grace have can triumph over anything. And I will go ahead and start the pool right now. I put my money on the first baby being a croc." He took a twenty from his pocket and slapped it down on a nearby table. "To Mason and Grace and the eternal peace between the bears and crocs."

I saw that while he was giving his toast, he kept looking across the room at a certain bear shifter in Mason's clan. Hailey was her name. I made a mental note of it as the night went on, and we ate and resumed dancing. Sure enough, over the hours, I caught Adam dancing with Hailey several times.

"I think there might be a competition for cutest bear/croc couple," I said to Mason as he held me close and we danced.

He looked to where I nodded. "Huh. Well look at that. I never thought Adam, of all people, would be next."

"Well, you know how it is. When fate leads you to the person you're supposed to be with, you don't have much of a choice."

He returned his gaze to mine and kissed me. "Thankfully, fate led me to you."

20

GRACE

EPILOGUE - ONE YEAR LATER

The pain was becoming too much for me. I knew it was going to hurt; I'd talked to all our friends who'd had babies and they'd each given me their birthing stories, so I thought I was prepared. But this was insane. It felt like my whole torso might implode at any moment.

I gripped Mason's hand so tightly, it was leaving a mark. "You're doing great, honey. I love you."

He kissed me and I wished it helped.

"Okay, Grace, I think you should change." Addie had said it, and Britt, Jessie, and Sophie agreed.

I'd always known what a group effort shifter births were; when my mom had me, she had four or five friends there with her to help. I thought it was a good way to go. They had been so supportive and helpful that I was grateful for their presence.

I shifted into croc form, and now I needed Sophie more than anyone. She shifted, too, as we'd planned; that way, I'd have an easy mental link to communicate. Mason also shifted. Though he and I could communicate telepathically since we were husband and wife, it was still easier to default to my own clan's link. And this way, I'd have him and still have Sophie. If the bear ladies had shifted, I'd have no way to talk to them at all. Mason would have to pass messages, which was just pointless. It was better for them to be humans for this part anyhow.

We had gotten a baby pool, knowing that at some point, I would probably get in it. But, being a mixed species couple, we had an added complication. If Mason was a croc, this baby would be a croc, no doubt. But there was only a 50% chance he or she would end up as a croc. Our child could just as easily have been a bear. Shifters often gave birth in their animal form because they found it easier, and if they did, that meant their baby would be born in animal form, too. Too bad that I couldn't have just laid an egg like a pure croc, though; it seemed like it would've been so much easier than delivering the baby, head, limbs and all.

Being a croc shifter, I had to try to predict which way things would go based on signals from my body. Britt had been helpful for this part. She and Ezra ended up having a bear child, and she said that when she was in panther form, she could tell something wasn't right. As soon as she shifted back to human, the baby was born with no problems and they had to assume he was a bear until he had his first shift. He smelled like a bear, though, we all agreed.

Because we were a mixed-species couple, I had the same challenge: I had to feel it out and see if things felt right or not. But that was my first baby, and I had no idea what was right and what wasn't. It hurt like hell; that's all I knew for certain. I did have the notion, though, that once I shifted into my croc form, if the baby was a croc, I should be able to feel whether or not the baby changed through my belly. Britt had tried, but a panther had too many similar parts to a human for it to be telling. That's one benefit in being so very different from a bear: there would be no denying a long croc tail and short, little legs.

When I shifted, I said to Mason, *Feel and see if you can tell.*

We'd had this discussion beforehand of course, and my croc doctor thought there was a good chance it would work. As he felt my stomach with his paws, though, he made a confused face.

I think Addie or a human should try, he said. *I can't tell with my paws. I think there's a tail?*

Sophie came over, too, and tried to figure it out. *No idea; sorry, hun.*

Britt seemed to pick up on what we were doing. I'd talked to her about the whole interspecies thing many times. "Want me to see if I can tell?"

I nodded my croc head and she felt my swollen belly with her human hands. "Um..." She made the same confused face. "Well, I do feel a tail. But I also feel an arm, I'm pretty sure."

Can a baby partially shift inside its mother? I asked Sophie and Mason mentally.

Neither of them seemed to know. But if there was a tail, then it had to be a croc. I slithered into the pool, and when the contractions were stronger and Addie told me to push, I did.

It took some time, but before long, a tiny baby croc floated into the pool and Mason scooped it up with his massive bear paws.

He cuddled the baby and told me, *Girl!*

I felt the surge of joy, but something else was happening. Something felt very wrong inside me. The pain was still there. That shouldn't be happening after I'd already given birth, should it? I let out a hiss and caught everyone's attention. What was going on?

I shifted back to human form and reached out for Addie. "Something's wrong."

"What are you feeling?"

Mason had shifted back and held our baby in his muscular arms, who was already starting to shift to her human form. When she'd come of age, she'd begin her routine shifting. That was normal, they'd all said, for a baby born in animal form to shift back quickly if he or she were to be surrounded by humans.

Mason was at my side, though, looking extremely concerned. I wanted to hold the baby, but I couldn't bear the overwhelming pain that racked my body.

"It hurts," I cried.

"Delivering the placenta shouldn't be too painful," Jessie said.

"Unless there's a problem," Britt added.

"What sort of problem?" Mason asked. "Do we need to get to a hospital?"

"Wait." I felt another contraction. A strong one. The instinct to push was there, so I did. If there was a problem with the placenta, it would be better to get it out, right?

"Oh my god!" Tori shouted. She crouched in the catching position and I felt her hands touching me. "Push again!"

I did and heard something splash into the water.

Mason let out a cry of shock. "Twins!"

"What?" I asked. There was no way we'd just had two babies.

He laughed and tears streamed down his face. "It's a girl! Again!"

"You've *got* to be kidding me."

But then Tori placed a wet baby girl on my chest. The pain had subsided and was replaced by minor contractions, which I had expected.

"We have twins?" I blinked through my tears at Mason. "How did we not know that?"

He laughed again. "I don't know."

We switched babies and I gazed adoringly at both of my daughters.

Mason closed his eyes, taking a long sniff of our second daughter and gave me a mischievous smile. "She's a bear."

Mason positioned both babies on my chest and stood back to gaze at us. "My ladies. I love you all so much."

He bent down to hug and kiss each of us. "Guess Adam won the pool, since our croc girl was first."

I chuckled. "He'll be thrilled."

I thought about what our babies meant for a moment. Twin girls. One croc and one bear. These interspecies siblings were the first of their kind.

We had truly brought the clans together forever; first, through our love, and now, through our family.

We were finally one.

THE END

ABOUT THE AUTHOR

Meg Ripley is an author of steamy paranormal and science fiction romance. As a child, she had recurring dreams about being abducted by aliens and has been obsessed with extraterrestrial life ever since. A Seattle native, Meg can often be found curled up in a local coffee house with her laptop.

FREE BOOK SERIES!

Download Meg's entire *Caught Between Dragons* series when you sign up for her newsletter!

Sign up by visiting Meg's Facebook page:
https://www.facebook.com/authormegripley/

CPSIA information can be obtained
at www.ICGtesting.com
Printed in the USA
LVHW111028211022
731236LV00010B/49